Other Books by Rock W

Silver Enigma
Silver Search
Silver Victory
Revolt at Zeta Doradus

ALERT
STATUS
ONE

AN ISC FLEET NOVEL

ROCK WHITEHOUSE

ALERT STATUS ONE

AN ISC FLEET NOVEL

Copyright (c) 2022 by Rock Whitehouse

Published by BOHICASquared, LLC

www.iscfleet.com
www.rock-whitehouse.com

ISBN: 978-1-7327666-8-6 (e-book)
ISBN: 978-1-7327666-9-3 (paperback)

This is a work of fiction.
Any similarity to actual persons living,
or dead,
or yet to be born,
or any actual event,
past, present, or future,
is either pure coincidence or blind dumb luck.

Slava Ukraini!

Author's Note

Welcome to the fifth novel in the ISC Fleet universe! I hope you'll enjoy this next chapter in the story of Carol and David, et al, but you don't need to read the first four to enjoy this one. It might help, sure, but it's not required.

You'll find an appendix for the Traenah time system at the back of the book. There is also more background material on iscfleet.com, and I'm always happy to answer questions through my author page on goodreads.com or email me directly at rock@iscfleet.com.

Please leave a rating or a review wherever you purchased the book. I do read them all, even the snarky ones. Just please give the book more than five pages before you give up.

Enjoy the ride! I'll see you in the Afterword.

Rock Whitehouse
North Ridgeville, Ohio
August 2022

TRAENAH

Chapter 1

Traenah
Just outside the Gathering Dock
The Fourth Spin of the Eleventh Subcycle of Cycle 2497

The noise was deafening.

The relentless rain crashed down on the tent city, a muddy, dripping mess just outside the docks. Kirah stood just inside the edge of her temporary home, watching the water cascading off a low point in the roof. It seemed to fill and empty in a strange rhythm: splash, fill, drip, then splash again. And again. And again.

"You know this is crazy, right?" a Norther boy yelled at her across the sloppy path between them. She looked up at him in surprise. Norther boys didn't usually speak to Souther girls. Her first instinct was to ignore him, but after a moment, she decided not to.

"What? The rain? The mud?"

He smiled, looking surprised that she would answer. "No! This whole crazy idea — the comet, the ships, all of it." He looked down, shaking his head, then lifted it again to look across at her. "It's nuts."

Kirah paused, unsure where this conversation with a Norther boy was going, if anywhere. She looked at him carefully. He was not handsome; his ears were a little too big and not nearly erect enough for that. They were a bit too high on his head, too. His eyes, though, were open and sincere. And the fur-covered legs that held up his stout middle were strong and attractively colored. His hands, too, had some attractive features, the dark blue color of his opposing digit fading out through his three fingers, gradually merging into the medium brown of his arms. She found him interesting despite his visual and geographical shortcomings.

"So, you are not a believer? Your parents will disown you!"

The Norther looked around to make sure they were not nearby. "And how, exactly, would that be worse?" Without waiting for her response, he turned and walked back deep inside his tent.

Kirah waited a moment and then returned to the small nest of temporary partitions that held her family. Poorly lit, it stank of sweat and dampness and the uncontrolled excretions of her baby brother. Soon enough, he would learn how to wait, but he was still a cub, too young to know any better.

Her sister Selol, on the other hand, was just a few cycles younger than herself and already full of an independent, sometimes unregimented mind of her own. Kirah slipped into the small 'room' she shared with her.

"So, talking to Norther boys now, are we?" Selol whispered.

Kirah rolled her eyes. "I just didn't want to be rude. And besides, how do you know?"

"Mother saw you. She didn't hear what was said but saw you talking."

Kirah clasped her hands in frustration. "Mother only sees Tmoot. We don't matter much anymore." She flopped on her stiff fabric cot. "Just baggage."

Selol laid down on her own cot next to her sister. "What did he say?"

"Not much, just how lousy the rain is."

"That's all?"

"That, and how crazy an idea it is to go meet a comet when it hits your planet."

"But, no, it's not just a comet! We'll be joined with The Messenger! You know what the cleric Lanos said: There will be a *transformation*!"

Kirah looked at her little sister, her earliest playmate and friend, with pity. She loved her so much; she couldn't bear to keep up the lie anymore. "The only transformation will be from a solid, thinking person to a cloud of atomized plasma. Your very atoms will be stripped of their electrons."

Selol was less sure of the science, but one message was clear. "Will it hurt?"

"Not for long."

"Are you afraid?" she asked, finally.

"No."

"No? Why not? I wasn't before, but I am now."

"Because there is no way I am getting on that accursed ship to go over to East and die." Kirah left the partition and walked back to the edge of the tent, but the Norther boy was not there. She sat down on a dry spot and waited a spedset for him to reappear. After a sixteenth of a spin, with the light fading as Tetanna set behind the clouds in the west, she gave up and walked dejectedly back to her bed.

Early the next day, the rain began to abate, and a few rays of light broke through the clouds to brighten up the tents. Steam rose in curly, wispy clouds as they dried in the warmth of Tetanna's light.

"Oh, great," Kirah said aloud to herself. "Now we go from cold and wet to hot and wet."

As she stood in the food line a little while later, the Norther boy appeared behind her.

"Hello again," he said quietly.

Kirah didn't turn around. "Aren't you on the wrong side of the road?"

"Yes, I am. The Messengerites feeding us won't care. They feed everyone. But I also have a reason."

She half-turned to look at him. "A reason? I didn't know Norther boys could think that well."

"Surprise! We can." He leaned forward. "And we can think up ways out of here and back to the spaceport."

Kirah stiffened. She had hoped to find some way out of her family's determination to follow the cleric to East, but up until now there had not been any sign of a chance. "Oh? What did you have in mind?"

"Not now. Meet me tonight, right after sunset. Same place."

Kirah gripped her right hand in a fist of agreement quickly, then turned away before her parents could notice.

Kirah waited for her parents to settle in with her little brother Tmoot for the night, leaving her and Selol to themselves. She slipped out of their small enclosure and moved quietly to the edge of the tent. The Norther boy was already there, waiting on the other side. He looked carefully around before crossing the still-drying dirt path that separated them.

He looked around again, then pulled her down behind some cases of supplies to sit on the tent floor. "I can get an autowheel. My parents left it by the road."

Kirah looked past their hideout. Seeing no one, she looked back at him. "Are you sure? I saw hundreds of them parked out there."

"I went out there last night. I can get it."

"There won't be enough charge to get us to the spaceport. Nothing can go that far."

"It doesn't need to. It's a newer StreamLiner with a long-endurance battery. We used to go way up north to watch the stars and the comet on Peak Night. I checked. There should be enough charge to get us to the first recharge station."

"You're sure?"

"Yes, but even if it runs out, we'll be far away from here, far from the impact. We'll at least have a chance." He stopped talking and looked at her for a moment. "What is your name?"

She laughed slightly. "Kirah."

"I am Staal."

"My sister comes, too."

"Can she walk? I mean, fast, and far? Just in case?"

"Yes. Selol is younger than I am, but she'll be fine."

"I can't coddle a child!"

"Selol is no small cub!" Kirah continued sarcastically, "She even knows her sixteens, even that a long sixteen is sixteen times itself."

"Fine."

"She knows even more, like that a mileah is a long sixteen of paces by some long-dead scientist, and —"

"Enough! She can come."

Kirah remained skeptical of this young Norther.

"You can run an autowheel?"

"I can."

After a long silence, Kirah asked the question that had been most worrying her. "So, Staal of North, what is this going to cost me?"

"Cost you?"

"You must want something from me."

Staal looked at her for a long moment. "I won't deny that you are an attractive female, Kirah, strong, with fine features. But I will ask nothing of you. We both want to escape, and I think we have a better chance with the two of us instead of either of us alone."

"Those are good words, well-rehearsed. I just hope you mean it."

"Rehearsed? Someday later, perhaps, Kirah of South, you will think better of me. But, for now, I give you my best assurance that you and your little sister are safe with me."

"The assurance of a North boy? Seems not very assuring."

"That is all I have to give you." He looked at her again, trying to understand what she needed to hear. "So, are you in or not?"

Kirah hesitated only a teoset, hardly long enough to form her decision. "When do we leave?"

"Two spins. A ship docked this spin. They need to clean and resupply it before another trip. Before dawn, they will start calling us out, both South and North. I will wait for you in the last tent. When your family makes it to the final queue, turn and run away. You'll see when you get there. It's not hard. The push from behind will keep them moving...I've been watching how they load the ships, and there is just a chance at the last moment to get away where they can't follow."

"How will I find you?"

"I'll be at the last tent, the one nearest the road. My parents are less observant than yours, and I am older, able to make the final decision myself. I'll sneak away earlier and wait for you."

"They won't follow? Won't try to convince you?"

"No. They have my little brother convinced, and they will gladly take him and leave their apostate behind."

Staal took another quick look around and then moved back across the path to his own tent. He turned and gave Kirah a grip of agreement, which she returned.

The plan was set. Kirah retained a bit of doubt about the Norther boy, but the probability that Staal would betray or harm her was infinitely less than the absolute certainty of death under The Messenger.

She'd gladly take those odds.

Chapter 2 (Twelve Cycles Earlier)

Traenah
South Observatory
Spin 5, Subcycle 12, Cycle 2485

His favorite old office chair creaked as the old astronomer leaned back, his dark eyes burning from long periods spent pouring over reports, student papers and theses, and what seemed like an unending sequence of astronomical observations. But today, he smiled slightly as he picked up a report from his former student Nadon, now the Chief Astronomer of East. He thought pleasantly of his last visit with her several cycles earlier, at her new observatory on the high cliffs facing the ocean on the northeast corner of that island continent. The Easters knew how to build well, he thought, blending aesthetics and practicality into a meaningful whole.

Which, as he reflected on it, was very much like Nadon herself.

Focusing back on the report, he was only to the second paragraph when he suddenly sat upright. By the fourth, he struggled to his feet and carried it, with his cane in his other hand, to his assistant's desk.

"Stien? Have you read Nadon's analysis of the fireballs?"

Gkeze's young assistant looked up from his studies, relieved at a chance to look away from the deep mathematics that was a required part of his advanced physics coursework. It seemed such a fine way to overcome insomnia that he felt it best reviewed at bedtime. He shuffled a few papers, found the document, then looked up at his mentor.

"Yes, sir, I have. She makes an alarming case for the increased intensity of meteors coming off The Messenger after each Peak Night."

Peak Night. The night each fourth cycle when the comet known as 'The Messenger' made its closest approach to Traenah. There would be a Peak Night this very cycle, and one item on Gkeze's to-do list was the prediction of the exact date when the comet that many in his society worshiped would be at its closest and brightest. It was not a task he cared for, as it lacked much potential for new discoveries, but it was his duty as the Chief Astronomer of South to make the prediction. He awkwardly settled into the hard-backed chair next to Stien's small desk. The pain in his leg radiated up into his hip and down to his heels and never seemed to leave him alone. The memory of the autowheel mishap that broke his bones also never seemed to leave him. The pain and the grief were all parts of him, like a single foreign entity that felt alive within him.

Stien pointed to the document. "She demonstrates a clear pattern, sir. After each Peak Night, the fireballs are larger, and that pattern continues even as we traverse the same space in subsequent cycles."

"More fragments that come off The Messenger, of course. Remnants."

"Yes."

Gkeze flipped to a page. "She reports a large fire from one encounter, where the meteor fragmented near the surface, and the impact started fires, and then the blast pressure crushed many homes. Four whole blocks of the village burned down."

"Yes, sir, it is a frightening prospect that such a thing could occur."

"We have no such reports in South? Anything reported in North?"

"We do not get much from North, sir, as you know, since the war recommenced. But I have heard nothing in the media."

Gkeze gripped his agreement. "Yes, if old Hulis was seeing anything, he would discuss it with Nadon, and she would confer with me."

"Yes, sir, I would expect so." Stien flipped through a different stack on his well-cluttered desk. "There is this, sir, occasional reports of thunder with no evident storm from the countryside. Those could be fireballs exploding out in the wilderness to the south or west."

Gkeze read to the end of Nadon's report as Stien waited. He wasn't just reading: he was visualizing the movements of Traenah and The Messenger, trying to bring the incidents into an understandable context. He finally looked up at Stien.

"I must talk to Nadon." He stood, painfully, and went into his small office. The far-talker connection didn't take long. After some initial pleasantries, Gkeze got down to business.

"I have read your paper, Nadon. It is alarming."

"Not as alarming as what happened here last night. Out in the far desert, there was an enormous explosion. I have seen media reports of a crater a half a mileah wide."

Gkeze flipped open Nadon's paper, finding the section he was looking for. "But that would mean an even larger object than what struck the village! There has been no such impact here in thousands of cycles."

"Yes, I know. I fear what all these fireballs and impacts might mean."

"What does your government say?"

"They're in a disaster mindset now and asking me for an explanation. I don't have any answers for them yet."

"I will study the matter, Nadon. Can you send me the location and images of this new impact?"

"When I get them, yes, I will send them by courier. The location is off in the far east, not far from the coast. It is an uninhabited area."

Gkeze looked at the map of Traenah on his wall, quickly locating the area Nadon referenced. "How fortunate. A little change in timing would have cost many lives."

"Yes. If it were only a spedset later, Elenath would be gone."

They terminated the connection and Gkeze sat for almost a ductset as he considered what all this new activity meant. Finally, he came out of his office and walked slowly to Stien's small desk.

"Find The Messenger, Stien. Observe it for a half subcycle and then we will see what it is doing."

Stien shifted in his chair, turning to face the old scientist. "You are concerned, sir? Eight nights will impact the observation schedule."

Gkeze thought briefly about telling the young male the truth but chose a convenient, temporizing lie instead. "For the moment, I am only curious."

"The other researchers will not be pleased to lose their time on the instrument."

"Yes, I am sure of that. Look at the schedule and see if you can work yourself in between the others. Perhaps we can just reduce their time, not cancel it altogether?"

As Gkeze returned to his workboard calculation, Stien reached for the far-talker on his desk to cancel his social plans for the next eight nights, as he would be here making observations of the famous comet. If his current love-interest Ketir cared to visit him here, that would be lovely, but it was ultimately boring work, and she would likely tire of it very quickly. Still, he would ask her to visit.

Her company would certainly brighten the monotony.

Eight spins of Traenah later, Gkeze was rubbing his longish nose as he looked at the most recent data points Stien had collected. They didn't follow the pattern he had come to expect. *But,* he thought, *that means...*

He suddenly sat upright.

"Stien!" he called, "Would you please rerun the long-range prediction chart?"

Stien rose, shook off the fuzzy disorientation of inadequate sleep, and walked to the autocalc's controller. He ran the chart the old master had requested, then pulled the chart from the printer and carried it to him.

He was used to Gkeze's habit of mumbling to himself as he worked; it was the result of long years spent working alone, or so he said. What Stien was not used to was a sudden, lengthy silence. He noticed the change, even looked up from his desk and across the room at the old one but decided to leave Gkeze alone and turned back to his studies.

He was surprised shortly thereafter to find Gkeze standing over him, his face devoid of expression. Gkeze would always remember this day, the thirteenth spin of Tlovni, the twelfth subcycle of the current cycle around Tetanna.

"Stien, did you look at this chart before bringing it to me?"

"No, sir. I just ran it and brought it to you. I wasn't aware you — "

"Yes, yes, that's fine, Stien. But please look at it now."

Stien took the chart from the old scientist and studied it for a moment. As the realization of what the chart meant dawned on him, fear gripped his heart as it began to accelerate. His fight-or-flight instincts were intact and now fully engaged. "But, sir, this means — "

"Yes. In twelve cycles we will all be dead."

Gkeze and Stien spent the rest of that day going back over Stien's recent observations, and those of previous cycles, verifying that each and every one had been accurately entered into the autocalc.

Stien was discouraged. "The autocalc can't make a mistake, sir. It can't."

"Yes," Gkeze said gently. "That much is true. But *we* can. In our data or in our instructions. We must make sure both are exactly correct."

Stien spent another spin re-calculating past Peak Nights and confirming them against actual observations. The predictions were perfect. The autocalc was not incorrect.

They were all going to die.

Stien's discouragement quickly devolved into despair. "'But, sir, I have plans! I have been pursuing a young female. I like her very much. What am I to tell her now?"

Gkeze touched his heart. "You will speak of this to no one, am I clear? No one. I must consult with my peers, and we must together decide what to do."

Stien looked away. "Will you tell North?"

The war, Gkeze thought, *everyone thinks the war is the most important thing.* "They share our planet, Stien. They will share our fate, too."

Gkeze walked slowly to his personal office, a tiny book-stacked cubby with a small dirty window to the outside. It was a rainy spin, and the dull gray sky and wet splatter on the glass seemed to match the gloom he felt growing inside himself. He picked up the far-talker and requested a connection to East, specifically, to that beautiful university observatory on a high bluff near the northern edge of the island continent.

Nadon picked up almost immediately. Her crisp voice with its distinctive East emphases was pleasant to hear, almost comforting in its familiarity. She had been his assistant long ago, and now, cycles later, her discoveries rivaled his own. He could not be more proud of her.

"It is good to hear your voice again so soon, Nadon," Gkeze began.

Nadon could hear the stress in the old male's voice. She carried the far-talker to the wide window in her office and looked out at the blue ocean far below. It was a pleasant, bright day, with rolling waves breaking against the stony shore. A few fair-weather clouds dotted the sky.

"And to hear yours, too, old master, but I fear what a call from you might mean so soon."

"Yes, I understand. Have you been tracking The Messenger at all?"

She paused briefly. "Yes. I have been looking at it every night for two subcycles."

Ever since she published the paper! Gkeze thought. He could tell she wasn't offering what she had to already know. She was waiting for him to confirm it. "I have observed it for the last eight spins. Tell me, what do your observations tell you?"

"If you have been observing it, then you already know the answer to that question, my old teacher. You already know."

"Have you reported to your government?"

"Only to the Science Ministry, who agree with me that it must be secret, for now, even from the administrative divisions. I was planning to call you and Hulis tomorrow."

Gkeze paused just a moment. "Ah, Hulis. I have not spoken to him since their offensive ten cycles ago. Many died in my home village."

Nadon turned from the window and walked back to her desk. "I spoke to him last cycle about my research, and he sounds as sad as you."

"You have more observations than I. What exactly is your prediction?"

She paused again, stress now creeping into her voice. "In twelve cycles less fifty-three spins, The Messenger will strike a lowland in southern East."

Gkeze closed his eyes in recognition of the truth.

"There is nothing we can do to stop it," Nadon continued, " I know you know that. The comet will strike."

Gkeze slumped back in his chair; he had held back the enormity of the disaster from himself, hoping Nadon would find some flaw in his conclusion, but now it came fully to realization. "It will be the end of The People, Nadon, the end of everything."

"Yes, indeed. But we don't have to be here to see it, now do we?"

Nadon took on the task of contacting Hulis and arranging a three-point conference with Gkeze. With the war still smoldering, such contact could only be done from the neutral East. In fact, most citizens of East considered the war between North and South an immoral, petty, internecine dispute that could easily be settled by the brief intercession of rational adults. Unfortunately, from East's viewpoint, there didn't seem to be many such adults available on either side.

Hulis listened quietly to Nadon's explanation of her study of the increasing fireball activity, and her further discovery of a close encounter between The Messenger and the gas giant planet that was a bright light in Traenah's night sky. That gravitational encounter had shifted The Messenger's orbit by only a small amount, but over the next twelve cycles it would be the difference between a spectacularly bright Peak Night and a global catastrophe.

"Does Gkeze now condescend to speak to his former friend? His long colleague in science? Shall he break his silence?"

"I speak your name, Hulis, now as I often have. It is a name tinged with pain for me, as you well know."

"And as you well know, I know of and regret your pain, which I did not cause. The military does what it does, and it consults me not!"

Nadon waited for the two giants of her scientific domain to trade jabs. As they retreated in silence, it was her time to mediate.

"The data is clear," she declared. "We have run dozens of projections and they all have the same result. There is really only one question."

"What to do," Gkeze said quietly.

"No. Who to tell, and when." Hulis offered.

They never agree, Nadon remembered, *At least, not at first.* "I must agree with Hulis on this. But when this is revealed, it must be done equally to all three governments, same time, same data, same conclusions. We are scientists telling the world a terrible disaster is coming. There can be no question about our intentions."

"Yes, I believe you are correct," Gkeze said. "Hulis, have you reviewed the data?"

"I have, and I have confirmed what Nadon sent me with our own observations."

"Very well, then. Nadon, can you draft a document for us to release? I believe your reputation for integrity and objectivity will help expedite general acceptance of our conclusions."

Hulis gripped his agreement, not that Gkeze or Nadon could see it. "Yes, I agree. A neutral author with our joint concurrence would be best."

"I can, yes. But we still have the question of who to tell."

Hulis had always been skeptical of his society's power structure. It had disappointed him more times than he could count. "The governments must have time to prepare, but we cannot permit them any opportunity to keep it secret."

Gkeze agreed. "We will give them the document, then allow them five spins to decide what to do. Then, we release it to the news systems with full data and an explanation that even a layman can follow. Hulis, you have always had a talent for that."

"Yes," Nadon said. "I think that is a reasonable course. But everything we say and give to The People must come from all three of us. We must be united in this."

"There is no question of that," Hulis said quickly. "We must report what is going to happen, and no war, no politics, no belief in a transcendental spirit riding on the comet will change any of that."

Nadon drafted her document, then sent it by personal courier to Hulis and Gkeze. Hulis, unable to send anything directly to Gkeze, sent his edits to Nadon, who forwarded them. It was an awkward delay, raising the anxiety levels of all three scientists and their assistants and co-workers. All knew the need for secrecy, but all were also making private plans for what to do when the news got out.

Chapter 3

Traenah
South Military Air Base
Spin 10 of Subcycle 7 of Cycle 2485

South Air Squadron Leader Dsanik threw his half-finished water bottle in the trash in rage as the politicians, backed by scientists, announced the coming disaster. He was far angrier about his sudden recall from the skies over the border with North than the thought of any impending doom. He had seen his nemesis on the other side of the border and had just turned to engage when the order came for an immediate return to base. He and North's Wing Commander Tmoyan had tangled above Traenah many times, sometimes with near-fatal results. Today, Dsanik was up-star and had the drop on Tmoyan. He could have rid himself of his main antagonist once and for all.

But, no. Not today. And now, perhaps, never.

As Dsanik stood there cursing at the video, the immense import of the news began to settle in and crowd out his disappointment. His fatigue from long days in the air began to overcome his rage, and he settled into one of the comfortable chairs in the pilots' ready room. The announcement over, he had begun to relax when his commander arrived.

"Dsanik! I have orders for you."

Dsanik didn't stand but merely looked up at the old wing commander. He'd been Dsanik's instructor long ago and still commanded the respect due to someone both older and better at his job than even Dsanik. "Yes?"

"You saw the news, and you now understand the reason for the recall?"

"Yes, commander. But I almost had him, sir. I was ready to shoot when the order came."

"There will be no more of that."

"What do you mean?"

"The governments of North and South have declared an immediate and permanent cease-fire. It seems we are to join against our new shared enemy."

"That will be difficult for many, sir. For me, in particular. My family home..."

The commander looked at him for a moment. "I believe there will eventually be some kind of evacuation, but how that could be accomplished is unclear at this point. But in any case, it has been decided that you and Tmoyan from North will lead that effort."

Dsanik was instantly on his feet, his tired legs forgotten. "Tmoyan? He's a renegade! He's...he's...my enemy! It would be treason to even speak with such a person!"

The commander didn't react to Dsanik's yelling but simply handed him his orders. "It would now be treason not to."

The orders were plain, and they came from the very top of South's military command. He read them twice, brief as they were. Dsanik looked again at his teacher and mentor.

Chastened, he replied, "I am a warrior, sir. I know my duty. I will follow my orders."

"You could resign, you know."

Dsanik waved off the thought. "That, sir, would also be treason."

"Good. Congratulations on your promotion to wing commander. It is well deserved, and you can now engage Tmoyan as an equal. The far-talker ban has been lifted, and I have spoken to Tmoyan's superior. You should know his reaction was about like yours." He handed Dsanik another document. "This is a permit for you to enter North. You will meet with Tmoyan at Bordinata tonight."

"But sir, *we* hold Bordinata. We took it back more than thirty spins ago."

"Much is changing, Dsanik, and quickly. Bordinata is on the north side of the last consensus border, from before the quake and the change in the river's course. We are already pulling back our forces, and North is moving in to restore control."

"But, our losses...so many lives. What, then, was the point?"

The commander was taller than Dsanik. He was, in fact, almost too tall to be a pilot. He looked down on his shorter pupil and spoke sternly but quietly. He knew how Dsanik felt. He felt much the same himself until this morning.

"None of those old disputes matter now, Dsanik. Don't you see? We must work together, or we will all perish."

Dsanik's strong posture wilted slightly as he fought his disappointment with the realization that he no longer need risk his life in combat. But he had a new fight now, one that would be far more important. "If I am to be at Bordinata by dark, I must leave soon."

"My autowheel is outside." The commander handed him his autowheel token. "The document I gave you will get you across the border. Tmoyan will meet you after you cross the bridge."

Dsanik took time to wash up and put on a clean flight uniform. It would not do to meet one's fiercest opponent with grungy, salt-flecked fur and a sweat-soaked uniform.

Soon he was headed north in the old wing commander's autowheel. It was an ancient and well-worn four-wheel vehicle, but it had a full charge, and he would have no problems getting there and back.

Tetanna was almost touching the western horizon as Dsanik arrived at the border crossing just outside Bordinata. He left the autowheel and passed easily through South's exit checkpoint. After crossing the river, he arrived at North's barrier, whose crew appeared to have been on the front lines for some time. Their faces were dirty, and their uniforms were muddy and stained. Dsanik could not even read their ranks.

"What is this?" one yelled. "We don't take Souther deserters!"

Dsanik suppressed his instinctive impulse to anger and handed over his permit. "I have authorization."

"Who cares?" the big ugly one yelled, his face so close Dsanik could tell what he'd last eaten. It wasn't pleasant. "You're just another damned Souther we should eliminate and toss in the river. The fish can feast on you!"

"Have you not seen the news? We must work together!"

They laughed. "Oh, yes, we've seen it. We in the North will live. You dim-wits will do us all a favor with your deaths!" Two of them grabbed Dsanik and began pulling him back up the bridge.

"SOLDIERS OF NORTH!" came a shout from beyond the barricade. The unkempt group around Dsanik looked back at the source and were suddenly still. The crisply dressed officer hopped easily over the low fence and came to where they surrounded Dsanik. He looked hard at Dsanik and then stood in front of each border guard in turn, finally stopping nose to nose with their supervisor.

"Has this warrior of South shown you his permit to enter?"

"Yes, sir."

"Then why is he still here? And by what right do you threaten his safety?" The officer stared at them for a long moment. The supervisor had no answer as the officer walked slowly around the group. The officer pointed at Dsanik. "I have fought this warrior many times. He has tried to kill me and I him. But he has never disrespected me as you have him today. I am *ashamed* of you! Everything is different now, you stupid little cubs, *everything.* You will never, *never,* treat someone at this post in this manner again. Clear?"

"Yes, sir." The supervisor said no more, fearful of punishment.

"Now, Dsanik, if you would accompany me?" They moved through the North barricade and into the town.

"There is a cafe nearby, a quiet place where we can talk. Is that acceptable? And, yes, I am Tmoyan."

"Thank you for the rescue. I was badly outnumbered." Dsanik responded, then continued quietly. "Yes, the cafe would be fine."

The little cafe was small and dark, with high-walled seating areas perfect for private conversation.

"Have you eaten? The blouke is excellent here."

"It should be," Dsanik said bitterly. "This place used to be in South."

Tmoyan looked at his counterpart carefully. "We cannot re-litigate our disputes now, Dsanik. Besides, I have come to appreciate some South cuisine, blouke most particularly." They ordered food and plain beverages.

As they waited, Dsanik spoke. "I hate this assignment. It was not what I was trained to do."

"Nor I, but there is an upside: we will no longer be shooting at each other."

Dsanik gripped his agreement as their drinks were delivered. "We have been worthy opponents. We have each defeated the other at least once."

"Three times for me," Tmoyan said slyly. "But we can't be counting those anymore."

"Yes," Dsanik said sadly, "But I cannot but mourn that all those lost in the fights were in vain. What then shall we say to them?"

"The dead are already dead, my new friend, and we need not answer to them. I am grateful that we who are living will go on living and not join their sad legion."

Dsanik took a sip of his drink. It was cold and very good. "It's all moot and meaningless now...all the arguments, all the death, are suddenly made futile by the mindless action of the universe."

Tmoyan raised his glass to salute Dsanik. "Yes. So let us not be so mindless."

"I understand what you say. Still, I feel like a traitor to all those dead as I sit here with my enemy."

"Your *former* enemy, Dsanik. You and I, we will never raise our weapons to each other in anger, ever again. I, for one, am pleased to be here with you."

"I am unclear about our mission, Tmoyan. The idea of evacuation seems very impractical to me. Where would we go, and how would we get there?"

Tmoyan set down his drink. "Yes, I have the same questions myself."

"I must ask, Tmoyan, have you heard the rumors of a new propulsion system in East? Could that be why they believe this can be done?"

"I appreciate your openness, and yes, we observed something strange just a few subcycles ago. East launched it and we tracked it to fantastic speeds until it disappeared."

"If East has made some kind of breakthrough…"

Tmoyan smiled. "Then perhaps not all is as hopeless as we think."

They fell silent for a while, a silence broken by the arrival of the blouke, a seafood dish prepared with spices only available in South.

"This is excellent," Dsanik said finally. "But where do you get the seasonings?"

Tmoyan finished his bite before responding. "Well, East is good for *something*!"

"What is your assessment of the scientists?" Dsanik asked. "I don't trust them. How many times have they been wrong? And this Gkeze of ours, the old one, is weak. He limps. He leans on his cane."

Tmoyan waved his disagreement. "I have listened to him speak, even read some of his lesser papers. You should, too. His body may limp, but his mind does not, and neither does his soul. He has the courage that comes from knowledge, the certainty of proof. I envy him."

"Perhaps. I will hope you are correct."

After they finished their meals, Tmoyan paid the bill in North military script and they walked back to the border through dark streets, hearing only the occasional sound of cubs and their parents preparing for bed. As they arrived at North's barricade, the formerly rowdy crew opened the gate and stepped back a respectful distance.

They said nothing.

Dsanik turned to his former nemesis. "I am told we can now talk directly. I will report our discussion to my superiors, and we will speak again soon."

Tmoyan agreed, and Dsanik started up the bridge separating the two countries. The stars were bright tonight, and as he walked slowly across in the darkness, he realized he had not just taken a moment to look at the stars in many cycles. His focus had been on his fight, the opponents on the other side of the border, and the danger of flight itself.

The autowheel trip back to his base was long and dangerous; the roads were still blacked out from the war, and Dsanik himself was weary from a day of combat and change. He arrived at his quarters quite late and fell into his bed.

He was asleep almost before he stopped moving.

Dsanik was awakened early the next morning by the unpleasant alarm of the far-talker. He picked it up to hear Tmoyan's excited voice.

"Turn on the news feed! Something strange is happening in East!"

Dsanik slipped out of bed and switched on his video, which was always set to the official South news feed. As a warrior, he was permitted nothing else, and he knew it was much the same for Tmoyan. The picture was of the central plaza in Elenath, the capital city of East. There was a large, dark object there and some kind of 'person,' certainly not one of The People, standing in front of it.

"What have they said?"

Tmoyan was a moment responding. "Not much. Just that this ship — I guess it's a ship — arrived just after sunrise, and this, um, alien, I guess, came out asking to talk to East's leaders."

Dsanik focused on the ship itself: dark, elongated, but with no obvious means of propulsion. What was it? "I don't know about this, Tmoyan, but I never trust outsiders."

Tmoyan was amused. "Outsiders? You barely trust me!"

"I have orders to trust you."

"Is that what it takes?"

"For now, yes, I follow my orders. Later, we'll just have to see."

"Well, then, I will consider myself on probation until the illustrious, self-righteous Dsanik decides I am worthy of his confidence."

"This is all still new. And now, we have things not of Traenah suddenly appearing in East. You will just have to be patient with me, Tmoyan. If you are the warrior everyone says you are, we will be fine. If you are as dishonest and cruel as I used to think, there will be a reckoning."

"Dsanik, fellow warrior, we have both been lied to — and about — more times that we can count, probably many more times that we know. Can we not start from last night?"

"We can. We are. But last night was only a start, not the end. It will — " Dsanik stopped mid-sentence as the video began to include the sound from Elenath. The 'person' was speaking.

"We are called by some stewards, by others, trustees," it said. "We are here to rescue the people of Traenah from the inevitable disaster that is coming."

"Rescue?" Dsanik said. "How can they do that?"

"Be quiet!" Tmoyan shot back. "Let's hear what he has to say."

"We have known for some time that the comet you call The Messenger would eventually strike Traenah, with tragic consequences. We have prepared a new home for you, similar to Traenah, a safe place on which your culture can continue."

Dsanik snarled. "I don't like this at all. Who are they, really? Isn't the timing just a little too convenient? Maybe they just want this place for themselves!"

"No, that makes no sense. You heard the scientists yesterday, Dsanik. Traenah will be uninhabitable for thousands of cycles. All the plants will die for lack of light and then all the animals will die, too. It will be long after our tenth descendants are dead before Traenah might be livable, and even then, it will not be the same."

"I don't trust them."

"I understand your concern, Dsanik, but let us see what they do, not just what they say." The video image pulled back to show crowds beginning to fill the plaza. "This could get dangerous. I think we are wise to be cautious, but it is also wise to listen to new voices."

The crowds filed in from side streets, filling the central plaza but keeping a careful distance from the strange object in the center. The leader of East, a mid-aged female, came out of the capitol building and approached the alien. They spoke briefly, and the leader led the alien inside.

Dsanik and Tmoyan decided they'd seen whatever they would see for the moment and dropped the connection. Dsanik dressed and headed out for his headquarters, unsure of exactly what he should be doing that day instead of chasing Tmoyan across the sky. For now, he thought, he'd go see his superior and see what was expected of him.

Just inside the East's Counsellory, the alien stood before a semi-circle of East's leadership. Just behind them stood a line of armed males, weapons ready.

The guards looked nervously at the alien, glanced at one another, and then back to the alien. Their lieutenant stood to one side, hand on his weapon, watching the stranger for any sign of threat.

The Chief Counsellor stood squarely in the middle of her fellow leaders. "Who are you, and why are you here?"

The tall alien looked around the enormous entrance hall, lined with beautiful stone quarried from the mountains of the north coast. "With utmost respect, Chief Counsellor, it is an honor to be in your magnificent capital."

"You haven't answered the question."

The alien bowed slightly; a gesture unrecognized by The People of Traenah. "We are an old race, and others have given us names like shepherds or guardians. We call ourselves The Trust, for much has been given to us, and is thus entrusted to our care."

"Go on. Why are you here?"

"There have been disasters like you are facing in other systems, and it is our charge to preserve, to rescue, if necessary, races like yours facing terrible fates. We have come to transport you to somewhere safe, somewhere we have made ready for your use. It is not far."

"Charged? By whom? And for what purpose?"

"It is the duty of the strong to help the weak, is it not? To lift them up, restore their strength? And the duty of those blessed with wisdom to instruct the novice? Such is our charge from ages past. As to our purpose, it is as I have described: to save those who would be lost, to ameliorate suffering where we can, to offer an open hand to those in need."

The Deputy Chief, an older male with deep ties to East's small military, stepped forward. "And what would you demand in return for this largesse?"

The alien lifted his hands, the naked arms a bright white against his dark clothing, palms up. "We ask nothing of you, sir. This is our life. We offer you what you need when you need it most."

The old male turned to the Chief Counsellor. "I don't believe him. He is alien. He has no ties to Traenah. His speech is suspect."

"He does speak like a Continental; that much is true."

"I have learned your language as well as my humble capabilities would permit. If my accent is offensive to you, I do apologize. I intend no insult."

"He's lying," the lieutenant said, looking now at the Chief Counsellor. "He is not to be believed."

"Quiet, young male. I will decide if he is to be acknowledged." She turned back to the alien. "Is this generous offer only to East?"

"It will be offered in the same manner to North and South. We are here to save all The People of Traenah, not any one nation."

A long silence followed as the Counsellors considered what the tall, hairless alien had said.

"I fail to see why we should trust you. What payment would you demand for such a favor?"

The old male took another step closer. "We have no desire to be enslaved, beholden to some unknown master for our lives."

The alien took a half step back, reestablishing his distance from the old male. "As I have said, we do this as the mission of our race. It is an unselfish mission, and we ask nothing of you. Your lives will remain your own, to rule or guide as you see fit."

"I still find no reason to accept this," the Chief Counsellor said. "You are the very definition of an Outsider, with no investment in this place or these people. Leave."

The alien paused a moment, staring at the Chief Counsellor. "I will, of course, if that is your decision, but I beg you to reconsider and secure the safety of your people."

"Leave. And you will not find a better reception in North or South, as if they could stop shooting at one another long enough to listen."

"As you say." He looked again at the enormous hall, still hearing the echoes of their voices ringing in the air. "It is such a beautiful work. It is regrettable that it, and you, will not survive what is coming. Still, I wish you well."

He turned and carefully descended the sixteen steps to the large plaza that was the centerpiece of Elenath. He looked around, as if to see it once more, then entered the black ship and was gone.

Chapter 4

Not long after Dsanik and Tmoyan went back to their normal tasks, a new face appeared on the news feed. Lanos was a small-time preacher who taught belief in The Messenger as a deity that guided and judged the actions of The People. The sect was a remnant of millennia-old superstitions, one from the days before science developed a better understanding of the universe. Still, aside from the regular cultural celebrations of Peak Night, the faith still had its adherents in both North and South.

"We must reject the words of these aliens!" he cried, waving his disagreement. "We know nothing of them and they nothing of us!" His face, twisted with anger and fear, calmed suddenly as he finished. "If The Messenger is coming to Traenah, we must meet it! This is our transcendental opportunity!"

The interviewer paused before asking, "But, from what the astronomers have told us, meeting The Messenger in the manner you suggest would be fatal, would it not?"

Lanos calmed himself and turned to the camera. "In a physical sense, perhaps, but we will be spiritually joined with it and become part of that which we worship." He gripped both hands to express his intensity. "I can't imagine anything more ecstatic."

The interviewer looked at his notes. "The astronomers say it is possible that The Messenger will actually strike the sea, not land. How, then, will you meet it?"

Lanos waved his hand dismissively. "At sea or on land, true believers will find a way." He turned to look directly into the camera. "Today, I am announcing a new foundation to build a worship space at the Locus of Unification where The Messenger will arrive."

"*Arrive?*" the interviewer asked with obvious skepticism. "The Messenger will strike Traenah with violence never seen, power one can calculate but hardly imagine."

"Again, from your limited, archaic, physical viewpoint, this may be true, but within the Locus, the supernatural transcendence of its arrival will be wonderful beyond words."

The camera moved to the younger male next to Lanos. "Lanos has been a leader in the Messenger faith for many cycles," Ilrosa said in a smooth, deep voice that dripped credibility and substance. "His understanding of the significance and meaning of The Messenger is far beyond what the rest of us know."

"Still — " the interviewer began.

"Still," Ilrosa interrupted, "he understands the mystical nature of The Messenger. He is the one anointed to speak for it."

"I see. And you, then, speak for him?"

"I am but his humble assistant, lacking his depth of wisdom and insights. Dear Lanos is the true guide."

"Thank you for talking to us. I am sure we will be seeing you again soon."

The picture moved to the interviewer, who quickly closed the segment and moved on to promote what was coming up next.

That night, the chapels of The Messenger were filled to overflowing, with Lanos broadcasting a sermon from his small chapel in South. As he called for donations, thousands of new believers transferred millions of currency credits into his account. There *would* be a Locus; that much was now clear. The desperation of a race with a well-defined date of death was suddenly all he really needed. They would follow him, praise him, even adore him. As the number on the autocalc continued to grow, his confidence grew with it. He just needed to keep up the message, keep bringing more into the belief, and the currency would flow in. It would be glorious!

He turned to his assistant and main apologist. "Ilrosa, as soon as the scientists are sure of where The Messenger will arrive, we must go there and obtain land for a welcome space, a place to join with it. The Locus must be prepared."

"Yes, Lanos, I see. I have been watching the scientists' reports, and current estimates indicate a plain in the southeastern region of East. It is sparsely populated, and we should be able to acquire the space we need economically."

Lanos laid back in his chair, gripping both hands in excitement. "Excellent. We will wait for a subcycle or two until they make a firm commitment, then we must move quickly before the owners can react."

"As you say, sir Lanos."

"It will be glorious, Ilrosa, a glorious, glowing transformation. Instant transcendence with The Messenger."

"Yes, I look forward to the moment."

"Ah, yes, yes, as do I. Tell me Ilrosa, what do you think of the alien who appeared in East today?"

"He is an outsider, and The Messenger does not know him. As you say, whatever their race and their claims, they are *alien*. It is an epithet to us, and they are not to be believed. They will be no obstacle to us."

Ilrosa made a last check of the incoming contributions, found himself surprised at both the number of contributors and the sum, then retired to his own room for the night. Tomorrow, Lanos would continue preaching of The Messenger, and he needed his rest.

Unlike Dsanik's journey to Bordinata, Tmoyan had no problem crossing into South. Dsanik met him at the bridge and drove him to a South military base a short distance away.

As they sat together in the base commander's small conference room, Tmoyan asked, "Did you read about this preacher, this, uh, Lanos?"

"Yes. He's insane, I think."

Tmoyan gripped his agreement. "I fear he will be a problem."

"How so? No one with any sense is going to follow him."

Tmoyan waved his disagreement. "I am less sure of that. He is well known in North, and many believe what he says."

"My own family have been Messengerites their whole lives. I am not. But, seeing it as a symbol of something holy and committing suicide under it are very different things."

"I hope you are right."

The news video playing in the background suddenly switched from replays of the alien in East to a shot of the North capital. Tmoyan reacted with surprise.

"What's happening in Nomiana?"

"What?"

"The video is showing Nomiana. Look — the alien is there now."

The same dark, featureless ship sat before the fine stone building that housed the First Minister's offices. Again, as in Elenath, the alien disembarked and approached the wide stone stairs. Tmoyan recognized the guards who stood shoulder-to-shoulder, blocking the entrance.

"Those are the executive security forces," he said, speaking to Dsanik without taking his eyes off the screen, "If the alien approaches any closer, they'll shoot."

Almost as if he had heard Tmoyan's warning, the alien stopped several meters from the massed security males. The video cut to a mobile camera, shooting from behind the guards.

The alien was speaking. "We are no threat to you here in North. We have come to discuss how to save the people of Traenah from the disaster which is sure to come." There was a plaintive, almost pleading note in his voice. Dsanik thought he heard a note of desperation in the voice.

The First Minister came forward, flanked by his military and political advisors. As he talked to the alien, there was a low but growing murmur of sound in the background.

"You went first to East, and now you are here. How are we to trust you?" the executive asked. "We don't know where you have come from or what you want."

"Where we are from isn't important. What we want is to evacuate your people to a new, safe place we have made ready for you. May we discuss this inside, away from the crowds and cameras?"

The First Minister waved that idea away. "All should hear what you have to say, alien. I see no reason to have secret talks with you. Both South and East will be suspicious."

"As you wish." The alien paused as if gathering his thoughts. "We have found a suitable planet for your culture. It is fortunate that it is not far from here. We can transport your entire population there."

"Such a gift you offer, I find it hard to believe. But if you are truthful, then what do you demand for such an enormous gift? What kind of debt will you lay upon us?"

There was a long pause before he answered. "Surely you have heard from East what I said there. But I will repeat myself here, so that you may be sure of us, that we demand nothing. This is our work, our society's mission."

"We will owe you nothing?"

"Nothing."

The camera moved quickly to the side, where a large crowd was entering the open plaza. They were chanting something neither Dsanik nor Tmoyan could make out. The sound increased sharply as they came closer.

"Transcendence not fear! Transcendence not escape!" they were chanting. The alien looked at the approaching people and stepped back from the First Minister.

"I cannot help you if you will not listen! Please! We can save all of you. If you refuse, many of your people will die needlessly."

The First Minister looked at the crowd, growing in size and volume as it approached, each one a voter, he was sure. "I suggest you depart, alien. I can no longer assure your safety here."

The alien stepped forward and said something more, but the chanting of the crowd drowned it out. He moved quickly back to his dark ship and in a few moments, it silently lifted off and rose out of sight.

"What just happened?" Dsanik asked.

"The mob of fanatics just won the first round," Tmoyan said grimly. "I fear it will not be the last, and I wonder now what will happen to all of us. I feel we are foolish to cling to our narrow, provincial thinking with the death of our planet staring at us. The comet will strike, Dsanik. If we are not evacuated, we will die. It is just that simple."

They went on to the practical business at hand, the dismantling of border checkpoints and the joint work of securing weapons while allowing pilots to maintain their skills. Dsanik and Tmoyan were now the de facto heads of their respective air forces, charged by their leadership to ensure peace in the skies. Their quick friendship, somehow based in their long and near-lethal competition in the air, was the foundation. They were not by nature trusting officers, but they trusted each other, perhaps because each saw something of himself in his partner, and from that bond they were able to craft the conditions that would support the cooperation they would need to survive. It wasn't an easy sell to their subordinates, but each side knew how to obey orders, even unpopular ones, and they hoped the peace would hold.

Now, if they could just find somewhere to go, and a way to get there.

Traenah
Spin 3, Subcycle 14, Cycle 2485

The spin Tmoyan and Dsanik had both hoped for and dreaded had arrived. Today would be the meeting of the leaders of South, North, and East, together in one place. War and simmering resentment had kept the leaders separate, isolated, and distrustful of each other. On this day, they would meet in the capital city of East to discuss what to do about the coming apocalypse. Despite Lanos' distracting exhortations about The Messenger, the governments kept searching for a solution, some way to save their race from an unspeakable fate. Still, they bickered over timing, seat placement, and even how many escorts and assistants were allowed. It was East's Chief Counsellor who publicly cut through the delaying tactics and trivial objections, leaving North and South little choice but to take part.

Dsanik was about to walk out to his aerocraft when he was interrupted by the shrill alarm of the far-talker.

"So, old friend," Tmoyan's voice boomed, "what do you think of this new re-route?"

Dsanik scowled. "I had not planned on any sightseeing, but the Easters want our leaders to see this new crater."

"Yes, but I, too, want to see it. It should be instructive."

"I suppose. We will be on channel twenty-two."

"We are on fifteen. Monitor six, too; it might be good to talk as we circle the crater."

Dsanik hung up the far-talker. His deputy was standing next to him, wondering about the conversation. "Tmoyan just wanted to coordinate communications." He walked to his waiting craft and climbed the ladder. A crater half a mileah wide? Such a thing was wider than the length of his takeoff strip! It would indeed be something to see.

As they crossed the seacoast heading east, Dsanik was on the left flank of five craft. The large aerocraft in the center carried South's Governor, an older female known for her determination and, some would say, ruthlessness. She was a strong leader for a wartime country, and Dsanik admired her. Tmoyan despised her, of course, and made no secret of his skepticism that she would be effective now that the war was over, and they needed to unite all three countries if they were to survive.

Dsanik thought about Tmoyan's strident opinions as he watched North's delegation on his sensor display: seven craft on his left about ten-sixteens mileah away. They would have to moderate their speed to conserve fuel, as the crater was in the far east of East, which required them to cross most of that small island continent before they could see it. Dsanik didn't mind, really; he loved flying, and more time aloft was always better. It was a clear day and the air at their altitude was perfectly smooth.

There was no need to hurry.

As the enormous wound in the landscape crept over the horizon, Tmoyan looked at his communication panel but decided to forego calling Dsanik. North's delegation would be the first to circle the crater, flying east to the north edge, then making two circuits around it before proceeding back southwest to the meeting in Elenath.

Tmoyan keyed his microphone and ordered his fliers to spread apart so they could better observe the crater without endangering each other. As they arrived just outside the north edge, he commanded the slow right turn that would take them completely around it. Even from two mileah above, Tmoyan could clearly see how the rim was pushed up. He also saw scattered smaller craters he assumed were caused by the fall of large pieces of the object and the underlying rocks tossed out by the impact. The center of the crater still glowed slightly red, here a half-cycle after it had happened. He had sat through the same briefing with the rest of the pilots, where the scientists reported that this damage was caused by something no larger than a typical residence. *Incredible,* he thought. *So much power in something so seemingly small.*

As they finished their second trip around the crater and began turning southwest, his communications panel indicated something on channel six. Dsanik? Once they were settled on course, he switched over.

"Dsanik, were you calling?"

"Yes!" he responded immediately. "I can't believe my eyes!"

Tmoyan smiled. "Believe them, but I feel the same. It is an awesome sight. Frightening."

"Agreed. We are almost there."

"See you on the ground."

"Yes."

The two military delegations parked their craft close together on the wide tarmac at Elenath's airfield. After the South's Governor and North's First Minister had departed, Dsanik and Tmoyan and their pilots met in the pilot's reception room. It was an awkward gathering of strong males who had spent their careers trying very hard to kill one another, and on each side were pilots who had killed friends of those on the other side. Tmoyan and Dsanik reminded them of their own near-fatal battles and used their example to show the rest their commonalities, their warrior ethic, and the shared experience of air combat.

They walked to the meeting site together, freshly determined to make a show of their unity in the new fight to survive the oncoming disaster.

It was the first in-person council of all three leaders in recent memory. The meeting place was a small round plaza set down into the ground such that one entered at the top. The leadership was seated around the middle of the plaza. Dsanik and Tmoyan and their fellow pilots sat in the back row, some standing behind but all close enough to hear the conversation. Tmoyan looked at the inner circle of chairs, four sets, each occupying a quarter of the circle. The three governments faced the fourth group, which he saw included Gkeze, the old astronomer who had first discovered that The Messenger would strike the planet. There were others with him: Hulis, North's Chief Astronomer, and between the two old men, he saw a much younger, strong-looking female. Behind them sat a large group of Easters, based on their dress, who Tmoyan took as other scientists or engineers. They certainly didn't have the look of warriors.

Cedas. the Chief Counsellor of East, welcomed the other leaders, and thanked them for participating.

"We must unite to save our very civilization, and I am made more hopeful by your presence here." She walked around the circle, finally standing in front of the scientists, facing the government delegations.

Tmoyan felt the star's warmth on his face, the breeze cooling his ears and head as it swept by. He was happy to be there, relaxing for a moment in peace with his compatriots and now-former foes.

"We have all today seen the destruction caused by the meteorite impact here in East. I call Nadon, our own Chief Astronomer, to describe her findings."

Nadon stood and began to slowly pace the semi-circle facing the gathered leaders. "What you have seen today, a crater larger than seen here on Traenah in a thousand cycles, was created by a fragment of The Messenger less than a sixty-fourth of a mileah wide." A sudden silence met her ears. They were listening! "Something not even as wide as this plaza struck and left that enormous hole in the ground." She walked back and forth as the leaders whispered among themselves.

"We have measured The Messenger several times in the past and calculated its mass from its movement, its orbit. The Messenger is more than eight sixteens mileah wide, with a mass, well, enormously more than that small fragment." She paused a moment. "I could quote the mass, but I don't think the number, by itself, could carry the true meaning of it."

She looked again across the gathered leaders and their assistants. "We have determined that it will leave a crater sixteen times sixteen mileah wide. The mass of evacuated stone and the enormous heat generated can be estimated from smaller impacts, but, like the mass, such numbers tend to lose their effect when so unimaginably large."

She stopped pacing and stood in the middle of the leaders.

25

"The very sky will be hot enough to burn. The falling melted rock and bits of the comet will start fires everywhere there is dry land. The whole planet will burn, and if we are still here, we will burn with it."

The First Minister of North spoke up. "You paint a dire picture for us, astronomer Nadon. We knew The Messenger would strike but did not believe it could be such a global tragedy. I see little hope in this for us."

"I am not in the business of providing hope, sir, but I do have some. It is my duty to report the facts, and yes, I hope that you will use those facts to craft actions beneficial to us all."

The Governor of South stood. "Your forthrightness borders on disrespect, scientist. There are considerations beyond the mere 'facts' as you present them."

Nadon met the Governor's stare and, without looking away, asked, "Why is that?"

The Chief Counselor of East stood again, eager to cut off any conflict. "Thank you, Nadon, for helping us define the problem so clearly."

Nadon broke her stare at the Governor and re-took her seat across from the leaders. The Chief Counselor turned to face her peers.

"It is clear what is coming: a tragedy for everyone, for every living thing on Traenah. But. I stand before you with new hope."

Tmoyan and Dsanik glanced knowingly at each other, and both sat up straighter in their seats. A murmur spread through the crowd.

"We have a new discovery to share with you."

Sudden silence.

"As you all know, the graviton drive has been used for perhaps two sixteens of cycles to power aerocraft beyond the atmosphere and place satellites into orbit. We have all used it for research and scientific exploration. But now, the scientists and engineers of East have made new discoveries about this method of propulsion, which has an immediate impact on the danger to our society. We have created an artificial graviton propulsion system which can achieve previously impossible velocities."

Dsanik and Tmoyan shared another quick look but suppressed any further reaction. This was very new and must have been a closely guarded secret. The Chief Counsellor continued her stroll around the inner circle, coming to a stop between the North and South delegations.

"We intended this innovation for exploration, to allow us to see other stars and planets close up. But now, it can take us to safety if we can but find a suitable place to go."

North's First Minister tried to suppress his shock at this announcement. "We have heard nothing of this!" He stood and addressed Hulis. "How is this possible? Have you kept East's secret from us? Defend yourself!"

Hulis stood slowly, staring at the First Minister. "How dare you question my loyalty! I know nothing of this."

"He speaks the truth," East's Chief Counsellor said. "We have told no one until now. Our research has been done in extreme secrecy as we had no desire for this to be misappropriated as a weapon."

The First Minister of North returned to his seat, exchanging an angry stare with South's Governor.

"Fine, then. But how are we to apply this?" he asked. "And, how are we to decide where to go?"

South's Governor was no less alarmed. She rose and pointed accusingly at East's Chief Counsellor. "We cannot simply set out only to die of starvation or thirst while searching!"

East's Chief Counsellor came very close to challenging her. She was a tall female, an attractive, even intimidating physical presence.

"No one has suggested anything so absurd, illustrious Governor." She stepped back, defusing the confrontation.

"We have reported, openly and withholding nothing, a new innovation that could, and I emphasize the *possibility* and not the *certainty*, be an escape for us. For *all* of us." She returned to her seat. "We are undeserving of such exaggerations."

Gkeze watched this display with the disdain of one who uses known facts and verifiable data to control his actions, not the votes of the ill-informed or latest opinion polls. The leaders' histrionics were unnecessary: no one was going anywhere until there was somewhere to go. Besides, Gkeze had serious doubts that East's new evolution, whatever it was, could be scaled up efficiently to construct evacuation ships large enough to matter. Small explorations were one thing. Ships large enough to move a whole population were something quite different. He stood, pulling hard on his cane to get up.

"If I may, leaders?" All eyes turned to the old astronomer. "There are many questions to be answered, many steps to take before we can know what course is correct."

Dsanik leaned over to Tmoyan. "I have always laughed at how the old one limps, but he's the only one making any sense."

"Yes. He is only weak on the outside. Our leaders both seem very weak on the inside."

Gkeze continued: "I ask this council to permit me to work with Nadon and Hulis to understand how we might find a suitable new home, then see how we might travel there. If this new propulsion is all East thinks it is, it may well save us."

Sensing an escape from their self-induced embarrassment, the leaders agreed to reconvene the next morning.

Later that afternoon, the three scientists met with the engineers who had enhanced the artificial graviton system.

The lead engineer spoke first. "We are honored, sir Gkeze, to have you here. You have been an inspiration to all, and your student Nadon is a beloved, if stern, taskmaster."

"Do not forget, sir, Hulis was also her teacher. But she is successful because she is Nadon, not so much because Gkeze and Hulis opened the door for her."

"Yes, sir, I do understand."

Nadon waved away the attention. "Enough praise! Tell them of this revolution you have made. Can it work as we hope?"

"It will work." He turned to the old man. "Sir Gkeze, I understand your skepticism, but we have already surpassed the speed of light, and we believe it will scale as necessary."

"That is impossible," Hulis said. "Nothing can go that fast."

Nadon smiled at her colleague. "But it can. I have seen the data myself only a subcycle ago. I am sorry to have kept it from you, but secrecy was required."

Gkeze thought for a moment. "Until today, I would have agreed with you, Hulis. Impossible. A fantasy. But you know as well as I, Nadon would not be misled, nor would she mislead us. Therefore, it must be true."

Hulis started to rise to object, then slumped back in his chair. "So, everything we have known up to now, everything I have taught countless students, is false?"

"No." Nadon reached over to touch him. "It's just that the universe is different than we might have thought."

"Tell me, then," Gkeze asked, "what exactly have you done?"

"Yes, sir. We started with a small spacecraft which we launched normally with a chemical propellant, then activated the graviton drive. It traveled to the fifth planet, took photographs, and then returned under the graviton drive."

"All at speed greater than light?" Hulis asked.

"No, sir, that work was done separately. On our first successful flight, we sent a small spacecraft to the tenth planet and back within four spins. We can show you the data on its timing. The speed of light was exceeded by a factor of four."

"Indeed, you have done quite well!" Gkeze was sincere in his compliments but also ready to move on. "What are you thinking to do with this, Nadon?"

She stood and faced the collected engineers and scientists. "There are only a few stars nearby that might be suitable for us. We need to send probes to explore if there are compatible planets."

Hulis was looking out the window at the ocean in the distance. "And how fast can this propulsion system take us?"

"We have already been to sixteen times the speed of light, sir, with later development. Four sixteens may be within engineering reach, but perhaps not for a large vessel."

Gkeze stood and moved slowly around the room. "The nearest star that matches our own Tetanna, I mean, of course, Mehonnh, is then, if my mind can still do arithmetic, only something less than three sixteens of spins away?"

"Yes, sir. Three sixteens less five, assuming that maximum speed."

Hulis looked at his old friend Gkeze, then back to the lead engineer. "And how do you plan to power this, this, miracle?"

"A small fission reactor should suffice. That is what we have been using in our engineering prototypes."

"What about Eiglanni?" Nadon asked. "It is also similar to Tetanna but a little further away."

"Yes, I think we should investigate that, too. Hadaat is yet another candidate."

Gkeze spoke again. "If we have only three stars to choose from, I don't hold much hope for us. Habitable planets are fairly rare, or so our theory goes. I would have argued that alien life is even rarer and likely impossible to encounter, but these 'Trustee' aliens have cleared that question conclusively."

Uncomfortable laughter circled the room. No one knew how to interpret the alien offer. Were they sincere? Or, as The People were prone to think, were they just a dark threat in disguise?

In the end, the scientists settled on the three stars to investigate. The three probes would take more than three subcycles, some fifty spins, to construct. It would therefore be at least eight subcycles, a full half cycle, before they could expect any answers. Still, there were twelve cycles before the comet struck. There would be time.

Perhaps, Gkeze dared to hope, *enough time for all to live.*

The next morning, the leaders met again, away from the cameras, crowds, and collection of bureaucrats and assistants. They came to an agreement that while they awaited the exploration results, East's engineers would begin working up plans for the evacuation ships. Clearly, they could not wait to plan the evacuation until they knew where they were to go.

At the same time, East's engineers met again with the three astronomers to discuss the complex problems they faced. Larger ships could carry more but would then require more power, environmental systems, and supplies to keep everyone alive. Smaller ships, on the other hand, could be faster, simpler, and cost less, but would carry fewer individuals. It was not a simple tradeoff, and the engineers argued well into the evening before arriving at a consensus.

Nadon, again, was instrumental in pointing out compromises on both sides that appeared to allow enough time and capacity to evacuate their entire population. Some ships, she argued, should be dedicated to materials, tools, and other supplies which do not require food or any kind of life-sustainment systems. The mass otherwise required could then be reallocated to cargo. Other vessels would then be designed specifically to move The People and could therefore be optimized for that purpose.

But it would take most of the industrial capacity of the entire culture.

Nadon stood at the end of the discussion. "Well, I think we can manage without new aerocraft, entertainments, or autowheels."

"Or weapons," Hulis added.

Gkeze sat speechless as he looked at the figures the engineers had splayed across the workboard: *They could do it, after all, if they just had the will. It could be done!*

Chapter 5

Traenah
South News Bureau
Spin 4, Subcycle 14, Cycle 2485

Growing weary of the interviewer's direction, Lanos declared, "There is no need for this so-called evacuation! The Messenger is coming, and we should all welcome its arrival!"

Ghanor was an older male, a hard-news reporter who had sat across from hundreds of difficult subjects. But today, disturbed by this one, he squirmed in his seat.

"But, sir Lanos, aren't you really calling for mass suicide? Anyone in the impact area will certainly die."

Lanos looked aside at Ilrosa, his deputy and some-time communicator and chief apologist, then directly into the camera. "Like many of the uninitiated, Ghanor, you conflate the physical with the spiritual. The Messenger's arrival will be an event of unequaled spiritual transcendence!"

"And where will the transcendence take believers?"

"Wherever the Messenger wishes us to go."

"Can you be more specific?"

Lanos looked up dramatically, then again back to the camera. "To a place of peace, contentment...and ecstasy."

Ghanor paused, wanting to make sure Lanos' claim was clearly heard. "And, how do you know this?"

"I have the ancient writings, passed to me from cycles untold, which give me the guidance I need."

This was new. Ghanor had never heard of any writings, ancient or not, about The Messenger. Belief in it was personal, nonspecific, and more a cultural phenomenon than something of the eternal. "And where have these writings come from?"

"As I said, they were given to me from cycles long past. Only I have them; only I have the insight to express what they say."

"And the rest of us cannot have access to these writings? We are to take your word for what they say?"

"Sir Lanos has lived these writings his whole life," Ilrosa interrupted. "His honesty and wisdom are unassailable!"

Ghanor thought just the opposite might be true, but the clock was running down, and it was time to quit. He turned to the camera.

"So, friends, new information today from Lanos, chief priest of the Messengerites."

As they walked off stage, out of earshot of Ghanor, Ilrosa turned to Lanos. "Writings? You never mentioned writings before."

"Have faith, Ilrosa. They are here in my heart, where they were given to me by the cycles long past. I see them every day."

"I see."

"Do you doubt me, Ilrosa? I need your faith most of all!"

"No, Lanos, I do not doubt you. I was surprised, that's all."

"There will be more surprises, my friend, before this is all over. The contributions are flourishing?"

"Yes. The believers are very generous."

"We must continue to spread the truth of The Messenger and fight this impulse to flee. All should come to The Messenger, and to *me*."

Ilrosa paused a moment before responding. "Yes, I agree. We will persist in this sacred endeavor, and we will bring many more to The Messenger's truth."

Lanos gripped his agreement, and they left the news studio, bound for another gathering of believers and seekers. Fertile ground, Lanos knew, for more contributions, but, more importantly to him, to be immersed in new adoration. The glow of their praise aroused him, filling his inner self with momentary satisfaction. Clearly, The Messenger had heard him and was blessing his work on its behalf. And tonight, afterward, Lanos hoped, there would be more inspiration, just for him, in a dark, quiet place.

But there must be more, always more. Suddenly realizing he had stopped walking, Lanos pushed down his dark desires for the night ahead, regained control of himself, and proceeded with Ilrosa to the waiting autowheel.

The far-talker rang in Dsanik's room, waking him. It had been a long, scattered-sleep night, full of frightful visions of the comet's strike and his failure to evacuate in time. He was shaking off those visions as he picked up the far-talker.

It was Tmoyan.

Again.

"That accursed priest Lanos is holding a rally in Bordinata tonight. I think we should go see what he's saying."

"He's an idiot. And insane to boot."

"Yes, and a dangerous one at that. But I think it would be good to hear what he says."

Dsanik thought about his schedule for the day. Yes, he could get an autowheel, and he could probably make it to Bordinata in time.

"Fine. When?"

"He is supposed to speak at the thirteenth spedset, so, just after dark."

"I will see you there."

As the time for Lanos' rally approached, Tetanna was setting in the west, the sky clear and typically reddish towards the horizon. Dsanik had no problem finding it, what with the crowds flooding over the same bridge where the North guards had hassled him just a few subcycles before. Now, the guards and barriers were gone, and Tmoyan was waiting on the north side. Together they followed the mass of Messengerites as they walked to an open area just outside the village. There, a stage had been erected, flanked with bright lighting and loudspeakers.

They found a spot on the very edge of the crowd so they could leave easily. It felt safer there, too, outside the crazy crush of bodies. Right on time, Lanos' assistant Ilrosa came on stage, his trademark long beard flowing as he walked.

"Fellow believers!" he began, generating a deafening chorus of cheers from the crowd. "Fellow believers! Our guide Lanos has been in meditation all day, and he has new insights from the wisdom of cycles past to share with you tonight." More cheers, but less volume than before. Ilrosa went on to explain where the waste booths were located and where the attendees could purchase Lanos' new book about The Messenger, 'The Coming Transcendent Existence.'

"But most importantly, fellow souls, we need your tangible support. It will take substantial reserves of currency in order to build The Messenger a proper welcome in the East. We can do it, we know, but we need your support to make the Locus a reality!"

Finally, Lanos himself appeared. The crowd rose as one, and the deafening cheers went on for a full ductset.

"Can you believe this?" Dsanik yelled into Tmoyan's ear.

"I can. I've seen it before on Peak Nights in North."

Lanos walked from side to side, holding up his left hand while gripping his right. The crowd eagerly responded to his expression of solidarity, of commonality.

"We are all one tonight, my fellow believers. We are one. Do not listen to those on the news streams, those who doubt me. They complain and accuse, but all of you know it is completely false and without any possible foundation. *They* are the fakes! *They* are false! We follow The Messenger, we will greet The Messenger, and we will be the ultimate victors!"

Screams of support shot out from the audience.

"Yes, yes, and they doubt me, don't they? Unbelievable how deep is their skepticism and terrible unbelief! I've done all I can to open their eyes, but still they sneer at me, and you, too!" Lanos went on in this general vein for some time; each short pitch, tinged with complaint and the impression of oppression, generated more cheers from his followers. "But remember this, my fellow believers. Those who cling to their so-called objective truth, to their, shall we call them, *facts*? They call us blind and call you credulous, even gullible for following me. But they, they are the ones blinded by their self-induced

33

rationality to the larger truth at hand, the larger truth I have shown you, and you have now seen for yourselves!"

More cheers, more shouts from the crowd. Dsanik turned to Tmoyan. "He's wrapping up."

"Yes. Same speech every time, same result."

The two pilots moved off, determined to avoid being caught in the crush after the rally was over. As they reached the bridge, they could still hear Lanos' exhortations for contributions.

"Help us, fellow believers, help us welcome The Messenger. For now, good night!"

Tmoyan looked back once more, then waved his disbelief as he and Dsanik separated and headed back to their quarters.

Lanos walked off the stage, but not before surveying the excited attendees in the front few rows. Ilrosa went out to dismiss the crowd. As he came back, Lanos was waiting just behind the screen.

"Where am I staying tonight?"

"A small hotel right here in Bordinata. We bought all the rooms, as you asked."

"Good." Lanos slipped just outside the screen. "They don't want to leave!"

"Yes, Lanos, they are inspired by your words."

Lanos continued to watch the crowd as it slowly broke up. "That's good, but I could use some inspiration of my own."

"Oh?"

"See the young female, the one just right of center? She will do. Invite her."

"Invite her?"

"Yes, I have some personal revelations to share with her, *only* her. Tell her she's been called to the service of The Messenger. She'll come."

Ilrosa, as always, did as he was told and easily convinced the female, who he made sure was not quite too young, to come to meet Lanos in person. It would be a long, inspiring experience of mystic revelation, he told her.

The next morning, Lanos and Ilrosa moved on, and the young female, told she was now a member of Lanos 'inner circle,' went home with a different appreciation of what 'revelation' meant.

That night, there was another rally, and another female to lead Lanos to inspiration. At breakfast the next day, Lanos sat alone with Ilrosa in another small hotel dining room.

"The night in Bordinata went very well, Ilrosa."

"Yes, the contributions were very generous."

Lanos let out a satisfied sound. "Indeed, and contributions of every kind continued through the night."

Ilrosa did not respond.

"In the future, we must continue to use these small hotels. We must be careful of our security. There are many who question us, doubt us."

"Yes, sir Lanos. I will see to it. They will be less costly, as well."

"Your help the last two nights is appreciated, Ilrosa. Our work is exhausting, as you know, and I will require such renewal and inspiration again."

Ilrosa knew exactly what part of his work Lanos was referring to. He set aside his personal thoughts in favor of the quest he had taken on with Lanos. He was a believer, and that meant he did the bidding of the priest without question, reservation, or guilt.

"Yes, sir Lanos."

Chapter 6 (Twelve Cycles Later)

Traenah
Just outside the Gathering Dock
Spin 7, Subcycle 11, Cycle 2497

Just as Staal had predicted, well before sunrise on the second spin after their meeting, there were shouts and lights came on to get the pilgrims moving towards the waiting ship. It was now only a few spins until the comet would strike, and these ships would be the last to cross the strait to East.

Kirah and Selol went quickly over their plan.

"What about Tmoot?" Selol asked quietly. "He is so small. He doesn't know."

"Mother will never let him go."

"We have to try! We have to!"

Kirah looked at her little sister and her determination failed a little. Could she really leave her brother behind? Would she go on to certain death if she couldn't? No, she decided. Tmoot was barely weaned and not yet in control of his body.

"He will slow us down, Selol."

"He's so sweet, Kirah, I can't bear — "

"Fine, we'll try." Kirah cut her off, fearing their long conversation would alert their parents. She leaned in close to her sister. "But if Mother puts up a fight, we leave him and run. Understood?""

Selol's eyes fell. "Yes, Kirah." They slung their packs over their shoulders, packs containing all they had been permitted to bring of their former lives: a few changes of clothes, a book or two, perhaps a memento of something dear, and began the long walk to the docks.

Kirah always hated crowds, and she now found herself in the largest she had ever seen. The lines filtered out of the tents into an enormous assembly area. The Messengerite escorts kept pushing them forward, gently but insistently, as the fences gradually narrowed to where only a single family would fit. Kirah saw the moment coming and touched Selol on the arm to alert her. The fence around them was low, easily scaled, but a higher, completely impossible barrier was ahead. There was much grumbling and pointed conversation in the families behind as they approached, and Kirah could tell there were others like her, others who questioned what was about to happen to them.

As was the custom, Father led, with Mother second, carrying Tmoot. Kirah, the oldest child, was last, with Selol ahead of her. They were approaching the barrier where the fences became twice as high, and the line was forced into single file. This was the point that Staal had told her about. If they jumped the fence at the last moment, the press of those coming behind would prevent

Mother or Father from pursuing them. She looked around nervously, but there were no guards outside the enclosure, no one to stop them from fleeing. *Perhaps they don't care if you don't go,* she thought. The Easters running the ships of the exodus were not much for The Messenger, or so she had heard. But they were not much for interfering with anyone's personal beliefs, either. They would no doubt be making their own escape as soon as the ships were loaded. She thought this might be part of their obvious impatience.

"Mother, can I hold him?" Kirah was initially alarmed at Selol's question but quickly realized her little sister had a plan of her own.

"I will keep him safe," came the dismissive response.

"But Mother, you have been carrying him so long! Don't you want a rest?"

She was good, Kirah thought. Very convincing. But they had come to the moment.

Mother seemed to relent and began to turn towards Selol just as Kirah tapped her back. Selol, unable to wait another moment, grabbed at Tmoot, who screamed in fright at the grip of his sister's hands.

"No!" their mother yelled as she and Selol wrestled over the cub. The fight was over when Father placed his strong hand on Selol's face and pushed her to the ground, the crowd behind beginning to step over her. Kirah was already over the fence.

"Selol! Let's go!" Selol thought to make one more attempt, but now Father stood between her and her brother and they were steadily moving away. She pulled herself over to join Kirah.

"It's insane!" Kirah yelled. "You're going to die for nothing!"

Father screamed back at her, something unintelligible but still carrying his full fury of anger and betrayal. By then, Kirah and Selol were already running in the opposite direction. They ran along the low fence until they came to the end of the mass of people slowly moving forward. There, they climbed back over and ran down the maze of dirt paths to where Staal should be waiting.

No one stopped them. No one even called out to them. But no one followed them, either. Kirah had held out a small hope that many of her age would be inspired by their rebellion and come along. None did.

They slowed to a fast walk as they approached the meeting place Staal had given them.

He was there.

Staal waited in the last tent. Quiet and empty, its former residents were now queuing up for the journey East. He looked up as the two South females approached. They dropped breathless next to him, and he handed each of them containers of water.

"How was it?" he asked.

Selol broke down, crying and repeating her brother's name.

Kirah rubbed her back and turned to Staal. "She tried to get our brother, but Mother caught on and would not let go."

"I tried...and failed! He will only remember that I hurt him! I frightened him!"

Staal looked at her with sympathy. "Dear girl, I am sorry, but your brother will not live to remember anything at all."

Selol collapsed in another convulsion of pain and regret.

"You tried," Staal continued, "and that is admirable. Now, we must make good our escape. The autowheel is ready."

"Where are we going?"

"My cousin is a commander of North pilots. He told me he would be taking the last evacuation flight and when it would leave."

"How long do we have?"

"Until just before the comet hits, so, three spins."

"Three spins to cover two sixteen times a long sixteen mileah?"

"We can do it in two, Kirah, if we're careful. Cousin Tmoyan told me the last fission plant will be kept online until just a few spedset before the end. That will power the charging stations enough that we should be able to make it. But we have to leave now, and we have to be ready to keep going no matter what."

Kirah didn't miss the stress in his voice. "What are you afraid of?"

"Violence born of desperation, of second thoughts, or the sudden realization that they've made a fatal mistake."

They rose and moved out into the large open area where the pilgrims had left their autowheels. Kirah thought it was surprisingly neat, the vehicles parked in rows with space to get in and out. It reminded her of Peak Night events outside the city, where crowds gathered to watch they sky and parked their vehicles just this way.

Staal had brought his family's autowheel to the front the night before. They strapped themselves in as he turned it on. Staal grasped the control wand with his right hand and moved it gently forward. They moved ahead, then turned onto the empty road that ended at the docks. Or, for them, began there. Tetanna was up behind them, perhaps a fifth of the spin already spent as they rushed off to the west, away from the ships of death headed east to the 'Locus of Unification.' Away from their family and all they had known and loved.

But towards life, towards escape.

If, that is, they could make it.

Traenah
On the Road to Nomiana
Spin 7, Subcycle 11, Cycle 2497

Staal's head began to sag as the spin wore on. "Kirah, time for you to drive."
She waved her disagreement. "I don't have a permit, and I've never done it!"
"It's easy, and I will show you. And there's no one left to check for a permit."
"I'll try!" Selol's voice came from the back of the vehicle.
Staal smiled. "Your turn will come, young one." They pulled into a charging station and as they waited for the batteries to charge, Staal explained the controls to Kirah: start switch on top of the control wand, then forward for speed, left and right to steer, and back to stop.
"Simple, right?"
"I've watched Father operate ours, so, yes, I mostly understand."
"Good."
A spedset later, Tetanna was approaching the horizon in the west as they prepared to resume their travels.
"I'll rest a while, then when it gets dark, I'll drive again."
"We're going to drive all night?"
"Only until this charge is gone. There's another station ahead. It will take about four spedset to get there. Then we'll stop until dawn."
Kirah looked around, nervous. She saw Selol resting in the back seat. "Staal, can we do this? Can we make it in time?"
Staal also glanced at Selol before answering. "I believe we can, but we must keep moving. There have been no other autowheels on the road, which I think is good, but that can always change. We run, we charge, we run some more."
They disconnected the heavy electrical cables and Kirah gingerly moved the vehicle out onto the road, heading northwest.
As the star ambled slowly behind the horizon, Kirah thought about what a beautiful day it had been, sunny but not too hot, with some decorative clouds breaking up the dark blue sky. The roads had dried out and the countryside seemed to be returning to normal.
Not for long, she thought. *In a few spins, it will all be dead.*
As she drove on, her growing confidence allowing Staal more rest, she saw small creatures of the night crossing in front of her bright lights, creatures who had no clue that they were doomed, their end both certain and imminent. She'd read the reports and studied the analyses in the daily news. First, there would be an unimaginable explosion, violent ground quakes, and uncountable blazing stones falling from the sky, heating the very air to fatal levels. Finally, fire, fire, and more fire: an inferno to engulf the whole landmass of the planet. Then darkness, cold, and a barren future for whatever had the misfortune to survive to see the star's light again.

Her family would see none of that, and she wondered which was preferable: almost instantaneous incineration or a slow struggle to keep from being burned to death, frozen to death, then starved. What was preferable, she thought, was to walk away from those hideous options and escape to safety. If only her parents had listened to rationality instead of absorbing Lanos' spiritual exhortations.

Staal stirred next to her. "Kirah?"

She snapped out of her recollections. "What?"

"Are you all right? You've been silent for a whole spedset."

"I am fine. Just thinking about what's going to happen."

Staal gripped his understanding. "Yes, it's easy to obsess on that, but we need to think about where we are and what we're doing." When she didn't answer, he continued, "We should be at the next station in about eight ductset. How's the charge?"

Kirah looked down quickly, then back to the dark road ahead. "Ten percent."

"That will do."

Before long they began to see the lights of the charging station in the distance.

Staal pointed to the bluish glow on the horizon. "I know this place. We stopped here on the way to the docks. We'll charge, then move the autowheel back behind the building for the night."

Kirah didn't recall seeing this station on her family's trip to the coast. She might have slept through that part of the trip. It was enormous, with room for perhaps thirty vehicles to charge at once. It was still brightly lit, an island afloat in an ocean of darkness. After charging, Staal moved the autowheel behind the station, carefully putting them out of view of the road in either direction. As he was pulling out blankets for the cool of the night, Selol came out of the back of the vehicle and walked around to the waste booth on the side of the station.

"Do we have any food?" she asked as she returned.

"Only what we've already eaten. In the morning, we'll check the station," Staal answered. "There should be something."

Kirah crawled into the small back seat with her sister. Staal sat in the front, slightly reclined in the left seat.

Well into the night, Staal awoke and headed to the waste booth himself. As he came out, much relieved, he noticed lights in the southeast. Watching from the corner of the building, he could see that it was another autowheel, approaching very fast; too fast, he thought, to be safe. There were many large, lumbering grazers afoot at this time of night that loved the residual warmth of the road. They'd sleep on the pavement or blunder about looking for forage. Raised properly, they'd make a fine addition to a meal, but striking one in the wild at high speed could be fatal. His own father had such an encounter coming home late from a Peak Night. The animal was killed, and Father's autowheel barely made it to the next station before the leaking electrical storage ruptured and it was destroyed in flames. Staal had been quite young then, but the memory was as clear as if it had happened yesterday.

Staal watched as the vehicle sped on past, not slowing or stopping to charge. Strange, he thought. He'd memorized the list Tmoyan had given him of the location and status of all the charging stations on their route. Even a long-range autowheel like his family's would be unlikely to make it to the next open station at the profligate speed they were making. Once the lights were out of sight over the next rise, he returned to Kirah and Selol and tried to get back to sleep. Tomorrow might be more dangerous, but they would have to manage that as it came, one moment at a time, constantly on the lookout and constantly reducing risk as best they could.

As the sky began to show the first hints of dawn, Staal awakened the sisters and they looked to see if there was anything to eat in the station. The doors opened easily, and inside they found some packaged foods and drinks. At the pay station was a sign: "The Messenger will pay for you."

Kirah and Staal laughed.

"I wasn't planning to pay, anyhow."

"So, another Norther thief?"

"With the help of a self-righteous Souther girl, of course!"

When they returned to the autowheel, Staal kept Kirah outside as Selol made herself comfortable in the back and began organizing their ill-gotten provisions.

"I was up in the night," he said quietly.

"Why?"

"I needed the waste booth."

"Oh."

He looked around before continuing. "While I was out, I saw another autowheel go by."

"What of it?"

"It was going very fast, too fast to make the next station."

"Someone in too much of a hurry?" She was awfully smart, he realized. Not a child.

"Yes, in a panic, I think. They made a foolish mistake by not stopping here to charge."

Kirah looked carefully at his expression. "But that means we weren't discovered. Why does this worry you?"

Staal hesitated, looking down the road where the mystery autowheel had disappeared, then back at Kirah. "I expect we will find them ahead, either crashed on some dead animal or out of charge on the side of the road."

"What should we do about it?"

"I don't know. We'll have to see at the time and decide."

"Yes, I agree."

Tetanna was just cresting the eastern horizon as they moved out of the charging station.

"We've done well. We should be able to make the spaceport before dark," Staal said as they settled in, Kirah taking the first turn driving. "There is a station in eight long sixteen mileah. Then they become more frequent as we get closer to Nomiana. The spaceport is just this side of the city."

"Nomiana," she said quietly.

"What of it?"

Kirah sighed, her shoulders slumping slightly. "Enemy territory."

Staal looked out the right window, then back to her. "No more, Kirah, and, frankly, not for twelve cycles."

"I know. I mean, really, I accept what you say in my mind. But in my soul, there is fear, and... disquiet...about what I might find there. My home is South, and all else is suspect."

Staal gently waved his disagreement. "What you will find there is rescue. You will find the open arms of my people, and yours, ready to take all of us, North and South and East, away from this doomed place."

She gently gripped her agreement but was silent for a time. "I do love Traenah. It is my home, and I can't imagine feeling this way for any other place."

"I love it, too, but we both know it will not be like this for long. Let's leave while we can remember it as it is now. If we're late, we'll see a very different Traenah, right before The Messenger kills us."

Chapter 7

Traenah
On the Road to Nomiana
Spin 6, Subcycle 11, Cycle 2497

Kirah drove for half the morning. Selol then had her first lesson and took the second turn. She had just returned to the back seat, and Staal was driving when they spotted a figure walking next to the road two mileah ahead.

Staal stared at the lone figure growing larger in the distance for a long moment.

"What do we do?" Kirah asked. When Staal didn't answer, she asked again, "Is this the kind of trouble you were worried about?"

"Yes," he finally responded. "What is he doing here?"

The figure, hearing them approach, turned and raised his right hand, palm open.

"A Norther," Staal and Kirah said together. A Souther would have raised his left hand.

Selol stirred in the back, tired from her stint of driving. "What's going on? Why are we slowing down?"

"There's someone on foot, alone."

Selol sat up far enough to look out the window. "Ignore him. Keep going."

"Mercy, little one, is its own reward. Let's see what he has to say," Staal said as he slowed the autowheel to a stop twenty meters from the man. The man didn't approach the vehicle but waited for them to exit.

"Stay here," Staal said to Kirah.

"Not likely," she responded, "This affects Selol and me as much as it does you. I'm coming out."

Staal waved his frustration but said, "Keep your distance from him. I will search him before we talk."

Staal and Kirah exited on opposite sides of the vehicle, stopping just past the front.

"Thank you for stopping. I was afraid I would die out here." The stranger's voice was smooth, educated, and clearly Norther. Staal could tell he was handsome, with good ears and fine coloration. This was no factory worker, no foot soldier, no careless wanderer lost in the wild.

"You still might," Staal responded coldly. "Set down your pack and step back."

Kirah looked over at Staal with surprise, "Stay here," he said quietly. "If anything happens, get back in the autowheel and get out."

"Staal, I can't just —"

"Just do it, Kirah."

"As you say."

Staal turned back to the stranger. "Step back!"

"I am no threat to you! I am Ntasik."

A Norther name, Kirah thought. If he was lying, he was well prepared. Or he could just be telling the truth.

Staal knelt five paces in front of the man and searched his pack. Clothing, water, food, currency, and an identity card. Just as he expected. But, no weapons, which Staal took as a good sign.

"Do you plan to rob me, stranger?" he asked, seeing his money in Staal's hand.

Staal completed his search before he responded. "Rob you? Rob you of what? Worthless currency? What would I buy with it? A faked identity card? Who is left to be fooled by it?"

The man stood silent as Staal returned everything to the pack and threw it aside.

"Hands out and turn around."

After the man turned, Staal drew his knife in his right hand and approached him. Kirah suppressed her alarm – she hadn't seen a knife on Staal and was surprised when he drew it.

"I am going to search you. Cooperate and you will not be harmed. Resist and I will separate you from your life." Staal searched the man's clothes with his left hand, finding nothing unusual. He put his knife away.

"Turn around. What is your name?"

"As I said, I am Ntasik."

"No, your *real* name."

"I am Ntasik."

"What was your work, Ntasik, before the comet? And why are you out here alone?"

"I was a minor executive in a service company in Nomiana. I took my wife to the port but chose not to go myself."

"Where's your vehicle?"

"I fell asleep. The vehicle continued on autonomous control until it ran out of charge. I hid it off the road because I was afraid. I've been walking since before dawn, hoping someone would come by or I would find another transport."

"What is your wife's name?"

"She was...is...Mehon." Again, the right name. A respectable Norther name, but not one Staal was familiar with. It could be true, could be false. Still, something about the man bothered him. The fur on his head was neatly trimmed, and his clean face was pale, as if he had recently shaved a beard. On the other hand, many Norther men looked just like this, carefully groomed with no facial hair. He trimmed his own face at least weekly. It should not feel suspicious, he thought, but he remained skeptical.

"Wait here." Staal turned his back on the man and walked back to Kirah. "There is something I don't like about him, Kirah, but he seems to be who he says."

"The voice. The voice sounds somehow familiar. The face I can't place."

"Is it just possible his voice resembles someone you know? Could that explain it?"

"I can pay!" Ntasik called to them. "Whatever you ask."

Staal turned to him. "Under the conditions here and now, I can ask a great deal, far more than you are carrying. But we are not thieves, either. Be quiet!" He turned back to Kirah. "He is unarmed and alone. I think we should take him to the next charge station, at least."

Kirah gripped her agreement. "I will sit in the back with Selol. He can sit up front with you."

"Yes, that would be safer. I'd tie him down if I could."

Kirah laughed a little. "I'll keep his bag in the back with us. That'll help keep him under control."

"We need to get back on the road." He turned to Ntasik. "We will take you to the next charging station. Then, we'll decide whether to leave you behind."

Ntasik stepped towards his backpack.

"No!" Staal yelled. "I will take that. Kirah will hold it in the back."

"Kirah?" Ntasik responded, looking at Staal. "You have a Souther female?"

"If that bothers you," Kirah called out, "you can always keep walking."

"And what, fellow Norther, is your name?"

"I am Staal. Get in the right seat. And, she is not *my* female, nor will she be *yours*. Understood?"

Soon they were back on the road, Staal pushing the autowheel a little harder, the landscape having flattened out after the long, rolling ascent from the sea. They rode mostly in silence, Kirah studying Ntasik from the back seat, trying to place where she thought she had heard him before. On the news? Unlikely. Somewhere, though, she was almost sure.

For Kirah, that meant he was not who or what he claimed, but until she could prove it, she'd let him ride.

After two more spedset, they came to the next charging station. Staal escorted Ntasik to the waste booth, then used it himself. Together they searched the station for another vehicle but found nothing.

As they stood by the autowheel while it charged, Ntasik spoke. "So, what will it be, Staal? May I continue with you, or will you leave me here to die?"

"I am sure you are lying about something, Ntasik. I just don't know about what."

"And what if I am? Do you judge me deserving of death for some imagined falsehood?"

"Maybe," Kirah said. "But you can continue to the ship with us."

Selol came out of the station with more supplies of food and drink. Ntasik watched her intently as she climbed into the rear seat.

"Be warned," Staal said to him, "they are under my care, and I will protect them."

"I have done nothing wrong."

Staal waved his skepticism. "Your eye betrays you, Ntasik. Your thoughts are dark and selfish."

"Nonsense," he replied. "Can we continue now?"

They got back in the autowheel and continued towards Nomiana.

The autowheel continued at high speed as they came closer to the spaceport just outside Nomiana. The streets and residences of the outlying area rushed by at a rate that would be suicidal in normal times. Tetanna's bright light was just sinking below the western horizon as they made the last turn to the north, off the wide main highway and onto the access road to the spaceport. It was well worn and rutted, having absorbed far more traffic in the last cycle than it was ever designed to take. But then, as long as it was passable to the end, it met the need and there was no interest in repaving or improving it since there would be no one left to use it.

"Only five percent," Kirah said, looking back at Staal. Ntasik was in the passenger seat, Staal in the back with Selol.

"That should be enough. I can see the top of the evacuation ship already."

As they approached the spaceport, they found another large autowheel storage area. Staal coached Kirah into a parking slot. After they got out, he looked at it for a moment, then threw the token back on the front seat before giving the door a final slam. No one would likely be taking it anywhere, and, really, if they needed it, they were welcome to it. It was of no more use to Staal. There would very soon be no one left on the planet to drive it.

Throwing their packs over their shoulders, they ran through the gates, the guards eagerly waving them on. As Staal joined the queue waiting to board the enormous vessel, he saw a familiar face standing next to the entrance hatch.

"Tmoyan!" he yelled. The North officer looked up and smiled, then trotted to them, another officer with him, a Souther from the shape and color of his uniform.

"Staal! You made it!"

"Yes," Staal responded breathlessly. "I stole Father's autowheel."

Tmoyan smiled. "Congratulations!" He turned to the other officer. "Dsanik, this is my cousin, Staal, the one I told you about."

"A Souther?" Staal asked, surprised.

"Yes, and a fine friend he is. Who is this with you?"

"More Southers! This is Kirah, and her sister, Selol."

Dsanik greeted the females, "Welcome. We are glad you made it, but you have been very lucky. Time is short."

The tall, handsome male standing behind the females reached to greet Tmoyan. "I am Ntasik. Staal rescued me along the road."

Tmoyan gripped his understanding. "Well, congratulations again, all of you."

"The line is long," Dsanik said, looking back towards the ship. "But it moves fast enough. Tell the lodging officer at the door what your desires are for accommodations, and he will get you set up."

"Kirah is not my female."

Dsanik smiled. "No need to be defensive, young Staal. No one will question you. Just tell them what you want."

Ntasik leaned forward and spoke again. "I require privacy."

Tmoyan and Dsanik looked at each other. "That is not impossible," Tmoyan responded, "but it is unlikely. Speak to the officer at the door."

"But don't delay," Dsanik added. "The comet will strike in less than a spin, and we must be off the surface in half that time."

For Staal, the line seemed to move at a crawl. They separated themselves from Ntasik by pretending to need to have a discussion of how they would board, thus letting several newly arrived groups move ahead of them. A few more people rushed in behind them, each relieved to have made it in time.

Kirah waited for Selol to leave for the waste booth, then touched Staal on the arm and looked directly into his eyes. He wasn't all that terrible looking, she decided. The ears could be stronger, but, well, no one, including herself, was perfect. "You have been exactly as you said, Staal, but if you wish a female, I would — "

"No, Kirah. I cannot...do...that." He looked at her for a moment. "I have enjoyed our time together, if such a time could be enjoyed, you have made it so. You've been a good partner."

"So?"

"So, it is too soon. There is a long journey to come in the ship, and then, well, who knows?"

"Seventy-six spins, I know. But I would walk those paths with you, Staal. And whatever comes after, too. And if we were together, we could better protect Selol."

Staal made a quick fist of agreement. "I did not care for how Ntasik watched her. He was far too intense in his eyes."

"Let us be bonded, then, if only to protect her. I will do whatever you ask."

"I cannot accept a female who feels indebted to me, Kirah, and if you think about it a little more, you would be ashamed to make such an offer. It is unlike you. You will regret it."

"But — "

"No," he said, cutting her off. "You and Selol will get a cabin for the two of you. I will ask to be nearby, but I'll likely not be alone. We'll see how it goes from there. It's a long trip."

Selol rejoined them. "I feel better. So, have you two decided to be bonded or not? I can't stand the suspense anymore."

Kirah suppressed her instinct to laugh. "No, little sister, we will not be bonded. At least, not yet."

"Fine. I would have been OK with it, just so you know. We don't need a civic recorder, as if we could find one. You two could just agree and tell everyone later."

Staal looked at Kirah. "It seems your little sister is ahead of us."

"Yes. Frightening, isn't it?"

Dsanik was also ahead of them. He took the lodging officer aside and made sure Kirah and Selol got a double cabin near Staal, who was paired with another young man from North. Tmoyan saw to it that Ntasik got his single cabin, if only to ensure some degree of sanity and peace on the seventy-six-spin trip. Tmoyan could tell from Ntasik's imperious tone that he would have been a recurring problem if not granted his request.

After the line had played out, Tmoyan, as second in command, climbed to the small control room and reviewed with the crew there the detailed status of the enormous vessel. He found it ready to proceed. The vessel had already been to New Traenah twice, and this third trip would be its last. He and Dsanik then walked to the gate and stared out into the darkness for a long time, hoping to see more of The People coming. As they stood there waiting, a loud crack plunged them into darkness as the lights above suddenly went out. The last fission power plant had shut down, dropping its neutron-absorbing control rods completely into the stacks of uranium, the enormous turbine generators spinning slowly down as the automated encasement process began. There would be no one left to endanger should the reactor have some later accident, but all three countries wanted to leave whatever life came next with the best possible chance to survive.

Besides, they said, we will certainly come back to explore in the future, and we will need it to be a safe place.

The two pilots made their way back by the lights from the ship. The hum of its machinery was now the only sound they heard on a world that would soon be dead. Looking up, The Messenger was an unmistakable presence in the sky. It did not seem to be moving, but they knew it was approaching at an incredible, ever-increasing speed, a terminal velocity that would incinerate hundreds of thousands of their race in just over half a spin.

At the door, Tmoyan took a last look around. "I will not see this place again, Dsanik. At least, not in this way. My family will almost all be dead tomorrow, and there is nothing I can do."

"I, also, have family in the East. Fools, I told them. It will kill you! I pleaded with them, Tmoyan. Begged. But they were undeterred."

"Then they have chosen their fate and we cannot help that."

"I hate them, Tmoyan. I hate the foolish waste of their lives and that of their cubs. It is immoral."

"Yes, I agree."

"I will not cry for them, Tmoyan. I refuse to grieve. As you said, they have chosen their fate, and I will leave them to it."

"What do you think, Dsanik? Why did they go there?"

"I don't know. But I think they were fooled by a myth and a charlatan."

"So many? How could so many of The People be so gullible?"

"The Messenger has been in our skies for many generations, and the myths about it seem to grow with each encounter. I do not understand it."

Tmoyan looked up at the stars. The coma of the Messenger was just appearing above the horizon in the east, larger and more breathtaking than ever. "Even the name, 'the Messenger.' Doesn't that imply that there is someone or something else for which it is bringing messages?"

Dsanik gripped slightly. "Yes, but logic and proper thought seem to have been lost recently."

"Do you suppose there is something else? Is it the hope of something truly transcendental that they followed there?"

"I do not know. I am only a warrior, and this I have always been. My father fought your father and on back through the years. I do my duty; I keep my word. These are the things I can do. If there is something 'more' as you describe it, I can't tell."

"I would like to have hope that this is not the only life we have. I would like to know what is beyond."

"This is not for us to see, Tmoyan. When the darkness falls, the mystery remains forever."

Tmoyan stepped down from the ship, standing briefly once again on Traenah soil, staring at the coming disaster. Dsanik remained on the short ladder that led up to the entry hatch. He looked at his friend, then up at the comet, then back.

After a moment, Tmoyan turned. "Time to go. We need to be off soon."

Dsanik tightly gripped his agreement and stepped into the ship. Tmoyan paused just a moment to take one last look at his doomed home, then pulled the heavy steel hatch closed and secured it for space travel.

Chapter 8

Evacuation Ship Five
Nomiana
Spin 7, Subcycle 11, Cycle 2497

Dsanik stood in the small control room of the evacuation ship, Tmoyan seated just behind him and to his left. "Declare your status!"

The technical leaders all turned to face him.

"Reactor is ready, sir."

"Propulsion is ready, sir."

"Course is prepared, sir."

"Internal systems are ready, sir."

He turned to Tmoyan, who gripped his agreement but said nothing. It was up to Dsanik to give the command.

"Start the AG unit, turn to the west and continue until we are well out of the atmosphere."

The long grey giant rose slowly from its berth, turned on its axis, and began moving higher toward the west, away from the incoming comet.

As Dsanik sat down, Tmoyan leaned over. "We have one more task before we depart for New Traenah."

"Yes, we must observe the impact. I will inform Gkeze." He called for a runner to find the old astronomer and get him to the observation room.

The profile defined by the scientists placed them far from Traenah, well away from the comet's path. As they approached the designated observation position, the comet was an overwhelming vision outside the windows, its bright coma filling the sky.

Dsanik left the control room to see the impact himself. He found Kirah and Selol at the observation windows.

Gkeze was there, too, leaning hard on his cane as he watched the spectacle outside the windows. "It would be beautiful if it were not such evil."

Selol moved to stand next to the Gkeze, "How long now?"

"Very soon now, child, our home will die a violent death." He looked at the chronometer over the door to the next compartment. "Five and a half ductset."

"How fast is it going now?"

"Very fast, female cub, very, very fast. The numbers no longer matter." Gkeze turned to look at her. "I am very glad you are here and not in East. What is your name?"

"I am Selol. I could not save my brother. I loved little Tmoot. I was a good sister, sir, I was, but still I could not save him."

"Well, Selol, I am Gkeze. I am very sorry about your brother. There are many I love that I also could not save. We did all we could, did we not?"

Selol's shoulders slumped at her memory of her last moments with her family. "I tried, so hard, but Father pushed me away and then Kirah and I ran away."

"Kirah?"

"My older sister. She and the Norther boy Staal got me to the evacuation."

"Then we should be thankful to your good sister, Selol."

"I am, I guess. I just wish Tmoot were here."

"As so I. But let us share this moment, shall we? The old and the young together?"

"Yes, sir Gkeze. I am honored to be in your presence."

"Oh, child, be not too impressed by the vast knowledge of the old. We've had far more time to accumulate it than you have!"

Selol slipped her arm around Gkeze's weak side, helping hold him steady as the moments ticked off the timer.

Looking out the windows, the comet seemed to hardly move, but move it did. Dsanik went around the room, making sure every observer was wearing their darkened glasses. Many more watched on video monitors in their cabins or the dining areas of the ship.

He turned to speak to Tmoyan when suddenly the compartment was filled with a white flash, which quickly faded. Only quatsets later the light returned, even brighter, as an enormous glowing dome grew over the impact. It kept growing larger and brighter for what seemed like an impossible time. The intense light blinded them to the clouds of ejecta now falling back to the planet.

"Tmoot..." Selol cried softly. "Where is my Tmoot now?" She let go of Gkeze and slowly settled to the floor at his feet. Kirah came to kneel next to her and they held each other.

For most of a spedset, a sixteenth of a spin, the glowing fireball remained over the impact site, all the while filling the observation room with a brilliant and bizarre white light. As it finally collapsed, they could see that all East was aflame, with fires starting to burn in North and South, too.

Tmoyan looked over at Dsanik. "The spaceport is gone, Dsanik. All of Nomiana is burning."

"Remember Bordinata, that which we fought so fiercely over?"

"Yes, I especially remember that little cafe where you and I first met."

"Gone, too." He looked around the compartment. "I think it is time we got moving."

Tmoyan quickly gripped his agreement, and Dsanik, in command for this last voyage, returned to the control room. In only a few ductsets, the covers fell over the observation windows, and the ship began its long trek to New Traenah.

The meal that night was taken mostly in silence. It wasn't an idea anymore: it was real. It had happened just as Gkeze had warned twelve cycles earlier.

All of Traenah was burning, and not in some simulation or report or scientific forecast, but there before their own eyes. The Messengerites and their families weren't merely misguided anymore.

They weren't anything anymore.

It was sixteen spins, a full subcycle, into the trip to New Traenah, with sixty to go. Kirah and Selol had amused themselves at first with games and music in their cabin but soon found a better outlet helping with the small cubs in the nursery. There, no spin was like any other, and the variety and challenge of it kept their spirits up.

After a longer-than-usual spin in the nursery a subcycle and a half into the trip, Kirah and Selol stopped in the dining hall for a meal. Some old news programs were playing on the video monitor, giving the travelers a touch of home for entertainment. No one seemed to acknowledge that all of the places in those reports, and many of the people, no longer existed. It was happy insanity, like believing a child's tale just because it made you feel better or safer, even when you knew it wasn't true.

Ntasik stopped to eat with them, making his usual inane and condescending small talk and staring too long at Selol. Kirah was glad when he left. As she discussed with Selol what to do about him, or, more specifically, what not to do with him, she heard Ntasik's voice from behind her. Turning to see what he was talking about, she saw only the news report and was suddenly struck rigid. The preacher Lanos and his assistant Ilrosa were walking away from the camera. Many people in the dining hall were now yelling at the screen, many yelling obscenities and curses that would embarrass most polite citizens.

Kirah turned back to Selol. "This is out of hand. Let's go."

That night, Staal made his usual visit to Kirah and Selol's cabin before he went to bed. He wanted to hear how their day had gone, who they had met, whatever they might want to share. Staal was working in the environmental area, watching over air cleaners and waste processors. It was unpleasant work much of the time, but it was necessary work, and he was glad to have something to occupy his mind and his muscles. He had a bright and adaptive mind, and he learned the ship's processes quickly. Dsanik himself had noticed and congratulated the young man on his progress.

But tonight, Kirah was silent, even surly. When asked, she dismissed his concern and asked him to leave. Surprised by her suddenly chilly attitude, he departed.

"What was that about?" Selol asked her sister after Staal was gone.

"Nothing. Go to sleep."

"You're lying. You always look away when you're lying."

She turned to meet her sister's eyes. "Don't question me, Selol. I am the eldest. Go to sleep."

"Oh, sure. That will be easy now that you have frozen Staal out. You remember Staal, right? That male that saved our lives and then you offered to be his female? Do you — "

"Quiet! I have my reasons, Selol."

Selol changed for bed, then came back to her sister. "What happened in the dining hall?"

"Nothing."

Selol waved her disagreement. "Another lie."

"Go to sleep. Leave me alone."

Kirah turned the lights down, leaving just enough to read as she studied the drawings of the ship they had been given just after departure. The ship was enormous, with four decks of cabins. Their cabin was on the highest deck, the same as the crew cabins and the control room. She'd casually looked through the ship's emergency procedures booklet just after they'd boarded, but it was quickly clear to her that there wasn't much to do if something went wrong on a spaceship. You'd most likely die, and quickly.

But there were places to get out, or off, in some cases. Perhaps one of those was what she needed. After a while, she found it.

She left the cabin, locked the door behind her, and walked aft. It was already late, and there were few people in the dark steel corridors. She worked her way down to the lowest deck and about three-quarters back toward the rear of the ship. There, in a dimly lit corridor, was the escape airlock she'd seen in the drawing. The controls were just as pictured in the booklet, with large, well-labeled controls most anyone could operate easily. There was a heavy window in the inner door, and after turning on the light she could see the space inside. She opened the door and looked around to see how big it was. Yes, there was plenty of room for what she had in mind. She quickly closed the door and studied the controls again.

She looked up and down the corridor. There were no cabins nearby. If there could be a truly private space on a ship crammed with people, this was probably as good as she would ever find.

She would bring him here, she decided, and he would find here the reward he deserved.

A few spins later, Ntasik again joined them for dinner. Staal was with them as well.

"So, Ntasik," Kirah asked, "what is your duty on the ship?"

"Private cabin, so, no work for me. I was able to purchase a deferment."

Kirah smiled. "So rich are we?"

Ntasik smiled back. "We? Yes, I am wealthy enough."

Staal looked at Kirah and frowned. "And what will the mighty Ntasik do on New Traenah?"

"There is always a place for organization, young Staal, for competent and efficient operation. Clear communications. Those are what I will use to find a new position."

"Yes," Kirah agreed, "it sounds very promising for you."

"I have no doubt," Ntasik responded. "Perhaps you would like to talk more later? I plan to be in the cafe in a little while. Might you join me?"

"I will have to see to Selol," she responded warmly. "But after that, perhaps I will."

As Ntasik left, a smug expression on his face, Staal grabbed Kirah by the arm. "What was that?"

Kirah pulled away from him. "I need to see to my needs, Staal, and since you're unwilling, I have to seek other options."

"Needs?" Selol gasped. "You're kidding."

"Be quiet little one. Your time will come."

Staal stared at her for a long time. "I thought you, that is, you said — "

"That was then, Staal. This is now." She turned to her sister. "Let's go, Selol."

Ntasik was indeed in the cafe later, a dimly lit place where spirits and casual foods could be purchased for a small amount in ship currency. Kirah prepared herself carefully, combing her head and trimming her face in a fashionable manner. She was an attractive female, she knew, but she wanted to make sure Ntasik would understand her intent.

She left the cabin late, instructing Selol to be quiet and go to sleep. As expected, Ntasik was already in the cafe, several drinks ahead of her.

"I am fascinated by your potential," she said quietly, sitting very close to him.

"Really? It was clear to me in the autowheel that you much preferred Staal to me."

She carefully pretended to sip her drink, unwilling to surrender any of her wits or strength. "Oh, Staal has turned out to be a disappointment. I have to move on and look to my future."

"Well, in that case, I am happy to see you."

She continued her solicitous conversation until Ntasik had consumed several more beverages, and she just a tiny part of her first. She leaned into him. "I know a place we can go."

Ntasik looked at her in unfocused surprise. "But I have a private cabin."

She waved that idea away. "That corridor is far too public. Someone would see us, or see me leave, at least."

"So?"

"So, I don't want to be fodder for gossip. I do have a sister to consider. My embarrassment would be hers, too. Meet me at the escape lock on deck four, the one aft."

"An escape lock? Won't that be cold?"

Kirah leaned in closer. "Oh, I will make sure you're warm."

"Five ductset?" he asked. Kirah thought that would be too long. He might change his mind but decided not to fight it.

"Yes. I will be there."

Standing outside the airlock, Kirah watched him approach, his gait a little uncertain. She touched him when he arrived, and he murmured his pleasure. She gently moved him to one side as she opened the inner door. As he stepped in, a sly, anticipatory smile opening on his face, she gave him a strong push and slammed the door behind him.

"Kirah! What are you — "

"Justice, Ilrosa. Justice for my family and all the others."

"Ilrosa? I am Ntasik!"

"Liar!"

"What is this, Kirah? How much do you want?"

"All of it."

"All my currency? Fine. Open the door, Kirah! Yes, I am Ilrosa. You can't lock me in here!"

"Currency? You think this is about money?"

"What, then?"

"This is about my mother and my father and what you convinced them to do."

"That was Lanos, not me."

"You are as guilty as he, Ilrosa."

"What now? You're going to lock me in here? Turn me in?"

"No. I think you should spend the rest of your life in there. Actually, since there is no jail on this ship, I think you're going to do just that."

"What do you mean? I am begging you, Kirah! I'll do anything!"

"Begging? Who, coward, listened to little Tmoot's begging? Who listened to his need to live? No one will listen to yours, either."

"But Kirah, I didn't take him there. What do you want, Kirah? What do you *want*?"

Kirah looked at his eyes, now wet and pleading.

"I want all of the breath in your lungs, Ilrosa."

He seemed suddenly confused. "All the, the, what?"

She opened the controls and started the vacuum evacuation of the lock. Ilrosa, deeply intoxicated, pounded the door and screamed at her until there wasn't enough air in the sealed room for the sound to travel. Kirah turned off the interior lights and sat on the floor for a ductset just to make sure. Then she got up, turned the light on, and let the air back in. As she stepped in, Ilrosa was sprawled on the floor just inside the door. *So much the better,* she thought. *It will be a while before anyone finds him.* She took out a pen and wrote his name across his face. She took one last look at him, closed the door and turned off the lights. She looked up and down the corridor but there was no one around. She had not been seen.

It had been painful to mistreat Staal as she had, but she knew how to make that up to him. It had been necessary.

Justice was done.

She smiled and headed for her cabin.

Chapter 9

Evacuation Ship Five
En Route New Traenah
Spin 4, Subcycle 14, Cycle 2497

It was Dsanik's unpleasant duty, as the commander of this last evacuation voyage, to investigate any serious issues, criminal or otherwise. Still, the discovery of a rotting corpse in the aft escape airlock was a new low for the evacuation ships. The ship's physicians removed the remains to the hospital, where they were unable to determine a cause of death.

"So," Dsanik asked the gathered physicians as they stood around the corpse, naked and ugly beyond description as it lay on the operating table, "Please explain what you have learned."

"There are no wounds on the body that we can detect. There are no broken bones, no punctures, no bruises. Given the condition of the body and the place in which it was found, we believe he suffocated."

"Suffocated? Alone in an airlock? With an inside door release within reach?"

"Well, the chamber was closed. Sealed, of course, so, again, we believe he ran out of oxygen."

Dsanik waved his skepticism. "How long would that take?"

"Based on the size of the airlock chamber, most of a spin. It would be something of a race between the loss of oxygen and the accumulation of carbon dioxide, but our analysis is that hypoxia would be fatal within a spin."

Dsanik looked around at the physicians across the table from him. They seemed strangely quiet. "But, he would have been conscious for much of that time, no? Could he not have attracted attention to himself in there?"

"Yes, he would have been conscious for most of that time, actually. Whether he could have made his presence known to others or not would be more your area of expertise."

Then, of course, there was the matter of the name written across his face. *Ilrosa,* in unmistakable dark ink.

"Can we confirm that this is indeed Ilrosa?"

"We cannot. If we had Ilrosa's medical records or even a clean-faced image to compare, we might be able to tell. As it is, we have nothing useful to make a match."

Tmoyan looked away from the gruesome corpse to Dsanik. "His identification document is gone, too. Who is missing?"

"Ntasik. You will recall him, Tmoyan. He came in with your young cousin and the two young females. This... corpse...resembles him well enough."

"And there's the fact no one has seen him in at least a subcycle. Why was that not reported?"

"He demanded a private cabin, and he made no friends that anyone will admit."

"But someone thought enough of him to murder him?"

"So it would seem, unless we accept that he locked himself in an airlock to die a slow, terrible death."

Dsanik directed the physicians to preserve the remains pending further orders. Ntasik/Ilrosa could wait in frozen storage for now. If they needed to incinerate him later, as was their custom, that could be done after they arrived on New Traenah.

He and Tmoyan returned to the small office they shared near the control room.

"What now?" Dsanik asked.

"Well, if he was Ilrosa, he had the blood of millions on his hands. No one will grieve him, and no one will care if we simply ignore his death."

Dsanik waved his disagreement. "A murder has occurred, Tmoyan, under my command, and it is my duty to see it investigated."

"It could have been murder, yes. One could also argue that Ilrosa was consumed by guilt and killed himself."

"That would be too convenient."

"Think about it, Dsanik, Ntasik is missing at least sixteen spins...a full subcycle...and *no one* asks about him? Not a single inquiry into his welfare?"

"That is odd, true. But even a loner must be defended, his death verified and those responsible punished. There must be an accounting!"

"Yes, I understand, Dsanik, but balance that against who has been killed and what the investigation will do to the emotional environment of this ship."

"Yes, it would be hard to solve. We don't even know when he went in there, exactly, just that it was at least a subcycle ago."

"It could have been more. And, you have no evidence to work with!"

"Whoever did this, Tmoyan, and I reject the idea that he was overcome with remorse — he certainly didn't seem the type when I spoke to him — planned it very well. How they got him there, how they got him inside, I have no idea."

"Assuming they vacuumed the lock room to kill him, they were smart to re-pressurize it. He would not have decayed so quickly in a vacuum."

Dsanik gripped his agreement. "That, and the red warning light on the airlock door would have attracted attention and sped up his discovery."

"True."

They sat in silence for a few quatset, Dsanik alternatively gripping and waving his hand as he wrestled with his decision.

"What would you do, Tmoyan? How would you respond."

"I am not in command of this voyage, my friend. You are."

"Still, I would have your thoughts on this."

"Out of sheer convenience I would declare it a suicide, swear the physicians to silence about the 'Ilrosa' part, and leave it at that."

"An unexplained tragedy instead of a malignant act?"

"Exactly."

"I grasp the expediency, but I fear the consequences. We cannot have a lawless ship where murder goes unaccounted."

Tmoyan waited patiently as Dsanik wrestled with his decision.

"Case closed," he finally said. "Ilrosa committed suicide when he feared his real identity would be revealed."

"So, he both revealed it on his own terms, then ended his life to avoid the consequences?"

"Yes."

"I will support you in this decision. No need to investigate it further."

Dsanik made a general announcement at the next mealtime, outlining that the individual known as Ntasik was actually Lanos' despised assistant Ilrosa. In fear of being revealed, Ilrosa had taken his own life. His remains would be kept on board and disposed of properly when they arrived at New Traenah.

Cheers filled the dining halls. No one ever questioned the circumstances or showed the least interest in the details.

They were all too glad he was dead.

Staal responded to Kirah's note to meet him in her cabin. When he arrived, he was surprised she had sent Selol to the evening entertainment in the dining hall.

"Whatever you do," Selol said as she left, "clean up afterward, OK? I hate the smell."

Kirah didn't respond. Staal came in and sat where Kirah indicated. She looked outside the door, then closed and locked it. He looked at the locked door for a moment, wondering what was on her mind.

"So, what is it that is so important?"

Kirah sat across from him, their knees close. She looked directly into his eyes. "It was in the dining hall more than a subcycle ago. I saw a news report. When I heard the voice, I knew Ntasik was Ilrosa."

"Ilrosa? You're sure?"

"Yes."

Staal hesitated a moment, then responded, "I see."

"No, you don't. I went to the cafe with him, Staal. That evening I left you and Selol alone, I was with him."

"But, why would you give yourself — "

"I never did, Staal, never. But I let him believe I would."

"I don't understand, Kirah. He committed suicide."

She held Staal's eye for a moment. "He did not. I executed him."

When Staal didn't respond, she continued: "I lured him to that airlock, pushed him in and vacuumed the chamber. After he was dead, I wrote his name on his face and locked the door."

Staal gripped his understanding. "So, that's how they knew? His name was on him?"

"Yes."

Staal looked away. "Why are you telling me this?"

"I wanted you to know why I was so cold to you. I didn't want to hurt you, but I had to convince him to come with me."

"That can't be all."

"If you want to turn me in, I am ready to face it. I would do it again. He killed my family."

"He killed many families, although, I would say he was the lesser of the evils, but still, responsible."

Kirah's eyes flared with anger. "Are there lesser evils?"

Staal thought for a moment. "Perhaps not. I would have helped you had you asked. My family went to East, too."

She waved that idea away. "I could not ask you that. I had to do it myself and be prepared take the blame if I was found out."

"So what now?"

"You have my confession. I wanted you to know who I am, what I am capable of, before..."

"Before?"

"Before I offer again to be your female."

Staal paused a moment before answering. "We had this discussion before we left Traenah. I am prepared to wait until we arrive and are settled into our new lives."

"Yes, we said that. But I would rather arrive ready to face it together."

"But the debt you feel — " Kirah stopped him, waving away the thought.

"I am grateful that you invited me, yes, but we helped each other escape. We did that together, and I would like to do more."

"You are a little young for this commitment, Kirah. And what of Selol?"

"I have aged many cycles in the last subcycles since the docks. And I have learned those of North are not my enemies, far from it. We have always been but cousins fighting for no good reason."

"And, Selol?"

"She will stay with us. She is still my little sister, although not so little anymore. She has also aged too quickly."

"I will think about it. You are an attractive female, as I think you know. I understand about Ntasik. I don't think that is something you would ever do again."

"No."

"I do care for you, and Selol, and I am warmed by the thought of a life together on New Traenah."

"But?"

"But let me think on it. We have yet many spins on this ship. There is time."

After Staal left to return to his own cabin, Kirah flopped down on her bed, wishing she could somehow convince Staal to accept her. Perhaps he was right, she thought. Perhaps it is better to be a little patient, but she felt very much impatient at the moment.

Selol returned on time, full of questions Kirah had no interest in answering, and some were far too personal, and some far too graphic, to ever be answered even between sisters. They settled in for the night, and Kirah fell asleep in thoughts of a new place, a new role, and a new hope for her sister and herself. And a pang of small nagging guilt for Ntasik. He deserved death, she knew, but it was not her right to take that from him.

No matter, she concluded. *He's dead, and I will not be blamed.*

DISCOVERY

Chapter 10

Hansen/Powell Personal Quarters
Ft. Eustis, VA
Tuesday, March 26, 2086, 0630 EST

Commander Carol Hansen woke slowly to the sound of birds outside. Still drowsy, she turned over to see David still sleeping beside her. He woke at her movement and looked over at her with a small smile.

"Is this a dream?" she asked quietly as she closed her eyes again, putting off the day.

"Yes," he answered, "but it is also real life."

She pulled the covers back up over herself. "Hmm. That makes no sense."

He reached over to gently touch her cheek. "This is the life we dreamed of, remember? We are *fleet officers*! Remember all those winter evenings hitting the books? Those scorcher summer days doing field exercises covered in cow dung? It all brought us here."

She seemed to snug herself even deeper into the blankets. "Oh David, you're such a romantic. Yes, I remember the cow dung. And the rotting pig guts. Still...I think something is missing."

David had a sly smile. "Well, there is — " He was interrupted by the abrupt arrival of a five-year-old that looked very much like his father.

Carol sat up with a wide grin and the boy ran to her. "Yeah, that's what I was missing."

Later that morning, Carol sat across from Admiral Kieran Barker, Chief of Fleet Operations, her posture firm, her eyes fixed directly on his.

"No thanks, sir. Hard pass."

Kieran Barker unflinchingly met her gaze. "Commander Hansen, I'm not really giving you a choice."

Carol stood up, pacing in front of FleetOps' desk. "The last thing I need, sir, is a shadow following me around, writing down whatever dumbshit thing I might say. I never wanted to be known, never wanted to be the face of the fleet, or the war, or whatever — "

He raised his hand to stop her. He looked down at his desk, then back to Carol. "I understand, Carol, really, I do. But like it or not, people know what you did in Inoria and at Beta Hydri and what happened at the end on Alpha Mensae. Those stories are everywhere, even now, six years later, your name is known, and despite your aversion to the media, you're greatly admired." He paused a second. "CINC feels this would allow people to get to know you better."

Carol stopped pacing and grabbed the back of the chair she had just been sitting in. "But, Kieran, I don't *want* to be known better! Mom and Dad have problems enough already with the crazies that show up at the farm once a month."

Kieran spread his arms wide. "CINC wants this. The Fleet *needs* this."

"Oh, well, then, let us all bow down to the sacred International Space Council, the fabulous ISC, who pays for all our fun and buries all our dead!"

"Carol, that's uncalled for and you know it!"

She spread her arms in frustration. "Send them with Fiona! She's the beautiful famous admiral with the enormous brand new ship!"

He shook his head. "CINC doesn't want Fiona. She wants you. More importantly, the journalist wants you."

She sighed in resignation and flopped back into the chair. "OK, fine, bring them in. Who the hell is it, anyhow?"

"Wren Freya Thomas."

Carol perked up as she recognized the name. Thomas was a feature reporter for a major network, known for long-form interviews and fair, accurate coverage of her subjects. Her reputation seemed to say she was no hack looking for a nasty scoop. Thomas had covered the Fleet from the early days after Inoria, asking some pointed questions in the very first public briefing by then-FleetIntel Ron Harris. Carol had seen several good pieces by her about the Fleet during the Preeminent War. But try as she might to get them in front of a camera, Carol and the other survivors of *Liberty* had held her at bay.

"Well, I guess it could be worse."

"She came to CINC about this a year ago. We sent her away twice."

Carol thought for a moment. "I really hate this idea, Kieran. But if I have to do this, it has to be about *Endeavour* and not all about Carol Hansen. She follows orders, she keeps her mouth shut when I tell her to — "

Barker held his hand up again. "Why don't I get her in here and you can say that to her instead of me?"

"Fine. I need a minute."

"That works. She's waiting in Donna's office."

Carol stood up and returned to pacing as Barker picked up his phone and dialed the Fleet Chief Public Information Officer, Captain Donna Wright. After a short conversation, he looked up at Carol as she aggressively patrolled the carpet in front of his desk, hands jammed deep into her pockets.

"Five minutes."

Four and a half minutes later, Carol was standing beside Barker's desk, arms crossed, face set as if in stone as the office door opened and Wren Freya Thomas entered the room, with Donna Wright following just behind. She was shorter than Carol expected, with carefully groomed long blonde hair that looked natural. Bright, quick blue eyes accented her obviously camera-friendly features. Carol recognized, and suppressed, the immediate urge to like her. No doubt, she thought, her looks were part of her brand, part of how she got people to talk about things that might better be left unsaid.

"Hello, Captain Wright," Carol said, ignoring Thomas for the moment.

Donna, who knew Carol well, picked up her attitude and responded in kind. "Good morning, Commander Hansen. This is Wren Freya Thomas."

Thomas reached out her hand. "It is very good to meet you at last, Commander."

Carol paused just a second, then, remembering her manners, took the offered hand. Thomas' handshake was gentle without being limp.

Carol got immediately to the point. "Fleet Operations says you want to participate in *Endeavour*'s next cruise."

"Yes, Carol —:

"*Commander Hansen*, Ms. Thomas."

There was a second as Thomas was sitting down when Carol thought she might get back up and leave. Instead, she looked at Barker, who simply looked back, and then at Wright, who offered no help.

She nodded slightly. "As you wish, Commander, but I had hoped for a more cordial discussion, something more engaging — more, well, informal."

Carol didn't move, using her height advantage to tower over the sitting journalist. "I have been ordered to accept you. I want you to understand that before we proceed. This is not my choice."

"I see. Do you understand the power you have, Car —, um, Commander? People admire you; they want to know more about you."

"These would be the same people that showed up at my parents' farm last month, looking for me with a hunting knife? Or who sneak on to the base and walk around searching for my name, or Lieutenant Commander Powell's, to get a souvenir or a picture of us? Or our children? We've moved three times, Ms. Thomas, *three times,* and now we live in a house with someone else's name on it."

"Those incidents are regrettable, yes."

"Regrettable? *Regrettable?* They're damned dangerous, Ms. Thomas. And the spotlight you plan to put me under only increases the danger. I will not, I absolutely will not participate in something that places my family at even more risk."

Donna Wright looked at Carol, their brief exchange her attempt to calm Carol down and lessen the volume in the room.

Thomas stirred. "If I may respond, Commander, I do honestly regret such incidents. They are the bane of many well-known individuals. But I am in the business of communicating — "

"That's a lie."

Thomas blinked twice, then responded, "It isn't, and you didn't let me finish."

"It is a lie. Your actual business is attracting eyeballs to sell ads that maximize the profits of the network you work for. Otherwise, why would they keep you on the payroll?"

"I don't see it in such crass, vulgar terms."

"Well, Ms. Thomas, I suggest you open your eyes and read your contract."

Thomas turned to Donna Wright. "Perhaps this is not such a good idea."

"You can come," Carol said, cutting off her escape. "But the story has to be *Endeavour*, not Carol Hansen. You have a reputation for honesty, Ms. Thomas, which I am sure is the only reason Donna brought you in here."

"I have always tried to tell the complete story, Commander, not ignoring or exploiting the negative when the picture is larger than that."

"Nice turn of phrase, there. Rehearsed, I assume?"

"Really, Commander — "

"Here are my terms. They are not up for discussion. This is a one-time, take-it-or-leave-it offer. I know you will have to include something about me since I am in command, but nothing more. Nothing personal about David, our marriage, our children, or my family. You can have the run of the ship, within reason, but should something unforeseen happen, you will do exactly as you are told. You may see things that I will subsequently forbid you to ever report."

"Yes, Commander."

"If any crewmember refuses to talk to you, that is the end of it. You don't get to ask again, and you may not mention them in your final product. I don't want my crew followed around and harassed for scoops and then shamed for their uncooperative attitudes."

"I promise I will not be a problem, Commander. I have no desire to offend or annoy anyone. That's not my style."

"We'll see."

Carol stared the woman down for several seconds. *Maybe,* she thought, *this will not be so horrible after all.* Or, it might be completely intolerable. *Well, I can always lock her in her cabin.*

"Our first stop is the star Gliese 245. It will be a forty-one-day traverse, so I suggest you stock up on books and entertainment for the trip. FTL travel is dishwater dull."

"May I ask a question?"

Carol paused just a heartbeat. "Yes. One."

"The *Liberty* crew, Commander — "

"What of them?" Carol interrupted.

"*Liberty* was lost in the first minutes of the war. The story of those who survived on the surface was heroic. But they all refused to talk to me, or, for that matter, to anyone else."

"Yes."

"Why?"

Carol thought for a moment that she should just tell Thomas to go to hell. But it was a question that probably deserved an answer.

"This is what we will call *classified*, Ms. Thomas. I will share with you what happened, but you may not repeat a word of it."

"I don't understand, but, yes, I accept your terms."

"It's really quite simple, Ms. Thomas. I am surprised that anyone still asks us about it."

"Still..."

"Fine. I led that crew meeting, not that anyone needed much convincing. We were five days away from Earth aboard *Dunkirk*. By then, we had all heard how you people splashed Commander Michael's picture, and Captain Carpenter's, and mine, all over the news channels, making famous people of us without our knowledge or permission. We had all kinds of offers thrown at us, ranging from the prurient to the profitable."

Carol moved to stand in front of Barker's desk, looking directly down at Thomas.

"We would never dishonor Dean Carpenter, or Nicolai Roskov, or, especially for me, Marty Baker, my best friend on the ship who bled to death right in front of me. A few steps one way or the other and I'm the one bleeding out on the pavement, and he's here talking to you. Ever watched a friend's life literally drain from his eyes?"

"No."

"I hope you never do. We all agreed we would not soil their memory by padding our bank accounts with their blood. Do I make myself clear?"

"Yes, Commander, I see. I am sorry for those losses, and I said so at the time. But I wish you would let me tell some of these stories. It breaks my heart to hear such pain, but you give me no way to let people know what you have endured."

Wow, Carol thought, *she really is good at this.*

"Every word was, as I said, classified. You may not use a word of it."

"Yes, I understand. But in my own defense, Commander, I do try to tell an honest story, to give an honest picture of the subject, whatever or whoever it is. I should think you would want someone like me to tell your story, not someone with less consideration for the truth of it."

Carol turned to Barker. "OK, she can come. Get her something to wear on the ship that's not too distracting."

"Distracting? I have always dressed professionally, Commander. There are others who dress more, well, provocatively, but I never have."

Carol shook her head, "That's not what I mean." She pointed to her uniform. "Out there, we all wear this boring dark grey work uniform. You need to fit in."

"What do you suggest?"

"Donna understands. She can help you." Carol pulled out her phone to verify *Endeavour*'s schedule. "We pull out for GL 245 at 0600 on 14 April. Be at the

69

shuttle port at 1500 the day before. The XO will bring you up with the last few crew members."

"That would be young mister Dean?"

"That would be Senior Lieutenant Jayvon Dean, yes. He is an *Antares* veteran. He might be an interesting first conversation for you."

"Thank you, Commander. I will be ready."

Carol took her leave of Kieran Barker and headed home. In ten days, David would be taking *Onizuka* to Gliese 262, a star even farther away than her assignment. Two weeks later, she'd have to take their children Leon and Terri out to the farm to spend a few months with Grammy and Poppy. For the kids, it was an extended vacation, complete with tractors, dogs, and horses, far away from the dull routine of a military base. For the grandparents, it would be a busy time of bliss with small people they once thought might never appear.

It would not be so easy a time for the absent parents.

Meantime, Kieran picked up the phone and called CINC Patty Cook. "She accepted, but, wow, she is really not happy about it."

"Did she mention Powell's assignment? They'll be fairly close together."

Kieran looked at his notes. "No, she didn't. But, I'm not sure I'd consider seventeen light-years all that close."

"We could change it, you know, and send him elsewhere."

"These two signed up for Fleet duty long ago. They're pros. They get their assignments as the list bubbles up, Patty, just like everyone else. I don't think we should be catering to them."

There was a pause at the other end. "Yes, you're right, I know. These should be routine trips, anyhow. We have no reason to think there is any more risk in these stars than any others."

Kieran smiled. "Which is also to say no less risk. There is always a risk, but since the war we haven't seen any other modern cultures."

Another pause. "You think Thomas is as honest as Donna thinks? I'm worried about Hansen with the additional exposure."

"She stood up pretty well to Carol's obvious opposition."

"But Carol relented?"

"Yes. She set some hard expectations, but she agreed."

"OK, then, we'll see. I'll hope for a routine cruise."

"As will I."

They hung up, both sure that Carol Hansen could handle herself and her ship, even with the added baggage of a reporter observing her. The Fleet was taking a lot of questions lately about its size and particularly its budget, now that there was no war to fight. The ISC was looking to increase profits, and the Fleet was the one organization that did not directly contribute.

But, as CINC Patricia Cook had argued, should some problem culture appear, they would want the Fleet instantly available. She made it clear that they could not have it both ways, and, for now, the ISC had relented. But those ideas would not disappear, and she knew she'd be making similar arguments in the same place sometime in the not-too-distant future.

Chapter 11

Space Fleet University Campus
Northern Ohio
Wednesday, April 3, 2086, 1500 EST

Lieutenant Commander Declan Moore got up from his desk and closed his office door behind yet another student who had all the right stuff for success but wasn't choosing to actually use it. She'd probably be cut before junior year, and Declan decided he would not be too sad to see her go. There were less gifted but harder working students he could do a hell of a lot more for than this last smart-but-lazy slacker. *But,* he thought to himself, *they will all be someone else's problem soon.*

As he turned back to his desk, through his second-floor office window he noticed a familiar figure sitting alone in the courtyard a level below him. Lieutenant Commander Natalie Hayden could be found there frequently in the mid-afternoon, sipping from the oversized coffee cup she always carried. She sat very still, he thought, as she looked off into the distance. Declan knew first-hand the story of Natalie and her late fiancé Ben Price. Declan had been on *Intrepid* with them, watching with everyone else and silently rooting them on as their relationship grew. Ben had brought out a whole new Natalie, one more relaxed, more relatable, than the previously hard-nosed, all-business version. Declan had always respected her for the high quality of her work, but the whole wardroom felt lighter when she and Ben were around.

He was there too when they brought Ben's remains up from the battle with the Preeminent on the planet at Beta Hydri they called 'Big Blue.' And, when they took Ben and the others off for burial the day they returned to Earth. Declan had also sat with others from *Intrepid* near the back of the beautiful nineteenth-century church where Ben's family held his memorial service. The arches and stained glass harkened back to a simpler time, one Declan knew existed only in their communal nostalgia. The past was never as simple, serene, and beautiful as people liked to think. After all, on the very day that beautiful chapel first opened to worshipers, there was probably horse dung piled in the street outside.

But today, he was looking out on a pleasant spring day in Ohio, one where the brisk winter winds had begun to abate, and the sun was starting to warm the place up. The crocus had peaked already, and the tulips were in bud. As Declan looked further outside, leaves were just beginning to show on the trees. In a few weeks they would be fully green, and the slightly dingy landscape before him would be transformed into a lush green. But by then, both he and Natalie would be very far from the University, very far from spring itself. He thought about those orders as he considered the woman across the courtyard. In a moment, he made a decision he'd been putting off for weeks and picked up his jacket.

Natalie looked up as Declan came out of the double doors and started across the brick pavers towards her. She smiled slightly as she recognized him.

"Declan! Something up?"

He shook his head as he sat next to her, carefully not too close. "No, not a thing." He leaned forward on the bench. "I just had my last session with Morgan."

"Oh, that one." Natalie shook her head. "She'll never make the line for third year."

"I told her as much. She really didn't seem to care." After a pause, Declan looked at Natalie again for a moment. "Walk?"

She looked back at him, her head inclined slightly as if unsure what he had asked. "Sure, why not?"

They set off through the tall stone-and-brick arch that invited them out of the courtyard, out into the wide lawns and occasional scattered clumps of trees that dotted the campus. The sidewalk led directly through one, inviting the walkers to continue. They walked side-by-side for a few minutes in silence.

"Somehow," Natalie finally said, "I get the feeling you have something other than Cadet Morgan on your mind."

"Ah, well, I guess after working together this long, you read me pretty well."

Natalie smiled. "Well enough. I suppose. Declan, what's really on your mind?"

Declan took a breath, placed his hands behind his back, and plunged headfirst into the deep end. "I was wondering if you'd be willing to meet me for a drink after work tonight."

Natalie didn't break stride. "Declan, are you asking me out on a date? Me?"

He grinned, embarrassed. "I was thinking of it more like a pre-date, you know, just to see if there could be a date."

She answered quietly. "Aren't we kind of old for this kind of thing? I mean, gold oak leaves and all?"

He shook his head. "Not at all. I mean, really, I'm thirty-six, and without asking, I'd guess you're about the same, maybe even a little younger. Besides, I don't ever want to think I'm too old to find something new, something that might be rewarding."

"Rewarding?" she responded with a small laugh.

"OK, make all the fun you want of my word choice. Will you?"

They took several steps before she responded. "Yes, I will. But what brought this on now? *Enterprise*?"

"That has something to do with it, I think, but it's not all of it. I just decided it was time."

"Time?"

"Time to stop hiding that which should not be hidden. Time to reach out for that which might be..."

"Rewarding?"

Declan smiled. "Good word choice, but I think *worthwhile* might say it better."

As they approached the building on their return, she stopped and touched his arm. "Declan," she began gently, "I said I'll be there, and I will, but I can't make any promises. I'm just...well...I'm still..."

"I know, Natalie. I was there. I don't need any promise beyond that you'll be at *The Cookie Factory* at six."

"OK, fair enough."

They headed back inside, out of the warm April sunshine and back into the antiseptic, brick-and-steel-and-glass environment of Space Fleet University.

As she returned to her desk, Natalie's cheeks were flushed a little, and not completely from the fresh breezes outside.

It was just before six as Natalie sat at the end of the bar, sipping her margarita. She looked down and asked herself aloud, "What the hell am I doing here?" She hadn't been in a place like this since her last night ashore with Ben, and after his loss, she'd had little interest in anything that felt even faintly romantic. There had been a few invitations over the last years, all of which she had declined. As she thought of Ben, she unconsciously touched the gold cross Ben's mother had given her at his wake six years earlier. She could still see the sad tears in the old woman's eyes and felt her own welling up at the memory. She looked down at her hands as they surrounded the tall glass, focusing especially on the finger on her left hand where there would have been a ring, probably two by now, had he lived.

But Mila Price never wanted her to grieve forever and frequently reminded her of that. So, Natalie had accepted Declan Moore's invitation for an after-work drink. As he had said, it was a pre-date: a check-in to see if there was any interest in pursuing it further. He was a good man, she thought, a more than competent, hardworking officer. Declan had been the Maintenance Officer on *Intrepid* throughout the war, beginning right after Ben's pal Joanne Henderson took command. Declan was handed the ugly job of cleaning up a mess that an incompetent ensign, someone whose swagger far outweighed his skills, had made of the department.

A year after the war was over, he'd been reassigned to SFU to teach Ship Systems, his office just two doors down from hers. For the last three years they'd shared a few lunches, random coffee breaks, and many cadet counseling and discipline sessions. The combination of Natalie's wartime credibility with Declan's direct approach to students was enough to correct most problems. They seemed to make a good team, and Natalie enjoyed working with him.

Declan arrived right at six and slipped easily next to her at the end of the bar. He surprised Natalie by ordering a Southern Comfort, double, straight.

"What, no gin-and-tonic? No scotch?"

"Not tonight. Still learning to be a good Yank."

"Ah."

"Besides, have you *seen* the price of good scotch lately? Scandalous."

They chatted for a few minutes about the day, the weather, and the students they shared at the University.

After a particularly long pause in the conversation, she looked over at him. "I haven't been out much, you know..."

"Since Ben?"

She nodded. "It has been a long time."

Declan took a sip of his drink, buying time to think, then turned to face her. "I remember him clearly. It was a stretch for Henderson to make a Warrant her Intel officer, but Price was excellent. I thoroughly enjoyed his briefings...always a little humor lurking somewhere in the details." He paused. "Listen, if this is not a good time for you, I can wait." When she didn't react, he turned back to his drink. "I'm willing to wait."

Natalie shrugged. "I don't know if there will ever be a good time."

He looked her in the eye for a moment before responding. "Are you afraid you'll never feel for someone again like you did for Ben?"

She was suddenly still, her body hit with an unexpected rigidity. He was too close, seemingly already in her head, well past her defenses. *How did that happen?* "Yes."

He shrugged. "Well, you know, you might not."

She smiled as she fought back the tears welling in her eyes. "You're not helping yourself here."

Declan laughed. "Maybe not...maybe not. But it was a special, unusual time, what with the war on and so much uncertainty. And, he was an unusual man."

"That he was."

He looked her in the eye again, then back down the bar. "I've enjoyed working with you, Natalie, enjoyed watching how you work with people, students, instructors, custodians, whoever. You always treat people so well."

She quickly wiped her eyes and nodded. "Good manners were always a priority in my house."

"It's more than that." He paused for a few seconds. "There's a fundamental respect that you give everyone. I think that says a lot about who you are, and it's what draws people to you."

Natalie leaned back and shook her head. "Draws people? To me? That hasn't been my experience of it."

Declan nodded slightly. "People like you, Natalie. That's easy. But not everyone can be in a relationship with a woman as strong as you are. Or, as smart as you are."

Natalie looked at him for a moment. She had never felt like an object around him like she did with some of the other instructors. She'd never noticed him staring at her or watching her as she moved around a room. "But you can?"

"Yes, I can. I've been around them all my life."

She thought carefully about him, his obvious but unobtrusive intelligence, and how he also treated everyone around him with the same kind of respect he saw in her. *He's hard not to like,* she confessed to herself. *How is this guy still single?* she wondered, then remembered what a Fleet life was like and how it took real dedication to make any relationship work.

As she set her drink back down, he reached across her back and gently grasped her shoulder to bring himself a little closer. She was surprised but didn't resist.

"But Natalie," he said quietly, "I am not Ben Price, I can never be Ben Price, and I know no one can take that place in your heart. I accept that he will always be with you, but there is still a whole life out there ahead of us, and I'd like to see what we can share of that."

Natalie sat up a little straighter but didn't shake off his touch. She took a sip of her drink and turned toward him. "My time with Ben was unique. It was...intimate...in every way possible. I never had such peace in my heart before him. I never felt so comfortable as myself before I knew him."

He nodded and dropped his hand from her shoulder. "I see."

"I'm not sure you do. You knew him, and you know what we had together. But Declan, if we're to have any kind of connection ourselves it can't be about Ben, about replacing Ben, or how you're *not* Benjamin Price. It has to be about Nat and Declan. And honestly, I've spent the afternoon thinking about it, and I'm up for it. Really, I'm willing to see what might be there. But if we can't find that as just us, then I'm not sure I see the point in all this."

He looked out across the restaurant, thinking about what she said. She paused to absorb the feeling of his touch. There had been none of that in the long years since Ben's loss. Suddenly missing it, she consciously leaned slightly into him.

"OK, so, what happens now, Commander Moore?"

"Dinner?"

"Yeah, dinner would be good. I'm starved."

Declan slid off his bar stool to go find the hostess.

They stood outside for a minute after dinner, admiring the stars in the clear night. Finally, Declan touched her gently on the arm.

"Goodnight, Natalie. See you in the morning."

As he walked towards his vehicle, she called, "Thank you, Declan. This was...lovely."

He turned back to her, smiled and gave a slight bow. "My pleasure."

Natalie watched his vehicle silently pull out of the parking lot and disappear around a bend in the road to the west. Then she walked the short distance to her own transport, a small electric ASV, and sat gently in the back seat.

"Take me home," she said, her voice distant and distracted. There was much to think about, and she wondered how much sleep she would find in the night ahead.

Price Residence
Frederick, MD
Monday, April 22, 2086, 1400 EDT

Natalie held on to Ben's mother Mila for a long time, then finally released her and stepped down the old wrought-iron steps to the brick sidewalk that framed the narrow Frederick side street. Her rented ASV pulled up right on cue and she got in. She turned to look back at Mila and Logan, and they shared one last wave as she departed. Once away, she wiped away her tears and prepared herself for what was to come next.

As the vehicle headed southeast, she leaned back in the well-padded seat and closed her eyes, thinking about the last few weeks: about those final days in her classroom and long evenings spent preparing for *Enterprise*, frequently with Declan across the table from her. Systems and Weapons were inextricably entwined, and his job keeping everything working had a direct effect on her ability to employ *Enterprise*'s vast arsenal. Often, they would study the drawings and flowcharts side by side, and Natalie welcomed the feeling of him being close to her. She was beginning to feel the easy comfort of a genuine relationship, of growing affection well-seasoned with admiration and respect.

Mila and Logan Price were delighted with her news. They insisted she bring Declan to see them. Soon. After all, they said, she was like a daughter to them. But there was one more person she needed to visit. One more pilgrimage to what was to her a sacred place

A half-hour later, the ASV parked in the last lot on Sugarloaf Mountain, and Natalie climbed the stony, irregular path to the summit. There, she stood by the boulder where she and Ben had first confessed their feelings for each other and where she had come many times since, alone, to grieve. It was a beautiful, peaceful place, a place to which Ben had such an intense connection. She wasn't sure what she wanted there or what she was looking for there. To feel his permission to go on with her life?

No, Ben would not have felt that she needed either of those. He loved her fully but never possessively. His love always surrounded her but never encased her. She stood at the boulder they always shared, Ben on the right, she on the left. She sat carefully and placed her hand where he would have been.

"I love you," she said quietly. "I always will."

Instantly his answer flashed into her mind, his voice as clear as if he were physically present: *And I will always love you. But the time is here for new chances, new happiness. Seize it!*

She nodded to herself, smiled slightly, and gave the stone a last touch. "Goodbye, Ben."

As she descended the stone path, she could feel him fading from her, almost as if he had needed her to release him. He was now free, and she was now equally free to experience her life anew. By the time she sat in the ASV, she was smiling, feeling a new lightness as she anticipated a pleasant evening in Norfolk before leaving tomorrow for *Enterprise.*

Three days later, Natalie stood in the passageway just inside the port forward airlock, waiting for the *Enterprise*'s new contingent of Fleet Marines to arrive. She checked herself in the glass of the door, then stopped. *I'm not that vain,* she thought. *So what is it?* she thought back. She didn't need to answer. She knew the reason she wanted to be here, and he was just on the other side of the airlock door.

As the door swung open, all Natalie saw was Liwanu Harry's bright smile. He stepped out of the path of the Marines following him and embraced her. She held him close, surprised but pleased.

"Hello, Commander," he finally said.

Natalie turned him loose. "Hello, Liwanu. I am glad to see my little brother again!"

"Not so little anymore! See?" he laughed as he pointed to his two silver bars.

"That's great. I'm still one up on you."

"Yes, ma'am. You look well. Is Commander Moore aboard?"

"Yes, things are going pretty well right now. And yes, Declan is already here. What about you? How are things with Kamaria?"

Liwanu watched as his Gunnery Sergeant went by. "Good, ma'am, very good. But I best be going, Commander."

"Of course. See you in the wardroom."

Liwanu trotted to catch up with the back end of the Marine contingent, his first solo command. *Enterprise* was enormous, with the ability to land ground forces as well as mix it up in the kind of ship-to-ship combat they had experienced during the Preeminent War. Liwanu's light rifle/recon platoon had AI-capable drones and advanced weaponry they had lacked during the earlier conflict. The force-multiplier aspect of their technology helped keep the complement small, less than thirty individuals. But they could pack a significant punch.

Promptly at 1800, *Enterprise*'s Executive Officer Commander Mazablaska Dawes entered the wardroom and called everyone to attention. As chairs squawked and rattled behind knees going straight, a thin, short woman with deep auburn hair followed Dawes into the room. Fiona Collins had offered to return her star to CINC in order to command *Enterprise*, but Patty Cook turned her down. She kept the star but still got the ship.

The admiral walked amiably to her place at the head of the table. "At ease, everyone, please go ahead and sit down. And, let's not do that again, OK Maz?"

The officers responded with a short laugh, sat, and the conversation level rose dramatically. It died just as rapidly when Fiona stood again.

"I'm glad we're finally all here." She stopped a moment to look around the table. "Thank you all for coming along with me. I want you to know that you're here because I specifically wanted you here. CINC gave me every opportunity to have the crew I wanted, a crew to match this fantastic ship we've been given." She looked around the table again. "Enough talk, though. We're leaving 0600 tomorrow for GL 188, thirty-eight days, as planned. Enjoy your dinner."

Natalie sat between Declan and Liwanu, talking animatedly with both and often pausing to bring one or the other up to speed on what they were talking about. As Liwanu listened and watched her face, he saw flashes of the Natalie he had known on *Intrepid*, someone he had come to admire and to envy, just a little, for her relationship with Ben. Back then, he'd hoped for something like that for himself with someone, and it was beginning to come true with his fellow Marine officer Kamaria Allen, another veteran of the final fight at Alpha Mensae. But watching Natalie now, he smiled inwardly at her return to her complete self. He would have to talk to *Intrepid*'s Captain Joanne Henderson; she would be pleased, too, to see Natalie this way.

For now, it was a thirty-eight-day traverse. He had Marines to train in how to manage themselves aboard ship; Fleet Marine basic training was great but didn't do much to teach them about the nuts and bolts of ship life. He also had to train the fleet crew on the basic weapons the Marines carried. The lessons of Beta Hydri, especially, taught the necessity for the whole crew to be ready to pick up a 2K7X if necessary. He smiled at the prospect. It would be fun, especially if he could get Natalie to drop in once in a while.

Chapter 12

Endeavour
En Route GL 245
Monday, April 29, 2086, 2215 UTC

It was late in the evening when Wren Freya Thomas strolled onto the Bridge, looking for Carol. She stood at the foot of the three steps that led from the floor of the Bridge to the command position. "Might I have a moment, Commander?"

Carol looked down at her, then nodded and indicated the XO's chair to her right. "Have a seat."

She set her NetComp down and turned to Thomas. "So tell me, how are you getting along? Two weeks out is often a difficult time for newcomers. The novelty is usually worn off by then."

Thomas sighed. "Yes, I underestimated how much reading material to bring, and I ran out of movies a few days ago."

"Are you getting to know the crew?"

Thomas looked at Carol skeptically. "Well, the captain is somewhat stand-offish, as you know, but the rest are being open enough. They're quite nice to the neophyte, very accommodating to her odd requests and lack of understanding of simple concepts."

"Yes," Carol smiled slightly, "there are many subtleties of shipboard life not covered in the Fleet recruiting material or the training manual." She paused a moment before continuing. "I did instruct the officers to cooperate to the extent they felt comfortable."

"I appreciate that. But what of the captain? Will I ever get a juicy exclusive from her?"

Carol could not help but smile. Thomas was likable, even if she suspected it was just an artifice to get stories.

"The captain has her responsibilities. She does not wish to be the story herself."

"Yes, you made that clear at the start. But, if I could ask some simple questions? Not about you personally?"

Carol tapped her fingers for a few seconds. "OK. A few."

"The ship is not as cold as I expected. I mean, I brought sweaters, but I've never needed one. Space is very cold, or so I have read."

"Well, you're right. Space is incredibly cold. We basically steal heat from the reactor and distribute it throughout the ship. The insulating layers in the outer sections and the thick stealth coating on the outside of the ship then help contain that, keeping us nice and warm inside and reducing our external IR signature as well."

"Can I ask how fast we're going?"

Carol looked over at the Nav status display. "The top speed of these ships is classified, but we're only doing one-point-three right now."

"Only?"

Carol nodded as she picked up her NetComp to calculate the speed in terms Thomas would understand. "Let's call it 475 times the speed of light."

"That's incredible. I don't feel any sense of motion."

"Well, if you did, it would not be for more than a nanosecond. No one knows what would happen if the Drive were to fail, but we're pretty sure it wouldn't be good."

"Oh?"

Carol looked out over the Bridge for a second, smiling at a memory. "I had the same conversation with Greg Cordero, you know, the linguist? Anyhow, on our way out to Beta Hydri, he wondered why we stood watch in FTL since the ship was basically running itself. I told him if it was going to turn us all into x-rays or quarks or whatever, I'd rather someone be watching when it happened."

"That can't be all."

"No, true, there is always work to do: communications to monitor, systems to maintain, exercises to run, that kind of thing. But I learned from Captain Michael to keep it very informal during a traverse. Off duty, it's damned boring, as you've learned. But once we arrive, it's time to buckle down and get serious."

"Speaking of arrival, I'm not sure I understand why you do this."

"Do what, in particular?"

"Go all the way out here yourselves. Wouldn't it be more efficient to send some AI-powered probe to check out these stars? I guess without a war to fight, I don't get the point."

Carol smiled and nodded. "I've heard the same question many times." She looked out on the quiet Bridge, then back to Thomas. "It's not a simple thing to answer. It's partly a reconnaissance to look for new threats, partly scientific exploration, part prospecting for the miners who pay the bills, and part curiosity, too."

"But you have no astrophysicists aboard to make those scientific observations, right?"

"True, but our process for each system is designed by astrophysicists and astronomers based on what they know about it, and our data is open sourced as soon as we return."

"I wasn't aware that it was shared so publicly."

"Yes. Our instrumentation is very good, and we generate enormous amounts of data on every cruise."

"I see. I am told you hold a Bible study and prayer meeting every Friday?"

Carol looked at her for a moment, then decided it was, after all, part of the ship's culture. "There are a dozen or so folks that attend regularly, sometimes it's as many as eighteen. I consider myself more of a facilitator than a leader. Each week, someone picks a passage or a question and we talk about it. It's nothing formal. You're welcome to join if you like."

"I might. But, why Friday?"

Carol shrugged. "Old Testament Sabbath, I guess. Somehow it got started back on *Antares* and that's where it's been ever since."

Thomas nodded her understanding. "Do you have a favorite passage?"

"Yes. Romans 8:38."

Thomas looked away. "Remind me?"

"For I am convinced that neither death nor life, nor angels nor rulers, nor things present nor things to come, nor powers, nor heights nor depths, nor anything else in all creation, can separate us from the love of God in Jesus Christ."

"Ah, yes. I have heard that many times. It is, um, reassuring somehow?"

"I identify with the heights and depths."

"Yes. I can see how you might. How do you feel about your faith now, what with all these intelligent alien species about? Does it affect your thinking?"

Carol thought for a moment. "I think the lesson of alien intelligence for a Christian is humility."

"Humility? How so?"

"It is not for us as followers of Christ to limit the creativity of the creator. Life is seemingly everywhere; the universe was apparently designed for it to be so."

"An interesting point of view. I would have expected something more, well, more narrowly drawn."

Carol smiled and moved the discussion away from herself. "Have you been to the Saturday night jam in the hangar?"

"I was there the last two Saturdays. It is enormous fun. The crew really seems to enjoy it."

"It's a creative release for sure, a chance to just be themselves for a few hours. There is an amazing amount of talent in the Fleet, all kinds of stuff that has nothing to do with spaceflight."

"I saw a few drinks in there. I thought alcohol was forbidden on US-commanded Fleet ships?"

"It is, but I confess I do deliberately look the other way for one evening during a traverse. We don't exactly have weekends aboard, but I do my best to lighten the schedule for Saturday and Sunday to give people a little break. But it's only for that one evening and the crew knows it. I haven't had to discipline anyone for alcohol use, but I would not hesitate to do so if it were necessary."

"I am told there is a stranger who sometimes attends the jam, hiding in the back of the crowd behind oversized sunglasses and a floppy hat."

Carol grinned slightly. "I have heard that same rumor from time to time. I think she, or he, was there last Saturday. Whoever it is, I suspect they're there to hear the music and laugh at all the jokes at the captain's expense."

"Yes, perhaps...you mention *Antares*...I know many of the *Liberty* survivors followed Captain Michael to that ship. How many *Antares* crew are aboard?"

"Well, you already know about the XO. Jayvon was the Comms officer on *Antares*. There is a handful of *Liberty* crew here, mostly chiefs and senior techs now. My Reactor Officer, Denise Long, is probably the senior member of that club. She was literally a kid just out of college when Inor was attacked. She's a solid veteran officer now. I was at HQ for several years after the war, then a year as XO of *Sigma*, so some of the *Liberty* folks have left the Fleet or been promoted away from me."

"How long have you been captain here?"

"Three months. *Endeavour* came out in the summer of 2080, just after the war. Last year it was time for her refit, so when she was ready, Denise and Jayvon and I went out to Tranquility II and brought her back."

"Just the three of you?"

"Well, there were about a dozen altogether. You need five FPI staff and at least four for the reactor. But, a small group."

"Tell me about the experience at Beta Hydri. I've read some amazing things about that planet."

Carol shook her head. "What happened there, the Seeker culture, the ground battle with the Preeminent, that's all well documented, as is my part in it."

"You lost people there. Surely you have feelings about that."

"I did, and yes, I do. What happened there, as I said, is all very well documented."

"Senior Lieutenant Dean speaks glowingly of your time in command of *Antares*. What was your experience of it?"

"Aren't we a little off-topic here?"

"I am trying to get a fuller understanding of your leadership, Commander. There are so many stories about you floating around. I would like to know what's real and what isn't."

"My experience in command began when Terri Michael's chest exploded and the dart that killed her damn near killed me, too."

Thomas looked up from her notepad. "Must you always be so graphic?"

"Must you always be so naive? It was a war, Ms. Thomas, complete with battles, blood, and guts, and I do mean all of that literally."

Thomas consulted her notes, and Carol noticed for the first time that Thomas used a paper notebook and pen, much as she and David did for their journals.

"You use a notebook? Doesn't that make it hard to organize?"

"Oh, I have my system. And with paper, I can write in the margins or doodle or write notes to myself. I could do all that with a tablet, I suppose, but this just feels more natural to me." Thomas looked up from her notes. "Is it true that you and Commander Powell keep paper journals that you exchange periodically?"

"Off-limits, but who told you that?"

Thomas looked up, as if looking at something far away. "It's a very romantic idea, right? Lovers sharing thoughts even when they're light-years apart?"

Carol looked at her for a moment. "As I said, off-limits."

"That's not a denial."

"Nor is it a confirmation. What else is on your mind?"

"You mentioned the dart. How is your leg today?"

"OK, we're veering pretty close to the edge now, but I guess it is part of the story. It's fine; it annoys me by itching at the margins sometimes, but I am completely recovered and have no lasting physical limitations."

"That sounds like a quote from a fitness report."

"It is."

Thomas slumped in the chair. "I would like to earn your trust, Commander. I would love to be able to tell your whole story because just what little I know so far is so inspiring, so beautiful, that I think people should hear it."

"And your network could sell ads at exorbitant prices for people to watch it."

"That, again."

"Yes, that again. You're a product, Ms. Thomas. Something sold for a profit. The Fleet is not. I...am not."

Thomas paused, then said, "I promised you fair coverage, a full story of you and your ship. I think the public would like to know if the person is anything like the legend."

"The public, Ms. Thomas, has not been particularly kind to me or my family. Unlike some in the public eye, I do not crave their approval or adoration. I am just not that concerned about what they want."

"I would like to talk again if we could."

"Sure. And, I will consider what you've said. I don't watch much of what comes streaming out of the news studios these days, but Donna believes you can be trusted. So far, she seems to be correct."

"I appreciate that. In a few days, then?"

"Fine. Meantime, I will ask my admin to give you access to the unclassified partition of the ship's library. Most of the Library of Congress is in there, along with a number of entertainment options: music, movies, old television, that kind of thing."

"Thank you."

"Good night, Ms. Thomas." Carol turned back to her NetComp.

Wren Freya Thomas was not accustomed to being dismissed. She paused a few seconds and then rose and left without another word.

Carol watched her leave, now unsure of her opinion of the woman. Was she sincere, or was this all just a con to get a headline? She'd certainly invested her time: four months in space, and, therefore, not in front of her audience was quite a commitment. Perhaps she had misjudged the woman.

Carol decided to talk to her XO and see what he thought. Jayvon was a good judge of people, one of those people who could quickly spot a fake.

Onizuka
En Route GL 262
Wednesday, May 8, 2086, 1730 UTC

Lieutenant Commander David Powell sat in the command position on the Bridge, reviewing on his NetComp the astrometric data available on their destination. *Onizuka* was already more than fifty light-years from home, with nine more days of travel yet to go. This was David's first long traverse in command, and it was longer even than *Cobra*'s covert sprint to Alpha Mensae back during the war. He had a good crew, but six weeks at FTL was hard on everyone, and there were only so many books and so many workouts and so many games of Spades one could play before boredom began to creep in. He counted himself lucky to command *Onizuka*, a fast new frigate with the latest evolutions of the Forstmann Drive and reactor, making her capable of cruising at incredible one-point-four light-year-per-day speeds.

As David refreshed his memory, the star Gliese 262 was very similar to the Sun, slightly larger and brighter, but still a class G star likely to support terrestrial planets and, therefore, life. Astronomers believed there were no close-in gas giants there, but the detection of smaller, Earth-size planets was iffy, and the data gathered to date was ambiguous.

Well, he thought to himself, *we'll know soon enough.*

David was glad his Space Fleet University classmate Larry Covington had signed onto *Onizuka* as Chief Navigator. They were now all 'plank owners' in the old Navy parlance: the first commissioning crew of a new ship. His Weapons officer was Grayson Lopez, a new Senior Lieutenant only a few years out of the University. David had reservations about handing Weaps to such a junior officer, but David's good friend, the very dependable Natalie Hayden, had recommended Lopez as one of her best students, so David agreed to take him. He also recalled how Captain Terri Michael had handed his wife Carol the Weapons position on *Antares*, well before she was ready 'on paper,' and he felt keenly that it would have been slightly hypocritical of him to turn the man down.

He had no such qualms about his XO: the bright, beautiful, and battle-scarred Melinda Hughes. Sometimes, Hughes-Clark. David was never sure what she and Mike had decided about their names, and it seemed to change from time to time. David knew her well from his time on *Columbia*, knew first-hand of the courage and determination that had damn near killed her in the critical battle above 'Big Blue' at Beta Hydri. If he ever found himself in trouble, he would be glad to have her at his right hand. And if he were to be lost, he knew he could count on her to carry on.

David was equally pleased to have First Lieutenant Sabrina Herrera leading his small detachment of Fleet Marines. Sabrina had been with him in the adventure on Zeta Doradus (b), where they had managed to keep the natives from starting a revolt just when they were about to be freed from Preeminent rule. Since then, Sabrina had gone through OCS and graduated second in her class. She was another strong asset in his wardroom.

He was pulled out of these thoughts as Larry slid out of the Navigation workstation just below David's command position and dropped into the XO's seat next to him.

"Still thinking three AU?"

David nodded, then looked again at his briefing materials. "Yeah, hab zone is one point two or so. I'd like to be close but, you know, not too close."

"No problem. We'll throttle back to point-five a few hours out and look to cut the Drive at five AU and coast down to three."

"Sounds right. Thanks."

"Heard anything from Scheck?" Larry asked.

"Last I saw, Joe was headed for *Enterprise*," David answered with a grin. "Like half the officers I know. Fiona Collins is trolling the whole fleet to fill out her assignments...It'll be the cream of the cream if she gets her way."

"She will. It is a monster, after all."

"Five hundred meters long? Yeah, that's a monster all right. Saw a report the other day that Nat Hayden is going there as Weaps, and Jack Ballard is off *Cobra* to be the Intel chief."

"That's all very fine, you know, but I'm glad to be where I am."

David smiled up at his old classmate. "Well, it's less crowded for sure."

Larry stepped down from the command position, his dark six-six frame still at David's eye level as he moved to the Navigation station to instruct his techs. There were still a few days to go, but better to brief them now so there would be no question about the commander's intent. Larry then waved to David as he moved on aft for a short visit to his office, then to his cabin for a night's rest.

David remained a while, then left for his Duty Cabin just behind the Bridge, leaving the Conn officer in charge.

The next morning David was reviewing the status of his weapons when there was a rap on the hatch to his Duty Cabin.

"Come!" he called, and Lieutenant Sabrina Herrera slipped inside, closing the hatch behind her.

"Good morning, Sabrina. What's on your mind?"

Herrera sat in the one chair available, across from David's small desk.

"Rifle training."

David had taken the lesson of the Battle of Seeker Woods at Beta Hydri very seriously and mandated basic weapons training for every member of the crew. They were spacefarers, for sure, but the experience of the war with the Preeminent made clear that a crew could find themselves on the ground in unexpected circumstances. Most ship captains now did the same, and new ships came with a small weapons range on the lowest deck.

"OK. So, how is it going?"

"Fine, mostly. My gunny is a good instructor."

David leaned back in his chair and smiled. "I expect you were a pretty good instructor yourself."

She smiled slightly. "Yes, I was. But it is his job now, not mine, and I try to be careful to not overstep."

David nodded, then leaned forward with his elbows on the desk. "Good. So, what part of it is not 'fine'?"

"We have three holdouts. I've talked to each of them more than once, but they refuse to take the training."

"What do they say?"

"Generally, it's a 'not what I signed up for' argument. I've told them that excuse doesn't cut it, but they're not budging."

"Who are we talking about?"

"A medical tech and two from the reactor team."

David thought for a moment. "Give the med tech a pass. If we wind up in some kind of shit, I'll need them more as a medic than a rifleman."

"And the others?"

"Talk to them once more. If they still refuse, Melinda can talk to them. If she fails, then we'll let it go. It will go in their personnel record, but I doubt they care much about that."

"Yes, Commander. I'll talk to the XO."

"If anything happens, we'll just have to work around them. I can't physically force them to do it."

"Yes, Commander, I understand."

The conversation seemed to be over, but Sabrina didn't move. "Something else?"

She paused for a few seconds, looking at him, then stood. "No, Commander. Thanks for your time."

"Of course, Lieutenant. Any time."

Chapter 13

Onizuka
GL 262
Friday, May 17, 2086, 0930 UTC

A week later, *Onizuka* was approaching GL 262, coasting out of FTL towards the star. Surveillance Officer Lieutenant Scarlett Walker was supervising the survey of the new system. A few hours after they passed the 3 AU mark, an alarm sounded on the panel.

The duty tech sat suddenly upright. "Possible blue dot, Lieutenant, but...the reflectance spectrum is off...I'm not sure it really is one."

Walker leaned over the young man to examine the data on the planet the automated surveillance system had decided was habitable.

"Show me the breakdown," she said in her crisp Australian accent. A few motions by the tech and the spectral analysis was up on the main viewer. "Water vapor, nitrogen, CO2, oxygen, but, yes, you are correct. Something is off."

"No chlorophyll signal. With these gases, there should be plant life."

Walker shrugged. "Maybe...but don't forget the universe has a twisted sense of humor about these things." She looked again at the spectra they were still gathering. "Wait, look here...do we see a very low peak in that band? Barely above the noise level?"

"Perhaps, yes, Lieutenant," the tech responded, his skepticism plain.

XO Melinda Hughes stepped down from her position a few steps above the main Bridge level to see what Walker was talking about. It didn't take the former Surveillance Officer long to make her decision.

"Conn! Alter course and take us to this planet."

"Yes, ma'am! Heading for the weirdish blue dot." The Conn officer issued the command, and the Nav workstation got busy moving *Onizuka* right and towards the oddball planet.

Melinda stepped back up into the Command position and picked up the ship's phone. "Powell...it's Melinda. We've spotted a possible blue dot, but it's not like one we've seen before. I've altered course to observe." She listened for a moment, nodding unconsciously as David spoke, then hung up. "Lieutenant Walker, please keep up the overall survey of the system. Commander Powell wants the full picture before we start focusing on the possible blue dot."

"Yes, ma'am, will do."

A few hours later, David was up and back on the Bridge. Walker delivered her assessment of the system: two smallish gas giants well out from the star, four beat-up terrestrials in close, with the outermost rocky one being the strange 'blue dot.' As they approached within a few million kilometers, the picture became clearer, and David made his decision.

"Comm! Send a flash to CINC and FleetOps: Atypical blue dot GL 262. Details to follow."

"Yes, Commander, right away."

As the Comm techs were transmitting his SLIP message, David stepped down and stood with Melinda and Lieutenant Walker.

"What do you see so far?"

"Still too far for details, but there are oceans, and clouds, but the land we've seen so far seems barren. The planet is in a great spot for life, so I'd expect it to be really green."

One of the techs spoke up. "Uh, Lieutenant Walker, ma'am? I might have the explanation." He placed the latest image of the planet on the large viewer over his workstation. There was a long silence as the three senior officers stared at it.

"Ho-ly shit," David finally said. "How big is it?" Walker went to work on the image, trying to measure the enormous crater that had appeared on the planet's surface as they came closer.

"At least a hundred klicks," she answered.

"So, at least as bad as Chicxulub?"

"Yes, sir. At least."

"How deep is it?" David asked.

Walker shook her head. "Too far to tell, sir. We'll need a little time to accurately measure it."

David turned to Melinda. "See if Intel has anything on impact craters. I want to know if they can tell us how long ago this happened." As Melinda headed aft, he turned to Walker. "I'll put us in a polar orbit...let's get the planet imaged and see if there was any tech here."

"I doubt we'll find any survivors, even if there was anyone here to begin with."

"Unlikely, true, but hardly impossible. Keep looking. I want to know what's down there." He walked to Larry Covington at the Nav station and explained what he wanted, then returned to Walker.

"Scarlett, let's get the radar up and see if there is anything in orbit."

"Yes, sir, will do."

David stood behind the Surveillance station as the tracking display began to light up with targets.

"Wow," was all he said as Scarlett Walker stood next to him.

"Twenty?" she said as the target counter stabilized. "Looks like most are in geosynchronous orbit. Some lower."

Melinda Hughes joined them. "I expect there will be more targets like those as we complete a few orbits."

David looked at the multiple targets on the three-dimensional radar display.

"Wait...so we have a technically advanced civilization wiped out by an asteroid strike? Am I seeing this right?"

Scarlett nodded. "Yes, sir, so it would seem."

On their second orbit over the southern hemisphere, a few hundred kilometers west of the crater, the AI surveillance alarm went off again. David and Melinda watched as the techs zoomed in on a large open area near the eastern coast of the main continent.

"That," Melinda said, turning to David, "is a goddamn airfield."

Walker turned to the command position. "There's more. I can see a wrecked city just south of the airfield. Looks like everything was blown over by the shockwave."

"Do the edges look fuzzy to you, Scarlett?" Melinda's eye for detail didn't miss much.

Walker zoomed in on the image. "Yes. Probably fine dust and ejecta from the impact."

"Any more satellites?"

"Yes, we've found a few more. Still, the majority are in geosynchronous orbits."

"So, weather, surveillance, that kind of thing?""

"Yes, Commander, that would be my assessment."

David got up from his Command chair and headed for the Comm workstation. "OK, time to tell the boss what's going on."

```
FLASH 208605190930UTC
TO: CINC, FLEETOPS, ALLFLEET
FROM: ONIZUKA
SUBJECT: BLUE DOT

NOW CLEAR THAT BLUE DOT GL 262 (d) SUFFERED LARGE ASTEROID
OR COMET IMPACT.

THERE IS A 133 KM CRATER ON ISLAND CONTINENT EAST OF MAIN LANDMASS.

SATELLITES, AIRFIELDS AND COLLAPSED STRUCTURES PROVE PLANET
SUPPORTED INTELLIGENT SPECIES.

CONTINUING OBSERVATION BUT AS YET HAVE SEEN NOTHING ALIVE.

POWELL

END
```

"Almost four days..." David mumbled to himself as he was finishing. It would be more than a week before he would hear back from Fleet HQ. As he was complaining inwardly about the slow speed of FTL communications, his Intel officer Lieutenant Ethan Reyes brought his report.

"OK, sir, so, a crater that big implies an object the size of Halley's comet."

David looked again at the image of the crater. "An extinction event then?"

"No question. This thing was maybe twice the size of the Chicxulub impactor."

"Shit."

"Yes, sir, a really, really bad day."

"How deep is it? I saw some incredible shadows on the first images."

"About a klick and a half, sir. Again, an incredible feature."

David looked at the image again. "That thing will be there for a million years."

"Yes, sir, I think so."

"Is the AI pulling anything else out of the images?" Melinda asked.

"There are areas of crushed structures all over the main continent, so we're looking at a large population. The smaller continent to the east, where it hit, also has some signs of roads and cities and such, but it was really beat up by the impact.

"Can you tell me when this happened?"

"Not really, Commander. The skies have cleared and surface temperatures seem to have recovered, based on our models of what the climate is supposed to be, so I'd say it was several years, maybe as many as ten. We're still looking for data on cooling rates for the crater itself."

"Anything else?"

"Well, the edges of the crater are still sharp, as are the large ejecta craters around it. There's no indication of weathering."

"Fine. Keep looking. I want to know how long ago this happened."

Ethan didn't move despite the obvious dismissal. "There is one more thing, Commander."

"Oh?"

"We think we see a spaceport on the main continent."

David looked at the young lieutenant carefully. Carol liked him immensely, having worked closely with him in FleetPlans. He'd been to cookouts at their house at Fort Eustis a few times, so he was hardly a stranger to David. "So?"

"So maybe they got off before it hit? If they have aircraft and space travel, they should have known it was coming."

David smiled slightly. "Keep looking. And put someone on where they might have gone."

"GL 252" came the immediate answer.

"Wait...how far is that?"

"Seven point six. It's another class G star, a G0V actually: hotter but a similar absolute magnitude. Definitely a workable alternative."

"Planets?"

"Like here, sir, none reported."

"OK, stay on it, Ethan. Thanks."

"Sir, yes, sir."

David was slightly amused at the formal response. "Get lost."

Ethan turned to head back to Intel. "Getting, sir."

Melinda slipped close to David. "Another dead world?"

David smiled, recalling the supposed genocide of the Seekers culture at Beta Hydri, which turned out to be somewhat less than that.

"I guess, but at least we're not looking for an enemy..."

Melinda could tell he was not finished, his face suddenly blank. "David?"

He turned to her. "I was thinking about the race the Zeds called the 'guardians'...what we think is the same species the Preeminent called the 'shepherds.' They might have done this."

Melinda sat up in surprise. "What? Dropped an asteroid on an inhabited planet?"

David waved his hands. "No, no, not that. They've moved whole species before. Why not this one? The strike would have been predictable."

"Wait. You think these people were transplanted?"

David nodded slightly. "I think it's possible, yes."

"OK, so how would we know?"

"Dunno. We'll see what Surveillance and Intel turn up."

Melinda left for her cabin aft as David returned to the Command position. *How would they know? Could they know?*

David had no answers to his questions. They would just have to keep looking and see what turns up. As he watched the planet moving past in the bridge windows over the main displays, his NetComp vibrated with a message. He picked it up and saw that he'd received a personal message from back home. *That will have to wait,* he thought. *I need to focus.*

Onizuka
In Orbit at GL 262 (d)
Saturday, May 18, 2086, 1700UTC

Over the last week, *Onizuka* had mapped the entire planet in high-resolution, a panorama of tragedy and disaster. Reyes could not tell if it was an asteroid or a comet, but it didn't really matter very much. The impact occurred in a flat region of a small island continent to the east of the main landmass, which was a wide strip of terrain running mostly north and south.

As David studied the composite maps and photographs, he could not help but wonder about the race that lived there. Once the survey was complete, he asked Intel Officer Ethan Reyes to brief the officers on his conclusions.

After describing the geography of the impact, and his assessment of the immediate aftermath, Ethan put up a slide of what they thought was a spaceport. "I have a couple observations about this location." He zoomed the image in close. "First, you can see here the cradle that the ship was in. It wasn't small, and, most importantly, I see no evidence of rocket propulsion."

Larry Covington's head came up. "So, you think they have a Drive?"

"Yes, Lieutenant, I think that is almost certain. There are four of these facilities in this area. If they were using rocket propulsion, the whole thing would look much more like Canaveral or Baikonur than it does."

David looked at the image for a moment. "Go ahead, Ethan."

"Yes, sir. The other interesting thing is in this area." The image moved slightly to show row on row of small objects.

Melinda leaned forward, elbows on the table, her chin in her hands. "Looks like a parking lot."

"Indeed, ma'am, that is our assessment. We've seen plenty of examples elsewhere that they seem to have had wheeled transportation, much as we do. But the interesting part here is that there is no evidence of any activity post-impact."

David leaned back in his chair. "Well, if this was the exit point, or maybe the evacuation point, everyone who drove those cars there is gone, right? So, no surprise that they're just sitting there."

"That's true, sir, and we talked that through as well. But this location is just outside a major city, and there is no evidence of any post-impact activity."

"Show him the power plant," Scarlett asked.

Reyes pulled up a different slide, showing a domed structure on the eastern seacoast. "This is obviously a nuclear power plant. IR shows it is cold. The facility itself and the water nearby register as the expected ambient temperature. We've seen a dozen of these small plants and they all look alike. You can see the power lines...here...where the towers were knocked down by the impact."

Melinda was intrigued. "Any other power source like wind or solar? Coal?"

"No, ma'am. Just the nuke plants."

"But clearly, they shut these down before leaving."

"Yes, ma'am. We think that indicates that the departure was very well planned."

"That's encouraging. What are your thoughts on the timeline?" David asked.

"Well, take the cars. The fine ejecta has been washed off, mostly, and you can see how it flowed downhill and into drains and streams. The climate here is not dissimilar to ours, so we think the rain gradually washed the fine stuff away and uncovered the other wreckage we can see."

"Continue."

"There are still small craters and evidence of smaller fallout, stuff less than a meter in size, all around." Ethan paused to take a sip of water. "We don't see any large vegetation, like trees or whatever, but there are some grasses, maybe, starting to rebuild themselves."

"OK, so?"

"So, while some areas have been cleaned, like the cars in that parking lot, some ejecta remains around them. We can't be positive but think this happened within the last ten years."

"What does the crater tell us about that?"

"IR says the surface temp is 320 degrees Kelvin, which is obviously warm but not extremely so. Based on the research papers we have available, we would need to get down there and sample the temperature further down if we want to time it out more accurately."

David smiled. "Nope. We're not going down there."

"Yes, Commander."

"Thanks, Ethan."

Reyes, understanding that his presentation was complete, sat down next to Scarlett Walker.

"OK," David began, "If they have a Drive, where did they go?"

"We still think GL 252 is the most likely," Scarlett said. "It's close by. It's a class G, but both hotter and brighter than this G4V."

"What about GL 255? It's similar," Larry asked.

"Yes, that's a possibility, sir. But it is dimmer and cooler. There are other candidates, but they're further away, are binaries, or have other issues we think make them less likely as a destination. GL 252 is a decent match, sir."

David nodded. "And you're thinking this race could manage the differences, assuming there's a suitable planet?"

"Yes, sir."

"But," Larry said, "it's a big universe, there may be no suitable planets at 252, and they might have gone elsewhere."

Melinda Hughes smiled and inclined her head. "What you're saying, Larry, is that we may never know?"

"Yes, exactly that."

"All true," David said, seeming to close the discussion. "But I agree with Scarlett and Ethan. We head for GL 252. Now." He turned back to Larry. "And step on it!"

"Yes, sir, full speed ahead, sir!"

David turned to his Communications officer. "Inform FleetOps for me, please? After Larry gives you our ETA?"

"Yes, sir."

The group broke up quickly, with Covington heading to the Bridge to get the ship moving. GL 252 was less than eight light-years away. At flank speed, they'd be there in less than five days. It would press the Drive a little, but when David asked for full speed, Larry knew exactly what was expected.

ISC Fleet Headquarters
Ft. Eustis, VA
Thursday, May 23, 2086, 1230 UTC (0830 EDT)

Fleet Ops Admiral Kieran Barker made his way to CINC Patricia Cook's office, *Onizuka*'s message on his NetComp.

"You've seen Powell's report?"

"Yes. Strange, don't you think? An advanced species hit with an asteroid?"

"Intel says there are two or three likely stars where they might have evacuated themselves."

"Yes, I saw the same report."

"Well...*Enterprise* isn't that far away."

Cook looked across at her Chief of Operations with surprise. "You want to send them to one of these other stars? The species at GL 262 would have to be incredibly lucky to find another blue dot close by."

"True, they could be anywhere, even something around a K- or M-class."

Cook nodded her agreement, then stood and looked out the large windows at the back of her office. She recalled how Connor Davenport had done much the same when he was CINC. The physical motion seemed to move her mind, too, and it gave her a few seconds to gather her thoughts. "Back to *Enterprise*, I'm not sure I like redirecting Fiona on her first cruise. That's asking quite a lot of a new crew."

"It is."

" I'll think about it. But still, what about Powell?"

Barker shrugged. "I don't have anything to tell him that he doesn't already know."

"Well, I want him to know we got his message. Tell him we advise caution but to proceed as he sees fit. Relieve him of whatever his next star assignments were."

Kieran smiled. "Hansen is at GL 245, not far away. She could pick up the last two of Powell's systems."

Admiral Cook sat back down, shaking her head. "How do those two do that?"

"Do what?"

"Manage to place themselves close together whenever there's a crisis?"

"They're a lucky pair, I guess. I'm not sure this is a crisis, but do you want me to send her over to assist *Onizuka*?"

Cook shook her head as she sipped her coffee. "No, she's got her own list to work on. And, they're so far out there, by the time we'd tell her to go help, it would be too late."

Kieran looked up from his NetComp. "OK, I'll tell *Onizuka* to follow this GL 262 thread as he sees fit. Likely they're already doing that."

"Fine. I am sure he'll report more details as they study the planet."

"No doubt."

Barker stood and left CINC's office, which was still decorated as Connor Davenport had left it. Davenport's NetLink had sent out the alarm on a warm Sunday afternoon as he worked on some contingency plan or another, but by the time the medics could get to him, he was dead of a massive heart attack. The so-called 'widow maker' had struck him with no warning whatever. Barker missed Davenport, but Patty Cook was a more than competent replacement: experienced, smart, flexible, consistent. He was less confident in his own elevation to Chief of Operations, but so far, so good. His staff kept him afloat much of the time, and he was learning the rest as quickly as he could.

He dictated the message to *Onizuka*, then went back to reviewing possible destinations for the race at GL 262. That was FleetIntel's job, really, but his curiosity had been aroused, and he thought it useful to have a good understanding of anything more they would be reporting.

Endeavour
En Route GL 245
Tuesday, May 28, 2086, 0530 UTC

It was early in the morning, ship time, as Commander Carol Hansen looked up from her NetComp to the chronometer over the Nav console. It was driven by the ship's triple-redundant Cesium atomic clocks, but it always seemed to run slower at this time of the night. She'd been unable to sleep, and after an hour of tossing and checking and re-checking the chronometer in her duty cabin, she'd given up, dressed, and relieved the Conn officer on the Bridge. He, at least, could get a little extra shuteye.

As she looked back to the tablet, a single tear escaped her eye as she studied the new picture of little Leon James Powell and his younger sister Teresa Marcia that she had just received from home. The four-year-old boy sat up so very tall on Carol's horse, Capella, his grandpa smiling broadly beside him, the little sister seated in front of her brother. The latest iteration of the Fleet's SLIP FTL communications system supported images and short audio files. It was an enormous improvement, even if the resolution was hardly photographic quality. And while a SLIP message could cover a light-year every ninety minutes, it still seemed damnably slow when over fifty light-years from Earth.

Carol set down the tablet and quickly flicked away her tears as she looked up at the Nav status display, looking for their current estimated position. So far from home. So far from everyone she loved. She thought about what it felt to have them inside her, to feel them grow into being. She smiled at the memory of how much she and David had laughed the day little Leon James was conceived, after the celebration of how far she had recovered from her PTSD and David had just returned from Zeta Doradus. It was a perfect day, made that much more perfect by the small but loud consequence that arrived thirty-nine weeks later.

But all that was literally trillions of miles away now. She started to do the math in her head, calculating just how many trillion miles they were from her, but she quickly gave up. *After the first couple trillion,* she thought, *what the hell did it matter?*

As she glanced around, she realized her XO, Senior Lieutenant Jayvon Dean, was looking at her. She had not noticed him coming onto the Bridge and taking his place just a meter to her right.

"Good morning. Something on your mind, Commander?"

Carol leaned back in her chair. "I'm trying to understand how a little farm girl like me got way the hell out here."

Jayvon smiled. "Same way this little street kid from Milwaukee did. We asked. Or, in my case, you asked."

She nodded. "True."

"Might I ask, Commander, why *did* you pick me?"

Carol sat up and turned towards her second-in-command. "Well, Jayvon, it's actually pretty simple. First, you were a fully qualified candidate. Second, I knew you from our time on *Antares*, so I knew how you would react under stress. Third, I just kinda liked the whole idea."

"I thought you'd pick Alex or Lori or someone like that. Someone more senior."

Carol shook her head. "Nah. They have their own good qualities, believe me, but I'd rather have someone who comes from a different place, with different ideas. I need that."

"I guess that's me."

Carol leaned back in her chair, stretching. She nodded slightly. "But that's not all. I knew you were scared shitless when *Antares* was hit with the beacon-mines. I could see it. I was, too."

Jayvon shrugged and looked away. "Hardly seems a credit."

Carol smiled slightly. "But you kept going. You never hesitated, never froze, never fumbled or screwed up. You got the job done despite your fear. That's who I want next to me in a fight."

He nodded slowly. "It almost felt like a dream, you know? Like some kind of waking nightmare that wasn't real."

"Yes, I remember wondering who was screaming so loud, then realized it was me!"

Jayvon smiled and looked back at her. "Loud, Commander Hansen, doesn't begin to cover it. I never heard anything like it before or since."

Carol caught herself gently scratching at the ugly scar on the outside of her right thigh. She could still feel the dart that had passed through Captain Teresa

Michael's heart before slamming into her leg. She stopped and placed her hands back on the armrests of her command chair.

"Still bothers you?"

"Yeah, itches sometimes. Doctors said it should stop eventually. Sometimes I wonder if it's all in my head."

"I doubt that, Commander."

Carol looked around the Bridge, quiet at this early hour, then leaned closer to her XO. "So, Jayvon, just between us, what's your assessment of Thomas? Is she for real, or is she just hunting a scoop?"

"Well, she is fascinated with you, there's no denying that. Every second question has your name in it."

"I was afraid of that."

"But, ma'am, I don't think it's cynical. I think she genuinely sees something in you that she would like to be able to show to the world."

"Do I want to be shown to the world?"

"Well, Commander, that's a different question and one only you can answer. It's one thing to dismiss her because you think she's just looking for a salacious headline, but quite another to decline the exposure for your own reasons."

"Jayvon, remember we were talking about why I wanted you for my XO?"

"Yes, of course."

"This is why. Thanks."

She looked back at the Nav status display. "We'll be at GL 245 in two days. Another G-class star."

"Yes, correct. With a debris disk...I'm curious about that. I wonder if we will actually be able to see it just with the naked eye."

"Yeah, me, too. But that disk is way out — like 300 AU or something. I wonder what's right around the star."

"We'll know soon enough. If I might ask, where is Mister Powell?"

"Jayvon, as my XO you may certainly ask whatever is on your mind. *Onizuka* should be at GL 262. They're about seventeen light-years from us."

"Just around the corner? Should we drop over for a coffee?"

Carol smiled. "That would be lovely, yes, but orders, my dear XO, are orders."

"OK, on to 245 it is."

Their conversation moved on to less personal matters: crew status, ship maintenance issues, search plans for the new star. There was time to prepare, but Carol hated to wait until some theoretical optimum time before arrival. Something always seemed to come up and shred their carefully drafted outline. Better, she thought, to prepare well before it was necessary and be ready when the moment finally arrived. She and Jayvon didn't always agree on that, but he was learning the wisdom of her approach day by day.

Chapter 14

Onizuka
GL 252
Wednesday, May 29, 2086, 1045 UTC

David's well-founded skepticism about this new star evaporated shortly after they came out of FTL.

"Blue dot, Commander, high confidence, right place."

"Comm!" he responded. "Flash to CINC, Blue dot GL 252."

"Flash to CINC, yes, Commander."

"Wow," he heard Melinda say. "Right where it's supposed to be."

David looked over at her, seated a meter away in the XO position. "Supposed?"

"OK, nitpicker, make that 'hoped,'" she responded.

David nodded slightly, ending the discussion. If indeed this was where the GL 262 race had fled, he would have to be very careful. Their society was at least as technologically advanced as his own, and what surveillance methods and weapons they might employ were unknown. And, therefore, a threat. Or, at least, a potential threat. "Nav!" he finally called out, "As soon as Lieutenant Walker can tell us how it's turning, get me in a high polar orbit — say, two orbits per day."

Larry Covington waved his understanding as he towered over the Surveillance workstation, watching Scarlett Walker's tech focus on the new planet.

Walker stood and turned to David. "We're still more than an AU away, so it will be most of a day. I'm assuming you want the usual approach? North up?"

"Yes, please."

Walker put her hands on her hips. "You do know, Commander, if science had started where I grew up — "

"Then clocks would run backward, and the globe would be upside down."

"Something like that, yes. Just sayin'..."

"I understand, Lieutenant, but do humor me, OK?"

"You are in command, sir, so humoring you is our daily burden."

Melinda covered her mouth and turned away to hide her laughter.

David made his best faux-offended face. "Walker?"

"Yes, sir?"

"Just watch the damned planet."

"Sir, yes, sir."

David looked at the chronometer over the Nav workstation and turned to Melinda. "I'm going to get some rest. Just in case, let's set Minimum EMR by 0500."

Melinda glanced at the clock before answering. "Kinda early, don't you think? We'll still be a half-day away at least."

"I know, but what we saw at 262 was a technological society at our own level. If they're here, I think we need to be really careful. Last thing I want to do is alarm them."

"OK, David. I'll be on until 2300, and then I'll leave word for the Conn officer."

"Very well," he responded as he rose and walked the short distance aft to his duty cabin.

The Captain's Duty Cabin was supposedly a perk - a benefit of being in command. David wondered about that idea as he slipped into the small space and closed the narrow hatch behind him. Every ship he'd been on, from *Sigma* to *Columbia*, *Cobra* to *Antares*, this space all looked just the same: a bunk along the far bulkhead, a small desk welded to the left bulkhead with chairs for the captain and one visitor, a tiny bath on the right. A ship phone hung on the wall between the bunk and the desk, easily reachable from either. Driven by its own distributed array of processors, all he had to do was pick up the receiver and speak a name or position. The system would find the individual or station and instantly make the connection. While the rest of Terran society was nearly completely wireless, including his wrist-mounted NetLink, personal phone, and NetComp tablet, the ship's internal communication system was hard-wired, un-jammable and un-hackable, with six redundantly routed fiber-optic connections. It would take a near-fatal blow to take the system completely offline, and, so far, that had not happened.

Or, David thought as he stared at the phone, *it had not happened where the survivors lived to tell about it.*

Not since the war had both he and Carol been 'out there' at the same time. She had been busy in FleetPlans, then off to *Sigma* for a year while he continued in FleetIntel. Finally, he attended the same Deep Space Command School she had been working through while he was at Zeta Doradus, trying to pull a peace rabbit out of a hat full of insurrection and the knife-edge of violence.

But now, here he was commanding *Onizuka* some sixty light-years from home, just as Carol was running *Endeavour* a dozen or more light-years away from him at GL 245. The Fleet was determined to extend the examination of the local stars to a hundred light-years in all directions, which was actually a surprisingly large crap-ton of stars. The new CINC, the previous Chief of Fleet Operations Admiral Patricia Cook, was adamant that there were to be no more surprises, no such disasters as they had at Inor at the beginning of the war with the Preeminent.

He pulled off his day-old slate-grey uniform and took a longer-than-usual shower to shake off the apprehension he felt about this new society. After drying off, he sat at the little steel desk and opened his journal. David and Carol had kept personal journals during the war, exchanging them every time they met, and once it was clear they were both headed back to deep space, they renewed their commitment to a daily virtual ink-and-paper conversation.

Before opening his well-bent notebook, he pulled out his NetComp and displayed the picture of his children Carol's dad had sent, what, four days ago? The little boy — the big brother — sat tall and proud on a beautiful brown horse. The little sister sat in front of him, with the still-tall grandfather behind them, clearly making sure there would be no falls. David stared at the image for a full minute, taking in the faces, the sunshine lighting up the farm fields in the background, and the knowledge that the doting grandma was behind the camera. David smiled as he recalled Laura's tears as her daughter placed her first grandchild into her arms. She hugged little Leon James Powell so tight David thought for a moment he'd be crushed. But even new grandmas know just how hard to hold, and he reached for her nose just as a tear escaped down it, and she laughed a laugh of joy David had never heard from his own mother. His throat tightened at the memory. It was so real, so genuine, so deeply loving that he found himself basking in the moment even five years later.

He shook off the memory, set the NetComp up against the bulkhead, and opened his journal.

Wednesday, May 29, 2086

My Dear Carol -

I'm looking at the picture Papa Ols sent - Leon looks so confident up on your horse, doesn't he? Capella never looked happier, I think, if a horse can look happy. And little Teresa — I still kinda choke up when I see her. So much of you in her, and, luckily, so little of me! What a smile on that kid!

We're at GL 252 now, and sure enough there is a blue dot. Assuming they could, it would make a lot of sense for the 262s to come here. I am worried about what they might be like, but Melinda seems more sanguine about it. Trusting soul, she is. Just love her - so smart, so brave. Not sure I could handle this job without her.

Miss you desperately. That's not news to you, I know, but just writing it out seems to blunt the pain a little. I still say it, again and again: I would not change a thing that brought us to right here, right now. It will be a long time before I see your face again, but I still feel you here next to me, as if you were hiding in my shadow. Be safe, my love, and look forward to that day we'll be together once more. It is all that keeps me going.

> *All I am, is still yours.*
> *-David*

He set the journal back in the desk drawer, took one last look at the chronometer and ship status display across from his bunk, and turned in for the night.

New Traenah
Home of Kirah and Staal
Spin 3, Subcycle 2, Cycle 2510

Kirah bid Staal a good day and began the long walk up the hill to her job at 'The Tracker.' Mehonnh was just moving above the eastern hills, a very different dawn than what she remembered from Traenah. There, the land was quite flat near her home, and her home star would make a majestic, slow appearance at the start of each spin. Here, the planet turned so fast that she thought at a glance she could see Mehonnh moving.

Staal would be leaving shortly, too. His journey to work was much shorter as he took public transport to the airfield. There were aerocraft there that needed his detailed attention. They had committed to their bond just after arrival from Traenah, with Selol, Dsanik, and Staal's cousin Tmoyan there to celebrate with them. It all felt like very long ago to Kirah, but her perception of time was distorted by the new planet, what they called New Traenah. Its faster spin truncated both day and night. Adding to her disorientation was New Traenah's much longer orbit about its star, making a 'NewCycle' almost twice as long as what she had grown up with.

And, there was no short-period comet here to mark the time or comment on their spiritual and cultural progress. Kirah saw that as a distinct improvement.

Selol, meantime, had completely acclimated to the new environment, and in the six new-cycles since their arrival, she'd completed her primary education and was now in an advanced school for medicine. There were many males circling around her these spins, all subject to Staal's suspicious eye and Kirah's stern warnings.

Kirah arrived at 'The Tracker,' an enormous, movable structure that could detect artificial gravitons. It was based on a new application of the same technology that powered their evacuation ships and also enabled the aerocraft Staal maintained to easily operate in orbit. But, instead of generating artificial gravitons, it could detect and locate them. Many in the leadership remained fearful of any contact with new alien species, and the Tracker was their first line of defense.

In the four new-cycles she had worked there, she had risen to be an expert on the theory and operation of the device, something she thought of as almost magical in its simplicity. Today would be a quiet day, she thought, with no exercises or performance tests, so she brought some books along, something to further her education.

Kirah's head snapped up from her reading when the detection alarm sounded, flashing lights demanding her immediate attention. With a few commands on the autocalc, she displayed the contact. She leaned back in her chair to re-check the exercise schedule posted on the grey steel wall. Nothing this spin. No regular space flights, either.

She reset the alarm, but in only a few teoset, it went off again.

Now, there could be no question. Something was out there where nothing was supposed to be. All the People of Traenah were already here. She herself had arrived on the very last evacuation ship, a witness to the impact of the comet on their home planet. Nothing should be out there. But that was why they kept the Tracker operating, was it not? They were away from their home planet and wary of any other species that might be about.

She thought back to the first day of her training on the Tracker:

"We know that they're out there! One alien came and tried to take us from Traenah at our moment of greatest weakness. We must constantly be on guard against such forces. This is why you are here! You are our defense against the evil that may be all around us."

Those words seemed prescient to her now as she reached for the far-talker and requested a connection to her commander.

He was not impressed.

"Surely, Kirah, you're mistaken! When was the last time we checked that device?"

Kirah suppressed her annoyance. *Did he think I just made this up?* "Sir. as you know, we run regular tests against our own aerocraft. I have no reason to think there is any problem with the Tracker."

Flight Leader Aytila looked out the window at the small craft scattered on the pavement outside the Operations Center. The tech was right, he realized. They did test the huge detector from time to time, but nothing had been seen since the evacuation.

"Fine. Where is whatever this is?"

Kirah paused to re-check the track on her display. "It is approaching but not coming directly at us. I think it will go into orbit on the south end of New Traenah, perhaps a very high one."

"I see."

"One more thing, sir. This signal is very precise, very narrow. I will speak to Nadon, but I believe this is a very powerful vessel. The power distribution is clearly unlike our ships. I've never seen anything like it."

"Thank you for that." Aytila hung up the far-talker and waited a moment, trying to think what he would say to Wing Commander Dsanik, his superior. He knew the old warrior would first be asking him what he'd already done to fix whatever problem he was reporting, so Aytila chose action first, call second. Getting up, he trotted to the maintenance facility.

"Staal! Find your supervisor! Have him get everyone outside and get every craft under cover. If you can't get them into storage, get them covered with something, anything."

"Sir? Is there some threat?"

"I don't know. Just get it done, and I'll explain later."

The supervisor and other technicians were surprised. They hadn't needed to hide an aerocraft since the war ended back on Traenah, and Staal had never heard of such a task.

Aytila went back to the far-talker and requested to speak to Dsanik.

Back at the Tracker, Kirah was similarly making a connection to Nadon at the Observatory south of the city. She would want to know and, Kirah hoped, might have some insight into what this new intruder might represent.

His long day finally done, Staal stepped off the public transport and walked down the small lane to the cottage he shared with Kirah and Selol. He was greeted warmly, then proceeded to bathe before dinner, as was his custom. He did not like to be covered in work dirt at meals. In short order, he was back in the kitchen, clean of body and clothing, feeling much refreshed.

Kirah brought plates to the table. "Strange things today," she said as she sat down. "We detected a ship like we've never seen before. We think it's alien."

Staal gripped his understanding. "That would be why we hid most of the aerocraft inside and pushed the rest to the edges of the parking area and covered them."

"Something is happening?" Selol asked between bites.

"I think so," Kirah answered. "I spoke to Gkeze today — "

"YOU spoke to Gkeze, the astronomer?" Selol almost choked from surprise.

"It's not the first time, little sister. I work at the Tracker, right? I had much to learn about how it worked, and Gkeze and Nadon were the main teachers."

"You never mentioned that before." Selol mixed her food around, then added sea seasoning.

"Well, it is not something to boast about."

Staal smiled. This was something he knew, but he and Kirah had not discussed it in much detail.

Kirah looked across the table at her sister. "Besides, you have also spoken to Gkeze!"

Selol looked back at her sister, perplexed. "I have? When?"

"When we watched the impact! Do you recall the old male who comforted you?"

"I haven't thought of that moment in a long time. I do remember how kind he was to me."

"That was Gkeze."

"I had forgotten that. What is he like?"

"He is a person, like any other. He is kind and helpful to students. Nadon, on the other hand, is very tough. She has no patience for slow thinking or slack work. One must be well prepared to study with her."

"So, what of this alien?"

Kirah set down her utensil, thinking about how to describe what she knew. "It approached and has entered an orbit. We trained with evacuation ships, small fighters, and all kinds of areocraft. But this one was very different. Nadon said their propulsion was very powerful, very advanced. It is likely even faster than the evacuation ships."

"Hard to believe!" Staal responded. "The evacuation ships flew many times the speed of light. If this vessel is able to go even faster, what else can they do?"

"Well, the military is in charge now."

"Yes," Staal said, "they ordered all the aerocraft into the storage building, and whatever we couldn't fit we had to cover with tent fabric."

"I feel like I should be afraid," Selol said quietly.

"It is too early for that," Staal answered. "We will know eventually, but for now, we continue."

Selol looked around the table. "Well, I saw no aliens and conferred with famous scientists, but I had an interesting day, too."

"Oh?" Kirah said. "Tell us!"

"The four of us in training have been given a research project. There have been very few cubs born since we came to New Traenah. Not enough, in fact, to keep the population going. My professor is very concerned."

Staal laughed. "Of this I know! I am harassed daily about the beauty of my female and my lack of production in cubs!"

Selol wasn't amused. "It's not just you two, although I have been careful not to ask if you are trying, or even if you desire cubs." When they didn't answer, she continued. "There are two main possibilities. First, Mehonnh is hotter and brighter than Tetanna. Radiation and UV levels are slightly higher but should be safe. The other is the spin."

"It's too fast!" Kirah responded quickly. "Only thirteen spedset, and a little more, per spin? I have trouble keeping track."

"Yes," Selol agreed, "Even after thirteen old cycles, it feels odd for the days and nights to be so short. We don't yet understand how that might affect our internal feedback systems, how it might make females unable to produce."

"So, what is your task?" Staal asked.

"We will use the autocalc to process the statistics, to see what might be the real determinate factor. It will take a subcycle or so to enter all the data and devise the calculation process."

After kitchen cleanup, they passed the evening quietly, Staal spending some time reading a technical manual, then moving on to a favorite work of fiction.

Kirah filled a page in her kitchen journal with how she had prepared the meal, how it had been enjoyed, and how she might improve it next time. Her mother had kept such a record, and Kirah remembered the thick, detailed book on the kitchen shelf fondly. But it would be gone now, most likely burned up in the fires that followed the comet's impact.

Selol had more than just her research project to worry about and invested most of the evening in a physiology text. The information was dense and complicated but vitally important to understand fully if she was to competently care for her future patients.

Onizuka
GL 252 (c)
Thursday, May 30, 2086, 0830 UTC

Onizuka closed the distance to the blue dot, the third planet in this small system, in less than a day, with liberal use of the Forstmann Drive to pull her into a high polar orbit. David relented in his Minimum EMR routine only far enough to leave the Bridge window covers open. They'd leak a little more visible light and infra-red radiation that way, but the view was amazing, and from better than thirteen thousand kilometers, David didn't see much risk. Scarlett Walker was doing a good job at Surveillance, and after a day in orbit, David had numerous detailed images to review. Ethan Reyes called him back to the Intel workroom, much as David had done many times for his commanders on *Sigma*, *Columbia*, and *Cobra*.

Reyes swung his thin legs over a chair, sat backwards and rolled up next to his captain, dropping a pile of printed images on the worktable. "I think we've found the 262s, sir. The level of technology looks about the same. There are a few airfields, but really, only one very large one, near the main city."

David sorted through the pictures, stopping to look at the notes Reyes had made on them, keeping some and flipping some aside. "Sure, makes sense."

"Yes, sir, kinda obvious if you think about it."

"What else?"

"There are eight large ships in a high orbit."

"Evacuation ships?"

"That is our assessment, yes. They're stone-cold in IR, so if there is a reactor or whatever aboard, it's quiet."

"How high?"

"Fifty thousand kilometers, more or less. We think they're parked there for safe storage."

"Well, fifty thousand is pretty high. It will be centuries before they decay, if ever."

"Correct. There are also a few small satellites in geosynchronous orbit."

"Weather? Communications?"

"Well, there is really just one large city, so we're thinking weather, but we could not exclude comms."

"We still have six sleuth kits aboard. Do you want to pass one by one of those satellites and see what we can collect?"

"That might be interesting, yes, sir, but we have not brainstormed that scenario. It might be a little too aggressive at this point."

David smiled. "Fine. Let me know if you want to do it. What about population?"

"Can't tell yet, sir, but we think many hundreds of thousands at least. There are vehicles on the roads, which appear to be paved in something like concrete, but we don't have enough data for a count."

"So, you want more time?"

"Yes, sir."

"Fine." David leaned back in his chair and picked up his coffee. "We'll be staying here for a while. I've updated CINC and the nearby ships about this. She may want to send additional help, but for now it's up to us, that is to say, *you*, to gather whatever we can as fast as we can."

David pushed the photographs back to Reyes and started to get up. "One thing, sir?"

"What?"

Reyes frowned as he looked up at David. "The airfields are empty, sir. We need more images at different times of day, but with the size of this parking ramp, I'd expect several dozen aircraft at least."

"But?"

"But we haven't isolated even one object that looks anything like an aircraft."

"OK. I'll have the Nav shift our orbit maybe a quarter sol. That should get you some fresh perspectives."

"Yes, sir, that's fine."

David paused a moment to consider what the lack of aircraft might mean. As an old Intel man experienced in such things, he could conjure options from 'there aren't any' to 'we've been detected, and they're hiding their combat strength to fool us,' but he didn't really consider either of those extremes very likely. The reality, like a lot of things in the Intel world, was probably something far more reasonable, more prosaic, likely even boring.

He left Intel and headed back for his Bridge without further comment.

Chapter 15

New Traenah
Above the Atmosphere
Spin 6, Subcycle 2, Cycle 2510

It was just two spins after the alien had been first detected when Dsanik arrived above the atmosphere, looking out on the universe as it stared, unblinking, uncaring, clearly unaware, back at him. He'd never lost that first sense of wonder he'd felt as he left the atmosphere and the cheerful twinkling of the stars faded into the steady gaze he now saw. He sat silently in the recon ship, floating high above New Traenah. It had taken him three spedset to get here, but the beauty of the universe around him quelled any impatience he might have felt about his mission. They had moved a long way from Traenah to escape the comet, but most of the constellations he'd known since he was a cub were still recognizable. He craned his head around to look back at Traenah, or, more specifically, Traenah's star, Tetanna, glowing just behind his head. It was not the brightest star in his new sky, but it could be easily found if one knew where to look. Dsanik knew. *What was happening there now?* He wondered. *Was anyone still alive? Was anything still alive?*

As he waited for the mysterious alien craft to meet him, he thought about the last time he was this high in a combat craft and how he and Tmoyan had chased each other twice around Traenah in a deadly contest that, fortunately, came to a draw. It had been very close, twice, to a conclusion not in Dsanik's favor. But his dogged determination and quick reflexes had saved him from North's superior technology. But it had been a very, very close match.

A tone from the artificial graviton detector plates on the wingtips of his ship brought his attention back to the task at hand. The technicians at the Tracker complex had calculated the orbit of the intruder, and he was now waiting for it to come back around the planet. That wait had now come to an end.

The intruders had placed themselves in orbit over New Traenah's rotational poles, which seemed like an enormous waste of time to Dsanik and Tmoyan until Gkeze explained how that would put them over every bit of the planet within a few spins. Whoever they were, Dsanik realized, they were experienced, careful, and therefore dangerous. Gkeze had also explained that at that orbital altitude, they would probably remain undetected indefinitely.

In fact, the old scientist had said, without the Tracker, "We would not know they were here."

It would be wise, Gkeze had said with a grin, not to spoil their sense of security.

Dsanik squirmed against the harness of his seat, which seemed far too tight given his weightlessness. Still, it did keep him from floating around the recon aerocraft's tiny cabin, which was probably a good thing. The indicator on his panel displayed a large gap between what he was seeing and what had been predicted. They had changed their orbit. After a few ductset, he had a good estimate of their new course and moved his ship further up and started looking for his target. The display on his instrument panel gave him only an estimate, good within a few sixteens of mileah, of the intruder's position.

Then all at once, the detector's track display was moot. He saw it first as a regular pattern of stars winking out, then returning. He approached and moved in behind the enormous black shape as it slid by him. A few touches of his controls, and he was so close he felt he could reach out and touch it.

Dsanik could not help but be awed by its size. It was enormous, larger even than an evacuation ship. In the aft end, he saw what looked like an AG propulsion unit, but it was much larger and different in configuration than he had ever seen. He stopped staring long enough to turn on the recon ship's recording system. It would now collect images every five teoset, using the cameras all around his converted fighter. Whatever he might miss with his own eyes could be seen when he returned to the surface. One side of the ship held an enormous disk that covered almost the whole height of it. He recognized this as likely a radio listening device of some kind. As he pulled forward, he could see small openings in its dark skin, and in those openings he saw a glint that had to be glass. *Lenses? Heat detectors?* he wondered. His ship's skin was as cold as the space around it, and while he could see outside, the heat-reflective glass around him would not allow the warmth of his body to escape. In his insulated pressure suit and helmet, he was as good as invisible.

Or, so he'd been told. If not, he'd know soon, but perhaps not for long.

On what he thought of as the belly of the ship, he noticed a round apparatus rising through the dark material that covered the ship. What that might be, he didn't consider. He was too distracted by the even larger opening slightly forward through which the end of a large telescope could clearly be seen. He'd almost flown right in front of it! No competent alien observer would have missed him if he passed in front of it, he was sure. He moved left and up the side of the ship, continuing forward.

Still, the enormous beast had not reacted. Like the universe itself, it seemed unaware or uncaring of his presence.

As he came near the forward end, he could see a hint of light escaping from a wide opening in front. As he focused on it, he could see what looked like thick covers that had been pulled back. He slowly moved forward until he could just see where the light was coming from.

He was surprised to see a reflection of the planet. Windows! They were in there, he realized, *right there*, so close to him, looking out at New Traenah. He pulled back, allowing the evil-looking black ship to slowly move away as he watched it go. He held his speed and course as the phantom faded in the distance, but he could not wait too long. He had to complete his re-entry while the intruder was out of view and get on the ground and under cover before they came back around again. There was just enough time for all this, but the timing was tight, and he was not where he had planned to be.

He re-engaged his propulsion unit and started moving down towards the planet. There would be much to discuss once he was on the ground. The thing was as thoroughly dangerous as anything he'd ever seen. It was enormous, powerful, and built for stealth. It was unquestionably a warship. There had been no such disguise on evacuation ships. No, this beast was evil, and they would have to find a way to repel it or destroy it.

Either choice was acceptable to Dsanik, but he preferred its destruction, for then it could not reappear and re-threaten his new home.

Yes, he thought, *destruction of the alien should be the goal.*

Onizuka
GL 252 (c)
Friday, May 31, 2086, 2330 UTC

It was several orbits later before Intel Officer Reyes called David back to the workroom. As David entered, the room was very quiet, unlike the usual banter and casual conversation that flowed out of the space. Reyes was looking at a picture with two of his techs. It was several seconds after the captain had arrived before he looked up. They snapped upright.

"Sorry, Commander."

David smiled and waved off their concern. "Never mind that. What have you found, Ethan?"

Reyes pointed to the large video display on the forward bulkhead. "Over here, sir. The change in timing was very helpful." He dropped the photos on the worktable. "I need to zoom in closer than these show." One of the techs put up an image of the airfield. There were several zoom-pan-zoom-some-more iterations until the image settled on a lumpy object in one corner of what they believed to be the aircraft parking area.

"What is that?" David asked.

"It's about fifteen meters on the long axis, maybe eleven on the shorter axis. We think it's an aircraft, camouflaged to keep someone from seeing it."

David crossed his arms, but his eyes remained locked on the picture. "Someone? Who did you have in mind?"

"Us."

David looked at Reyes. "You think they know we're here?"

He turned to a tech. "Show him the rest." The tech displayed eight different images, all about the same dimensions, all near the edge of the tarmac. The coverings varied in color and reflectivity, Reyes reported. "This was done in a hurry, sir. And there is no evidence of activity elsewhere on this field, or any other airfield." Reyes turned away again. "Show him the hangars."

An image of large buildings with wide doors appeared. "They're not like ours, sir. The door is only twenty meters wide, and, as you can see, it's very long instead of wide, but it's clearly a hangar. We've been watching these all this sol, and nothing is moving. I think they're hiding."

"Any heat signatures on the pavement or in the buildings?" David asked.

"None, sir."

David sat on the edge of the table, rubbing his chin. "Ethan, if they've detected us, how did they do it?"

"I have no idea, sir. Luck?"

David smiled. "I don't believe in luck, and neither do you."

"Still...a lucky telescope hit? Some kid in his backyard with a pair of binoculars?"

David shook his head. "It would take more than that, Ethan, and you know it. Anything else?"

"Well, we've been looking around, you know, more generally, and there is another object we don't understand."

The tech put up the image of a large rectangular object. "From the shadows, it's mounted several meters off the ground, so it might be steerable. We've been trying to get it from different angles, but it hasn't been as high a priority as the airfield."

"How big is it?"

"Fifty meters by twenty, more or less."

David looked at the image for a long moment. "Stay on it, Ethan. If it's a phased array radar or something, it might be more significant than you thought."

"Yes, sir, that was the plan. For what it's worth, there's no evidence of RF energy directed at us. There is some VHF radio traffic we can't understand, which is no surprise, but nothing pulsed or even constant wave that might represent a tracking device."

David thought for a moment. "OK, so, let's test this idea that they know we're here. With this polar orbit, we've been giving them large blocks of time when we're out of sight. We've done enough mapping of the surface for now — I've got what I need there. It's time to move."

"Synchronous orbit?"

"Exactly, we're going to go higher and sit right over that spot and watch what happens for a few days."

David walked back to the Bridge and let Larry Covington know what he wanted.

"Can we make those moves on the other side of the planet?" he asked.

Larry thought for a moment. "Sure. Do you want this as a gradual move, or all at once?"

David looked up and out of the Bridge windows at the beautiful vista of the planet below them. He took a few seconds to drink in the sight and to stall for time to make his decision. "OK, let's do it all at once as soon as we're out of sight. The airfield is well off the equator, which stinks, but I still think a synchronous orbit is the way to go. Give me a small inclination, so we can get a little closer once in a while."

"Understood. We'll get it done."

"If they really have detected us, that large a move should break any tracking lock they might have on us."

"Agreed." Larry leaned over to give instructions as David headed aft to talk to Ethan about the imagery they'd already seen. Something, he couldn't say what, was bothering him about them.

New Traenah
Traedenath Central Airfield
Spin 6, Subcycle 2, Cycle 2510

"WHAT?" Dsanik yelled at the far-talker.

"We've lost them, sir. They didn't come back around from their last orbit."

"Aytila, get your crew on the problem, then ride them until they *find them again! Am I understood?"*

As Dsanik slammed down the far-talker, Tmoyan was looking at him with disapproval.

"It's not their fault. The alien ship has maneuvered, which should come as no surprise. Maybe they saw you?"

"They didn't. There was no reaction."

Tmoyan smiled. "My old nemesis, you know full well that doesn't mean what we would like it to mean."

Dsanik stood abruptly, walking to the window that looked out on the empty aerocraft parking area. He studied the fabric-covered lumps at the far side, eight of his own squadron, hopefully hidden from prying eyes above. "What would you do if it was us up there and them down here?"

Tmoyan looked up at his friend. "I don't know, because I don't know their intentions, or their capabilities. What do they want, Dsanik? Tell me that and I can predict what they'll do."

"So, it remains guesswork."

"Yes."

Dsanik walked out of the Operations Center and out into the open. Why were they hiding, anyhow? Were they not as strong as any alien they might encounter?

That thought brought back the memory of the strange aliens that had come to Traenah just as the news of the comet was announced. It seemed so convenient, so suspicious that they would happen to arrive just at the right moment. Dsanik had been skeptical, but the discovery of New Traenah gave him second thoughts. Here was a planet much like their own, even with the same vegetation and wildlife. Whatever this place had been before, someone had prepared it for them, and that must have been the ones that called themselves the 'Trustees.' He wondered now why his mind had been so closed. Were these aliens above him the same ones? Were they evil, as most assumed? Or were they something else?

Still, prudence and caution justified keeping their own capabilities under wraps for now. Tmoyan came out after a few ductset.

"We need to be inside, Dsanik, especially now that the alien has slipped our track."

Dsanik gripped his agreement. "Aytila's crew will find them if they're still here."

"Yes, I think so, too, but just to be safe, let's get back inside."

"As you say. Feels so good to be outside, don't you think?"

"I do, but..."

"Yes, back inside."

Dsanik took one last forlorn look around, then followed Tmoyan back inside.

Onizuka
In Orbit GL 252 (c)
Saturday, June 1, 2086, 1215 UTC

David leaned back in the stiff Intel work chair, pulling the front legs off the floor. He'd spent many hours in just such a hard seat in his first years in the Fleet. He rubbed his eyes, then carefully sorted out the images of the dark rectangle that was the focus of his curiosity. There were more than a dozen high-quality images, and David dealt them out face up like blackjack cards. As he did, something lit up in the back of his mind.

"Ethan, do we have a current image of this thing?"

"Yes, sir, taken just as we came into range, maybe three hours ago." Ethan printed the fresh copy and handed it to his commander.

"I'll be damned," David whispered.

"Sir?"

"This image, Ethan, north is up?"

"Yes, sir. What is it?"

"Hold on." He picked up the ship phone. "Walker...Scarlett, this is Powell. I want a high-res of that suspected tracking device north of the airfield...When? Now, of course...OK, that will do." He hung up and turned back to Ethan. "Put the feed from the hi-res on the viewer. It will be a couple minutes."

The picture on the viewer moved at a nauseating rate as the large-aperture telescope slew from its previous target to the object David had asked them to focus on. Finally, it stopped and snapped into sharp focus.

"Gotcha," David said with a smile. "Print that, please, Ethan?"

Ethan waved to a tech to get the image for the captain.

"Sir, if you don't mind..."

David looked at him pleasantly. "Always expect the unexpected, Ethan. Now, look at all these older images. What do you see?"

"A dark rectangle."

"And what do you see in the one you got three hours ago?"

"Same device."

"Yes, but...what?"

"It's the same, sir. I don't get — "

"No, it isn't the same. Look again." Ethan scanned the photos again, then came to the one that David had pointed out.

"Damn. I missed it."

David smiled. "Missed what, Mister Reyes?"

"In every other picture, the device appears as a perfect rectangle. It's pointed right at us. In the picture after we maneuvered, it's not pointing at us."

"All correct. But where *is* it pointing?"

"Oh shit, sir. It's pointing where we should have been, coming around the north pole in our previous orbit."

"Also, right. Now, look up at the monitor."

There was a long silence as the whole room studied the familiar shape. "Dammit, sir. They have us again."

David nodded. "This has been bothering me since about the third image. Something about the picture just seemed off, like it had been faked or whatever. It wasn't until I saw that last one after the orbit change that I realized what was so strange about it."

"So, what will you do, sir? Other than kick my ass, that is?"

"Ethan, I just figured this out myself, and I am a fairly notorious spook. Take the lesson and do better next time. Better than me, even, next time."

"Yes, sir. But, what will you do?"

"Honestly, I am not sure." David picked up the ship phone and called his XO, Navigator, Surveillance Officer, and Forstmann Propulsion Officer to the Intel room.

XO Melinda Hughes was asleep, so she was the last to make her way there, carrying a sizeable mug of coffee from the galley. Intel Officer Reyes briefed the group on what they had learned, showing them several pictures of the strange rectangle that seemed to be tracking them.

"What about the reflectance spectrum?" the FPI engineer asked. "What is it made of?"

Reyes shook his head. "It's painted, I think. The reflectance shows some absorbance lines from metals and such but no obscure stuff like iridium or lanthanoids. So, no help there."

"Tell me," David asked the FPI engineer, "what is the power consumption of the Drive when we're just hanging out in orbit?"

"I'm not sure I'm allowed — "

Melinda would have none of that. "We know, sir, from long observation and experimentation that this ship emits almost nothing. No radio, only a trace of IR, no gamma rays, alpha rays, nothing. But this race is tracking us. To me, as absurd as it sounds, that leaves the Drive."

"To keep the Drive warm and ready requires about a kilowatt."

David looked over at the now-chastened engineer. "And we need about fifteen minutes from cold start to full power? Am I remembering that right?"

He recovered quickly now that his expertise was needed. "Yes, correct. We can start generating power in about eight minutes, but FTL is not possible for the full fifteen."

Melinda looked at David and nodded.

"OK, shut it down."

"What?"

"You heard the man," Melinda snapped. "Turn it off."

He hesitated. "I am not sure I can do that."

David smiled. "I could just call the Reactor Officer and have her pull your breaker. How would that be?"

He paused again. Every ship had a Forstmann Propulsion Incorporated (FPI) engineer aboard. FPI never sold its technology, only licensed it, and a hard requirement was that only their employees could handle the Drive. It was a strange arrangement, but if you wanted to go really fast, FPI was the only game in town.

"It's...unprecedented."

Melinda looked hard at the engineer. "So is being tracked. We're never *tracked.*"

David looked at Melinda, then back to the engineer. "Get it turned off."

"Yes, Captain. It will take a few minutes."

"Fine. Dismissed." The FPI officer stood up and headed aft to see to shutting down his only reason to be aboard.

David turned to Larry Covington. "Once the Drive is off, I want a thruster burn, just enough to move us out of the previous orbit."

Larry nodded. "Yeah, sure. I can move us a few k-p-s, and it shouldn't disturb our observation much. Maybe a slightly lower inclination?"

"Actually, I'd take a higher inclination. It would give us more apparent movement from the ground, not less, which makes us a little harder to find." He paused a second. "Or so I hope."

116

"Understood, sir." Larry stood and left the room. He had to calculate the attitude and burn times and instruct his techs.

David pointed to the image of the presumptive tracking device as he turned to his Surveillance Officer. "Scarlett, I want you to keep the hi-res on that device. We'll stay with it for a while after we turn off the drive. How it reacts may tell us something interesting."

"Yes, Commander."

David looked around the table. Seeing no more questions, he left to return to the Bridge. "Conn, close the Bridge windows."

Melinda looked at him with curiosity as they returned to their positions.

"No variables, Melinda. We close up nice and tight and wait to see what happens."

"Ok, David, I get it."

As they watched, the colorful vista of GL 252's blue dot was erased, replaced with the dark grey of the insulated covers. David looked away from the windows to the viewer displaying the tracker, wondering how its operators would react.

Time would tell.

Chapter 16

Endeavour
GL 245
Sunday, June 2, 2086, 2125 UTC

Carol looked down at her Bridge crew from her raised Command station as they scanned the GL 245 system. They'd been there almost a week, and in a couple days, it would be time to wrap up and move on. She looked back at her NetComp, reading the troubling messages again from *Onizuka* about the culture they had located at GL 252.

Next to her sat Senior Lieutenant Ronan Murphy, her Weapons Officer, working his shift as the Conn Officer.

"Wondering about 252?" he asked.

Carol set down the NetComp and looked over at Murphy.

"Yes."

"Sensing trouble, Commander?"

Carol shrugged. "The potential for trouble, anyhow. But there's nothing obviously threatening yet."

Ronan looked over at the Nav status board, which displayed their current position. He entered a few commands on the Conn workstation and new figures appeared over the Nav.

"Almost eighteen light years...so...thirteen days eight hours at one-point-three, eleven-point-eight if we can get one-point-five."

Carol responded, "I'm aware."

When she didn't say anything more, he cleared the route information off the Nav display and went back to monitoring the ship's systems and current status. Hansen could be warm and engaging at times, much more so than the typical ship's captain, but there were other moments when she was flatly unreadable. She couldn't possibly not be worried about *Onizuka* and her captain, but she wasn't letting on that *Endeavour*'s plans could change as a result. Their next stop was GL 295, another G-class star almost twenty light-years away and still over fourteen from *Onizuka*.

"Leaving for 295 on schedule?"

This time Hansen didn't even look at him. "Some reason we shouldn't, Lieutenant Murphy?"

Ronan, chastened, replied quietly. "No, captain, just making conversation."

Carol immediately regretted her curt response. "Sorry, Ronan. Yes, we'll head for 295 as planned. Yes, I'm aware of Commander Powell's situation at 252. Should he need our help, we'll certainly oblige him. But meantime, we stick to our orders."

"Yes, captain."

She stood. "Goodnight, Ronan. I'll be in my Duty Cabin if you need me. Nav will be coming on to conn at 0600, and he will get us moving to 295."

"Yes, ma'am."

Carol walked to her cabin just a few meters behind the Bridge. She had a quick shower and pulled out her journal as she waited for her hair to dry.

6/2/86
Dear David -

Here I am again wondering what you're thinking right now. The tracking by the 262s bothers me — it reminds me of how the Preeminent tried to track us with the SLIP apparatus. You (well, Leah and you) saved us from that, so I'm hoping you can do it once more. Got another trick up your sleeve?

I confess I am worried about you, but I'm even more worried that my crew is starting to pick up on it. I'm not that far away but I can't just abandon my orders and run to hubby's rescue. Until, of course, he asks me to! Meantime, we're going to play it straight and stay on plan. It's hard to write that, you know? I'd love to zoom over and give you a hand, but, like I said, orders.

I'm sure by now you've seen the picture Mom took of Leon and Teresa. They look very happy there, Dad included. It's a comfort to know they're where they're so completely loved.

Just as I do you.

Carol

She slipped the journal back into the desk drawer and pulled out her Bible. It was starting to show the wear of near-daily use, but it still had far to go to be the close companion for her that her old one was. That tattered volume had been given to her at thirteen. It went through many young struggles and quests, only to be lost with *Liberty* in the first minutes of the war with the Preeminent. For a long time, she had wondered how she happened to be on the surface that ugly day, but with more distance, she saw the plan in it, one that saw David restored, with a family created, and an incredible conflict won. She opened it to one of her favorites, Proverbs 3, and began to read.

She read and re-read the short snippet of wisdom, hoping it would renew her confidence and strength. She closed the book and placed it carefully in the desk drawer next to her journal. She slid into the small bunk and was soon asleep, dreaming of certain small children and large horses. And one modestly handsome but engaging young man she loved with her whole being.

New Traenah
Traedenath Central Airfield
Spin 8, Subcycle 2, Cycle 2510

Dsanik and Tmoyan sat in the small pre-sortie briefing room. They had sent all the other pilots out so they could talk privately.

"Two spins, and we still don't know where they are," Tmoyan began.

"Gkeze told me yesterday that they must have figured out how we were tracking them. They've shut down their propulsion system."

Tmoyan waved his disagreement. "Gkeze is a scientist, not a warrior." He paused, thinking, then continued, "But, I admit, in this, he might be correct."

Dsanik pointed to the star map on the wall that indicated where the intruder was last seen. "They must not need it at the moment. We've never just sat in orbit, Tmoyan, but I would not expect to leave the propulsion system running if I was."

"Yes, they're good at hiding from a distance, but, as you demonstrated, up close they are as visible as anything else."

"The obvious problem then is how to get close enough to see it. I was perhaps a sixteen of mileah away when I made visual contact, and that was only because the stars started blinking. I had to get much closer to see the ship itself."

"If they are anywhere close to their previous position, and I don't see how they can't be, they will see us take off."

Tmoyan thought about that for a few moments. "So, we condition them that our operations are routine, normal, and not a threat. If they're watching, they will have seen autowheels on the roads. They will know that there is a civilian population here."

"I think I see what you're saying. We restart flight operations but in a manner that seems normal."

"Yes. But we must do this a little at a time, Dsanik. If we suddenly pull all our ships out at once, they will be alarmed."

"So, tonight, perhaps we'll uncover my eight ships and park them in a nice peaceful line?"

"Yes, very good. Then a few operations during the day, perhaps four, just to get started."

"And then?"

Tmoyan stood. "And then, we remove this threat. I am out of patience with them."

Onizuka
In Orbit GL 252 (c)
Tuesday, June 4, 2086, 0430 UTC

David was awoken well before 'dawn' on the ship by the shrill ringing of the ship phone.

"Powell."

"Reyes here, sir. They've uncovered their aircraft."

"Be there in ten." He dropped the phone back on its cradle without waiting for a response. He did his short morning ritual (toilet/toothbrush/comb/clothes) and was in the Intel workroom in nine.

"Show me," he said as he dropped into a work chair. Reyes pointed to the large viewer, which showed a mid-morning picture of the large airfield. There, in a neat line were eight objects, clearly aircraft of some type. "Interesting. When did they appear?"

Reyes shrugged. "Sometime overnight, I guess. We were off looking at the industrial areas and only saw this when we came back for the morning status check."

"What's your assessment?"

"Based on shadows, they look a lot like fifth- or sixth-generation stealth aircraft back home. Angular features, canted tails...it's like a trip back in time."

David studied the image for a moment, then looked at his Intel Officer. "So, Ethan, is their long holiday over, or is this flashy display for our benefit?"

"I don't know, sir. We don't know anything about them, but a holiday that lasts six sols? Seems like a long time."

"Are they trying to flush us out? Get us to move so they can find us? Or, is this just a normal cycle." David tapped his foot for a few seconds, thinking. "Anything moving?"

"No aircraft yet, but there are individuals moving around. Preparing for flight, I would assume."

David smiled. "Thanks for not calling them aliens."

"Yes, not sure which of us, if either, should get that name."

"Maybe both, right? We'll just keep calling them 262s for now. It at least has the advantage of being accurate. What else can you tell about them?"

"They're shorter than we are, maybe five feet or so, and I get the impression they're fairly light-framed."

"Thin?"

"Yes, I would say so. But the sample size is small. Hi-res is coming on target now, sir."

They turned back to the large display on the wall. There was movement around one of the aircraft, with one individual standing off to the side. The shadow then began walking slowly fore to aft.

121

David pointed. "Pilot. He's doing his pre-flight walk-around."

In the last few minutes, most of David's staff had arrived to see what the alarm was about. Melinda stood near the wall to study the image as closely as possible, Scarlett Walker next to her.

Walker's phone buzzed. "Walker...fine, thanks." She turned to Ethan. "IR is up on monitor five, Lieutenant."

In a few seconds, the IR display appeared on the second display monitor. The 262's showed up as warm objects, as did the outline of the aircraft.

David sat back in his chair, resting his elbows on the arms and folding his hands in front of his chest. "I somehow feel like I'm playing chess with a master. Or, maybe, tic-tac-toe."

Melinda turned to him. "Tic-tac-toe?"

"Yeah. If both players play the game perfectly, nobody wins, but nobody loses, either."

"But in chess?"

"You can get a draw, but it's hard, and you can get real close and still lose your ass with one wrong move."

Larry Covington pointed to the display. "They know we're here. Ethan already told us he figures the camouflage job was hasty."

David nodded. "OK, so what are you saying?"

"They did all that almost before we got here. Now, for some unknown reason, they've uncovered and look to be resuming flight operations."

"Again, Larry, what are you thinking?"

Larry waved his hand dismissively. "This is a show. It's for us to see and react to. Why, I don't know." He turned to Scarlett. "Any evidence they've detected us otherwise? Radar? Anything?"

"No. We haven't seen anything like radar."

Larry persisted. "But there could be a passive detection. Stellar occlusion, that kind of thing."

"Yes," she answered, "We talk about that a lot, maybe too much, because there's nothing we can do about it. A savvy observer with the right telescope might catch us. But, at this altitude, it's very, very unlikely. But, no, we would not know if they'd achieved that."

David nodded as Scarlett continued. "And, with the Drive off, there's *really* nothing we can do about it."

David looked around, but there were no more opinions to be had at the moment. "Right. OK, let's step up our surveillance. We can go look at other stuff, as Ethan or Scarlett think necessary, but I want a check on the airfield at least once every fifteen minutes."

It was very early morning, but there was no going back to bed for David. He touched Melinda on the arm and nodded towards the wardroom. It was time for some breakfast and hard talk about what to do next.

New Traenah
Astronomic Observatory
Spin 9, Subcycle 2, Cycle 2510

High in the mountains south of the new city they called Traedenath, the old astronomer looked wearily at his workboard. He'd written and drawn and erased it a dozen times already today, the problem of the moment refusing to either succumb to his intellect or allow him to leave it alone. He looked again at the reports and pictures from Dsanik's visit to the alien ship. It was enormous, bulky, and clearly not designed to travel in an atmosphere. It was, without doubt, a warship not so unlike those that had fought on the seas of Traenah for hundreds of cycles past.

He looked again at his last drawing, thinking about what he might do, were he the alien commander. He knew little of military matters, but physics and astronomy he knew intimately, and this was, in the end, a physics problem. The object of interest in his equation had been in one position. But it was no longer there. There should be limits to how much force could have been exerted on it. Therefore, he decided, there must be limits on the distance it could have moved.

He looked again at the pictures on his autocalc, expanding the image to look at the fine details of the aft end of the ship. He looked away from the image, leaning on his elbows. As he looked at his hands, he could not help but notice how his fine, richly brown fur was becoming marred with streaks of blue. He was getting old. Yes, perhaps, but not yet feeble. His old injury ached from time to time, turning his limp into a difficult shuffle. Today was one of those days, and Gkeze wondered if the stress the alien ship was causing him was the reason. Perhaps he was spending too much time pacing the workboard?

Gkeze closed his eyes and tried to visualize the alien ship, where it was when it was last seen, how it would move, how the star would appear to move with the turning of the planet, and where the city was beneath it all.

He sat upright, eyes suddenly wide.

"Stien! Are you here?"

His long-time assistant jumped at the sudden call. "Indeed, sir Gkeze. I am here." Stien moved to his master's work area. "What is it?"

Gkeze was writing quickly on his workboard. "Stien, we are still taking daily images of Mehonnh, are we not?"

"Yes, sir. As you directed, we began the long-term study of Mehonnh as soon as the telescope was unloaded and re-installed. The star was in a high-storm state when we arrived, but it has settled down over the last few cycles. We continue to monitor it at its maximum elevation every day." When Gkeze didn't respond but kept staring at his workboard, Stien turned to leave.

"No, Stien, I have a task for you. And please call Nadon on the far-talker. I will need her, too."

123

As Stien watched, Gkeze went back to his workboard, erasing part of it and then writing furiously with his right hand. His left hand was gripped tight.

Gkeze, Stien realized, had solved the problem.

Tmoyan set down the far-talker and looked out the window, puzzled. His commander had just ordered him and Dsanik to travel up the mountains south of the city to meet with Gkeze, the famous old astronomer that had first warned them of the Messenger's impact on Traenah. The scientist was as old as Tmoyan's second-past-father, but Tmoyan did not perceive any diminution of his intellect. Many in the military laughed at the old scientist, thinking him weak, but his mind was anything but. Tmoyan greatly respected Gkeze. He recognized the truth that had more People listened to Gkeze, instead of the rantings of the Messengerite preacher Lanos and his loyal apologist Ilrosa, many more would have been saved. At least, Tmoyan thought, there was some justice in the fact that Lanos had died with his delusion. But then, he did so with a legion of admiring followers. Some unknown person had given Ilrosa the end he deserved, too. Tmoyan often wondered how that had happened; who had learned who Ntasik really was, but he and Dsanik had expediently declared Ilrosa's death a suicide, and there was no one to contest that conclusion. He was perfectly content with that solution.

Tmoyan pushed his latent anger against Lanos and his ilk aside as he ordered up an autowheel to take up the mountain. Shortly, Dsanik landed and taxied his craft to its designated parking spot, first in line on the left. Dsanik strolled in, happy to have been airborne for a long sortie to the northern plains.

"Get changed," Tmoyan said. "Command wants us to go see Gkeze."

Dsanik looked at his friend in surprise but hustled to the pilots' lounge to take off his flight gear and put on a proper uniform.

They traveled for two spedset in silence, Tmoyan driving the narrow road up to the observatory. It was half a long sixteen of mileah above and eight long sixteens of mileah south of Traedenath, it had clear, dark skies and very little extraneous light or atmospheric particulates to dim the view. The viewing there was better than back on Traenah, Gkeze often said. They arrived just before dark and were ushered quickly to Gkeze's workspace. The old man rose to greet them.

"Thank you for coming. I have something very interesting to show you. But, please sit."

"What is it that you want to tell us, sir?" Tmoyan asked.

"When we first arrived, a high priority for the astrometric community was to understand the details of Mehonnh. We knew our old star Tetanna very well, its habits and phases of activity. We needed to understand Mehonnh to see if there would be large storms with dangerous levels of radiation flooding our new home."

Dsanik squirmed impatiently. "Yes, sir, I am sure this is all — "

"Let him finish," Tmoyan said.

A soft voice with a distinctive edge came from behind them. "As always, the warrior class is impatient for quick answers?"

The pilots turned to see that a female scientist had quietly entered the room behind them. Tmoyan instantly recognized her as the astronomer from East, an interesting, attractive female. They had never met, and Tmoyan was fairly sure she had not noticed him among the pilots there in the far back row at the meeting in Elenath.

"I am Nadon. Gkeze has asked me to explain what we have found." She moved to the workboard. "Now that master Gkeze has explained the why, I will show you the what." She pulled a stack of images from the worktable and handed the first to Tmoyan, who looked at the yellow disk carefully before handing it to Dsanik.

"What do you see?" Nadon demanded.

"A star, Mehonnh, I assume," Tmoyan responded.

"Correct. Now, look at this one." She handed over another image, which to Tmoyan's eye looked no different from the last. He and Dsanik looked at each other,

"Again, the star."

"Again, correct. But there is something else there, too." She handed over a third image, this one all yellow with a single speck of black in the center. "We have used the autocalc to examine the last ten spins of images. It was able to locate four in which we saw this single anomaly."

Dsanik's eyes grew wide. "Is this — "

"The alien vessel?" she answered. "Yes, we think so. We know from these images it is not a passing asteroid or other natural body. It's in a stable orbit, not that far from its previous position."

Tmoyan looked at Nadon carefully. She was hard of expression, as if she didn't want to be there, or perhaps didn't want to be here *with him.* Her accent was clearly East, a country that had remained studiously neutral as North and South had hammered away at each other.

"Nadon...you are the Chief Astronomer of East?"

She waved away his question. "I was. East no longer exists."

Tmoyan briefly considered arguing the point with her but decided it was likely a futile exercise. "Are you able to define their orbit from these images? And, therefore, predict their position at some later time?"

Nadon's surprise was obvious. "Bright for a warrior, are we? Yes, we can. Assuming they have not changed their orbit, we can predict where they will be at any moment. This, I assume, would be somewhat useful to you?"

Dsanik stood. "Listen, learned scientist Nadon, we are not — "

Tmoyan waved his friend off. "Never mind, Dsanik. We have what our commander sent us here to get."

Dsanik looked at Tmoyan in annoyance. "We are not the enemy here. She should know that."

"Oh, I do know, " Nadon responded. "And you needn't speak as if I am not here, pilot. But your petty arguments have cost many lives and disturbed even more. How many homeless, pilot? How many cubs with no parents? You set science back many cycles because we could not talk freely with one another for fear we would share something you could turn into a weapon against us. You will just have to forgive my impatience with your attitude."

Dsanik looked at her carefully. "Tmoyan and I understand what you're saying. Now, long after the evacuation, the dispute seems small to us, too. But we had our duty, and we did it with integrity."

"How many, pilot? How many innocent dead are required to satisfy your so-called duty?"

"That is enough!" Gkeze interceded, waving them all into silence. "We cannot undo what happened on Traenah many cycles ago. We must all forgive the past, or the future will be similarly unforgiving to us. Soldiers, Nadon, true warriors, do as they are ordered. If you would have recriminations, find those who truly held power!"

Nadon gripped her agreement, if weakly. "Yes, Gkeze."

The astronomer turned back to the pilots. "Use the information we give you wisely, Tmoyan. We do not even yet understand the aliens' intent. They may be peaceful, just observing and learning about us."

"Or they may be planning their attack," Nadon said, surprising the warriors. "I hate war," she said quietly. "But I do not know how to evaluate what I see. I must trust in your judgment, and that unsettles me."

Tmoyan looked up from the data sheet Gkeze had handed him. "We will be careful, scientist Nadon. We also question what is happening, and why, and wonder how we can tell if they are friend or foe." She looked at him, their eyes holding for a moment. "But I can say that the longer they remain, the more of a threat they present. Haste is not a wise course, and we will take what time we can to learn more, but inaction can be similarly foolish."

Dsanik gripped his agreement but added, "We will be patient while we can. But if they change their behavior, we may have to strike to ensure our safety."

The pilots drove carefully down the narrow mountain roads, lights blazing in the darkness. They spoke only sporadically about the alien ship and the unbelievable luck that a routine sun monitor had revealed it to them. Tonight, they would rest. Tomorrow, they would begin planning how to strike the alien, something which seemed more likely every spin.

But tonight, Tmoyan would be thinking about something else entirely, something not a 'thing' at all. Her voice. It was her voice, he realized, and the intense intellect that drove it. There was something about it that he just could not get out of his head.

Chapter 17

Enterprise
En Route GL 188
Wednesday, June 5, 2086, 1145 UTC

Lieutenant Commander Declan Moore, *Enterprise*'s Systems Officer, dropped into the chair in Natalie Hayden's small office outside the Magazine without looking up from his NetComp. "What do you make of this message from *Onizuka*?"

Natalie laid aside her notes and relaxed in her work chair, turning slowly from side to side. "The tracking?"

Declan nodded as he looked up.

"It's dangerous, of course," she responded. "If they can track a Fleet ship, however they're doing it, that's a problem."

He set down his NetComp and leaned back in the chair. "I hammered the FPI engineer about it, but he denies they're leaking anything."

"Hmm. Too strong a denial to believe?"

Declan folded his arms. "Maybe. Just feels wrong somehow."

"Well, the Preeminent had some kind of mass detector, or so we think. They never disclosed what those Type V ships were actually doing. I guess it could be a variation on that."

"Well, there was no pulse from the planet, or, at least, Powell didn't report one, and I doubt he would have left that out."

Natalie nodded. "Unlikely."

"But I was able to pull something interesting out of the systems database."

"Sysdirt? Oh, do tell."

Declan smiled. Her ability to make up words on the spot always both impressed and amused him. "Sysdirt? I like it. Did you know that once we turn the Drive on, it pulls power even when we're not using it?"

Natalie leaned forward on the desk. "How did you find that nugget?"

"Well, I kinda recalled that from the reactor requirements, and when this tracking issue came up, I went back and looked at all the system monitoring data we had related to the Drive."

"And there it was?"

"Yeah, like I said, I knew it was there but now that I focus on it, it surprises me. It's taking power, even when we're not moving. Those kilowatts are going *somewhere*."

Natalie tapped her fingers on her desk, thinking. "Forstmann swore to FleetIntel that it didn't leak anything. I read those transcripts from early in the war. He was adamant."

Declan met her eye as she looked up. "I read them, too. I believe he believes it. I'm just not sure I do anymore."

She inclined her head slightly. "Where are you going with all this?"

"We should get ourselves to GL 252 right now. We shouldn't wait for our work at GL 188 or whatever. I just have a bad feeling about it. Powell is going to need backup."

Natalie hesitated only a second before she stood up and grabbed his arm as she headed out the door. "Let's go!"

A few minutes later, they were on the Bridge, an impressive, imposing presence compared to what most Fleet command centers looked like. *Enterprise* was wider and taller than any other Fleet ship, and her extravagant double-level, extra-wide Bridge windows seemed to call attention to that fact. The section consoles were larger, too, each with an extra workstation. There were two wide main passageways on *Enterprise*, not the one narrow central passage as on other ships, and the command position stood between their large hatches. Declan and Natalie found Fiona in her command chair.

Natalie scaled the four steps and caught Fiona's attention. "Admiral, ma'am? Might we have a word?"

Fiona Collins nodded and quickly joined them in the passageway just off the Bridge. "OK, so what are you two up to? Do I even want to know?"

Declan spoke first. "I'm concerned about *Onizuka*, Admiral."

"As am I. Go on."

"This tracker, it's strange."

Fiona looked at Declan, then Natalie, then back. "Something makes me think you two have an idea."

Natalie took the NetComp from Declan. "The Drive, ma'am."

"What?"

"The Drive. It draws power even when it's idle."

Fiona let out a low whistle. "Yes, I remember that. So... you're thinking wherever that power is going, the GL 262 race is detecting it?"

"Seems plausible."

Fiona looked at them briefly, then turned and walked back inside the Bridge. "Conn! All stop!"

Every head turned to her. The Conn officer paused only a fraction of a second. "All stop, yes, ma'am. Nav! All stop if you please."

The call came back immediately from the Nav workstation. "Conn, going to all stop."

The normal low vibration of Drive operation went suddenly quiet. Fiona walked to the Navigation position, Declan and Natalie just behind her. "Figure out where we are, set a course for GL 252 and haul ass."

The junior navigation officer looked at her and could not help but smile. "GL 252 at haul ass, yes, admiral."

"Get me an ETA once we're back underway."

"Yes, ma'am, will do."

It took only a few minutes to define their position, and then they were off for GL 252 as fast as *Enterprise* could go. Fiona moved to the communications console and sent a warning to *Onizuka* and the rest of the Fleet.

She would get there as soon as she could, secretly hoping that this diversion was entirely unnecessary. But if it was necessary, she was bringing the newest, biggest, baddest club the Fleet could wield.

Onizuka
In Orbit GL 252 (c)
Thursday, June 6, 2086, 0830 UTC

It was a quiet morning on *Onizuka*'s bridge, but XO Melinda Hughes was unsettled, picking up her NetComp, setting it down, walking down to the Surveillance Station, across to Weapons, and back to her own position. Finally, she turned her XO chair towards David and leaned over close to him. "Can I ask a simple question?"

David put down his pen, leaned back in his command chair, and shrugged. "Sure."

"What the hell are we still doing here? This little cat-and-mouse game we seem to be playing with the 262s is freaking dangerous, David."

"I want to learn as much as we can before moving on."

"That's all well and good, but what more can we learn without making contact? We should be out of here already. *Sir*."

David laughed slightly at her heavy emphasis on 'Sir.' He never wanted Melinda to hold back because of rank, and she never had. "I understand your opinion, XO, but I don't think we're quite done."

"Fine. Just remember how hard Rodriguez tried to warn Len Davis, David. Don't overplay your hand."

David abruptly stood in anger, turned as if to yell at his XO, then slammed himself back down into his seat, arms across his chest, his eyes staring at the current image from the hi-res telescope. Len Davis had nearly gotten everyone on *Sigma* killed by not promptly retiring from an encounter with multiple Preeminent ships. David, as a Warrant Officer in charge of Intelligence, was the senior survivor and had, by luck and smarts, saved the rest of the crew and limped the badly damaged *Sigma* into the Tranquility II Starbase. The later read-out of the Bridge conversations showed how XO Linda Rodriguez had tried multiple times to get Davis to bug out, but he stubbornly refused. The final strike killed her and everyone else on the bridge; indeed, every officer on the ship.

After a full minute of hard foot-tapping, he looked up at the chronometer, then at Melinda. "All officers in the wardroom at 0930."

David looked around his wardroom. He had a dozen good officers, with no slackers, no problems. He was grateful. It made his job so much easier that they knew and did their jobs so well.

"OK, Ethan, current status of the 262s?"

"Yes, sir. There were four operations last sol, all about ninety minutes long. It's closing on noontime there now, and one aircraft departed earlier in the morning, about four hours ago, and has not returned. No other activity this sol."

"Four hours? Seems like a long time?"

"Yes, sir, it does. Perhaps there is a field somewhere we're not aware of, or they just have more endurance than I, at least, would have thought."

Melinda leaned into the table. "Different propulsion tech? Could they have installed a Forstmann Drive in something that small?"

"We have," David answered quickly. "Shuttles."

"We know from what we saw at 262 that they *must* have the Drive," the FPI engineer chimed in. "Now, we see some kind of graviton detector, something Forstmann has always said would be too enormous to be practical. They tracked us with it. Therefore, they understand what the Drive is."

Ethan Reyes was intrigued. "Are you saying their Drive tech might actually be ahead of us?"

"I think that's without question. Or, at least, they've been more flexible in their thinking about it. No one at FPI ever thought of building a graviton detector like they have."

David let that comment settle for a moment before continuing. "OK, now, all of you, have we been here long enough? Is there anything more to learn about this culture before we move on and leave it to the diplomats to make first contact?"

Reyes folded his hands on the table. "I believe we have done all we can at this point, sir. We have detailed imagery of the planet, and we've measured what we can from orbit. We have recordings of VHF radio transmissions, not that we can understand any of it."

"So, you feel you've done what you can?" Melinda asked.

"Yes, ma'am."

Melinda leaned forward. "Any chance we could establish communications with them?"

Ethan shook his head. "I don't see how, ma'am. We don't have any reference materials or any way to talk to them. We had Cordero to break out the Seeker language, and the Preeminent had their own translators. We have zip."

"True."

"And, as you know, the first contact with the Inori was totally peaceful. It took months but they were ultimately able to make a connection. We're being shot at, which doesn't bode well for a friendly talk."

David looked down the table. "Weaps?"

"I defer to Intel, sir. We're loaded and ready to fight, as usual, but I think Lieutenant Reyes is in the better position to advise you."

"Larry?"

"Yes, sir. My advice is to get moving. The unknowns are accumulating, including this last long sortie by one of their aircraft. Time to go."

David looked around the wardroom table. "Very well. You all seem united in your advice, which I understand and appreciate."

"And?" Melinda asked.

"And, we'll leave tomorrow. Larry, let's get back in a low polar orbit to get some final pictures. Execute whatever maneuver you need, then shut the Drive down soon as you can. We'll make a few low passes and then set off for GL 270 unless FleetOps wants us home."

As they were about to leave, the wardroom phone rang. Melinda, nearest, picked it up.

"Hughes." Her eyes grew suddenly wide and locked on Ethan Reyes. "Tech says the airfield is empty, and the hangar door is open."

David thought for only a second. "They're coming." He ran out of the wardroom, calling up the passageway. "Conn! Set Alert Status One!" He turned and yelled back towards the wardroom. "Get the Drive online!"

CONFLICT

Chapter 18

Above New Traenah
Near the alien vessel
Spin 11, Subcycle 2, Cycle 2510

Tmoyan was moving closer to the alien ship, but it was still not in sight. He could see his other seven aerocraft on his display, all behind and to either side of him. He moved cautiously, remaining clear of the telescopes and other detectors Dsanik had found on the alien ship. He had severe reservations about this attack, but the leadership had demanded it, and he would carry it out as ordered. The aliens had been here too long, learned too much, and now constituted an acute threat. Or, so their logic went. He had two small missiles aboard, designed to destroy craft like his own, not a monster like what was now slowly revealing itself outside his shielded canopy. There it was, right where it was supposed to be. Gkeze and Nadon had been right about that, at least.

Another alarm flashed on his panel. Their propulsion unit was coming alive. Had he been discovered? His ships began their dispersal, a move carefully planned to strike the alien from several directions at once. They used their own anti-grav propulsion freely, which told Tmoyan the alien had no such detection capability. Otherwise, they would have seen Dsanik and surely reacted to his approach. He needed only a ductset more to complete his flight's positioning. Patience, he decided. He would not react impulsively just because the alien seemed to be getting ready to move.

Patience. It would not be much longer.

Onizuka's Bridge was suddenly alive with the structured chaos of techs arriving at their combat stations, putting on their headsets, and setting their equipment up for a fight. David watched all this with some satisfaction. They were a lot faster than when he first arrived aboard, not surprising for a brand-new crew on a brand-new ship. But would they be fast enough?

Scarlett Walker suddenly turned to David. "IR DETECTION CLOSE ABOARD!"

David turned. "Nav! Do we have Drive yet?"

"Four more minutes."

"Then burn the thrusters, Larry, just get us moving! Comms! Flash, all fleet, under attack GL 252."

"Yes, Commander."

"More IR tracks, sir! Starting the radar!" Walker was making the right moves. David could only hope they weren't too late. A few seconds, she called out again. "Multiple incoming missiles...but they look small, sir."

"I have no lock!" Grayson Lopez yelled from the Weapons station. He was staring at the evolving tracks, trying to see where he might have a chance to intercept.

"Radar is up!" The flat panels mounted on all six surfaces of the ship had finally come alive. After perhaps twenty seconds, Lopez called out again. "Locks confirmed on eight incoming missiles. Firing Spartans."

"Roger Spartans!" David responded. "Walker! Backtrack and find me something to shoot at!"

The Spartan defense missiles were not designed to intercept a weapon as small as was headed for *Onizuka*, but they took out six anyhow. The ship shook briefly from two small impacts. The shocks didn't seem too serious to David until the ship status display started going red. He had no time to think about that yet, but he was vaguely aware that Melinda had left the Bridge to begin her damage assessment. David focused his mind back on the Surveillance display.

"Do we have them?"

"Eight ships, sir, small and close in."

David turned to the Weapons station. "Lopez, you are weapons-free. Fire as you have targets."

"Weapons free, sir. Firing Lances."

David left his chair to stand behind the Surveillance station where he could watch the engagement in detail, leaning back against the raised command platform. He felt better being on the same level as his officers and crew where he could communicate better.

Tmoyan was momentarily shocked and speechless at the violence of the alien reaction. Most of his attack weapons had been destroyed by a massive defensive response. His force had made some hits, but they were now the ones on the defensive as more weapons poured out of the alien and headed their way.

He opened his radio. "All ships fire second round and disperse! Return to base on your own! *Split up!*"

The second volley would do slightly better, he hoped, but he was now fully occupied with escaping the alien weapon charging in his direction. They knew where he was. He pulled his ship left, then pressed forward toward the alien, hoping he might break the tracking lock of the weapon closing in on him. Surely, they would not allow it to strike their own vessel!

A tech called out, "VHF traffic, close aboard, ma'am."

Scarlett started to respond but was interrupted by flares on the IR display. "New tracks! More incoming missiles."

Lopez waited only a few seconds, "Spartans on the way, sir."

Several flashes blinded some of the IR sensors, "Five hits, sir. One of them is charging us!"

Scarlett turned to David. "Evasive?"

David nodded. "He's just trying to keep from getting killed like his pals."

"Four more hits, sir, three Spartans, and one more ship."

Onizuka shook again from the impact of the 262s' weapons. David finally focused on the status display.

"Larry, tell me about the Drive."

"Offline."

David looked over at his old friend and classmate. "Offline?"

Larry nodded. "Down for the moment. We're still investigating."

His communications officer left his station to walk to David.

"Yes, Wyatt?" David asked, almost afraid to hear what had to be bad news.

"SLIP is gone, sir. I think it was hit by one of their first shots."

"Shit. Did we get our flash message out?"

"Yes, we did. Barely."

"Well, barely counts today, I guess. Thanks." David looked at the status board for a moment, then turned back to Scarlett Walker. "Where are they, Scarlett?"

"There was eight total. Two escaped, under Drive, I think. We had them for a few seconds, then all of a sudden, they were too far away to hold a track on. They really are pretty stealthy craft. I dropped the pulse frequency and raised the power, but we were unable to reacquire them."

"I see. It's fine, Scarlett. I would not have fired on a retreating ship in any case." After a moment, he asked, "Do we have any targets at this time?"

"No."

He returned to the command position and looked out on the Bridge. "Set Alert Status Two. Lieutenant Walker, keep the radar up for now. Let's talk about it again in an hour."

Tmoyan gently turned his ship back towards New Traenah, not pausing to enjoy the beauty of the view outside his canopy. He was glad to be away from the alien, counting his luck that he was still alive. He'd seen four explosions that could only be other fighters being destroyed. Hopefully, the others would make it home. His AG Detector still showed the alien ship, but the signal was very weak. Their radio detection device was still operating, the signal touching him every few teosets but clearly not tracking him.

Still, the alien response had been a nightmare. Weapons poured out of it faster than he could believe. The combat camera would tell him the story in detail, but this was a more formidable opponent than he and Dsanik had ever seen. If there were more of them, well, it might get very uncomfortable for the People of New Traenah. Perhaps the attack had been a mistake, but only time would answer that question.

Melinda Hughes returned to the Bridge after a dismal tour of the ship. The Bridge officers gathered around her and David.

"OK, first the bad news. Drive is out, and the whole FPI contingent is dead. We got very unlucky with where they struck and when. There's a lot of voltage back there as they initialize the Drive, and the missile blew out the rear drive module and the shrapnel from that decompressed the workspace."

"What's the good news?"

"There is no good news. SLIP is gone. We can see the external apparatus from the ventral inspection cameras. It's shattered."

"Casualties?"

"Other than the five FPI people, none. The weapons were small and didn't penetrate the inner hull. I suspect some didn't even get past the stealth coating to the outer hull."

David looked over at Larry. "Can we get any propulsion at all? Maybe from the forward drive module?"

"I'll see what we can do, sir. But it would only be local...we cannot do FTL without both modules fully functional."

"Are you still running thrusters?"

"No. I stopped when we only had about twenty percent left."

"Very well. See what you can do with the forward Drive module and get back to me."

He looked around the officers in front of him, *his* officers, and saw the worry on their faces.

"Listen, we're OK for now. They'll take a while to think things over. After all, they lost at least five of eight fighters deployed, and we're still standing. That is not a 'victory' anyone would want to repeat." He waited for them to smile a little. "We're hurt, for sure, but we're still here, and we're not without options. Ethan, stay with the XO and me. The rest of you are dismissed. Go talk to your people, let them know we're doing OK."

There were a few lame attempts at humor as their ad hoc council of war dissolved, most of which met with ridicule that just generated more laughter. Ethan moved to the far right side of the Bridge with David and Melinda.

"What's on your mind, sir?"

"Classified, understand?"

"Yes, Commander."

"We can't stay here indefinitely. If they're really serious about this, they'll be back with more and bigger guns, and we'll be in real trouble. I recall from your first briefing that there are some mountainous areas on the back side of the planet. The continent opposite of where the 262s are?"

"Yes, sir, that's correct."

"Climate?"

"Well, much like back home, sir, that depends. The sea coast is warmer than Florida, something like Belize, maybe. Up in the mountains, of course, it's cooler, more like, um, Colorado or Montana."

"OK, well, get with Sabrina, find me a place to hide two shuttles and eighty people."

Ethan looked at David for a few seconds as if waiting for him to smile and reveal the joke.

He didn't.

"Yes, sir. We'll get on it."

Melinda and David shared a long look after Ethan headed aft to the Intel workroom. They'd survived the attack, but could they stay alive long enough to be relieved? She pulled him further into the corner, away from the prying eyes and ears of the others on the Bridge.

"You're serious about leaving the ship?"

"I'm serious about evaluating all my options. Maybe we can stay up here, maybe not. A lot will depend on what Larry can do for us. But we're mute, Melinda. We can't call for help or let anyone know what's happening. We're on our own here."

"At least the flash got out."

"Yes, and a good thing that was. *Endeavour* is not too far away..."

Melinda paused a few seconds before responding quietly, "You know Carol will come."

David nodded.

Melinda turned and looked at the Nav display. "She should be here in about twelve days."

"Yes, *Endeavour* will come. So will anyone else close by."

"I hope she's in time."

"Yes, let's hope that."

"I still have some damage control issues to check out. Nothing major."

"Yes, fine, go ahead. I'll be up here for a while yet."

Melinda reached out and grasped his arm, squeezing it gently, then turned and headed back aft to see what else was broken. David paused a moment to organize his thoughts, then returned to the command position to see what might happen next.

Endeavour
GL 245
Friday, June 7, 2086, 0545 UTC

Carol was still fast asleep after a late night on the Bridge when the ship phone next to her bed in the duty cabin rang.

"Hansen."

"Flash for you from *Enterprise*, ma'am." Carol shook off the fog of being awakened and looked at her NetLink, which clearly showed the FLASH message notification. She'd somehow slept through it. She quickly got up and dressed. The Comms tech on watch handed her a NetComp with the message.

```
FLASH 200806052000UTC
TO: ENDEAVOUR
CC:  CINC, FLEETOPS
FROM: ENTERPRISE
SUBJECT: ONIZUKA TRACKING

ENGINEERING HERE BELIEVES TRACKING BY GL262 CULTURE MAY
BE RELATED TO RESIDUAL POWER DRAWN BY DRIVE WHEN IDLE.

ACTUAL TECHNOLOGY EXPLOIT UNKNOWN.

ENTERPRISE PROCEEDING IMMEDIATELY GL 252 ETA 208606200900UTC.

FIONA

END
```

Carol looked up at Zach Robinson, her communications officer. "Get Denise out of bed," she said wearily, "and call the FPI boss up here, too."

"Yes, Commander." Zach walked back to the comms station while Carol read and re-read the message from Fiona Collins.

Rylan Mosely was a veteran, a tall and good-looking bachelor with just a hint of grey spoiling his long dark hair. If he'd been in the Fleet and not working for FPI, he'd be a full Commander by now. He and Denise Long arrived within ten minutes. Carol handed over the NetComp with the message. He read it carefully, one eye squinting in lockstep with a raised eyebrow.

"Well, Mister Mosely?"

He looked up and handed the NetComp to Denise. "Yes, the Drive pulls a small amount of power at idle, maybe a kilowatt or so. I was always told it kept the Drive aligned and ready to go. I had no idea it would leak anything."

Carol turned to her friend. "Denise?"

"Beats the hell out of me. Sure, I knew that draw was there; after all, it's right there in the Drive interface requirements. Like Rylan, it never occurred to me that it was a problem."

Carol nodded. "But, if we were to shut the Drive down to defeat this tracking, the problem, of course, is the fifteen-minute delay to get it back up. We'd be unable to react quickly should something unexpected happen."

Mosely nodded. "Correct. I can check, Commander, but I am unaware of any shortcuts in that process."

"Neither am I, but please look into it."

"Yes, Commander," Rylan answered, Denise turned and headed aft to her cabin near the reactor.

Mosely hesitated.

"Rylan?" Carol prompted.

"Just thinking, Commander. I thought this mode had been pretty well tested. I'm surprised that it's suddenly suspect."

Carol stretched a moment and smiled. "Well, we learned from the Preeminent that other advanced cultures sometimes see our blind spots much better than we do. Check it out, and we'll talk later."

"Yes, Commander." Mosely left, leaving Carol alone on the Bridge but for the Conn officer and the various technicians on watch.

The Conn officer waited for her to depart. When she remained, the officer came to the side of the Command Station. "Something more you need, Commander?" she asked.

"No, Lieutenant. Just thinking."

"Yes, ma'am."

She looked over the Bridge for a moment, suddenly remembering another Bridge on another ship, a ship still today lying broken and useless on Beta Hydri's 'Big Blue' planet. They called her a hero for that achievement despite her repeated statements that it wasn't actually her idea. Without that one wildcat day Larry Covington and Joe Scheck had spent in the simulator senior year at the Fleet University, she'd never have known to try it. But she was in command of *Antares* when it happened, and that's all the upper levels cared about. She wondered for a moment if she was just as much a product for the Fleet as Wren Thomas was for her network.

Now, *that* was a revolting thought.

She pushed it away as she turned to the Conn officer. "I'm going to breakfast. Call me if we get any more messages."

"Yes, Commander, of course."

Carol took a final look around her Bridge, found all to be in order, and turned away to walk to the wardroom.

Chapter 19

New Traenah
Traedenath Central Airfield
Spin 12, Subcycle 2, Cycle 2510

Tmoyan sat in the briefing room, staring at the six names written on the message board. Six good pilots he had led to their deaths. Dsanik sat next to him, listening carefully to the report of the strike on the alien ship.

"The alien is still in the same position," Tmoyan heard the briefer report. "Astronomer Nadon has observed it today."

"What of their propulsion?" Dsanik asked.

"It was detected briefly during the strike but then went silent again. We believe it may have been damaged."

"What did you see from the combat cameras?"

"Of sixteen missiles fired, there were six confirmed strikes. One hit the aft end of the vessel, which may explain the subsequent lack of movement."

"Only six? Of sixteen expended?" Dsanik asked. "Other than the propulsion damage, what effect did the strike have?"

"We see no out-gassing in the images, nothing to indicate that the hull of the ship was breached. It is covered in a dark insulating material which may also provide some protection."

Tmoyan stirred, pointing to the image. "Not so much physical protection, I think, but the weapons likely detonated prematurely as they impacted this outer layer."

"Yes, sir, that is our assessment as well. But one more item, if I may."

"Continue."

"There is an object on what we consider the top of the ship, a hemisphere an arms-width or so in diameter. It was destroyed, but we don't know what it was or what its loss will mean to the aliens."

"So," Tmoyan began, "we have sacrificed six lives while inflicting little damage, and the only consequence is that the alien we wish would leave can no longer do so?"

The presenter paused a moment. "Yes, that is an accurate statement of the results."

"Such victories," Dsanik said quietly, "will be the death of us all."

The presenter shifted his stance, signaling a new subject. "The leadership has asked me to invite your thoughts on what should be done next."

"We need to strike again, drive them off once and for all!" Dsanik declared. "This attack was too limited, too tentative to be successful. From what Tmoyan reports, more craft and more speed are required."

Tmoyan looked at him with surprise. "We lost six of eight engaged. I don't like the odds of a new attack. They are certainly more aware of their danger and will be even more alert. You weren't there, Dsanik. You didn't see the huge weapons pouring out of it!"

"Perhaps, but more weapons deployed from further away, with immediate evasion, should make the difference. We can hurt them, and we should!"

Tmoyan was silent for a moment, then said quietly, "I was ready to get rid of them, too, but I now say that was a mistake. We've now set ourselves in opposition to a powerful race, and I, for one, fear their wrath in retaliation. They would certainly feel justified in striking out at us."

The briefer shifted his stance, moving away from the display. "Your recommendation, then, is to wait?"

"Yes."

This generated an emphatic "No!" from Dsanik. "Give me twelve craft, and I will inflict such damage on them that they will not recover. I've seen the ship. There are weaknesses you did not exploit."

"Such as?" Tmoyan asked.

Dsanik flipped through a pile of printed images, finally selecting one and passing it across to Tmoyan. "In the forward area, there are windows. That has to be their control room. If we can breach those, their leadership will be eliminated, and much critical equipment will be damaged. It will cripple them further."

Tmoyan gripped his understanding and tossed the images back. "But, Dsanik, what is our goal? Do we wish to destroy them as an enemy or drive them away? I don't see how inflicting further damage helps get rid of them. It's more likely to keep them here, and if they've been able to call for assistance, it also gives their fleet more time to arrive."

Dsanik stood, waving away Tmoyan's concerns. "There is no such choice anymore. Whether they were an enemy before or not, they are now, and we must rid ourselves of the danger. And, as to their fleet, if they even have one, how would they call for help? Any message would take many cycles to arrive. They are on their own until someone notices that they have not returned, and that will also take a very long time."

The presenter watched the discussion with interest. "I was expected to take back a recommendation to the leadership. In this case, I understand both of your opinions and will present your arguments to them. They will decide our course of action."

"Fine," Tmoyan responded.

"But in the meantime, Dsanik will assemble his ships and arm and instruct his pilots as he sees necessary. The strike can always be canceled, but I think it prudent to be ready for whatever the leaders command."

The presenter folded up his reports and left, taking an autowheel back to the city.

There was long uncomfortable silence after the presenter was gone.

"Your tactical approach is good, probably better than mine," Tmoyan finally said, "but I still believe it to be a strategic blunder. Their response was purely defensive. They have shown no trace of aggression. They have not even struck this facility, which they would have every right to do."

"Perhaps they can't. Perhaps their weapons are damaged. Perhaps they're still planning."

"We can continue this debate, but I think it better that you begin assembling your force. I will fly your wing."

Dsanik looked at him with surprise. "You would participate in a mission whose wisdom you question?"

"You and I have both done just that more times than we can count. If it is ordered, I will do all I can to help it succeed."

"Yes, but that was war. This is not. I would not question your refusal."

"I will go with you, my friend, even when we don't agree."

They moved to the status board, selecting available aerocraft and the most appropriate pilots. They would have to agree to go, as neither Dsanik nor Tmoyan felt it proper to order their participation. It would be very dangerous, and some, at least, were likely not to return.

Endeavour
GL 245
Friday, June 7, 2086, 1745 UTC

Carol Hansen was having a quiet dinner in the wardroom, chatting carefully about some background details of the ship with Wren Freya Thomas, when her NetLink message alarm went off. Just as it did, her Communications Officer came running in. She struggled to finish her bite before asking, "Zach?"

Ensign Zach Robinson took a second to catch his breath. "Flash from *Onizuka*, ma'am. They're under attack at GL 252."

"Shit." She left her meal unfinished and ran to the Bridge, blasting through the hatch at full speed. "Nav! I need flank speed to GL 252!"

"Yes, Commander!"

Wren Freya Thomas followed a few steps behind, placing herself out of the way just to the left of the opening to the main passageway, notepad in hand.

The duty Nav officer got his techs started, preparing *Endeavour* to turn away from the GL 245 system and head into trouble.

Carol slammed her fist on the command workstation. "Dammit all!! We're too far away!"

Jayvon Dean, dropping into his XO seat, responded, "We're the closest ship, Commander. We'll do what we can."

Carol had too many other things on her mind to respond. "Zach! Flash to all fleet, *Endeavour* responding GL 252."

"Yes, Commander."

In a few moments, the Nav Officer came to her position. "Looks like just under twelve days, Commander. We should be there about 1300 on 19 June."

Carol nodded her understanding. "See if FPI can give us any more speed."

"I already did, ma'am. FPI says they can do one-point-five all the way there, but that's all. The ETA I gave you is based on that speed."

Carol slumped down into her chair. "Very well."

"Yes, Commander."

Jayvon looked at his captain, the stress clear in her eyes. "We're coming as fast as we can, ma'am. We're doing — "

"Everything we can do," Carol snapped, cutting him off. "I know, Jayvon, I know. I just pray it's enough."

She got out of her seat and walked to the Communications position. "Nothing more from *Onizuka*?"

"No, ma'am. We will bring anything we get to you right away."

Yes, I know. Just wishful thinking, I guess."

"Understood, ma'am. We're on it, Commander. We'll let you know."

"Yes, fine, thanks."

Carol noticed Wren Thomas standing along the aft bulkhead of the Bridge. "Still gathering material?"

"Yes, Commander," she responded quietly.

Carol looked around the Bridge, suddenly alive with activity, and turned back to Thomas. "Well, Ms. Thomas, you're in for a more interesting ride than you might have anticipated. What you don't know is that *Onizuka* discovered a civilization at GL 262, which appeared to have been destroyed by an asteroid."

Thomas' face betrayed her surprise. "You mean, like the dinosaurs?"

Carol nodded. "Exactly like the dinosaurs. But no one was there. *Onizuka* was able to identify a star fairly close by where that race might have evacuated themselves. They located them there, but now *Onizuka* has been attacked by the natives."

"*Onizuka*...that is Lieutenant Commander Powell's ship?"

"Yes, but this isn't about David and me. We happen to be the closest Fleet vessel, so we're going there as fast as we can." Carol turned and looked at the Nav display. "As you heard, we'll be there in about twelve days. *Enterprise* is not much further away, and Fiona will be coming, too."

"Fiona?"

"Oh, surely you've heard of Admiral Fiona Collins? She was FleetIntel until taking over *Enterprise*."

"Yes, of course, I have. I'm just surprised sometimes at the familiarity you all have with one another."

Carol nodded. "Fiona has always been a good friend to David and me, from the first day he came home from *Sigma*."

Thomas looked at Carol for a moment. "But you must be very worried."

"Well, there will be time for worry later. Right now, there's a job to do."

She returned to her command position, trying to tamp down the insurgent panic in her chest she had just denied to Thomas. David was suddenly in combat with an unknown race with uncertain abilities. Sure, she was duty-bound to respond to any Fleet ship in duress, whatever the reason, but what she felt now was nothing like the normal apprehension before an engagement. She'd felt that many times during the Preeminent war, not the least as she, Nat Hayden, and Liwanu Harry (and maybe a hundred Marines and crew) held off two shuttles of Preeminent 'Combatants' with small arms. Jimmy Cornell had died in that engagement, a memory that returned to her frequently. She'd given her son his name along with that of Marine Sergeant Leon Jackson, who'd saved her life at least once, and earlier probably helped make her career. It was the best she and David could do to express their thanks, and their understanding of the sacrifices made by others on their behalf. Now, though, it was David's life, and those of his crew, on the line. She would need to manage herself carefully. This was not just about the one love of her life; it was about a ship in peril that needed her help.

Focus on the ship, she thought. *Save Onizuka, and you save him, too. Think about the ship.*

That might turn out to be very, very difficult.

She looked over to see Thomas scribbling furiously and wondered how much of her internal feelings were apparent to the correspondent. Hopefully, none.

Thomas left the Bridge after a short time, as there was, really, nothing more to see.

Carol was still on the Bridge eight hours later, anxiously awaiting more updates from *Onizuka*, when a message came in for her from FleetOps:

```
PRIORITY 208606051200UTC
TO: ENDEAVOUR ACTUAL
FROM: FLEETOPS ACTUAL
SUBJECT: GL 252

CAROL:

YOU ARE THE CLOSEST VESSEL TO GL 252.

YOU ARE AUTHORIZED TO ABANDON OR ALTER YOUR SYSTEM LIST
TO ASSIST ONIZUKA SHOULD CONDITIONS WARRANT.

CONTINUE TO ADVISE HQ OF STATUS AS NECESSARY.
```

```
KIERAN

END
```

Carol read the message from FleetOps several times, listening in her head to Kieran Barker's elegant English voice and carefully parsing his words. This was personal, more directly from Barker to her and less from the Chief of Fleet Operations to the Captain of *Endeavour*. She smiled grimly at Kieran's now-moot message.

Her Communications Officer came to the command position. "Any answer to the FleetOps message, ma'am?"

The message had been directed to her personally, so Zach had not seen the content. Carol handed him her NetComp so he could read it. When he looked up, she was smiling slightly.

"I think our message earlier today tells the admiral all he needs to know, don't you think?"

"Yes, Commander, I do."

"Carry on, Ensign."

"Ma'am."

It was nearly 2300 when she finally gave in and retired to her duty cabin. There was nothing more to be done for more than eleven days, which felt like an eternity to her. The hours of silence from *Onizuka* gave rise to terrible fears in her heart, fears of pain and death and disaster that had occupied her for the entire day. She struggled to set them aside, reminding herself that silence was just silence and could have a multitude of explanations other than the loss of the vessel. David had pulled out of tough situations before, and if it was possible, he'd pull out of this one, too. Her confidence in him was complete, and she let that be the theme as she switched off the light and tried to sleep.

It was a fitful, episodic sleep, her mind not completely ready to let go. There would be more of these as the days went on.

Chapter 20

Onizuka
GL 252 (c)
Saturday, June 8, 2086, 0930 UTC

David looked out the Bridge windows at the planet below. It was the second day since the 262s had struck his ship. He hoped that help was on the way, but his ship was now deaf to whatever responses were coming from the Fleet. But he wasn't just deaf and mute; he was hobbled, too. Larry Covington confirmed that FTL was impossible without the complete Drive, but he could manage some maneuvering with just the forward module.

David called a meeting of his senior staff in the Intel workroom.

"Enough to change our orbit?" David asked after Larry had given his update.

"Yes, sure. But it will take longer than you're used to."

"Fine, we can probably work with that." He turned to his Intel Officer. "Ethan, I gave you a classified task. What did you find?"

"Yes, captain. You asked me to find a place on the surface to which we could safely evacuate the crew. I think I've found one."

Weapons Officer Grayson Lopez looked at David with alarm. "You're thinking of abandoning ship?"

"Keeping my options open, Lieutenant. Go ahead, Ethan."

"I found several candidates, sir, but take a look at this." He pulled up an image of a mountainous area. "There is a large meltwater lake...here...with a wide meadow adjacent, which is an obvious, easy choice."

"Somehow, I don't think that's where you're thinking we should go."

"Yes, sir. If we move west about fifty kilometers, there is a long valley with a smaller lake. And there is an open area...here...that would accommodate the shuttles. The valley is pretty deep, the walls almost vertical, but we should be able to get down there. The vegetation is quite high, weird-looking trees based on their shadows, but that should be a good place to hide ourselves."

"OK, I like it." David looked around the room. "Melinda, pick a pilot and get Ethan down to that location. I want you to scout it out before we make our move. Take Sabrina and a couple of Marines for good measure."

"Won't they figure out what we're doing?" Lopez asked.

"You won't stay there long, just long enough to check out the site."

"And then?"

"And then we move into some other elliptical orbit that we can get to easily but doesn't reveal our location."

Melinda looked at David. "So, you've decided?"

"I've decided to check out this location. Nothing more. If we can keep moving around, maybe we can keep them off of us."

Grayson Lopez leaned forward. "One more thing, Commander. You haven't mentioned a retaliatory strike. We could hit the airfield the space planes came from. Maybe teach them a lesson."

David shook his head. "No, we're not going to do that. Not yet, at least. I think they misunderstood our intentions here. Let's not reinforce that by hitting back at them."

"And," Melinda added, "they've already paid with six pilots. That had to hurt."

Ethan spoke up. "I actually have a different question, sir, if I may?"

David smiled. "As the Intel Officer, Mister Reyes, you don't have to ask."

"Yes, sir, but what was that attack all about?"

Lopez looked across the table at his fellow officer. "I don't follow."

"What was the strategic objective of that engagement? They must have had some reason to do it."

"I have wondered the same thing," David responded. "If they wanted to be rid of us, disabling our Drive is a bad way to do that. As I said before, it's likely they just misunderstood what we were doing here."

"They have modern technology; they're tactically sophisticated. They should have known what they were doing and why."

"Or," Melinda commented, "they're xenophobes. Or religious zealots. There could be any number of reasons why they would attack something simply because they perceive it as alien."

Lopez nodded. "In that case, we would be a threat just by our presence and not by any action we might take."

"Yes."

David shook his head slowly. "I don't think so. They have modern aircraft, they have a Forstmann Drive. They came here from almost eight light-years away. They might not have encountered an alien race before, but they would certainly have to acknowledge the possibility, right?"

"One would think," Melinda responded.

"It just feels off to me," David said. "I don't understand the strategy. As Ethan says, they must have had a strategic objective. My guess is they just wanted to be rid of us, but if so, it backfired, and now we're stuck here."

"Do you think they know that?"

"Yes. The tracker would tell them that."

Melinda shook her head. "No, the Drive was off. They found us without it."

"Right. That's something else that's been bothering me. How did they do that?"

"Sir," Ethan responded, "we have looked at some possibilities, but the only one that makes any sense, well, doesn't make much sense."

David suppressed a laugh. Carol had been dead right about this kid when she talked him into assigning him to the Intel post. "OK, so what is it?"

"A transit, sir. We went back and looked at our position, and we have been between the star and the city about six times since we've been here, all at about solar noon."

"Yeah, I get the noon part. We are, after all, in a synchronous orbit on the same longitude as the city."

Lopez shook his head. "So, you're saying they happened to take a picture of their star, at extremely high resolution, just as we happened to be there?"

Ethan raised his hands in submission. "No. I am saying that is the only plausible explanation Intel could craft based on the data we have available. If anyone knows something we don't, we're listening."

No one had anything to offer. David looked around the table twice before continuing.

"As absurd as it sounds, Larry, please figure transits into your calculations."

With nothing more to discuss, David closed the meeting and returned to the Bridge. *A transit?* he wondered; *could they possibly be that lucky?*

No, he decided. *It was too far-fetched.* Still, he'd have Larry keep them out of the star from now on. Far-fetched didn't mean impossible, and like it or not, they did it *somehow.*

A transit? Nah.

Melinda, in her typical fashion, assigned herself to fly the shuttle down to the planet with Ethan, Sabrina Herrera, and two marines aboard.

New Traenah
The Tracker
Spin 13, Subcycle 2, Cycle 2510

It had been a long, boring day at the Detector. There were rumors about that; the alien was still there, waiting for the right moment to strike, but Kirah saw no evidence of it on her monitors. Her shift was complete, and she was about to leave, turning her watch over to the next tech when the detector's alarm went off.

"They're moving!" the new tech called out.

Kirah looked at the spectrum and power display. "I don't think so...this is something different."

"Oh, you're right. This doesn't look at all like the first configuration we saw."

"It's weaker, somehow." She moved the giant detector slightly off-target, then let it re-find the signal. "Still there, right where we think the alien is."

Kirah called her superior, who passed the information to Dsanik.

But in just a few ductset, the signal disappeared. "What?" the tech said.

"They turned it off again," Kirah sighed. "They know we can see them."

"How could they do that?"

"I have no idea, but clearly, they're careful with their propulsion system. The pilots are sure that they've learned that we can track them."

"That's frightening."

"Yes." Kirah made the second far-talker call to Aytila herself, saving the evening tech the stress of his displeasure.

GL 252 (c)
The Meadow
Saturday, June 6, 2086, 2130 UTC

Melinda piloted the shuttle down to the area Ethan had located. It was high in the mountains, a narrow valley, less than a kilometer wide, just below some of the highest peaks. The cliffs on either side were impressive, a dark, brittle-looking rock she assumed was volcanic. The open space was right where Ethan said it would be, and she set up for a shallow descent between those dark cliffs, keeping the flat landing zone locked in her sights until setting down with only the slightest thump.

Sabrina and her Marines went out first, making a quick survey of the perimeter.

"I hope there aren't snakes in these trees," she said cheerily as Ethan and Melinda came out.

"Too cold for snakes, Lieutenant," he said, his breath obvious in the cool morning air. "Actually, we checked the area out with IR, night and day, and there didn't seem to be any predators around, and only a small population of animals."

"Strange."

"Yeah, somehow just doesn't seem natural."

They set off for the woods. The trees were thick at their base, with long bare trunks that split into heavy branches well over their heads. Ethan picked up some of their sharp green and spiny droppings.

"Evergreens?" he said, showing the needles to Melinda.

"Maybe, sure."

They walked a hundred meters into the forest, far enough to be out of sight of the shuttle. The further they went in, the trees seemed to get taller and thicker, which Ethan thought was a good sign. They could hide here. Walking back to the edge, he used his laser ruler to check the heights of the first few trees.

"We could actually get a shuttle under here," he said, almost to himself.

"What?" Sabrina asked.

"There is room under these to pull the shuttle in undercover."

She looked up for a few seconds, turning as she did. "Wow. That's hard to believe. You're sure?" Ethan handed her the laser ruler. "Oh, OK."

She looked back up the valley towards the mountains. "We need to check out the lake." They walked to the north end of the meadow, where it descended gently to the water. A small stream flowed out through the meadow and into the grove of trees to the south. Ethan took a sample and they headed back to the shuttle to check it out.

Melinda knelt down to feel the grass. It was smooth, almost silky, and cool in this early morning. It was darker than the grasses she was used to back home, but the darker blue of the sky seemed to match it.

Sabrina joined her by the lake. "A beautiful place, don't you think?"

"Yes," Melinda answered, "I was just thinking the same thing."

"Well, let's just hope it's not a death trap."

Sabrina turned and headed back for the shuttle. Melinda watched her go, her budding affection for this narrow alien valley now quashed. It was a good place to hide, Melinda thought, but maybe not such a good place to fight.

New Traenah
Traedenath Central Airfield
Spin 13, Subcycle 2, Cycle 2510

Dsanik put down the far-talker and looked across the table at Tmoyan. "There was a short signal from the alien ship this morning. The techs say it was not the ship itself, or they don't think so, anyhow."

"So, what do you think?"

"We damaged their unit. Perhaps they have some kind of backup?"

"That's possible. I don't know what else it might be."

"Could they be carrying a smaller craft, like a fighter?"

Tmoyan waved his skepticism. "It doesn't matter. We leave at dark, my friend, to finish what we started."

Dsanik looked out on the inside storage area where their ships were being prepared. "Sixteen is a good number, don't you think?"

"Yes, the best."

At dinner, Kirah told Staal about the strange signal she had detected from the alien.

"I don't think you'll be detecting them again."

Kirah looked up at him, surprised. "Why?"

"We spent the whole day preparing ships for an attack. They wanted almost every aerocraft we have ready to fly, so my supervisor and I had to make all these small repairs. I thought it would never end! Then the armorers came in and started loading weapons. Four per ship this time, when they're only designed to carry two."

152

"They're going to strike the aliens again?" Selol asked, a bit of fear in her voice.

"Yes. The pilots are furious that six of their fellows were lost in the last strike. If I am to believe their banter, it will be a very long night up there."

"But," Selol said, "how do they know the aliens are dangerous?"

"I don't know, but I am just a repairman, so I am not privy to such information, nor would I want to be."

"Why?"

"I don't have to keep a secret I don't know. And, I don't have to debate my conscience about things I had no part in."

"But you did. You made the ships ready for the fight."

"Leave it be," Kirah said, trying to redirect the conversation. "Staal does his job, and very well. What the leaders do with the craft is out of his control."

Staal gripped his agreement. "My only job, as I see it, is to keep the pilots as safe as I can. What happens after that, I can't control."

Selol dropped her utensil on her plate. "I understand, but I think they're making an enormous mistake, and I fear what the consequences will be." She got up and went to her room, picking up a medical text and pretending to study. After a moment, she looked out the window, wondering if she could see the battle. No, it was too far away, she realized, and her window was on the wrong side of the cottage anyway.

Chapter 21

Onizuka
In Orbit GL 252 (c)
Monday, June 10, 2086, 1300 UTC

David had just returned to the Bridge after lunch when the ship phone rang. He suddenly stood and slammed it down. "Larry! Take the Conn! Scarlett, you're with me!"

Covington looked up in surprise, replying "Yes, Commander," to David's back as he quickly headed aft.

The Intel tech was ready when he arrived, with a live image of the airfield on the viewer. "Something is happening, Commander...their aircraft are pulling out, one right after the other."

"How many?"

"We were late to the party, sir, but eight so far, and they haven't stopped."

"Late?" Scarlett asked.

The tech nodded. "It was just a routine check, ma'am. Lieutenant Reyes has us check the airfield regularly, and they rarely fly at night. But when we came on it, the planes were out and already hot, and the runway had a heat signature, mostly in the takeoff area. I don't know how many left before we got on them."

"I see." She turned to David. "When are Reyes and the rest supposed to be back?"

"Not for several hours. It's just dark here, so morning on the other side, right?"

Scarlett crossed her arms and leaned against the hatch frame. "So, mister former spook, what does this tell you?"

David looked at her, then back to the scene playing out on the IR display. He turned to the tech. "Get Lopez in here."

The Weapons Officer arrived as the last 262 space-plane was taking off.

"That looks like the last one, sir. Nothing more in line."

Lopez looked at David. "What's happening?"

"We're about to get struck, and hard. What's my weapon status?"

"This isn't a combat cruise. We came in with thirty-two Spartans, seventy-two Lances, and sixteen Bludgeons. We've expended half the Spartans and eight Lances."

"Shit." David picked up the ship phone. "Conn... Larry, it's David. Get us moving, whatever you can manage...yes, now." He turned to the tech. "I counted twelve."

"Yes, sir, so did we. But there were more before that."

"But it should be at least an hour before they get here, don't you think?"

The tech shrugged. "Out of my expertise, sir."

David shook his head as he left the Intel area and returned to the Bridge, Walker and Lopez right behind.

"What's the status?" he asked Larry as he climbed back into the command station.

"I don't have much power, so I'm slowing us down, not speeding up. I assume they're coming?"

"Yes."

"I thought if we could drop into a more elliptical orbit, it might make us harder to find."

David looked at him. "I knew there was a reason I hired you."

"You? Everybody knows Carol talked you into it."

"Get out of my chair, Covington." As Larry moved back to Nav, David stood in front of his chair. "Nav! I have the Conn."

"Captain has the Conn!" Larry responded.

David looked around the Bridge once more. Lopez busily working the status of his weapons, Walker keeping an eye on the airfield and the tracking system, which, she saw, was pointed right at them. Finally, there was Larry, standing at the Nav workstation, knowing what he was about to say.

"All stations set Alert Status One. Nav, close the Bridge window covers. And Larry, shut down the Drive soon as you can. They have to be tracking us, and I want to cut that off."

"Another ten minutes, Commander, and I can shut it down."

"Very well."

New Traenah
The Tracker
Spin 15, Subcycle 2, Cycle 2510

The alarms went off again in the Tracker control room, and the tech made the far-talker call to the military.

"They're already gone," Aytila answered.

"This time there is no question, sir. The ship is on the move!"

"Can you tell where they are going?"

"Not yet. It will be some time before we can calculate their new orbit."

Aytila debated what to do. The attack craft were still on the other side of the planet, climbing to altitude while they were hidden from the alien. He would have to call them after they came around. He fretted that the aliens might have slipped away, escaping their strike.

Time would tell, he thought.

Far above, Tmoyan was surprised when his AG detector went off as he came around the edge of the planet. They were moving! He watched the display for a few quatset, then used his own anti-grav propulsion to adjust his course. The ship's autocalc was sending him frequent updates to the alien's course, and Tmoyan finally let the autocalc pilot the craft, if only to reduce his mental workload. Hopefully, all the other ships in the force would be doing the same. Using the radio was out of the question, as he was certain the alien would hear them.

But down on the surface, Aytila could not wait.

Tmoyan jumped when the radio squawked, "Attack force! The alien has maneuvered."

He didn't respond. He could lecture Aytila on operational security later, but he knew Aytila meant well. The change would mangle their attack schedule, but that could not be helped. If every pilot followed his training, the attack would still proceed to success.

The AG detector announced the loss of signal, telling Tmoyan that the alien had again shut down his propulsion. *No matter,* he thought, *I have their course. I will find them.*

David looked around his Bridge. The hour was almost past, and the room was eerily quiet. He walked down to the Nav workstation, then gathered the other senior officers together.

"Melinda is on the surface. Larry, that makes you the XO for the moment. After Larry, it's you, Grayson, then Scarlett. Simple seniority, right?"

Scarlett nodded. "Yes, captain, but I doubt any of that will be needed."

"Let's hope not, for my sake, right?" They laughed, a nervous, uncomfortable sound in the near-silent Bridge.

"OK, Scarlett, let's get the radar up, full power. Grayson, you are free to fire as you find targets. Don't wait for me to pick them out. Everything out there is a threat, right?"

"Yes, Captain."

"OK, good luck."

The timing was very tight. Dsanik would have less than four quatset to fire once he acquired the target; a fourth of a spedset was all they had allotted. The plan was for every ship to pass the alien at high speed, firing all four weapons at close range. The alien would be hard-pressed to hit them at that speed, or so the discussion had gone.

A tone in his headset told him the alien had turned on their radio detection device. He heard it scan across him three times without pausing. They had not detected him. He was surprised they would use it at all since it would betray their location, and everything about the alien spoke of the need for stealth.

Clearly, the aliens knew they were coming and had decided it was better to see what was coming than to conceal their location. He used his receiver to confirm the alien's new position, and sure enough, the autocalc had predicted correctly. It would not be long now.

Scarlett paced behind her Surveillance station, anxious to see the coming danger. Waiting felt like torture.

"IR target, ma'am. Shows zero one zero minus five."

"Radar confirms! There is another at three two zero plus ten."

David looked at the Weapons station, but Grayson Lopez was already shooting.

"Lances away, sir!"

"IR TRANSIENTS BOTH TARGETS!" the Surveillance tech yelled, his excitement overcoming the Bridge's normal calm.

Scarlett turned to David. "Eight missiles inbound, sir."

This time as David looked over at Weapons, Grayson was looking back, the question obvious.

"Shoot at what you can, Lieutenant," David called. "When we're out, we're out."

Scarlett leaned over her lead tech, gently grasping his shoulders. "Just stay on it, just do the job. I'm counting on you."

In a few seconds, Lopez and his techs selected the most likely targets and dispatched the weapons.

"Four Spartans away, sir!"

"Radar contact one five zero plus fifteen."

Another few seconds and David heard, "Lance is away!"

He looked at the track display over the Surveillance workstation, trying to put what he saw and heard into a coherent picture. They were coming in from all around him, with no IR warning, at a speed that gave him no radar warning until they were almost ready to fire. They were good; he had to give them that. But what was next?

"Larry! Get us moving again."

"Yes, Captain."

"Lance hits on those first two targets, sir," Scarlett called.

"More radar contacts, sir. One seven five plus three, two zero zero minus thirteen."

The ship rocked slightly from multiple hits. They were getting better at this, David realized.

He was leaning over to speak to Scarlett when they were knocked down by an explosion close by, followed by the sound of glass shattering above them. Looking up, David saw that the outer layer of the Bridge windows had been hit.

Both windows were splintered, but the middle layer had not been penetrated, and the inner seal held.

David stood with his hands on his hips. "OK, dammit, now you've made it personal."

Larry was looking up, too. "Bastards tried to kill us!" The explosion against the Bridge windows shook everyone on the Bridge, but not for long.

"Two more Lance hits, sir. We've hit four of eight so far. Four more targets coming into range now!"

"They all fired before we hit them, right?"

"Yes, sir."

"Stay on them. Keep finding Weaps targets."

David felt more hits aft, his ship shaking briefly with each insult.

"All Spartans expended, Captain. All hits, but we're out."

"Very well. Larry, how are we doing?"

"Moving, but they're staying with us. I can't seem to shake them."

"Floor it, Larry, whatever you can do."

"Well, I can't get into a non-Newtonian solution, David. There are limits..."

David looked at his old friend, then nodded. Any escape that ended with an uncontrolled entry into the atmosphere would mean an ugly death for all aboard. If *Onizuka* had to absorb more punishment, that would just have to be endured.

Dsanik released his weapons on time, on target, and saw them explode against the front of the alien ship. He hoped to see some kind of effect: an out-gassing or debris flying out, but he was moving too fast for that. He flew very close over the top of the alien and turned immediately to return to New Traenah. A missile zipped by just over his head, exploding on a different craft just visible in the distance. He was frozen for a moment by fear and the shock of his near-death. Re-animated with the realization that death might still be hunting him, he pushed forward on his controls and accelerated his craft away from the alien as fast as he could.

Tmoyan watched two of his ships destroyed by the alien's defenses but managed to fire his weapons and make his escape, turning sharply to throw off anything that might be chasing him. He pulled his ship up, away from the planet and the alien, then turned back inverted so he could watch what was happening. He could just make out the alien shape, dark but illuminated by the star. There were flashes all around it now and more flashes as other ships were hit. His radio monitor told him they had detected him once or twice, but for now, he seemed to be safe.

The alien was moving again but not making much speed. Tmoyan adjusted his controls to stay with it. Three more explosions meant three more lost pilots. The work they had done on the weapons should have made them more lethal, but the alien was defending itself very well, he thought, and this second assault might not be enough.

Enough? he caught himself thinking. *Enough for what? To kill it? Cripple it? Force it to surrender?*

Again, Tmoyan found himself questioning the whole idea that they should strike the alien ship at all. What was the end game? How would this conflict end? Would a wounded alien behave like a wounded animal and strike out regardless of the consequences for either itself or the target?

His misgivings were reinforced by the speed and violence of their defenses. This was not their first battle, and he feared what other weapons they might deploy in retaliation. The leadership had led them down a road that might prove fatal, having likely created an enemy where none existed before.

As the attack played out and subsided, Tmoyan moved quickly away from the alien, hoping to avoid their notice.

Onizuka
GL 252 (c)
Monday, June 10, 2086, 1430 UTC

As the attack wound down, the surviving 262 ships fading from radar, David headed aft to the Intel work area. The techs looked up as he entered.

"Show me the airfield."

They retrieved the latest imagery of the 262's main airfield. David moved the image on the monitor around, seemingly searching for something.

"There," he said finally, having found what he was looking for. He picked up the ship phone. "Lopez...Grayson, come back to Intel, please."

In a moment, he was there. "Sir?"

David pointed to the image on the monitor as he looked at the Intel techs. "What are these spheres?"

The lead tech responded without hesitation: "We assess them as fuel storage, sir. Probably hydrogen tanks, from the design. Their aircraft seem to be a hybrid of sorts, sir, hydrogen powered jets in the atmosphere, then Drive powered in space."

"Fine." He turned to Lopez. "Three Bludgeons, Grayson. One in these tanks, the other two on either end of the runway. Time to put them out of the attack business."

Grayson nodded. "What about the hangars and support buildings? There could be more planes in there."

David moved the image slightly to display the buildings. After a moment, he turned to Grayson. "I'm not going to kill one single person I don't have to. I'll shit all over their runway, and I'll take away their gas. That should keep them on the ground for a while until we can get the hell out of here."

"Yes, sir, I see. What about the detector? That'll be a risk for the rest of the fleet."

"No. Too close to other buildings that might have people in them. Get it done, Lieutenant. Weapons free."

The chief tech spoke up. "Excuse me, Commander, but there are two other small airfields west and north of the city."

David looked at the tech for a moment. "Tell Ethan I said you're doing a great job." He turned to Lopez. "They should all be on the ground in three hours. Wait that long and then give the other two the same treatment. Gas and runway only."

Lopez nodded and left for the Bridge.

David turned back to the Intel techs. "Keep the hi-res on this target. I want to see a BDA as soon as the smoke clears." Without waiting for an answer, he turned and headed forward.

Larry and Scarlett were waiting. "Damage report, sir. There were sixteen spacecraft, each firing four small missiles."

"Sixty-four weapons? You're kidding."

Scarlett shook her head. "No, sir, that's the number. From the IR and radar signatures, I would say they were similar to old Sidewinders: fast, but with only a small warhead."

"How many?"

"We were struck about forty times."

"Forty? And we're still alive?"

"The warheads are small, and the outer hull and insulation helped. We took a few holes in the hospital unit, but no serious injuries. They're patching those bulkheads now. The lower decks were hit hardest, and we had to get the Marines out before they ran out of air, but we'll recover that in a few hours."

"What else?"

"They hit the forward Drive module. We're not going anywhere."

"Way to bury the lead, Larry. What else?"

"Exterior inspection cameras show we've lost a good bit of the insulation."

David shrugged. "Well, they're not tracking us with IR anyhow." He looked around for a moment, considering the news they'd just delivered. "Very well. I've instructed Weaps to hit the airfield and the fuel supplies."

"That should keep them on the ground for a while."

"Indeed, but now with no Drive at all, I don't think we can stay here." He looked at his NetLink. "Melinda should be back in a few hours. We'll get together then and come up with a plan."

"Yes, Captain."

"Do I still have laser comms? We'll need to let the shuttle know where we are."

"Yes, sir, laser facilities are intact, as are VHF.

"OK, that's something, anyway."

"The external NetLink apparatus is gone. We have service inside the ship, but if we go to the surface, we won't have NetLink comms."

David paused, again looking around, then returned to the command position. There was nothing more for him to do until the Bludgeons struck. Time to sit, to think, to consider options he'd never thought about before. He thought first of Carol, of what she must be wondering about his silence. She must be terrified, but she would not be showing that to her crew. She would be solidly in task mode, doing what needed doing to get to him and his crew. He was counting on her. He knew he could.

Then, there was *Enterprise*. That enormous, brand new warship was farther away than Carol's *Endeavour*. He smiled at the knowledge that Fiona would come full speed. He turned to Larry. "Larry, when do you suppose *Enterprise* will get here?"

Larry did some quick calculations on his NetComp. "Well, supposedly she can do 1.6...you think that's real?"

David, recalling his classified briefing with Fiona before he left, nodded.

"OK, so, twelve days, give or take, from GL 188. Carol will be here in about nine, assuming she left after our first attack message."

"When they get here, we'll need to let them know somehow what's going on, where we are."

"I'll stay aboard, David. Someone has to."

David looked up at his tall friend's dark face, so serious now, looking calmly back at him, not at all the comic act he was with Joe Scheck back at the University. "OK, I'll think about it. But you are correct. Someone needs to be here to bring the Fleet up to speed."

David returned to the Command position to think about what he needed to do. He had almost a hundred crew to shuttle off the ship. There was no hiding it from the 262s' tracker, but hopefully, once they got below the horizon, they'd be safe. That was a huge guess, he knew, but it seemed reasonable from what he had seen. Each of his two shuttles could carry twenty, excluding the crew who would have to return. So, he thought, two trips each, after some number of trips to get food, weapons, and whatever shelter they could devise down there. Maybe, he thought, four trips each shuttle, carrying a combination of crew and materials. But what then? Could they just use the shuttles as shelters? It would be more than twice the rated capacity. Their small reactors would provide heat and light, but how long would the toilets hold out?

Things could get primitive.

He looked over at Grayson Lopez, who happened to catch his eye, and nodded in response. He was dispatching the first batch of Bludgeons to disable the 262s' main airfield. Hopefully, there would be few casualties. But, David was fully aware that nothing like this is ever bloodless, and he might be killing people. He'd done what he could to reduce the chances, but they could not be zeroed out.

But he reminded himself, Carol was probably nine days away. The potties just might hold out that long.

Chapter 22

New Traenah
Traedenath Central Airfield
Spin 15, Subcycle 2, Cycle 2510

Staal picked himself up off the floor of the aerocraft repair shop, his ears still ringing from the explosions outside. Was it two? Three? More? He looked around, brushing the broken glass and bits of metal from his work clothes. His head stung, and there was blood on his hands where he had touched his temple, but he did not seem severely injured. As he became more aware of his surroundings, he heard his supervisor Sniat groaning beneath the aerocraft they had been working on. As Staal pulled him out, the sound, and his breathing, stopped. The blood from a large wound in Sniat's torso left a smear across the floor.

Still disoriented, he walked towards the doors, now buckled and hanging half-open. Outside, he found yet a worse scene of destruction. The hydrogen tanks that held fuel for the aerocraft were shattered. Bits of the insulated steel spheres were all around him, smoke rising lazily from them. The aerocraft parked on the tarmac were heavily damaged. Those closest to the fuel tanks were on their backs, burning.

An aerocraft whistled overhead, turning as if to land. Staal watched it align with the runway, then abruptly climb and turn away. He walked out past the burning craft to see that the runway was now filled with small craters. He could see more aerocraft overhead, circling, likely, he thought, figuring out what to do next now that their home field was unusable.

As the craft moved off to the northwest, Staal walked back to the hangar, wondering what he should do next. The repair commander ran to him, a worried look on his face.

"Staal! We must get you to the hospital!"

Staal looked at him in confusion. "Hospital?"

"Yes, yes, right away. Staal, can you hear me? You have a gash on your head that will need attention."

"If you say so, commander. Snait is dead."

"Yes, I saw him." The commander called one of his uninjured co-workers to take him to the hospital. "There is nothing to do here, Staal, until the fires burn themselves out."

Staal had just left in the back of his dead supervisor's autowheel when Kirah ran into the facility, then came to a stop as she saw the wreckage for the first time. Two aerocraft were upended, smoldering, their crews walking around, seemingly unsure of what to do next. The enormous door to the hangar where Staal worked was askew, its large windows broken teeth in its facade.

"Female!" the commander called to her from the building. "Get away! It is not safe here!"

Ignoring his warning, she ran towards the voice. "I am looking for Staal! Do you know where he is?"

The officer touched her arm gently. "You must be Kirah." She gripped as he continued. "He was injured, but not seriously. He has just now gone to the hospital."

She turned without thanking him and began her long walk to the medical facility in the middle of the city.

There, Kirah found him resting in a treatment room, his head covered with bandages. They talked quietly about what had happened, the death of this supervisor, the destruction of the fuel tanks, and the damage to the runway.

"Snait was the only one killed," she told him. "Several others were hurt, but not badly."

Staal closed his eyes and laid back on the bed. "He was a good male, a good teacher."

"Why do you suppose they didn't strike the building?"

"I don't know. Alien military strategy is somewhat beyond my understanding."

Kirah smiled and touched his face. "I think, Staal, that you understand far more than you let on. But, for now, rest. They say your wound is fine, and you can come home before nightfall."

He reached up and took her hand from his face, holding it tightly. "I will look forward to that."

The next morning, Gkeze and Nadon answered Tmoyan's call to come down from the observatory and discuss what they should do next. Dsanik joined them in the headquarters, just a few dozen meters from where the aliens had struck the day before.

"They have now struck the other two airfields," Tmoyan reported. "They waited for us to get on the ground, then damaged them in the same way."

"I am no strategist, Tmoyan," Gkeze said as he sipped his drink. "I am not sure what Nadon and I can offer you."

Tmoyan waved his disagreement. "You and Nadon are people of science, sir, people who use fact and logic to reveal the truth of the universe to us."

Nadon looked at him. "These are strange words from a warrior."

"Not as strange as you think, scientist. But the questions on my mind are these: First, why did they do this yesterday?" His arms swept across the view of destruction outside the window.

"And second?" Nadon asked.

"What will they do next?"

Nadon stood and walked to the window. Crews were moving the destroyed aerocraft off the tarmac. As they did, more techs moved in to pick up the small pieces of blackened wreckage left behind. "This looks terrible, doesn't it?"

"It is terrible," Dsanik said.

She turned back from the view of the wreckage outside. "Seeing this, what is your assessment of the wisdom of attacking them?"

"They are alien. They must be driven off!" Dsanik said.

"Yes, the hatred of the foreigner is deep in our culture. I think it was at the root of the long war between North and South, too."

"Go on."

"But you have *not* driven them off. If the observations of the Tracker are to be believed, you have actually kept them here."

"Yes."

"Gkeze and I have studied the reports of your pilots that struck the alien, and we have thought about the alien's strike here."

"Yes?"

"Had they hit this building or the storage and repair facility next door, there would have been many more deaths, correct?"

"Yes."

"The one death, the maintenance supervisor, is regrettable. But wouldn't you say that the circumstances of that death are, well, somewhat unlikely? He was hit with a random piece of broken glass. No one else was seriously injured."

"Again, yes, that is true. What is your point?"

Gkeze spoke next. "This attack by the alien, we believe, was designed to achieve a specific objective with a minimal loss of life. We believe that was a deliberate choice on their part."

"What objective?"

Nadon pointed to the window. "Can you fly? Can you attack them again until the hydrogen tanks are rebuilt and refilled?"

Tmoyan rose to meet her eye. "No. What you are saying is that this was actually a defensive move, something to protect themselves, not to punish us?"

"That is our theory of it. Of course, as Gkeze says, we are not strategists. But it seems logical to us. Had they wanted to truly punish us, obviously they have the weapons to do far more damage. They didn't."

Tmoyan looked at Dsanik. "We might have done better to simply leave them alone. They might have made their observations and left."

"And," Dsanik responded, "returned later with an invasion fleet. They may yet. This reticence they show for taking lives may be simple strategic reserve: not letting us see their true intentions until it is too late."

Tmoyan waved his disagreement softly. "Yes, that is possible, but I think it unlikely."

Gkeze stirred from his consideration of the wreckage outside. "Why do you suppose they failed to strike the Tracker? They know what it is, and where. Why leave it there?"

"I don't know," Tmoyan answered.

Nadon turned from her consideration of the damage outside. "How long, pilot, until the runway can be repaired?"

"Two spins, perhaps three."

"And how long to fix the fuel tanks?"

"That will take half a cycle, but we can bring in portable tanks from the hydrogen factory on the coast. What are you getting at?"

"All they have done, then, is keep you on the surface for a few spins. After that, you will be able to operate as before, correct?"

"Yes, I suppose."

She turned to Gkeze. "They have made time for themselves, a short time where they are safe from our attacks. What will they do with it?"

Gkeze waved away her comment. "I do not pretend to understand them. Also, we do not know what condition their vessel might be in after the second attack."

"I know I hit the control room," Dsanik said. "But I don't know how much damage I did."

Tmoyan looked over at Nadon. "We also struck the forward propulsion unit."

"So, now you've taken away any chance to escape?"

"Yes, we have," Dsanik said proudly. "They are at our mercy now."

Gkeze scratched his chin, the bluish fur there in need of trimming. "I am not so sure of that. You overwhelmed their immediate defenses, but their counterattack here reflects a much greater potential for harm, I think."

Nadon looked at Tmoyan as she pointed at Dsanik. "Is this one always so aggressive? So ready to strike?"

"He has always been so. Even when I almost had him in my sights, he was finding the angle to get back at me."

"Gkeze and I are not schooled in the military arts, but we suggest caution. The alien has neutralized you for a short time but made no attempt to completely destroy you or lash out at the People. We believe the wise course is to simply watch carefully and await developments."

Gkeze tightly gripped his agreement. "And, meantime, repair your facilities and prepare to return to the skies when it is safe to do so."

Tmoyan asked Nadon and Gkeze to remain in the city for a few spins, so they would be available should some new events occur.

It was late, and the small restaurant was nearly empty. As he entered, Tmoyan was immediately reminded of the first night he met Dsanik in Bordinata. Even the smell of blouke in the air was familiar. It had been a long day, full of questions and uncertainty. The runway repairs were underway, but it would be three spins, not two, before they could fly again.

Nadon was waiting in a small booth off to the side.

"Good evening," she said evenly.

"Yes, to you, as well," Tmoyan said as he sat across from her.

"It has been a long day for you?" Her tone was friendly, even concerned. Tmoyan was intrigued by her apparent change of attitude.

"Yes, very long. As you know, we lost a repair supervisor yesterday, and now we are unsure if his apprentice is up to the job."

"Surely, there are others?"

"Yes, some, but the male we lost was the most experienced. He was assigned to my aerocraft during the war."

"So," she answered, "not just a repair tech, but a friend?"

"He was someone who held my life in his hands. It is a strong bond, pilot and tech, especially in wartime."

"I see."

Tmoyan let the conversation lie a moment, then asked, "So, learned astronomer and scientist, why are we here?"

"I'm hungry. Some blouke, perhaps?"

Her abrupt change of the subject surprised him, but then, he hadn't eaten since sunrise.

"Sure, that would be fine. I'm famished."

They ordered dinner and tall glasses of baught, Nadon's favored distilled drink.

"Baught? That is a drink for soldiers and the working class, Nadon. One would expect a refined female like yourself to choose something, well, finer!"

Nadon waved away his comment. "I am no refined female, Tmoyan. I have worked all my life to achieve what I have. My parents died when I was young, and I was left to fend for myself with my father's idiot sister."

The baught came and they each took a long drink, seeking some comfort and to blunt the stress both felt.

Nadon set down her drink, then looked up at Tmoyan. "You surprise me, pilot. Your mind is not what I have seen in your type."

Tmoyan took another sip, thinking about how to respond to her. "I think you underestimate us. You made your disdain for us plain when we first met."

"I abhor pride and the deadly rituals of dominance you Continentals play. So many have suffered over these petty arguments."

"They did not seem petty at the time, and they were not so petty to those whose homes were invaded and destroyed."

"There were better solutions than killing one another."

Tmoyan gently gripped his agreement. "Yes, I know. You don't seem to understand that it is the fighter who most hates the fight."

She looked at him for a long moment. "I would have thought the quest for glory, for fame, would be foremost in your mind."

"Again, you misjudge us, and me in particular. I have lost many friends to the battle, good males who never saw a trifle of glory. I would prefer they had lived."

The conversation was interrupted by the arrival of the blouke. They ate eagerly in silence for a time.

"This is excellent," Tmoyan said finally.

"Yes, and it is very, very strange."

"Strange? How so?"

"Oh, Tmoyan, sharp-eyed pilot of North, look around!"

"I don't understand."

"This fish came from the ocean here on New Traenah. We are told by the fishermen that the population is small but rapidly growing."

"But, this is a fish from Traenah!"

"Ah, now he begins to see. The trees? The grasses?"

"The same as on Traenah?"

"Yes, at least here near the shore where we settled; less so farther away. Should we be equally surprised that there was a perfect landing area for evacuation ships, right here? Close to good water, close to an ocean already seeded with fish from home?"

Tmoyan looked away, then back to Nadon. "The first aliens."

"Yes, those that called themselves the Trustees, who said they had prepared a planet for us to evacuate to."

"This is that planet."

"Yes. I see no other plausible explanation."

"So, they spoke the truth. Is it possible, Nadon, that the aliens here now are the same?"

"Gkeze and I think not. Their ships do not appear similar at all, except that they are clearly designed to be hard to find."

Tmoyan paused between bites. "Nothing has been said of this, officially."

"No, but it seems The People have just accepted what this place is without thinking."

"They have had more important things on their minds: building a life, finding ways to make a living."

"Yes, exactly," she responded.

There was an uncomfortable silence, broken by Tmoyan. "I have enjoyed our time together. Might we meet again sometime?"

Nadon lightly gripped her agreement. "Indeed, when?"

"Tomorrow evening? Here?"

Nadon looked around the restaurant, then back to Tmoyan. "The menu is long. It will take some time to work our way through it."

They left soon after, Tmoyan back to his quarters at the airfield, Nadon to her small apartment in the center of town.

As he walked the dark streets of the new city, Tmoyan wondered at Nadon's sudden interest in him and what that might mean for his future. Their conversation was open, even friendly. He would not have thought that possible only a few spins before. He wondered which of them had changed.

Tomorrow, there would be a meeting of the council, who would decide what is to be done about the aliens. Tmoyan held out little hope they would be as reasonable and flexible in their thinking as Nadon.

Pity.

Chapter 23

Onizuka
GL 252 (c)
Monday, June 10, 2086, 2145 UTC

David paced the Bridge nervously, waiting for his scouting party to return from the surface. He was pretty sure the 262s were grounded, but one could never be completely sure what the opponent might have in reserve, hidden away from sight. He was relieved when they called in as they came back around the planet, and when they finally arrived, he was in the hangar, greeting Ethan, Sabrina, and Melinda as they exited the spacecraft.

"It's workable," Ethan reported. "We can hide there for a while."

David looked at Melinda. "Yes, it'll work. We can even hide the shuttles. The trees there...wow...you'll just have to see them for yourself, sir. Enormous in every way."

"That sounds very good." He turned to Sabrina. "Lieutenant?"

"Defensible, sir. There is good cover under the trees, water easily available."

"It's cool there, sir, up in the mountains. We need to be prepared for cold weather."

"OK, then, let's get the staff together and talk it out."

The argument in the wardroom went on for a half-hour. David was adamant that the captain could not leave his ship, and XO Melinda Hughes was just as adamant that he must go with the crew. Larry Covington tried to negotiate a middle ground, but it seemed hopeless until Sabrina Herrera, the new Marine Lieutenant who had been a Gunnery Sergeant with David on Zeta Doradus, closed the case: "The danger, Commander, isn't here. It's on the surface. We need a command presence there, not here."

David shook his head. "I don't like it."

"It's a shitty situation, sir, but you and I have been in shittier."

David was forced to smile at that. It seemed to him that Herrera had learned a few tricks in her Marine OCS, and her logic was beginning to turn his thinking.

"So, if I go, who stays?"

"I do," Larry answered immediately. "Someone has to contact *Endeavour* and *Enterprise* when they get here. I am the Communications Officer. It's my job."

"OK, assuming I agree to that, which I have not yet, who else?"

"I'll need a reactor tech to keep the lights on, maybe a weaps tech just in case."

David shook his head. "Reactor, yes, weaps, no. We're not shooting at anything."

Grayson Lopez leaned forward. "We're out of Spartans, anyway, Larry."

David paused, tapping his stylus on the table as he thought. "Nine days on the surface, best we can guess. Can we handle that?"

His Logistics officer explained they could, with some restrictions. "We might have to make a return trip up here to resupply."

David shook his head. "No, we can't. If you need to make a couple extra trips today or tomorrow, fine. But by three sols from now, if not two, they'll have their runways back up, and our safe space will be gone."

"Yes, captain. I'll see to it."

"Good. OK, first trip, Shuttle one: Marines and weapons. Shuttle two: medical and galley. After that, quickly as possible, half loads of personnel and supplies until we're all on the surface. Since you were so foolhardy to volunteer, Larry, you'll remain on board. *Endeavour* should be here in nine days. Carol will probably issue a VHF ping when she arrives."

"I estimated her time en route at 11.8. Given transmissions delays, etc., I would estimate her ETA as mid-afternoon on 19 June."

"Fine. If she hasn't sent a ping by 1800 that day, send one yourself every hour until she responds."

"Understood, Captain. I'll get it done."

He looked around at his officers for a moment. "Anything else? No? OK, Sabrina, get your people and the armory packed for transport. It's cold down there, so make sure everyone has their winter gear."

The meeting broke up quickly. Each officer headed to their section to brief their people and start the evacuation.

New Traenah
Spin 16, Subcycle 2, Cycle 2510

Kirah didn't want to go to work at the Tracker this spin. She argued with Staal that she should remain with him for at least another spin, but Staal stubbornly insisted she should go. Selol had no classes that day, so she promised to stay with him, making sure he had no unexpected symptoms from his head wound. Kirah left a little late, what with the long discussion, and arrived at The Detector after her shift was to start.

"It's back!" the overnight tech said.

"What is back?"

"The other vessel, the small, less powerful one."

Kirah looked at the display to confirm his observation. As she did, a second alarm sounded.

"Another one?" she asked, mostly to herself.

"Yes!" the overnight tech answered.

Kirah picked up the far-talker and requested a connection to Aytila. She reported the observations.

"Where are they going?" he asked.

"They're headed to the other side of the planet. I can't tell if they're going to orbit or land."

"This is the same type that was gone for half a spin, right?"

"Yes."

"That's all I need for now. Keep tracking them and let me know after they disappear."

"Yes, sir."

Kirah turned to her bleary-eyed co-worker. "I am sorry to be late."

"It is not such a problem. How is Staal?"

"He is doing fine, for now. He has a bad laceration that will take time to heal."

"You want me to stay? There are two targets out there."

"No, I will be fine. Go get some sleep."

Kirah watched the two tracks as they moved to the east and set below her horizon. When they were both gone, she called Aytila again.

"They are moving too slow to be in orbit. They are clearly landing somewhere."

Aytila hung up the far-talker and walked the few steps to the pilot's ready room.

"The aliens are landing somewhere on the other side of the planet."

Dsanik waved his skepticism. "How do you know?"

"Two small ships, moving east below the horizon, too slow to be in orbit."

Tmoyan shifted in his chair. "And last spin, there was just one, with a similar profile?"

"Yes."

"So, a reconnaissance, now a landing. Why?"

Aytila said nothing.

Dsanik looked from Aytila to Tmoyan. "Perhaps we damaged them more than we thought? Could they be evacuating their vessel?"

"Perhaps, but they would have to be very desperate to do that — to abandon the safety of their ship for the surface?"

Aytila gripped his agreement. "Unless the ship is now less safe than the surface. So, Tmoyan, what shall we do?"

"The north airfield should be operational tomorrow. I will go see what they are doing."

"Those craft would be slow, easy targets. Take those out, and you cut off those on the surface as well as removing any escape for those still aboard."

"No, Dsanik, we do not shoot at each other after we abandon our aerocraft. We will not do that to them either."

"What will you do?"

"Observe and try to see where they're going."

The next morning, Tmoyan read the Tracker report of the aliens' latest movements just before he took off from the north airfield. He climbed quickly out of the atmosphere and turned towards the course he'd been given.

Onizuka
In Orbit GL 252 (c)
Tuesday, June 11, 2086, 0930 UTC

Lieutenant Ethan Reyes refused to leave his station in Intel until the very last shuttle was ready to go. Weary of the argument and seeing something of himself in it, David reluctantly agreed and left on the fourth trip down. Logistics would need two more cargo-only runs to ensure that there were enough supplies on the surface, so Ethan wrangled a seat for himself in the cockpit of the last trip.

It was just after local dawn the second sol after the attack as Ethan made his periodic check of the airfields. As the high-res telescope focused on the airfield north of the city, he sat upright.

"Shit."

The dark shape rolled down the runway and out of his field of view. But, no need to follow it. He knew where it was going. He walked to the Bridge.

"Lieutenant Covington, sir, I have some bad news."

"We're full up on bad news, Ethan. We're only accepting good right now."

"Well, the good news is on backorder. They're flying again."

"Shit. How many?"

Ethan shrugged. "Can't be sure. I only saw one."

Larry sat at the Comm console and slipped a headset over his shaved head. "Shuttle one, Shuttle one, *Onizuka*."

Melinda's head shot upright at the sound of Larry's voice in her ears. She looked over at David, sitting right seat, who just nodded.

She pressed the microphone control. "One here, go Larry."

"Bandit, one each, just now."

"Dammit," was all David said.

"Roger one airborne. Keep us posted."

David looked out the windscreen of the shuttle. "Well, they're industrious. I'll say that for them."

"What do we do?"

David shook his head. "This die is cast, Melinda. We're right in the middle of a tactical redeployment, with most of the crew already on the surface. We stick to the plan and hope for the best." He looked across at her. "It probably was not the best idea for us to ride down together, you know?"

"Oh, well, thanks for that, boss. Before, I was just terrified. Now, I'm worried, too."

David crossed his arms and went back to watching the planet grow outside.

High above in *Onizuka*, Ethan went back to check the other two airfields. Neither was usable yet, but the 262s were hard at work. Later this sol, he thought, they'd be serviceable. If they could get fuel to them, they'd all be back in business by sunset.

He walked to the Bridge and reported what he had seen to Larry.

"Get some good images before you leave and brief Powell on the situation when you get down."

"I don't think I should go. I should stay here and keep observing."

"No, you're going. Look, Ethan, you have your orders."

"Still — "

"Still nothing. If you stay here, you're worthless to him. We're stuck in this dip-shit sorta-synchronous orbit where it will be weeks, if not months before I have a line of sight to that cool little valley you found."

"Yes, true."

"So gather whatever you have and take it with you." Larry looked up at the chronometer. "You've got about six hours. Make good use of it."

"Yes, Lieutenant."

Ethan took one last look around the strangely quiet, strangely empty Bridge, then turned and walked back to Intel. He started downloading as much imagery as he could to his NetComp, then printed hard copies of the valley and the surrounding area, just in case. This data dump would take a little time, but Covington was right. He was of no use to Powell aboard *Onizuka*. He needed to be with him on the surface with as much information as possible.

But, meantime, he'd also keep a close eye on the airfields.

Chapter 24

Endeavour
En Route GL 252
Wednesday, June 12, 2086, 0900 UTC

Wren Freya Thomas sat quietly in the waiting area of the captain's in-port office. She was surprised by the prosaic feeling of it. Other than the sterile paint design scheme, steel bulkheads, and airtight hatches, she could be in the outer office of any minor executive back on Earth. The admin tech looked at her from time to time as he worked through whatever paperwork Commander Hansen had given him. Music played quietly from somewhere behind the counter. Thomas could not quite place the source or the material.

There was no sensation at all of going upwards of five hundred times the speed of light, just the slightest vibration in the floor that she had learned was the Drive running at full power.

Still, she wondered, what was behind Hansen's resistance to her? Had she really been betrayed so terribly by the media? Sure, she hated being covered in the first days of the war. Who wouldn't? But, after all, she was in the middle of it and was young, attractive, incredibly brave, and intelligent. Or so the reports coming back about her said. It was a no-brainer story. Hansen brought viewers, and that's what the networks wanted. She made the Fleet look great, and that's what the ISC wanted.

Lots of people in the news don't want the attention, and Wren understood that. But the news was news, and interesting stories can give events depth and fuller meaning. And, as Hansen had repeatedly said with obvious scorn and derision, good stories draw viewers and sell advertising. There was no getting around that, but Wren felt Hansen was ignoring the positive side: that meaningful stories are a societal good beyond the crass considerations that network execs might be thinking about.

Finally, Carol came out and invited her into the inner office.

Thomas sat, then waited for Carol to take her place behind the desk. "Thanks for seeing me."

"Yes, we have several days before we get to GL 252, so this is a good time. We'll start briefing our approach tomorrow. After that, I will probably not have much time for you."

Thomas looked around. "I don't recall you ever being here. In this office, I mean."

Carol looked around, then back to Thomas. "This is what we call the in-port cabin. When we're out here, I feel it's important to be in the duty cabin, just a few steps from the Bridge. That's fine for me — really all I need. But, for meetings and small private discussions with staff, this office does make sense. The bathroom and bunk areas are bigger, for sure, but honestly, I prefer the duty cabin."

"So, are you ready to talk to me? I mean, really talk?"

Carol looked at the glorified beauty-shot photograph of *Endeavour* on the wall, with the Milky Way splashed dramatically behind her. There were also pictures of the NASA spacecraft that had carried that name: the command module of Apollo 15 and, later, a space shuttle.

"Yes. I have listened to you, and to my officers, and, finally, to my own intuition, and I feel you are someone who can be trusted."

"Thank you, I know how hard that is for you."

Carol leaned forward, elbows on her desk, and looked directly at Wren. "Well, there is one caveat...maybe two."

"Oh?"

"I see the final cut of whatever you're going to broadcast, and I have veto rights over anything about me or my personal life."

Wren sat up a bit straighter. "That ties my hands a great deal, Commander."

"I'm a reasonable person, Ms. Thomas. If you are who everyone says, I don't think there will be much of a problem. There is one more."

"Yes?"

"Nothing you don't use is ever published in any form. No behind-the-scenes intrigue, no extra-special exclusive scoop on the wonder girl."

Wren relaxed a little. "Is that how you see yourself?"

"It's how I believe many others see me, and I hate it. So, do we have a deal or not?"

Thomas looked down at her notes, then back at Carol. "Yes, we have a deal."

Carol leaned back in her chair and nodded. "OK then, where should we start?"

"Inoria. Tell me about Marty Baker."

Carol looked away and smiled as her eyes filled. "Had to go there first, did you?"

Thomas inclined her head, looking sympathetically at Carol. "That was a hard moment for you."

She nodded as she composed herself. "Indeed." She swallowed hard and let out a deep breath. "Marty and I were classmates at the U, acquaintances but not at all close until we were both assigned to *Liberty*. We were the two new kids, and we kinda struck up this friendship where we had each other's backs. The Fleet is rough on new grads, with high expectations and very little patience. It's something of a rite of passage."

"Was there anything more to it than that?"

"Oh, it wasn't long before I loved Marty and he loved me, but it wasn't romantic at all. He was just this hilarious guy, and we became the best of friends.

I had broken up with my boyfriend Rick before the end of school, and I was still stinging from that debacle. Marty was always looking for someone to connect with, to find something permanent was such an important dream for him. A very deep need. He and Denise had a dinner date or two aboard, I think, right before he was killed."

"Can you talk about that?"

Carol took another deep breath before answering. "It's been pretty well reported, and from what I've seen, the media accounts are accurate. We had taken the published tour of Inoria and stopped in a cafe when the Preeminent attack came. We were running for the shuttle when he was hit."

Wren flipped back and forth in her notebook. "You once asked me if I had ever seen someone's life drain from their eyes. That was about Marty?"

Carol took a second to clear her throat. "Yes."

"Let's move on to Beta Hydri."

"Yes, let's. Which time? I was there three times."

Wren smiled. "That's amazing in itself, but I was thinking about the scene on the beach with the Seekers and Doctor Cordero."

"Yes. Eaagher and Ullnii."

"Doctor Cordero gave an interview about that, where he talked in glowing terms about your interaction with the granddaughter."

"Ullnii, yes. A sweet child, gentle, and quite smart. The Seekers are naturally very strong, and I could feel her strength even as she held my hand. She was careful not to hurt me."

"I've tried several times to interview Natalie Hayden. She lost her fiancé there, right?"

"Yeah, good luck with that. Nat is one tough woman, but I have no better friend. And, you are correct that Ben Price was killed in the first ground engagement on Big Blue."

"Safe to say that broke her heart?"

Carol shook her head. "You would need to get that from Natalie. I'm not going to speak for her. But I can say that Ben was a wonderful guy, a great officer, and his loss was devastating to anyone who knew him, including *Intrepid*'s captain, Joanne Henderson. Natalie was always a serious officer, rigorous, and detailed. Ben brought something out in her I'm not sure she knew was there. I just love her."

"She was there at the end on Alpha Mensae?"

"Yes, David, Natalie, Liwanu Harry, and I were all in the room with The First. There were some Marines there as well."

"This was when Sergeant Jackson was killed?"

"Wow, you're really touring my greatest hits, aren't you?"

"These are the stories people have heard, and I'd like to hear your part of them."

Carol nodded slowly as she thought about how to tell Jackson's story. "Leon never called me 'ma'am' or 'Lieutenant;' it was always 'Miss Carol,' and I know that's such an anachronism today, so wildly out of fashion, but he meant it in such a caring yet respectful way it was so endearing."

"It does seem very old-fashioned. How was he killed?"

"We were attacking a barricade the Combatants had created, not very well, mind you, but it gave them some protection. As we started to move forward, he saw one rise up with a weapon, so he pushed me down and then wasn't able to get low enough himself and was wounded in the back. We thought he'd be fine, but he died of an infection in the hospital the next day."

"Who actually killed The First? I've asked but never heard a straight answer."

"He moved towards our translator, Asoon. We all fired almost at the same time."

"And Hayden finished him off? With a shot to the head? That really happened?"

"Yes."

"And, you're OK with that? Killing a defenseless enemy?"

"With four shots in his chest, he was dead. He just hadn't stopped breathing yet. Nat may have done him a favor."

Wren shivered. "That's cold."

Carol shrugged. "That's war."

"I am surprised at your comfort with this. You're a thoughtful woman, a woman of faith...how do you accept this so easily?"

Carol looked away, then returned to leaning on her desk and looked Wren directly in the eye. "Marty."

Wren looked into Carol's eyes, now cold, her face set in a determination she had not seen before. "I see. So, it's personal?"

Carol didn't move. "That moment was, yes. But I am a warrior, Ms. Thomas, and my faith aside, I have accepted the charge of protecting those under my care, to the death if necessary. I could not permit The First to harm someone under my protection."

"It's that simple?"

"For me, yes, it is."

Wren made some notes, thought for a moment, then asked, "How does this influence what you will do when we get to GL 252?"

Carol shifted in her chair. "Well, that will be an altogether different situation, with many questions to be answered. Sure, *Onizuka* was attacked, but we don't know why or what has occurred since. We believe the race there are the refugees from Gliese 262, and that has to be taken into account. Our priority is to recover the crew, of course, but what we do beyond that depends on the conditions and actions of the GL 262 race at the time."

"Your thinking is surprisingly flexible, Commander. I expected something more aggressive, considering who is aboard *Onizuka*."

Carol smiled and leaned back again. "This has never been about David Powell, Ms. Thomas. We were the closest ship, so it fell to us to respond. Others will come. Fiona Collins is even now pushing *Enterprise* to a millimeter of her limits to get there. This isn't Carol saving David. This is *Endeavour* and the rest of the Fleet coming to the aid of *Onizuka*. It's important that you keep that in mind."

"Yes, I see."

"I think this is enough for now. If you want to know more about Marty, you might talk to Denise."

Thomas smiled and shook her head. "She won't talk to me. Told me to go to Hell and added a few obscenities to help me on my way."

Carol nodded. "Ah, yes. She has become somewhat more colorful in the years since Inoria and Beta Hydri. In any case, you may continue to observe as you have been, and if there is more you would like to hear from me, we can talk on the way back home. There will be plenty of time."

"Thank you, Commander."

"Good day, Ms. Thomas." Wren looked at Carol for a moment, then rose to leave.

"Was there something else?" Carol asked.

"Must our time always be so distant? Can we not be friends?"

"Unlikely."

"I confess I am disappointed. Commander. I had hoped for something, well, more personal. Warmer, perhaps."

When Carol didn't respond, Wren paused just another second, then turned and left the office. She thought for a moment that she had pierced Hansen's armor, only to find that beneath one layer was another, even stronger. She returned to her cabin to collate the notes and add the little details of Hansen's face and body language that would add depth to the story she planned to tell. She had made progress with Hansen, but there was still a wall, still a vast distance between them. Hansen's distrust remained intact, despite her seeming acceptance, and she wondered how to gain her trust. She felt there was more, much more, that Carol Hansen could tell her if she could only get her to talk freely.

Chapter 25

On the Surface
GL 252 (c)
Wednesday, June 12, 2086, 2100 UTC

Marine First Lieutenant Sabrina Herrera knew her business. After all, she'd been a Gunnery Sergeant just a few years before, working with David on a clandestine mission at Zeta Doradus that suddenly went south when the natives decided to drive their Preeminent overlords out by force just as they were about to be liberated. She'd come away from that experience with a deep admiration for Powell, and an accompanying barely suppressed attraction as well.

Today she was right next to him, just inches away, as they surveyed their position on the planet, looking for where the 262s might threaten their encampment. They explored the woods to the south, moving downhill until they arrived at a small river, perhaps ten meters across, flowing gently but freely. The water was clear, and the river's speed and depth made it impossible to walk across.

"It would not be easy to get across that without some kind of bridging equipment," she said.

David agreed, and they generally walked east, the river guiding slightly north as they went. They came to narrow rapids, where boulders made a natural ford.

"Here, on the other hand, it would be easy," David said. They agreed to station pickets at that point, in a concealed position just back from the riverbank. They'd also place some in the southwest, near what appeared to be wildlife trails. Their camp was open to the east and north, the shuttles just barely under the tree cover. There would be Marines ready there, too, in case the 262s decided to strike them from that direction.

As they turned to walk back along the river, she grasped his arm just enough to stop him.

"Commander...David..."

"What is it, Sabrina?"

"I... I just want to say...how...glad I am to be with you again. I... well..."

David was aware of the conflict in her. After Zeta Doradus, one of her Marines had stopped into FleetIntel, asking to talk to him in private. *"She's a great leader, sir, really, but I think she talks too much about you. Watch your back, sir. That's all I'm saying.* David had filed that away for future reference, and while he knew Sabrina had asked to be on his ship, he didn't feel he could refuse her assignment based on second-hand speculation.

"Lieutenant Herrera," he responded. She looked at him as if he had slapped her. "Sabrina..." he continued more gently, "I welcome your friendship, but you and I cannot be anything else."

There was a long pause before she replied. "Yes, Commander."

"I mean it...I value you as a colleague, and I was happy to see you commissioned. You were an excellent gunny, and I think you have what it takes to be an excellent officer, too."

She lowered her head. "Yes, sir."

"I don't mean to demean you, Sabrina, or to hurt your feelings. But there have to be fences, and we're up against one now. Can you see the position this puts me in?"

She shrugged. "I guess so, yes."

David paused just a moment. "Good. Let's get back to the camp."

They walked back in silence, Sabrina now two or three steps behind.

That night, the pickets were in place, unsure of what they were looking for and what they might do about whatever might appear. Before placing them, Sabrina had briefed them the best she could, but there were still so many unknowns. She sympathized with their dilemma.

Finally, she just said, "If it isn't carrying a weapon, don't shoot it."

New Traenah
Traedenath Central Airfield
Spin 16, Subcycle 2, Cycle 2510

Tmoyan looked at the map of the planet, focusing on the mountainous area in the opposite hemisphere. He turned to Dsanik.

"I followed them down to this point..." He placed a finger on the lowlands near the seashore. "I had to leave them there because I didn't want to be seen."

"So, where do you think they went?"

Tmoyan pointed to the map. "Based on their course and rate of descent when I left them, they're hiding in these mountains."

"Why do you think that?"

"Well, think about it from their point of view. They wouldn't land if they couldn't survive. They made eight or ten trips with two small ships. That has to mean supplies as well as personnel. So, they're not sitting inside a sealed ship. They're outside, so they need air and liquid water at the very least. Not that different from us."

"But why the mountains? Cover?"

"Exactly. There have to be many sixteens of valleys they could hide in. The forests there are old, with large open areas underneath. It's almost a perfect place to get lost in." Tmoyan looked at the map for a moment. "Let's get some ships up in the morning and try to cover the middle altitudes in this range. They don't want to be up in the snow, but they'll want to be away from the lowlands, too."

"Yes, I see. I'll lead a flight to get there at first light."

Tmoyan nodded. He wanted to find them, these strange aliens, but he wasn't sure what he would do once he did. He sympathized with their dire circumstances, more or less alone on a strange planet. The xenophobia in him wanted them destroyed, but his warrior's heart respected their reserve, and something deep inside wanted more to secure their safety than destroy them.

The first task, then, was to find them. The rest would come later.

On the Surface
GL 252 (c)
Thursday, June 14, 2086, 0850 UTC

The mountain air was crisp as David stirred from his spot outside the shuttle. Melinda was on one side, Sabrina on the other, her weapon always at the ready.

"Short night?" Melinda asked brightly.

David smiled. "Yes. This place is as bad as Zeta Doradus. Spins like a freaking top. And I have no idea what the hell time it is."

Across the camp, those who had chosen to sleep outside were getting up, rolling up their beds, and preparing for their second sol on the third planet orbiting GL 252.

On the other side of camp, smoke was rising from a small campfire that some of the crew had started to keep warm. David looked at it for a moment, then decided to let it go. He'd have them put it out before long. No need to put out such an obvious IR signal.

"Melinda," he said, "tell them to have enough water on hand to put that thing out in a hurry."

She looked over at the fire, quickly coming to the same conclusion as David. "Yes, sir, right away."

Dsanik and his wingman followed the route Tmoyan had laid out based on the aliens' last position and direction. They flew well above the surface, throttled back to make as little noise as possible. As they flew east from the shoreline, below the peaks. The wingman was a three mileah left of Dsanik, and both of them were searching for any sign of the intruders. A several long sixteens of mileah ahead, the mountains rose to heights not seen on Traenah, where the snow and ice reached all the way to the base. Surely, Dsanik thought, they would not be that high up. No, they would be in the temperate area, where they could be comfortable, find water, and be concealed from view under the enormous trees of New Traenah.

They flew the first pass flying east and saw nothing, then turned before the high peaks and headed back west, the wingman now on the right and slightly behind. Mehonnh was behind them now, where Dsanik always wanted it to be. The air was still; the heat of the star had not yet generated enough thermal uplifts to rough up the air with turbulence.

Dsanik was surprised when his wingman spoke excitedly: "Smoke, sir Dsanik. Off to my right."

Dsanik looked where his wingman indicated and could see a small, isolated column of smoke rising out of the forest. If they hadn't had Mehonnh at their backs, they might have missed it. Dsanik looked at his map and marked the location.

His radio crackled again. "Shall we investigate?"

"No. Mark your map so we can compare when we land. Hold your course, and we'll break off at the shoreline and return to base."

"Do you think it is the aliens?"

"Yes."

Dsanik was surprised at their foolishness, such an obvious mistake in hostile territory. He would not have made such an error, he was sure. Perhaps they were not the tactical magicians Tmoyan seemed to think.

After they landed, Tmoyan found Dsanik's report almost impossible to believe. "They had a fire?"

"Yes. There was a single thin column of smoke rising out of the forest. We saw no others." They compared the positions from the two pilot's charts, each of which placed the smoke in a narrow valley just below a small lake.

"A medium-sized valley with a not very big lake, a small river running down towards the sea."

Dsanik gripped his agreement. "The valley is quite deep. It took some skill to land their ships there."

"But they built a fire? That makes no sense."

"Perhaps they thought we would not be looking for them?"

Tmoyan waved his skepticism. "It was a mistake, simple as that." He turned to Dsanik. "Get the recon ship prepped. I will fly a low-level mission to confirm their position. We need to know exactly where they are and how many are there."

Dsanik agreed and headed to the maintenance hangar to instruct the technicians to prepare the recon aerocraft, the same one he had flown up to the alien ship.

It was midday as David was walking along the stream that flowed out of the lake just north of their encampment. It was a beautiful place, he decided, the greens darker than home, which reminded him of Inor. The trees were unique in his experience, perhaps fifty or more meters tall, with thick foliage that began at least fifteen meters above the ground and incredible trunks of at least two meters in diameter. He thought about his defensive positions, which were about as good as he could manage. Not that they needed much. They were well concealed, and it would be hard for the 262s to find them in this narrow place. He allowed himself a thought of Carol on her way, how sweet it would be when *Endeavour* arrived to pull them out of this ugly situation. He was sitting by the stream when a sound invaded his pleasant thoughts. *Was that an aircraft?*

He was still there when a black shape whistled across the sky from west to east, just above the valley. David jumped up, running back to the shuttles and calling for everyone to get back under cover. The sound faded but didn't disappear, and the shape returned, now flying north to south along the center of the valley that was their temporary refuge.

Melinda joined him behind one of the shuttles. "That damned campfire."

David nodded. "They must have been up very early this morning. Fire's been out for hours. I never heard anything, and I was outside the whole time."

"Stealth?"

"Apparently. It flew a couple hundred meters over my head, and if I hadn't been alone, I might have missed it."

The 262 aircraft passed over the valley again, this time south to north. David peeked around the side of the shuttle to see it bank sharply for another pass.

"He's coming back."

Sabrina joined them. "He's not hiding anything. It's almost like he wants us to know they've found us."

David nodded. "Yeah, he's not showing any subtlety. This is a pretty clear demonstration." He looked at Melinda and Sabrina. "Stay here."

David came out from behind the shuttle to stand alone just outside the edge of the trees. The dark shape made one more pass west to east, then pulled up and turned back to the west. As it did, David could see the pilot, who seemed to see him too. David thought he saw just the slightest waggle of the plane's wings, almost a signal of recognition. Was that real, or did he imagine it? Or was it there but meant nothing?

As the sound faded to the west, Melinda came out and grabbed David by the arm. "What the hell was that?"

David smiled. "Yeah, here we are. I see you, and I know you see me. What now?"

"You think he got all that in what, a half-second?"

"I know he saw me, and he knows I saw him." David visibly relaxed. "Whatever is going to happen is probably going to take some time."

"I suppose. But this changes everything. I wasn't afraid before, David. I am now."

David gave Melinda a slight hug. "It's all gonna be fine. How about some lunch?"

Dsanik looked at the photographs Tmoyan had brought back. "They don't lack courage; that much is clear."

"Yes, this one," Tmoyan said as he pointed to a lone figure out in the open, "came out from their concealment to look up at me on the final pass. He wanted me to see him."

Nadon, sent by Gkeze to consult with the military about the aliens, asked, "Is this one the same as was by the stream in the first image?"

Tmoyan looked at the photos carefully. "Possibly. But they appear to wear uniforms, which makes them hard to tell apart from a distance."

She gripped her understanding. "So, this would be the leader?"

"No doubt. No one else would be so bold."

She looked at the image, then at an enlargement. "Bipedal, two arms, no breathing apparatus or protective suit, not much fur that I can see except on the head."

Dsanik looked at the same image. "Weapons?"

Nadon pointed to something on the alien's torso. "This could hold a small weapon. See how it wraps around the shoulder? But I don't see anything else obvious. They're really not all the different from us; taller, wider, probably physically stronger, but not extremely so."

Tmoyan looked at the same image. "They remind me of the aliens that came to try to rescue us from the comet."

"Yes," Nadon agreed, "but those were not so tall, and they had far less fur on their heads."

"Their dress was different, too," Dsanik added. "I do not think these are the same."

"I agree," Nadon said. "These aliens are different."

Tmoyan stepped back from the images on the wall and sat. "I am not sure what that means. Another alien species nearby? What does this mean for our aversion to outsiders?"

"Nothing," Dsanik answered. "The number of alien species makes our caution all the more justified. We must remove them."

Nadon looked at Dsanik. "Remove them? You mean, kill them?"

"They are here, Nadon, on our planet. They are a threat. They must be removed at all costs."

Tmoyan waved his disagreement. "We have seen the price of engaging them, Dsanik. The cost you quote so easily might be more than we can afford."

Dsanik sat still, unmoved.

Nadon rose to point at the images. "These are not the same aliens that came to Traenah to evacuate us. Gkeze and I believe that race set up this very planet for us, with plants and animals from Traenah."

"Your point?" Dsanik asked.

"Unless the, uh, 'Trustees' told them, these new aliens likely had no knowledge we were here. I don't think they represent any threat at all."

Tmoyan spoke quietly. "The leadership has asked us for our evaluation and recommendations for action."

Nadon sat and looked at Tmoyan. "So, what will you tell them?"

"First, we, you and I, will go. You will give them your estimation of what these aliens are. You can use the pictures I took this morning."

"What else?" Dsanik asked.

"I will discuss our military options, which are limited. We have no large explosives or artillery here. The only option we really have is to gather and arm enough males to surround and remove them."

Nadon quickly waved her disagreement, her face twisted in disgust. "It's a horrible thought, Tmoyan. What of your code of honor? You would kill these marooned aliens who have done nothing to provoke us?"

"Their existence is provocation enough," Dsanik said.

Tmoyan looked at his friend. "This is dangerous thinking, Dsanik, and I reject it. We are not on Traenah anymore, and we must understand what that means." He turned to Nadon. "To explain a military option is not to propose it. I would strongly oppose such a choice."

"That is comforting, but I have seen such ideas take on their own inertia, difficult to stop once in motion."

"Yes, Nadon, that can happen. And, if I am ordered to remove the aliens, I will be bound to do that with the least loss of life on both sides."

"How can you say that? Removing them is killing them, is it not?"

Tmoyan didn't move. "I will do everything possible to avoid that outcome."

"We have been given two spins to devise a proposal. Then, the council will meet to discuss what to do about the aliens."

Tmoyan and Nadon moved out of the small meeting room, silent, each trying to reconcile the thoughts of the other, to try to craft a proposal that would lead to an end they could both live with.

Two spins later, the Council was not receptive to their arguments. The aliens were to be removed, by force if necessary.

Chapter 26

On The Surface
GL 252 (c)
Saturday, June 15, 2086, 1748 UTC

It was dusk, two sols after the 262 aircraft had discovered them. The aircraft had not returned; at least, not that they could tell. With the high level of stealth the 262s had demonstrated, he could not be sure if they had been observed again or not. David, nervous about what was ahead for his crew, moved along the picket line, chatting quietly with his Marines, with Lieutenant Herrera walking just behind. As they finished at the last post on the southwestern edge, David decided to continue along the path that small animals had worn down along the edge of the forest beside the river. The trees here were lower and thinner and, David assumed, younger. There was also a dense undergrowth here not seen by the shuttles. Sabrina followed him closely.

They'd gone about a hundred meters past the last picket when David suddenly stopped. Across the river, a lone alien had appeared in a small opening in the undergrowth, his weapon pointed directly at them. David immediately gripped his M1911, and Sabrina moved to draw her P320, but without taking his eyes off the alien, David reached over to touch her arm, stopping her.

They stood there staring at one another for several very long seconds. David watched the alien's long fingers as they rhythmically gripped and released his weapon, his eyes flashing back and forth between himself and Sabrina.

"He's petrified," David said quietly.

"Yes. And dangerous," she answered.

David left this weapon in its shoulder holster and lifted his hands; his empty palms open to the alien. Sabrina followed suit. The alien looked from one to the other one last time, then abruptly turned and ran off through the forest.

Once his breathing had returned to normal, David turned to Sabrina. "Go tell the pickets. They must be getting close but likely just scouting us out. Tell the pickets, Sabrina, that they are not to fire unless they have no choice, clear? The last thing we need is an escalation into a ground engagement."

"Yes, Commander."

"OK, go on. I'll be there shortly."

It was by now too dark to write, but David knelt on the path and took a moment to try to set in his memory what he had seen. It was smallish, perhaps five feet five inches tall. Thin, as they had seen in the surveillance video back on *Onizuka*. The face was bare and dark-skinned, with wide-set eyes and a minimal nose. The rest of the alien was covered in fur, generally brown but with various color highlights. He was reminded slightly of the Seekers at Beta Hydri, but much smaller, and here the ears were obvious and high on the head. He came away with the strongest impression of facing a sentient German Shepherd holding a rifle.

Despite the planet's rapid rotation, it was a long, sleepless night for David and his officers. They quietly made the rounds of the pickets every hour, making sure they were alert and giving them encouragement. As dawn broke, Sabrina and four Marines scrambled across the boulders at the rapids into the woods on the other side of the river. They tracked the alien nearly a kilometer downhill until his tracks disappeared into a small stream. The undergrowth became denser as they moved downhill into a slightly warmer climate, and Sabrina was loath to get too far from their encampment. Every step felt dangerous, each one seeming to increase the possibility of encountering a larger 262 force. They walked back up the valley and then explored the woods along the other side of the river. There they found two more sets of tracks 262s had left on the damp ground.

She returned to camp chastened. Her worry was clear as she sat down with the other officers. "They know exactly where we are. And where the pickets are. The tracks we saw are all near our outposts, too near for my taste."

"But you saw no other evidence of them above the first stream?" Ethan asked.

"No."

Ethan laid out several of the high-res photographs he had brought from *Onizuka*. He pointed out the streams and then a narrow, low area around where the streams continued downhill towards a larger river. "This is a natural path into our forward position. There's a clearing, larger than ours...here...about three kilometers away." He pointed to the picture and made sure they all understood. "Then, they can walk up this path to within a klick or so of our outposts."

Sabrina looked at the images, which she had already studied before her exploration that dawn. "Should I go further along this second stream, maybe as far as the clearing? I could see if they're massing there, at least."

"No," David responded. "But we have three backpack drones." He looked at Sabrina. "Get one up right away and take a look at that area. If they're already gathering, we'll have to think about what to do. If not, we have some time to work with."

"Yes, sir. Right away."

David leaned forward, resting his chin in his hands, elbows on knees. "The alien we saw had no special equipment, just a weapon that looked to be a rifle. Make sure the pickets all have their night vision glasses tonight."

Melinda stirred in her chair. "You're worried they will come tonight?"

"I don't think so, at least, not in force. But they might be back to check on our reaction now that we know they're scouting us. We need to know what they're doing, that's all."

Ethan looked down at the photographs, then back at David. "When do you think they will come?"

David shrugged. "I don't know. I just don't know how quickly they can gather a large force and move it over here. The drone images will help with that."

"Well," Melinda said, "they did move their whole population seven light-years not that long ago."

"Yes, true. And I assume they'll use those ships stored up in high orbit to move them. We'll just have to keep watch and hope *Endeavour* and *Enterprise* get here first."

It was noon before David and the other officers went into the shuttles to get some sleep. Melinda remained outside to keep watch. As it was, it was a cloudy but quiet day.

The drone images revealed nothing interesting, not even a campsite for the 262 scouts. Wherever they were hiding, they were doing it well. But at least there was nothing imminent. David had time to think and hope that help would arrive before the 262s could assemble an attack. If, as he wondered, that was what this was all about. If.

As the next night after the encounter with the scout was falling, Sabrina moved from picket to picket, checking equipment and offering encouragement. She and David had agreed to augment the two Marines in each position with two armed *Onizuka* crew members. That gave them more eyes and more defensive firepower in case something truly unpleasant happened. She also organized reserve groups ready to support any hostile encounter. She placed herself on the south edge of the encampment, as close a point as she could find to all the pickets. It would be a long, nervous night.

The far southwestern post was just back from the wildlife trail. The Marines there had seen some small animals, something a little larger than a dog, move past them the previous night. They had wandered past, taking no notice of the human intruders only a few meters away. Before dawn, they had wandered back in the opposite direction. The picket team tonight decided to break their four-hour watch into half-hour segments, rotating both Marines and Fleet crew in and out of the forward position, the others moving just behind for a rest.

They had been watching for two hours when the sound of movement on the trail caught Marine Corporal Marleigh Barron's attention. She nudged her Fleet partner and indicated the direction of the sound.

"Good evening!" came a pleasant voice from a few meters away. All four pickets were immediately up, weapons ready.

Barron looked at her Fleet partner, who just shrugged. "Who calls?"

"My name is not important," the voice responded as it approached. "But I would like to speak to Commander Powell, if I might."

"Stay where you are!"

The voice continued forward. "Have no fear, my friends. I am unarmed. I would like to see David Powell, if I could, please, Corporal Barron?"

She raised her weapon again, pointing it directly at the voice. "How do you know my name?"

"Oh, my hearing is excellent. I was not far away when Lieutenant Herrera gave you your pep talk."

Barron flipped on the flashlight on her 2K7X, revealing a slightly-built individual, clearly not human, standing in the trail. He did not shrink from the light but stood still as they examined him.

"How did you find us?"

"That is not very important right now, Corporal. But it is imperative that I speak to your commander."

One of the *Onizuka* crew got up from her backup position. "I'll go."

David was sitting outside with Melinda and Ethan Reyes when a figure ran into the encampment.

"Commander!"

"What is it, Waters?"

"An alien, sir, and not a 262. He just walked up to our outpost and asked for you by name."

"By name?" David sat immobile, suddenly recalling Jack Ballard's words back on *Cobra* as they were headed home after the war: *If they don't want to be found, we'll never find them or any evidence of them. The only way we'll ever encounter them is if they want us to.*

On the other hand, he quickly corrected himself, *this alien might be something completely different.*

After a second, he was reanimated. "OK. Melinda, go tell Sabrina and have her send a runner to warn all the pickets. I don't know what this means, but they should be on guard in case this is some weird diversion." As Melinda headed off to find Herrera, David turned to Ethan. "You're with me."

They followed Weapons Tech Waters down to the outpost. As they approached, David could see the three remaining Fleet personnel standing a safe distance from a fourth figure.

"Hello, David," came the smooth, calm voice. "I have been waiting a long time to meet you."

David looked at the face, still lit up with flashlights. He was smaller than a human, and his features looked distorted, but it was still a face similar enough to be recognized as one.

"You have me at a disadvantage, sir. Who are you?"

The alien shrugged and looked away, hands on his hips, then looked back. "Well, that kind of depends on who you ask. To some, we're the 'Guardians,' for others, we're the 'Shepherds.' Either is fine with us, but I prefer *Trustees*. It's closer to how we think of ourselves."

Holy crap, David thought. *What would Ballard give to be here right now?* "Us?"

"Us, me, it's the same thing. I am part of a larger whole, same as you. I would like to talk, if you are willing, perhaps without all the weapons pointed at me? I am unarmed."

"Very well." David turned to the pickets. "Lower your weapons. If he is who he says, we'd already be dead if he wanted us to be."

"Could we speak in private, please?"

David turned back to Ethan. "Stay here."

"I should go with you, sir. Or, Hughes should, or Herrera."

"You have my word he will be quite safe with me, Lieutenant Reyes." Ethan looked back and forth from David to the alien, then stepped back.

The Trustee walked a few steps back up the trail, and David followed for thirty meters or so. "This will do."

"Do? Do for what?"

"Privacy."

David briefly glanced back towards the outpost. Yes, this was far enough. Whatever this alien needed to tell him, he wanted very much to hear it.

"You said you've been waiting a long time to meet me. If you really are who you say you are, you can't have been waiting that long. I'm not that old."

"Oh, no, David, even if you live a thousand years, or ten thousand like me, you live them just one sol after the other, right?"

"Time isn't different for you?"

The Trustee shook his head, which caught David's attention. "No, it isn't. Time is the one constant in the universe. It ticks inexorably forward. We can fool it a little by going very, very fast, but the truth is, it never stops."

David nodded. "We thought you all would have evolved into energy or something truly alien by now. "

"Well, it doesn't really work like that. As you know, once you've had a child your contribution to natural selection is pretty much over." He smiled. "And we've really evolved about as far as we want to, I think."

"So, just how old are the Trustees?"

"Oh, I don't know, our culture has been developing for something like a million Terran years."

"So, Trustee slash Guardian slash Shepherd, what should I call you?"

"My name isn't important, so just call me John."

"Well, John, you've made quite an entrance. So now, tell me, what is it you require of me?"

John seemed to dodge the question. "I admired your work at Zeta Doradus. You saved many lives there."

David stood still; arms crossed. "You were there?"

John waved his hand as if to dismiss the question. "We were aware of events there, yes. I can't say more than that."

"So, again, what is it you require of me?"

"Before we get to that, thank you for not killing the young scout at the river. He was terrified."

"You know about that? Yes, that made three of us. Sabrina and I came very close to dying at that moment."

"I was not far away. Can you tell me how Lieutenant Hughes is doing? She was very brave in the fight at Beta Hydri. Such unselfish valor does not come easily. I admire her very much."

"Melinda is fine. She has a few headaches from time to time, but nothing serious. Come back to the camp, and you can ask her yourself."

John looked in the general direction of the shuttles as if considering what David said. "No, I cannot. We try to keep our presence quiet, our exposure limited. I am sure you understand."

David looked back up the trail towards the parked shuttles. "Well, you're insightful enough to know what a grilling I am going to get when I return."

John laughed slightly. "Yes, I suppose so." His smile evaporated as he looked directly at David. "They're going to come after you, but I will try to stop it. Be ready to defend yourselves."

"We'll do what we can. We thought this might happen."

"Please, David, help me not fail them again. I will try to stop it, but if they come, you must not engage them directly. It will be a disaster for both of you."

"You know us. You know we can handle ourselves."

"I also know them, and it will not be so easy as you might think. I will talk to them. There are rational people there, too. I may be able to convince them."

"You've failed them before? How?"

"I tried to convince them to leave their home, Traenah, when they knew the comet was coming, but I was unable to break through to them. Many died because I could not overcome their hatred of outsiders."

"They're xenophobic? Is that why they lashed out at us?"

"Yes."

"You failed before. What makes you think you can succeed now?"

"First, they have seen the consequences of not listening. Second, much of the irrational segment of their society died under the comet."

David hesitated a moment. "I would like to hear more about that."

"Not now. I must go see them."

"Will we see you again?"

"Yes. I will translate with them for you."

With that, John turned and walked briskly down the trail. David watched him for a few seconds, surprised at the speed and agility of one so ancient, then turned and walked back to his pickets.

"What the hell was that?" Ethan asked.

David shook his head and smiled. "You know, Ethan, I'm not entirely sure. Let's get back to the camp."

The officers gathered in a shuttle. "OK, so, John the Guardian, Shepherd, Trustee, or whatever, says the 262s are coming to kill us. Or, drive us off."

Melinda looked at him in surprise. "John the Guardian slash Shepherd? Saviors of the Preeminent and the Zeds? You're serious?"

"That's what he said. Ten thousand years old, too, or so he says."

She shrugged. "OK, fine. Did he say why?"

"The 262s are xenophobes. He claims the Trustees, which is the term he says they prefer, tried to move the 262s off their home planet, called, um, *Traenah*, before the comet hit but they refused."

Ethan looked up. "So, a comet, not an asteroid."

"That's what he said. No reason to doubt it."

Sabrina pulled out the imagery they had of the area. "So, they're coming soon?"

"He was in a hurry to go talk to them, so I would say yes, soon. He wants us to not engage them directly."

Sabrina looked at him. "If they shoot at me, I am very likely to shoot back."

David smiled. "I would expect nothing less. But, let's see what we can do." He turned to his Intel officer. "Ethan, show me those photographs."

As they looked at the images, Ethan pointed out a narrow pass higher up on the mountain. "I knew this was here, sir. It's part of why I suggested we come to this location."

Melinda leaned in over the photo. "A fallback?"

Ethan nodded. "Yes, ma'am. It's a more defensible position. There is just one route in, only a few dozen meters wide, and then it opens up again. The walls are steep, but not too steep to climb, and covered in trees for half a kilometer until they end at the tree line. We could hold off a large force there for some time."

Sabrina nodded her agreement. "Too narrow for aircraft — too close to the peak. They'd be hard-pressed to strike us there."

"Fine," David responded. "Based on how alarmed John seemed to be, I expect they will be here sometime soon, so we need to get moving." He looked at Sabrina. "Can we defend the north end of the lake? Is that a line we could hold until we get everyone up through the pass?"

"Yes, we can hold there for a while, but it's susceptible to a flanking movement to our right. We'd have to withdraw if that happens."

"OK, done. Get your marines assembled for that."

"Yes, sir."

"Now, how will they approach us?"

Sabrina sifted through the stack of photographs until she found the one she wanted. "The streams converge here, just below the clearing. That area is large enough for one of their evacuation ships. There is a long curve in the smaller stream, here." She pointed to an area where the stream bordered the forest. "It flows almost west for a while before curving south above the meadow. This second stream flows out of the next valley over. The one we're in ends fairly abruptly about a kilometer south and joins with the one to the east."

"So, what are you thinking?"

"The largest part of the meadow is between the streams. That's where they will have to land. From there, it's a straightforward march uphill."

"How will they get over the stream?" Ethan asked.

"It's not that wide, Sabrina responded. "I expect they'll manage. But we could set up just this side of that to discourage them."

Melinda looked over at her. "Discourage them?"

Sabrina looked at her with a small smile. "We don't really plan to kill them, right?"

David answered, "No. What of the scouts?"

"Their tracks went across the lower stream, so I am guessing they're camped on the far side of the meadow. If we're quiet, we should be able to get into position without attracting their attention."

David rearranged the photos and crossed his arms. "So, we skirmish with them at the lower stream, just to slow them down and let them know they'll be resisted. If they come on, we fall back to the north edge of the lake. At that point, we engage them if they come on, understand? No more fussing around."

He looked around as his officers nodded their understanding.

"If they press forward, we push back hard, then reposition to the pass and hold firm there."

Sabrina asked, "When do we expect the Fleet?"

"Well," David answered, "the truth is we don't actually know. *Endeavour* should, we think, be here on 19 June, so, three or four days from now. Knowing Collins like I do, *Enterprise* is on its way here, too, but likely not for a few days after that."

David looked around his staff. "Depending on how fast the 262s move, that may or may not be soon enough." He turned to Sabrina. "I want another drone up at first light. Then keep one up as long as you can. If they're really coming, those will tell us."

"Yes, sir. I'll set up a schedule to keep all three flying in rotation."

"Very well."

The meeting broke up, each officer heading to their divisions to pass the word and get the crew ready to move uphill.

Chapter 27

New Traenah
The Astrometric Observatory
Spin 5, Subcycle 3, Cycle 2510

It was mid-morning as Tmoyan again drove up to the observatory south of the new city of Traedenath. The trip took him almost a full spedset, a sixteenth of a spin of his home world, Traenah. Nadon's message on the far-talker was immediate and alarming, pulling him out of the planning for the removal of the aliens that had first invaded their space and now seemed intent on invading the planet, too. Entering the cluttered workroom that Nadon shared with the old astronomer Gkeze, Tmoyan was shocked to encounter a new alien. Taller than himself, to Tmoyan's eye, it resembled the aliens that were even now defacing the surface of his new home.

"What is that?" he asked Nadon bitterly.

"Hello, Tmoyan," the alien responded, not waiting for Nadon.

Tmoyan stared at the alien. He sounded a little like an Easter, but Tmoyan detected a bit of South in his accent, too. A memory flashed in his mind: the alien that supposedly came to rescue us from the comet. "You are the alien that came to Traenah."

"Yes, that is correct. I am that Trustee."

"You now have new demands of us?"

Nadon stepped forward, placing herself between the alien and Tmoyan. "He is not here to demand anything. And, if you'll remember honestly, he didn't demand anything of us on Traenah, either. He offered us rescue and we turned him down."

Tmoyan looked at her with some annoyance. She was right, he knew, despite his instinctive aversion to outsiders, and they would have been much better off had they listened back then. Too late to think about that now.

"Yes, I suppose that is so. Why is it here now?"

"I am here on a new mission of rescue. You must stop the attacks on the humans."

Tmoyan waved his disagreement. "Humans? This is the label you give the alien invaders? You side with them?"

The Trustee was unmoved, apparently not intimidated by Tmoyan's attitude. "It is their name, not something I have given them. They are not your enemy. Do I side with them? Yes, but no more than I side with you."

"Nonsense."

"No, Tmoyan, it isn't. The humans meant you no harm."

"We cannot trust them. They are aliens."

The Trustee took a step forward, causing Tmoyan to step back. "Listen to me, Tmoyan, you must *listen!* The ship you struck, without warning or cause, is part of a Fleet that is enormously powerful." The Trustee looked away for a moment, then again directly at Tmoyan. "You have a choice here. You can control your fear and their power can make them a steadfast, indispensable friend. Or, let fear rule you and create a fearsome, terrifying enemy."

Tmoyan stood a little taller and leaned toward the alien. "I am not afraid."

"I know. You have never been afraid of conflict. That is part of your problem."

"They are alien. They are alone. They will be removed." Tmoyan leaned a little more forward. "As will you."

The alien looked at Nadon, then back to Tmoyan. "They will not be alone long. Two more ships will arrive in the next few spins and many more after that. You cannot defeat them."

"Impossible."

Nadon again moved to face Tmoyan, placing herself between him and the Trustee. "I have thought about this a great deal, fine warrior. I have tried to look at this as a scientist does, not that it is easy for me, and I know it is not easy for you. But I now see that yes, they are alien to us, but here in this place, *we* are alien, too. This is not our home."

"That is true," the Trustee said. "And, yes, this is the place we adapted for you. We knew long ago the comet you called The Messenger would eventually strike Traenah. It had to happen, so we made this place ready."

Gkeze stirred from his reading. "Tmoyan, the Trustee has spoken the truth from the first day he came to Elenath. They are an old culture, far older even than ours. They need nothing from us, so we have no fear that they might exploit us somehow."

"I do not share your confidence, old astronomer. He is an outsider, not to be believed."

Gkeze waved his disagreement and turned back to the alien. "Trustee, what was here before we came?"

"There were a few small grazing animals, as you have seen, and the trees, but no higher, sentient forms. We made sure it was compatible for you and safe from disease, then we stocked the ocean and brought more familiar vegetation."

"When did you do this?"

"As soon as we were sure the comet would strike. It was about sixty-four cycles past."

Tmoyan was unmoved. "I am still suspicious of these aliens. I do not trust them."

Nadon sat, her face radiating her frustration with this warrior male she so deeply admired. "Before, we were safe on Traenah, and we had the luxury of hating outsiders because they were really only ourselves, just from a different place. Now we are out in the universe, outside our beautiful little bubble, now all ash and death. There are races out here we do not know, yes, but we cannot just hate them all without reason."

"I cannot simply open my arms to aliens that arrive uninvited to my home. It is a perilous choice."

Nadon stood, facing Tmoyan closely, almost intimately. "Can you not see that *we* are aliens, too? After all, Tmoyan, what did the human ship actually do to deserve an attack? What violence did they commit before we committed violence on them? Don't you see it? We lashed out because we *were* afraid, because we feared their strength, and even more our own weakness. But what happened? They defended themselves, but only that. Even when they struck back, they only did what was necessary for their own safety."

"You believe this? You believe this fantasy that they are not a threat?"

"If we had watched what they did, not acted on what we feared they might do, we would not have attacked them. So yes, I believe it. I also believe the one who came to Traenah to save us all. The one we ignored, and millions died."

Gkeze looked up. "Lanos would have had his followers in any case, fools who believed his lies."

Nadon turned to him. "But there would have been fewer. Had the Trustee been heard, I know many more would have been saved. "

"It is possible," the Trustee said, "but I feel Gkeze is mostly correct. There were enough believers in the Messenger myth that many would have died anyway." He turned to Tmoyan. "Opening yourself to an alien race is indeed perilous. But this race is not belligerent by nature. They will not harm you without provocation."

"But once provoked?" Tmoyan asked.

"A conflict with the human fleet would be disastrous, particularly for you pilots and warriors."

"Fleet? How large is this so-called fleet?"

The trustee hesitated. "I will not tell you that, partly because I am not sure you would believe the number if I did. I will tell you there will soon be two more ships here, one quite a bit larger than the one you attacked, and four more in the near future."

Tmoyan looked at Nadon, who gently gripped her agreement as she reached out for his hand. He looked at Gkeze, who simply looked back at him, his cane at his side, a large map in his hand. "I did not think we could be over-matched," Tmoyan said quietly. "But if you speak the truth, we must not strike them. I am not interested in suicide, or I would have stayed on Traenah with the others."

The Trustee stepped back a little. "You are a good warrior, Tmoyan, and warriors are often necessary. But protecting one's home doesn't always require striking out. Sometimes, it means talking, understanding, and not allowing your fear of a possible threat to create an actual threat."

"This is not what I was taught, not how I have learned to view outsiders."

The Trustee looked at him sympathetically. "This is a new place, Tmoyan, and it requires new ways of thinking. You are a brave warrior. I believe you can face this and succeed."

Tmoyan and Nadon agreed to go to the ruling council to convince them to call off the attack on the humans. It would not be easy.

As they turned around to ask a question of the Trustee, he was gone. They looked at Gkeze, but he was again studying his map of the Tetanna system.

Nadon went outside with Tmoyan, Tetanna beginning its dive into the mountains in the west. "It will be rising soon on the humans," she said.

"They will be preparing, expecting us. I have to think the Trustee has already warned them. I don't know if I should trust him more or less for that."

"It would be fair, would it not, to talk equally to both sides? Would that not lead to a better outcome?"

"I struggle to place myself in their position. I see them only as alien, dangerous, and therefore my enemy. I respect their restraint, that much I can admit."

"Admit? To respect them is hardly a transgression! I admire them."

"Yes, I can see that you do. Do not let that admiration blind you to their threat. The Trustee may be correct, but conflict may be unavoidable. What I have not told you is that some things are already in motion — a small aerocraft has gone to one of the evacuation ships to bring it back to the surface."

"Then we should be moving, should we not? If we are to convince the council, we must get to Traedenath as soon as possible."

They climbed into the autowheel and began the long drive back into the city. They talked of which council members might listen, what arguments were most likely to succeed, and whether they could get a majority to agree. They arrived at the government building with only a small hope, but one that they would not abandon without a fight.

CONFRONTATION

Chapter 28

Endeavour
En Route GL 252
Tuesday, June 18, 2086, 2200 UTC

Carol pulled her senior officers into a late-evening meeting as they approached GL 252. She included Wren Freya Thomas after counseling her about the sensitive information she might hear.

"Here's what I want. The 262s tracked *Onizuka* with some kind of graviton detector, or so we assume, anyway. We can't let that happen to us. So, let's shut down the Drive as soon as we can once we come out of FTL."

Weapons Officer Ronan Murphy asked, "Will they detect our arrival? Do we want them to?"

"I believe they will, and yes, I want them to know we're there."

Carol turned to her Navigator, new Senior Lieutenant Bexley Farmer, on her first deployment aboard. "An interesting first cruise, eh Bexley?"

She smiled in response. "Yes, ma'am. Interesting is a good word for it."

"Soon as we have a reading on the planet, we'll have to maneuver for intercept. I want a flyby, something that gives us enough time to contact *Onizuka* but makes it hard for them to engage us."

"Yes, ma'am. We'll be ready."

"I want the Drive shut down as soon as we've made that adjustment. We'll bring it back online when we know what kind of orbit we need."

"Yes, Commander."

"Comms, we have to assume that *Onizuka*'s SLIP is out. So, we'll try a VHF ping. Hopefully we can get a lock on them and switch to laser."

"Yes, Commander. We were discussing that issue ourselves. We thought a ping at four light-seconds would be a good start, repeating every five minutes until we get an answer."

"That's all fine." She turned to Ronan. "Weaps, queue up a priority on Spartans. If we need to defend ourselves, let's be ready."

"Yes, Commander."

Carol turned back to Navigator Farmer. "We talked about a light-minute entry. Still good with that?"

"Yes, ma'am. That's pretty close to our limit." She looked at her NetComp. "We'll cut the Drive at, um, 14:52:03 tomorrow."

Carol sat back from the table. "Great. That's all, thank you."

Thomas remained behind, working on her notebook. Carol, seeing her still there, waited.

"Questions?"

"No, Commander. I can follow most of it...I assume any technical details are restricted?"

"Yes," she responded sharply. Then, more softly, she continued, "I doubt if any of that is relevant to the story you want to tell."

"No, probably not."

Carol nodded her agreement and left the wardroom. They'd be there in less than sixteen hours, and things were about to get very busy. It was time to get some rest. It might be a while before she got another decent night's sleep.

New Traenah
The Tracker
Spin 8, Subcycle 3, Cycle 2510

Kirah took her time confirming the new contact. Yes, there it was, a strong signal like the previous alien ship. But this was not the same ship. Perhaps the alien's friends had come for him? She tracked the target for a few quatset before the signal disappeared. Reluctantly, she picked up the far-talker and requested a connection to Aytila.

"A new alien ship is here. They turned off their propulsion just after they arrived, so I can't track them. But the signal is almost identical to the first one. No question, it is the same kind of propulsion."

Aytila thanked Kirah for her report, something he'd never done before. She wondered if that was good or very bad.

Aytila went quickly to the pilot's ready room, where he knew Dsanik and Tmoyan would be. "There is another alien ship."

"Where is it?"

"We only know where it arrived. They turned off their propulsion right after."

"So, they already know about the tracker?" Aytila turned at the sound of Nadon's voice. He hadn't noticed her sitting across the room from the pilots.

"Yes."

"How, pilots, would they know that?"

Tmoyan looked at Dsanik, who had no answer. "I don't know."

"Well, pilots, it can't be just luck. Somehow, the first ship was able to communicate with this new one."

Dsanik waved his disagreement. "But this ship may have been coming anyway, as part of their plan."

"Yes, Dsanik, I see that. But how did they know about the tracker?"

Tmoyan thought for a moment, then turned to Nadon. "Is it possible to communicate faster than light? Could the first alien have called for help when we attacked him?"

Nadon didn't answer at first, looking down at the floor. Finally, she looked up at Tmoyan. "Twenty cycles ago, I would have said travel at speeds faster than light was impossible. The equations demanded that travel at that speed would require infinite energy. It simply could not be done. The universe would not permit it."

"And then?" Aytila asked.

"And then, someone invented the anti-gravity propulsion unit, and I was proven wrong. And, understand, I was not just a little wrong. I was completely, totally, laughably, incorrect."

"So, you think communication at such speed might also be possible?"

"Logic demands it, Aytila, even if we don't understand the technology behind it."

Tmoyan looked at her carefully. "If that is true, we have to assume there will be others coming."

"Just as the Trustee told you."

Onizuka
In Orbit GL 252 (c)
Wednesday, June 19, 2086, 1415 UTC

Larry heard it clearly, right where it was supposed to be, right when it was supposed to be: thirty seconds of carrier on 121.5 MHz. *Endeavour* had arrived! The communications system quickly calculated the location and pointed the long, narrow laser transmitter at the source. Ten seconds later, his headset came alive.

"*Endeavour* calling *Onizuka*…Hansen here."

Larry smiled as he remembered the last time he'd talked to Carol in a crisis. "Hi, honey. How's *your* day going?" he answered.

There was a slightly longer delay, and in Larry's mind, he could see Carol's smile.

"Covington, you're a pain in the ass. But I do love you."

Larry smiled at the snippet of their old banter as he started the upload of ship logs and Ethan's intelligence summaries to *Endeavour*. All that would happen concurrently with his conversation with Carol.

He keyed the microphone. "Kinda lonely up here, what with the ship all shot to hell and everyone else on shore leave."

A few seconds later, her reply came through clearly. "Roger shore leave, Larry." A moment later, "Roger uploads, thanks."

A minute passed before his headset came alive again. "Larry, have you heard from the shore party?"

"Negative. Orbital geometry sucks."

"OK, let us talk and I'll get back to you."

"Understood. Not going anywhere anyhow."

Carol set down the Comms headset and called her officers for a conference on the right side of the Bridge. She turned to her Nav Officer.

"Bex, what's the story on *Onizuka*?"

Farmer flipped open her NetComp to the summary Larry Covington had sent over. "Drive is out. Battle damage. They have a good reactor, and the ship is otherwise not in too bad a condition."

"But she's not going anywhere anytime soon?"

"Yes, ma'am. Correct."

"I'd like to get Covington off, maybe get him some relief."

Jayvon nodded his agreement. "He has a dozen crew there, too. We should get them off as well. They don't need to be there anymore."

"Right." Carol thought for a second. "Ronan, you have a good idea where the crew is hiding?"

"Yes, ma'am. Lieutenant Commander Covington's information was very clear on that. We can find them."

"OK, then. Jayvon, who's the on-call pilot?"

"Finley Oliver."

"Tell Ensign Oliver he's headed for *Onizuka* to take the crew off. Bex, change of plans: we'll keep this course, then maneuver into orbit once we're out of sight of the detector. Give me a twelve-hour high-elliptical over the crew on the surface."

"Yes, Commander." She looked at her Nav display. "About two hours, ma'am, should do it. But the shuttle will be detected."

"Yes, I understand. Let them see what we're doing."

"Yes, Commander."

"OK, that's all." Carol walked back to the Comm position and picked up the headset.

"Larry, it's Carol. Still there?"

"Like I have somewhere else to be? Go ahead."

"I'm sending a shuttle for you and the remaining crew. You'll come over here for the moment."

Larry looked away from the Comm station, suddenly uncomfortable with the idea of leaving *Onizuka* completely abandoned. But, as he thought of it, they were only aboard in order to make contact with *Endeavour*, so why not?

"Understood. When should we roll out the red carpet?"

"We'll give you a firm time a little later, but figure three or four hours. Get your people ready."

"Will do."

"See you soon, my friend."

Larry smiled. "We can reminisce about the sim and other meaningless stuff."

"Sounds nice."

As she hung up, Carol was aware that Wren Freya Thomas was lurking nearby.

"Question, Ms. Thomas?"

"Well, I am surprised, I guess, at the speed of decision-making. There was not much discussion among the officers."

"Not in this scenario, no. It's up to me to decide what to do. But, if anyone had a disagreement, they would have raised it, and I would have listened."

"Really? I didn't think you left much time for that."

"Oh, they know how to interrupt me when I'm about to do something dumb. Anything else?"

"How long has Covington been alone on *Onizuka*?"

"Well, he's not exactly alone. There are a handful of other techs there to keep things working. Larry's been there about ten days, I think, so not too long."

"You seem to know him very well."

Carol nodded. "Classmate, and he was part of the study group David and I started. There were about six or eight of us that met almost every day."

"So, not a casual acquaintance?"

Carol grinned slightly and looked off into some indeterminate distance. "No, Larry is a dear, dear friend; and a wonderful officer."

"I look forward to meeting him."

Carol's eyebrows went up slightly as her smile returned. "Hmm, yes, that will be very interesting for you." She walked back up to the command station and took some time to study the intelligence summary Ethan Reyes had left for her.

After digesting that, she drafted her message to the Fleet:

```
FLASH 208506191530UTC
TO: CINCFLEET, FLEETOPS, ENTERPRISE
FROM: ENDEAVOUR
SUBJECT: STATUS AT GL 262

1) ARRIVED GL 252 208606191457
2) ESTABLISHED CONTACT WITH ONIZUKA.
3) ONIZUKA ATTACKED TWICE BY 262 CULTURE, DRIVE AND SLIP COMMS DISABLED.
4) 262 CULTURE IS A PEER TECHNOLOGICALLY.
5) THEY FIGHT WITH SMALL CRAFT ABLE TO TAKE OFF LIKE AIRCRAFT
AND MANEUVER IN SPACE.
6) ONIZUKA INTEL ASSESSES THAT CRAFT USE HYBRID JET/FORSTMANN DRIVE
PROPULSION SYSTEM.
7) ATTACK WEAPONS ARE SMALL 'SIDEWINDER' CLASS MISSILES.
8) MOST OF CREW CURRENTLY ON SURFACE IN HIDING, MINIMAL CREW
STILL ABOARD SHIP.
9) PLAN TO (A) EVACUATE CREW FROM SHIP AND (B) MAKE DIRECT CONTACT
WITH THOSE ON SURFACE.
10) WILL UPDATE AGAIN AFTER CONSULTING ONIZUKA ACTUAL

HANSEN

END
```

Enterprise
Approaching GL 252
Wednesday, June 19, 2086, 1645 UTC

Fiona was still reading *Endeavour*'s initial report as *Enterprise* came out of FTL near GL 252. She ordered a synchronous orbit over the single large city. Her Navigator programmed for an inclination that would bring *Enterprise* directly over the city once per sol.

The Nav then came to her. "Shall I shut down the Drive when we're in place, Admiral?"

Fiona shook her head. "No. Leave it on standby. Let them track us if they want. I'm not trying to hide. I'll have more for you shortly."

"Yes, ma'am, we'll be ready."

In a few minutes, she had laser communications with *Endeavour*. Carol relayed Larry Covington's *Onizuka* status report to *Enterprise* before calling.

"Good afternoon, Admiral," she began.

"Good afternoon, Carol. How are you doing? Any news from the surface?"

"Not yet, ma'am. We've only been here a couple hours ourselves. I'm generating a shuttle run to evacuate the dozen or so still on *Onizuka*, but I have not had a line of sight to call Commander Powell yet."

"I see. What's your status otherwise?"

"Drive is off to avoid detection. Otherwise, we're nominal."

Fiona shook her head. "Turn it back on. I want you over the *Onizuka* crew as much as possible, and I want you to maneuver a little every orbit to keep them guessing. I will be doing the same."

"Yes, Admiral. We were already planning a high-elliptical over them. We'll change orbit as soon as we get below the horizon."

"Very well. Let me know when you have comms with Powell. I need to know their status."

"Yes, ma'am, will do."

"And Carol, from Covington's report, they're all safe. That has to be a comfort."

Carol paused a moment before answering. "When they went to the surface, yes, but he hasn't heard from them in over a week. We don't know what's happened in the meantime."

"Yes, true. Keep me posted."

"Yes, ma'am, will do."

Carol dropped the connection and took a moment to look out the Bridge windows. It was a pretty planet, for sure, but then, all the habitable planets looked attractive, didn't they? Inor, Big Blue, Alpha Mensae, even Zeta Doradus. Was it just that she instinctively recognized something conforming to the pattern of where she came from? Would a different kind of life see this as dull and the clouds of a gas giant as attractive? Probably. Beauty, as the saying goes, is in the eye of the beholder: every individual places their unique interpretation on what they see.

After a moment, she looked away and got back to the task at hand.

Chapter 29

New Traenah
The Tracker
Spin 8, Subcycle 3, Cycle 2510

Kirah looked up in alarm as another target appeared on her monitor. Was this the first new alien reappearing, or was it a third ship? As she watched it for a ductset, she quickly realized this was yet another vessel. It was nowhere near the one seen earlier, and its power profile was deeper and wider. She was puzzled when this second new alien did not shut down its propulsion system. Shortly, there was another new target, identical to the first alien ship. She looked back and forth at the display before her, trying to bend her mind around what it was showing her, trying to understand where they were going.

Both vessels were still approaching New Traenah, likely, in her mind, heading for orbit. She asked the autocalc to correlate the sightings, and it estimated that the new target was the first new alien and not yet another. She waited until the autocalc determined the alien ships' courses, then she picked up the far-talker to call Aytila one more time.

Aytila returned to the planning room from another long discussion with the tech at The Tracker.

"There is a third alien ship."

"A *third?*" Dsanik asked.

"Yes, this one appears even more powerful than the first two. There is something else. They're leaving their propulsion systems on. The new one never shut down, and the previous ship has restarted theirs."

Dsanik looked at Tmoyan in surprise. "They don't care about being detected?"

Tmoyan waved away the comment. "No. They *want* us to see them. They want us to know exactly where they are and what they're doing."

"Why?"

Tmoyan stood and walked to the window, still cracked and pitted from the alien's strike a few spins ago and looked out on the aerocraft on the tarmac. "I don't know. Intimidation? Assurance that they are no threat? I have no idea."

Nadon looked at him. "Either is an invitation to inaction, is it not? Either by scaring us or comforting us, they want us to leave them alone?"

"That is one interpretation, yes," Dsanik admitted. "I don't know that we should comply with such a suggestion."

Tmoyan turned from the window. "Can we communicate with the Trustee? Has he made that possible?"

"No," Nadon answered. "But he said he would be watching and ready to help if needed."

"He regrets his failure on Traenah?" Dsanik asked.

"Very much. He sees conflict with the humans as a new disaster to be avoided." She stood and joined Tmoyan at the window. "I know how you feel about the aliens. I have the same innate revulsion myself, but the Trustee was truthful at Traenah. It would have been better to have accepted their invitation."

Tmoyan looked at her. "You believe we should trust him now and leave the humans alone?"

"Yes. I struggle with it, more than you know, but it makes sense. These humans may not be the only aliens we encounter out here, and we can't just strike out at all of them."

"We failed with the Council last spin, but with the two new alien ships, perhaps we should try again."

"Yes, we should."

Tmoyan yanked open the door, and they left for the government building nearby.

On the Surface
GL 252 (c)
Wednesday, June 19, 2086, 2105 UTC

Lieutenant Commander David Powell was napping in a shuttle seat, trying to get a little rest after a restless night in the outposts. His XO Melinda Hughes was in the next seat over, curled up in her winter coat, gently snoring. He was awakened by the communication alarm on the instrument panel. He got up and went into the shuttle's cockpit, where the laser-contact light was blinking. *She's here,* he thought. He pressed 'accept' and clicked the microphone control.

"Powell here."

There was a perceptible pause. "Nice to hear your voice again."

David sat back in the seat. "Yes, well, it's nice to be heard, especially by you."

"I got your position from Larry. How are you?"

"We're fine for the moment, but they know where we are."

"They know where you are?"

"Yes. No question."

"How did they find you?"

David shook his head. "It's not important. That they did is all that counts."

"I read Ethan's summary. They're pretty sophisticated."

"Absolutely. Very close to our technological level and tactically adept. They'd be a challenge to fight."

"Scary."

David leaned back in the pilot's seat. "We had a visitor the other night."

"A what?"

"A visitor. A Guardian."

Carol paused a long moment, trying to gauge if there was a punch line coming. "You mean, like, a Guardian of the Preeminent?"

"Or a Shepherd of the Zeds, yeah."

"Oh, do tell."

"He called himself John. He claims he was sent to rescue the 262s from the comet. He says he failed at that, mostly because of their xenophobia and something about a preacher. Not clear on that part."

"262s?"

David shrugged. "Seemed apt. 'Aliens' is too nonspecific at this point."

"Ok, yeah, I guess. So why is he here now?"

"He says they can't fail again, and he needs me to help him. He thinks if the 262s attack us here, you and Fiona will lay waste to their city, victimizing them yet again."

"I'm not sure that makes sense."

"I would do it if your crew was lying dead in a field. I think you would, too."

Carol shook her head, ridding herself of the visual he'd just given her.

"Maybe, maybe not. What did he look like?"

"What?"

"What did he look like? Was he eight feet tall with a massive brain case, or a little grey guy with triangular black eyes? What?"

David smiled and shrugged, not that Carol could see either expression. "He was normal looking, I guess. His face was very different, the eyes kinda wide apart, and the mouth seemed small, but really, he looked maybe like someone in their seventies. Not bad, nothing extreme."

"How old is he?"

"Ten thousand years."

"Really?"

"That's what he said."

"What is it he thinks is going to happen?"

"He says they're coming for us."

Carol nodded to herself and paused for a moment to think. "Fiona is here. How do you want to play it?"

"Well, *Enterprise* has a platoon of Marines. You have a squad. Mine are obviously already here: That makes at least part of a company."

"You want to stand and fight?"

"Stand, maybe, at least. I'm not sure just bugging out will solve anything, especially if we want to come back for *Onizuka*. We'll need a repair ship with new Drive modules and a week to install them."

"So, you're thinking we need to settle with the 262s if we're going to be able to do that?"

"Yes. I also think we need to make contact with these people and establish some kind of relationship. They don't need to be afraid of us."

Carol shook her head. "We have zero Corderos here and zero convenient books to drive translation. How do you propose to talk to them?"

"John said he would be here when we needed him to translate."

Carol looked off across her Bridge, thinking. "You think he already knows what's going to happen?"

"They don't seem the god type to me. He may have more insight than us, more experience maybe, but I don't think they're prophets or, uh, seers."

Carol paused before keying the microphone again. "I was worried."

David smiled. "I know. I was, too. Still am." David sat up straight, his mind now made up.

"Talk to Fiona for me. I did not expect her so soon, and that changes things. I want to move my crew off and get all the Marines we have down here. Ethan has found a redoubt a little way up the valley we can hold."

"So, you still think it will come to a fight?"

"I'm hoping that taking a strong position will prevent a fight."

"Negotiate from strength?"

"Always."

"OK, we'll get going."

"I have a new NetLink prefix for you, that'll put all of you in our loop. We'll be over you about ten hours a day."

David listened and took careful notes as she read off the sixteen hex digits required to resync their NetLinks to *Endeavour*.

"OK, fine. I'll get Melinda and Ethan to get this distributed."

After the comm link was closed, David gathered his brain trust just outside one of *Onizuka*'s now-tired shuttles.

Ethan looked to his CO. "So, what's the plan?"

"*Enterprise* is here, too. They must have stopped mid-course. I didn't expect them for several days." David sat down at the small table they had used for maps and meals. He handed a paper to Melinda. "New NetLink prefix. Get that distributed."

"Yes, will do. Meantime, what are we doing?"

"I want to settle with the 262s, not run away. But I want to do that from a strong position, so I recommended to Collins that we move the crew off and bring down all the available Marines. With what Sabrina has here, plus *Endeavour* and the platoon on *Enterprise*, we'd have about sixty, all fully combat-ready."

Ethan Reyes looked up. "I'd like to stay."

David looked hard at his young Intel officer. "You do know what holy Hell Nat Hayden will give me if you get even a small scratch?"

"I'd like to stay, *sir*."

"Approved. No one knows the ground like you do."

He turned to Melinda. "XO, you're in charge of getting the crew organized and off the surface. Leave the supplies and whatever else behind. Just get the people off as soon as you can."

"Can we get a run from *Endeavour*? With four shuttles, we can do it all at once."

David nodded. "Call them and request it." He waited a moment. "All of this is contingent on Admiral Collins buying off on my plan."

"She will," Melinda answered.

"Perhaps. We'll know soon." He turned to Marine Lieutenant Herrera. "Sabrina, you don't get a choice."

"No, sir, I don't."

"Captain Harry will take over when he gets down here, but I will need you to brief him on what you know and the lay of the land."

"Yes, Commander."

"OK, let's get to it."

The officers scattered, passing instructions to their staff, and starting the process of evacuating the camp. David was slightly sad to be going. It had been an unusual, interesting interlude after the attacks on his ship. He had hoped to just wait out the arrival of the seventh cavalry, but it hadn't quite worked out that way. Still, his crew would soon be safe back on board ship, and he would have the opportunity to make peace with a xenophobic race that had ignored the warnings of what was probably one of the oldest, wisest cultures in the galaxy, if not the universe, and who now seemed bent on killing him.

No sweat.

New Traenah
Traedenath Central Airfield
Spin 8, Subcycle 3, Cycle 2510

It was late in the evening as Tmoyan listened carefully to Aytila's report. The scouts watching the aliens now reported that they were preparing to leave, moving their ships out from under the trees and organizing themselves. The commander, or the alien Tmoyan believed was the commander, had walked up the valley with two others and briefly examined a narrow cut in the mountainside.

His long analysis was interrupted by the far-talker.

"Tmoyan."

"Sir, this is Kirah at the Tracker. There are two more targets, sir, same small vessels, one from each of the new alien ships."

"These are the small transports they have been using?"

"It would appear so, yes. They are heading towards the aliens."

"Thank you."

"Yes, sir."

Tmoyan hung up the far-talker. "Two more transports headed for the surface. Are they invading or evacuating?"

Nadon, now rarely seen outside his company, looked across the room from a seat by the window. "Are those the only two options?"

Tmoyan looked at her with some annoyance. She had a unique ability to find the small flaws in his thinking, flaws he immediately thought he should have detected on his own. "I don't know. Perhaps not. Aytila's report is that they are preparing to leave, but they have also investigated a second position. I am not sure what those facts represent."

Dsanik looked up from his maps. "The evacuation ship with the ground force will leave in time for the next dawn at the site. With two ships overhead, the aliens will be forewarned. There will be no surprise attack."

"If there will be an attack at all," Tmoyan commented darkly. "If the humans choose, that ship will never reach its destination."

"Yes, we have seen their weapons. If they strike it with the kinds of missiles they used on the airfields, it will have no hope."

There was a long moment of silence as they contemplated the ugly death that might be waiting for sixteen by sixteen males.

"Which means," Nadon said finally, "If the ship does arrive safely, it is because the humans *want* it to arrive. What would that say?"

"This may be the greatest test of their intent," Tmoyan answered. "But I am reluctant to risk so many males to find out."

"It is the council that risks them, not us," Dsanik responded.

Tmoyan stood abruptly. "I am going to have a look."

Dsanik checked the time. "We have just enough time to get there before dark."

Tmoyan gripped his agreement as they ran to the preparation room to change into flight gear. Aytila ran to the maintenance building to order two aerocraft prepared for a long flight.

Mehonnh was starting down into the mountains in the west as Tmoyan and Dsanik descended out of space and back into the atmosphere.

Tmoyan watched his AG detector as it tracked the small transports about to land. They were no threat, he knew. The ships in orbit were another question, but they'd made it this far, which meant that the humans were not planning to interfere with his mission. He keyed his radio. "Follow me over the location, then turn hard right to come back around."

As they came within a few mileah, Tmoyan turned on the cameras of his recon ship. They came from the west, out of the setting star, passing as low as possible over the wide meadow the humans had chosen for a refuge. The shadows of the trees were made even more enormous by the low angle of the star, so low that they darkened the entire field.

As he passed over the field, the sheer walls of the valley perilously close to the belly of his aerocraft, he caught a glimpse of four small spacecraft and a large number of individuals all around them. Pulling his ship hard right, Dsanik followed as they circled tightly to come back across the field, a little higher this time, and now there were only a few humans in view.

"Where did they all go?" Dsanik asked.

"Under cover, I would think. They would not want us to know how many they are."

"If they're leaving, why would they care?"

"Maybe they're not."

Tmoyan had an idea there would be one particular human waiting for him. "I believe the commander will come out. I am going to make another pass."

"I will cover you," Dsanik said as he circled wider and higher to look for any possible trouble. Tmoyan slowed down as he came back around and then turned into a slow curve around the open area. Sure enough, there in the middle of the field stood a single human, his right hand raised, palm open. He remained there, turning with him, as Tmoyan made two circuits of the field before turning back to the west. They would climb above the mountains before turning north to go back to Traedenath.

Back at their base, still in flight suits, they looked at the pictures Tmoyan had taken. "There are more humans here than were reported before."

Nadon nodded. "Yes, and they are dressed differently. Look at these with flecked clothing. They are not the same as the ones in dark gray."

As they looked at more images, on his second pass, the humans were nearly all gone, likely under the trees or into the four transports.

Dsanik pointed to the image. "They're just doing what any force would do if discovered."

"Yes," Tmoyan answered. It had been two spedset, two-sixteenths of a spin of Traenah since they had been over the humans' camp. Tetanna would be rising soon, but Tmoyan did not feel the fatigue of a long night. He looked at Dsanik. "Look at the last pass. The human commander came out again, just like the first time we found them."

They scanned through the images until they came to the best picture of the human commander. He stood alone, away from the transport ships, with one arm raised, palm open.

"He's showing us an empty hand. They made this same gesture with the scout, and clearly, he means something by it."

Nadon looked over their shoulders. "A hand with no weapon? A gesture that he is no threat?"

Tmoyan stared at the image, trying to see the scene from the human's point of view. This was difficult for him: to think of the alien as a person, someone to have empathy for. "I think so, yes."

Dsanik was fighting the same thought, pushing down his inherent hatred of the outsider, the *other*. "If they really are no threat, we cannot strike them. It would be improper."

Nadon gripped her agreement. "More than that, it would be immoral. A crime, really."

The pilots looked at each other. "We have to stop this, Dsanik."

"That idea is counter to all we have been taught, all we believe."

"Yes?" Nadon asked gently.

"But yes, I am convinced we must." He was still for a moment before turning back to Tmoyan. "How?"

"You and Nadon go back to the council." He reached for a picture. "Show them this."

"What will you do?" Nadon asked.

"I will go back to the humans' hideout and get between them and our attack."

Dsanik waved his strong disagreement. "You will be seen as a traitor! You might be shot with them!"

"Not if you get through to the council. But if you don't, I will stand there and demand that Hlatan stand down. I don't think the old soldier will shoot me."

"At his age, he might not know the difference."

"Thank you, Dsanik, for your encouraging words."

Nadon and Dsanik left for the council facility as Tmoyan called Aytila to find him a vertical landing aerocraft.

Aytila stood motionless. "What, sir, do you have in mind, exactly, if I may ask?"

"I am going to prevent a needless war, Aytila. Find me something."

Aytila faintly gripped his understanding and left to find the aerocraft that Tmoyan needed.

GL 252 (c)
On the Surface
Wednesday, June 19, 2086, 0145 UTC

David stood next to Marine Captain Liwanu Harry and Lieutenant Sabrina Herrera as the shuttle carrying the last of the *Onizuka* crew lifted off into the dark, starlit sky. In only seconds, it was out of sight, invisible as the night closed around it.

"No moon?" Liwanu asked casually as he looked at the sky.

"Nope. Nice stars, though," Sabrina answered. "I've had a few chances to just sit and watch. It's a beautiful place."

"Beautiful, yes," Natalie Hayden said, surprising them. "But freaking dangerous, don't you think?"

David looked back from the stars. "Natalie?"

She gave him her small, amused grin. "Hey, David. Happy to see me?"

"Always."

"How's my favorite student doing?"

"Ethan? Yeah, you nailed that one. He's great."

"As good as you?"

David grinned slightly. "Well…someday."

She looked at the stars for a moment, then turned back to David. "Fiona wants me here to help coordinate your fire support. *Enterprise* is moving into an orbit like *Endeavour*, offset about four hours. You'll have overhead fire available with no breaks."

"Good." He turned to Harry. "How are we doing, Liwanu?"

"Fine, sir. We've secured the entrance to the cut, and we're clearing the area above for aliens."

David smiled. "262s, Liwanu. We're all aliens here."

"Yes, sir, 262s it is, sir."

As they turned to move back uphill, there was a shout of surprise and alarm from their left. Turning towards the noise, they could see flashlights in a chase, bouncing through the low woods. The officers ran to the source, pulling up in surprise at what they saw.

There, in the light of dozen 2K7X-mounted lights, stood a single 262, his weapon up and swinging wildly from side to side. He tried to back away but found himself surrounded, his head flicking left and right, then behind, then in front, fear streaming from every movement. A corporal came to meet them.

"We found it in the underbrush, sir. It had this. It was trying to do something with it, but we got it away." He passed over a heavy metallic object.

"Another scout?" Liwanu asked David.

"Yes."

"But," Sabrina said, "if he is this close, and already behind us, there are more scouts than we thought, and they're probably all around."

David just nodded, watching the 262's fear grow as the lights bore into him. "Liwanu?"

"Sir?"

David spoke without taking his eyes off the 262. "Make damn sure the area above the entrance to the cut is clear. If they're this close, they could be up there, too."

Sabrina moved. "I'll check on that, sir."

"Very well." David broke his visual lock on the scout and turned to Liwanu. "What would you suggest, captain?"

"We could restrain him and hold him in the cut, sir, or — "

"What would you *suggest*, captain?"

Liwanu looked hard at David Powell, who was looking just as directly back at him. He knew the wife, at least, from Alpha Mensae: strong, courageous, and a dead shot. He had only met the male of the famous pair once, and briefly, at a Fleet party back at Fort Eustis. He seemed friendly enough then, and he had a reputation for smarts and an open mind.

Might as well test it.

"We don't want a conflict. Let him go, with his radio. Maybe we take his weapon for safekeeping."

David nodded slightly. "Close." He walked through the circle of Marines to the 262 and held up his hands to show he had no weapon drawn. The scout looked at the hands, then directly at David, and seemed to relax a little. David approached him, reached out and took hold of the weapon, gently pulling it down and away. The 262 looked down and released it.

"Good," David said quietly. The 262 looked up and David held out the radio. The 262 looked at the device, back to David, and then reached out and took it.

"Excellent." David turned to the corporal who had first found the scout. "Take three from your squad and escort him down out of the woods."

"What then, sir?"

"Let him go. Just escort him into the clearing and come back." David paused, then handed the weapon back to the 262, who took it with what looked like obvious relief.

"Yes, sir."

David pointed to the 262, then the corporal, then downhill. He did this twice before the alien lifted his empty hand and made and released a fist. Taking that as some sign of understanding, David handed the weapon over, stepped back, and the 262 started downhill towards the clearing, four Marines close behind.

"You think that message will be received?" Liwanu asked.

"I hope so, captain. I sure hope so."

"You want us to do the same with any others we find?"

"Yes. Just show them out as gently as you can."

As they walked back to the cut in the dark, Natalie gave David a little push. "Easy on my little brother, pal!"

David smiled. "He's great, Nat. I know that. I just wanted him to tell me what he thought, not what he thought I wanted to hear."

The young scout walked slowly away from the aliens, expecting at any moment to be killed. Once he was a two-sixteenth of a mileah from them, he began running all the way to the landing field below the woods. He had much to report, but the attack force was not there yet.

Soon, he knew, soon they would land, and he could give the commander his report. He didn't understand what had just happened to him, but he was happy to still be alive. Whatever the big ugly aliens had said, he'd gotten away with his life.

That had to mean something to someone.

As the night wore on, the Marines scoured the area for more scouts but found none. They worked over the narrow cut in the mountain three times, finding tracks but no scouts.

It was still dark as David called his team together. Sunrise, or star-rise as they tried, and often failed, to call it, was still three hours away. They huddled over a small table under a tent just inside the narrow entrance to the sharp valley they were holding. He laid out the photographs as Liwanu and one of his sergeants held up flashlights.

David turned to his Chief of Intelligence. "Ethan?"

"Yes, sir. We originally believed the 262s would land down the slope, past the lower woods where the streams converge." He pointed to the location on the map. "Now that we have pulled back, I think it more likely they will land in the clearing near our previous camp. There is enough space for one of their ships, and it's only about five hundred meters from our current position. That would be enough for us, so I expect it would be for them, too."

"You're assuming they know where we are? They know that we've moved?"

"I think the scout is proof enough of that."

"Agreed. When will they come?"

"We would already be here, sir. But given how that air recon happened last sol, coming at us out of the sun, I would expect them to come in at sunrise, out of the east."

David looked across the table at Liwanu. "OK. Get a drone up, now, and get a backup prepped."

"Yes, sir, will do." He looked at Sabrina, who nodded and headed for the drone crew to get the first one airborne.

"Won't we get a warning from *Enterprise* and *Endeavour*, sir?" Liwanu asked.

"We will." David nodded toward Natalie. "Commander Hayden tells me *Enterprise* is moving overhead to support us, but they will still be able to see them take off."

"But you want us to be ready in any case?"

"Exactly. I want you to set up a squad at the edge of the woods, just off the lake. Tell your people, very clearly, we are not trying to kill the 262s. I want them to fire over their heads. We may take a hit or two doing that, but I want to show them strength. Maybe it will warn them off."

"Yes, Commander."

"Then, if they come on, we pull everyone all the way back to the cut, and we hold firm. If they keep coming at us, then the gloves are off, and we have to defend ourselves."

One of the sergeants leaned into the light. "Should we fire on the ship itself, sir? Their Drive will have to use fore and aft emitters just like ours. We could take a squad in close and disable it."

David smiled. "Never cut off the retreat of an enemy you'd rather not fight, sergeant." There was friendly laughter around the table.

The sergeant smiled. "Understood, sir, yes, very wise."

More laughter.

"OK, get on it, everyone. Officers and NCOs back here in one hour, please."

Chapter 30

Enterprise
In Orbit GL 252 (c)
Thursday, June 20, 2086, 1545 UTC

Admiral Fiona Collins paced her bridge, stopping each lap to check the Surveillance display showing the location of the 262s' large ship on the ground. A few hours before, there was a crowd of individuals around, a crowd that was then lost to view as afternoon clouds drifted in off the sea. She was impatiently hoping the ill-timed overcast would move on before the ship departed. The blurry IR display showed the ship was still there, but there was no way to know how far they had come in their preparations.

Engineering Officer Declan Moore was also hanging out on the bridge, behind the large Surveillance workstation, leaning against the command platform.

"You're wearing out my expensive floor, Captain!"

Fiona stopped and joined him. "I'm not usually the nervous type, but this is such a strange scenario. I should just smack that thing where it sits and go get Powell and the rest and just bug out of here."

"That would be satisfying, I guess, in a way, yes, ma'am. But you're not going to do that."

"No, Declan, I'm not." She leaned over to him. "You're worried about Natalie?"

He smiled slightly. "Oh, some, I guess. But she can handle herself, and I'm equally worried about the other sixty or so we have down there."

"Equally?" she asked, amused.

"Well, *almost* equally," he responded.

The Surveillance officer stood up and walked to them. "We're seeing more VHF traffic. I can't understand it, but it feels to us like they're getting ready to depart. Two voices back and forth, short messages."

As she finished speaking, there was a call from her techs. The IR had suddenly become more intense, and as they watched, the ship emerged from the overcast and turned north.

"What do we do, Admiral?" Declan asked. Fiona stared at the image for a moment, struggling with her options. The ship was accelerating and rising out of the atmosphere. It would soon be in easy range of a Lance anti-ship missile, which is probably all that would be needed. One Lance. Should she destroy it, thus cutting short the threat to the people on the ground but simultaneously enraging this new culture? Or should she let it go and let Powell and Nat Hayden and the Marines deal with them? Powell had been amazingly reserved in his responses to the 262 attacks. He had done only that which had to be done for the safety of his ship.

Fiona finally shook her head and turned to the Comms officer. "Call Powell, let him know they're on their way."

David's NetLink buzzed with the message that the 262 ship had taken off from the city, moving north. *They'll come over the pole,* David thought, *then move to approach us out of the dawn, just as we would if the roles were reversed.* It would take them two hours to make the journey, or so *Enterprise*'s Intel shop thought.

The hour David gave his team was almost up as a faint sound seized his attention. It wasn't natural, that much he was sure of. It grew gently louder, and finally Natalie and Ethan came out from under cover to look around with him. It sounded to David like one of the 262s' aircraft, but there was something else with it. The Marines didn't miss it, either, and they prepped their 2K7Xs and moved into their positions. Dawn was coming, but still an hour away, and it was now light enough to tell the woods from the field, the sky from the ground. David thought it unlikely what he was hearing was a large ship, but then, he couldn't be sure. Ethan had no idea, either.

The sound got abruptly louder as an aircraft cleared the mountain above them. It turned quickly around and settled into the small open area above the lake and below the woods where they would be holding. David walked down the slope to the edge of the woods to find a small aircraft, clearly a jet, but with large bulges on the wings and tail.

Ethan was right behind him. "Are those Drive modules?"

David turned, surprised that Ethan had followed him down. "Maybe."

As they watched, a single 262 worked his way out of the cockpit, set his helmet back on the seat, and looked across at David and Ethan. As they stood there, David was suddenly aware of someone next to him.

"Hello again, Commander Powell," John the Trustee said quietly.

David turned. "That showing up unannounced thing, John? That's really annoying."

John stood firm. "I told you I would be here when you needed me."

Natalie looked at John. "Who the hell is this?"

"Oh, hello, Natalie. You can call me John." He extended his hand to her.

"How do you...David?" Natalie shook hands almost automatically, not thinking about what she was doing. The Trustee's hand was awkward, as if he was wearing a mitten.

"Natalie, meet the Guardian slash Shepherd slash Trustee. He calls himself John, but somehow, I don't think that's his real name."

"A Guardian?"

"In the flesh."

"Damn."

"Yeah, that was my reaction, too."

The 262 walked slowly around the back of the aircraft, then stopped and raised his right hand, palm forward. David recognized and returned the gesture. The 262's attention moved immediately to John.

He spoke quickly, in what sounded to David like a mixture of deep tones and sudden consonants. The sound surprised him, strong and low frequencies from such a small individual.

"What, Trustee, are you doing here? Do you favor the humans?"

John stepped forward, standing between the two warriors. *"No, Tmoyan, I am only here to translate."*

John turned to David. "He asks what I am doing here, and I told him I am only here to translate. I have met Tmoyan before. He is a brave warrior, a warplane pilot, and famous on his world."

The name came out of John's mouth in a way that David could pronounce, higher and less complex than what he had heard John say to the 262. David nodded. "I understand. What message has Tmoyan brought for us?"

John translated the question, and Tmoyan paused a few seconds before responding. John turned back to David. "He congratulates you on your bravery. Not every leader would stand out so alone in the face of a potential enemy."

"Thank him for that and tell him we deeply regret his losses in the attacks on *Onizuka*. We had to defend ourselves. I hope he understands."

There was another long exchange between John and the 262. Finally, John turned again.

"He understands the need to defend your vessel. He, too, regrets the losses. Tmoyan now believes those attacks were unjustified."

"I appreciate that. Tell Tmoyan we offer no threat to his people. We would prefer to be friends."

Tmoyan waved away John's translation. *"I doubt that we can enter into friendship with such aliens as these humans,"* he said. *"But we would not be enemies, either. There are now more ships in our space, and you, Trustee, tell us there are many more coming. How can we be sure there is no danger to The People?"*

"He's not sure friendship is on the table, but he wants to know how they can know you don't present a danger."

David shrugged. "Test our actions. We have taken no aggression on them, despite their attacks."

John translated, but David didn't wait for a response. "Why is he here, John? We know they're coming with a large ground force. We've seen it loading. It left the city an hour ago."

"Tell the human I have come to stop the attack on them, if I can be convinced that they do not pose a threat to Traedenath."

John translated this for David, then addressed Tmoyan again. *"The human commander asks merely that you consider what he has done. He has taken no offensive action on you, despite the attacks. He says this is all the evidence you need."*

David looked at John. "Tell him we have not fired on the ship they are sending to attack us. Ask him what that tells him."

Another long exchange.

"Tmoyan understands what you are saying, but his people are intensely suspicious of outsiders. It is deep in their culture. I can tell you myself that this aversion has caused many conflicts on their home planet. I find it a most regrettable trait in an otherwise modern culture."

"Can he stop them? Does he have the authority?"

"I cannot order it. I will go to Hlatan when he lands and try to reason with him. Others are trying to convince the council to stop it. They may yet succeed, but I have little hope of that. We have tried before to convince them to leave the humans alone and were unable to sway them."

David listened carefully to the translation, then looked directly at Tmoyan. "Tell Hlatan that we will not fire on him unless he fires on us. But if he does, we will use the same weapons on him that I used to cripple your airfields. Many will die, sir, who need not. Tell him this!"

John translated, then responded, "He says he understands."

David turned to face John directly. "Tell him, John, as emphatically as their language allows, I do not wish this conflict, but we must come to an understanding of each other. I am still here so we can do that. But if they force the issue, we will defend ourselves."

John listened to Tmoyan's response. *"So you say, but here you remain, armed and prepared to strike at us. How am I to interpret this other than as a challenge to our security?"*

David looked at the shorter, thinner 262. He fought the instinct to think of him as weak, even childlike. He was a pilot, a military leader who had come to him to try to avoid a conflict despite his innate hatred of outsiders.

"Had I left, we would not have had this conversation, nor had this chance to know one another. Someday soon, we will come back to recover *Onizuka*, and if I had just left, you would have seen that as a dangerous act. In the meantime, you probably would have attacked my ship again, causing even greater damage." He waited for John's translation. "And when we returned, you would again lash out at us. She is just one vessel among dozens in the fleet, but she is mine, and I am responsible for her. Surely you understand this."

John and Tmoyan had a long exchange before John turned back to David.

"Tmoyan says you have answered well, and he believes what you say. He will go to Hlatan and try to prevent his advance. Then, Tmoyan says, you must go. He will instruct his government that your return to salvage your vessel does not present a threat."

"And after that?"

John asked Tmoyan, then told David: "After that, nothing. They wish to be left alone."

David looked at Tmoyan again. "Both ships are now overhead. I can call down the same kinds of weapons I used on your airfield. There are enough over your position right now to kill your entire force. Don't make me call that kind of force down on you."

John translated, and Tmoyan turned abruptly and returned to his ship. He lifted off and moved downhill to set down on the edge of the landing area.

They would be here soon. David knew. He turned to John. "Are you planning to stay with us, or will you disappear into thin air again?"

"I'll stay, but enough of the insults, David. I have my instructions, too, you know."

They walked back to the small headquarters tent, just a cover, really, with a small portable table underneath. The officers and NCOs gathered around them, curiosity on every face. John greeted each one, looking squarely at each face as if to store them for future reference. His personal review stopped at the newcomer.

"Natalie Hayden, I must say how honored I am to meet you. I offer my sympathy for your loss at Beta Hydri. Such a tragedy. I hope your grief is passing?"

Natalie looked at David, who shrugged. "I have no idea how he knows anything, Nat, but he seems to know damn near everything."

Natalie looked down, thinking, then up and directly at John. "I appreciate your expression. It has taken me a long time, but I am doing well, thank you."

"Excellent!" John turned back to the table. "The race you have encountered here is from the planet Traenah."

"The one with the enormous fresh crater?" Ethan asked.

"Indeed, yes, that is correct. They call themselves the 'People' of Traenah. At least, that's the best translation I can make. 'Beings' or 'sentients' or whatever other word I can think of doesn't really capture the meaning. I went to them as soon as they discovered the comet would strike. We had known for almost a thousand Terran years that this would happen, and so we prepared this planet for them."

"When was this?"

"I contacted them as soon as they learned of the strike. That was about twenty-one Terran years ago. The comet struck almost exactly nine years ago."

"So, you brought them here?"

"Regrettably, no. I failed in that task. Their xenophobia, and one insane preacher, drove me out. They would not accept our help, and we cannot force anyone, even if it means thousands will die."

"Thousands?"

John nodded slowly, then continued. "The preacher gave them an insane, pseudo-spiritual interpretation of what would happen when the comet struck. We estimate several hundred thousand were at the point of impact."

"Oh my God," Sabrina said softly.

"Yes, instant incineration. Males, females, fathers, mothers, children of many ages, all gone in a flash."

David looked across at John. "I have been a poor host. Can I offer you something? Water? Food?"

"I would have some coffee if that were not too inconvenient."

"Coffee? Really? Coffee?"

John folded his hands in front of himself. "On all the planets I have seen in ten thousand years, not much compares to Terran coffee properly prepared."

Sabrina suppressed a laugh and looked at David. "I have that instant stuff in my pack. It's not terrible."

"That will do, thanks."

"I'll get it for him. Cream? Sugar?"

John shook his head. "Oh, no, that would spoil the whole experience. Black will be just fine. Thank you, Sabrina."

She paused, then looked at David as he stood. "Still weird to hear him call us by name."

David just smiled and nodded as Sabrina left to locate her rucksack.

As he took the cup from Sabrina a few minutes later, John looked across at David. "Go ahead, David, ask."

"Ask? Ask what?"

"Ask what you have wanted to ask since Zeta Doradus, or Beta Hydri, or now."

"Why are you here? And why now? We thought you confined yourselves to natural disasters. I get that would be the case at GL 262, the supernova that would have wiped out the Zeds, saving the Preeminent from the asteroid. Why inject yourself into a military confrontation?"

"Because it's my fault it is happening. I begged for a chance to redeem myself, and you're it."

"Scary, isn't it?"

"Not that much. I have faith in you. You are correct about the Zeta Doradus race: their binary system went nova only a few years after we evacuated them. As for the Preeminent, we didn't save them from the asteroid. They lucked out and managed to survive that on their own. They were very small then, not so different from the early mammals. They continued to evolve in isolation as the mammals grew strong."

"So, if they survived and were progressing, why would you move them?"

"Earth was prime for an advanced species to rise. We didn't move them to save them. We moved them to make room for you."

"When?"

"Oh, long before me. A half a million years, I guess."

There was a long silence that Ethan finally broke. "You know our names; you know things that have happened to us individually. Can you tell what we're thinking?"

"Well, telepathy is really overrated, and I think it would be very confusing if we could do that. Sure, I can tell something of what you're feeling, but it's only because I can hear your heartbeat if I try to. I can tell when you're sweating and perceive the flushing of your skin. But as far as reading your mind, no, that's not our business."

Liwanu looked up at John. "Is there a God?"

"A powerful question, Captain Harry, but one I cannot answer. I can tell you that I've seen an incredible range of creation, and while some races know nothing of a supreme, supernatural being, many do, and the idea of an envoy of God coming to redeem a fallen race has happened many times. Are all those Yahweh and his son Jesus? I have no way of knowing."

David picked up the thread. "What do you believe? What do the shepherds of the universe think?"

"You give us too much credit, David, and please don't accuse us by your question of some conceit about ourselves. We know what we are and, most importantly, what we are not. But I do believe in an ultimate architect because I see a fundamental design in all of creation, an underlying logic that sponsors the rise of life in an incredible variety of places. Is it nothing more than complex chemistry, an efficient system of energy transfer? Perhaps, but if so, what is the point? That we can have this conversation is proof to me that something larger is at work. But it is as far beyond my understanding as it is yours."

David nodded slightly. "I did not expect to find humility in you. So much time, so much power — "

"So much duty, so many responsibilities. We are charged to be trustees...caretakers...to help whenever we can. But never to interfere. It is a difficult line to manage." He finished his coffee, set the cup down on the table and looked up at the sky. "It will not be long now."

David looked at his circle of officers and NCOs once more, then took out his comm link earpiece, then looked quickly at his NetLink. "Combat network, channel six, encrypt code is five alpha seven." They quickly entered the settings, and the command link was up.

David pressed his microphone switch. "OK, everyone, let's get to it."

The ship came low over their heads just before dawn, an enormous, silent steel behemoth. It settled not in the meadow by their camp but well down the hillside where Ethan had first expected them to land.

Surprised, David turned to Sabrina. "Drone." She picked up the drone's display module and handed it to him.

In the lower meadow, just below the streams and the woods between that and their camp, he saw Tmoyan's ship, well off to one side. The transport was centered in the field, doors just opening and soldiers filing out. A single figure stood outside the hatch, waiting.

David pointed. "Tmoyan."

As they watched, another 262 came out of the transport and began a conversation with him. Their gestures were strong, the new one, likely the Hlatan that Tmoyan had spoken of, waving broadly.

John watched the display. "Hlatan is not convinced. That wave you saw? Think of that as disagreement, or when you shake your head."

"What about the fist gesture?" David asked.

"The opposite: yes, or agreement, like a nod."

As they watched, the presumptive Hlatan pushed Tmoyan aside and began moving away. Tmoyan moved to one side, paused, then headed for his ship.

"Failure," John said quietly. "They'll come on anyway."

The scout waited for the officers to finish their argument, then approached the commander.

"I was captured by the aliens," he told Hlatan.

Hlatan waved his skepticism. "And yet here you are still breathing. What happened?"

"They somehow saw me in the dark, I don't know how. I was well concealed, but they found me regardless. I ran, but there were too many, and they got behind me. Their lights were so bright, I couldn't see!"

"Go on."

"One of them came and took my weapon and communicator."

Hlatan pointed to his weapon. "And yet here you stand, holding both."

"They talked among themselves, but I could not understand any of it. When they were done, they walked me out of the forest to the clearing above the lake and let me go."

"They just let you leave?"

"Yes, sir. They handed back my weapon and my communicator and pointed towards the lower woods. I walked away and they let me go."

"What did you see?"

"There are more of the soldier types there now, all with large weapons. There are at least three sixteens, possibly more. It was hard to see in the dark."

227

"What of this alien that let you go?"

"He talked quietly. The others were very loud. I think it was the same one a scout encountered several spins ago."

"The commander, most likely."

"If you say so, sir. They are dug in above the narrow point, sir, but they have others watching on both sides."

"I see. Anything else?"

"No, sir. If I knew more about them, their language, I might be able to say more."

"Yes, I suppose so, but who wants to learn the speech of hated aliens?"

The scout left, moving back to their small camp just off the landing field. He was still feeling the panic from being surrounded and trying to reconcile that with his easy release. Back on Traenah, a captured scout would have been executed on the spot.

David looked at the display as the second conversation with the commander ended, then turned to Natalie.

"Can we get a couple of Bludgeons on the woods just uphill from them? Maybe we can discourage their advance."

"I'll clear it with Collins, but I don't see why not." She turned away to call *Enterprise.*

Three minutes later, she returned. "They're on the way from *Endeavour,* which is closer right now. ETA six minutes."

David stared anxiously at the drone display, watching the 262s assemble themselves and hoping they would not advance too quickly. Five minutes and fifty-three seconds later came four flashes, blinding in the dim morning light, and the sharp crack of the explosions was followed by the low blast of the shock wave, a hard, two-pronged attack on their ears. Leaves stripped from the trees initially floated up from the explosions, then slowly rained down on the 262s, carried in the light downhill breeze.

On the drone display, the 262s stopped moving. David could see Tmoyan get up from where the blast had knocked him down and walk back to Hlatan. They had another animated conversation, but this time Tmoyan seemed to be doing most of the talking.

"Do you see?" Tmoyan demanded, his face in Hlatan's. "Do you see what they can do?"

"I see yet another threat to us which must be removed."

Tmoyan waved away the comment. "If they were a threat, we would all be dead, and this evacuation ship would be in flames."

"Perhaps their aim is just that poor."

"So poor they could blast holes in my runways and fracture my fuel storage but not hit the maintenance building full of technicians or the residences nearby? *That* poor?"

"You are only a pilot, Tmoyan, famous and talented, I am sure, but you are not a soldier. You do not understand."

"I understand foolishness when I see it. And you are being a fool, Hlatan. If you assault them, you will die not from their weapons but of your own fatal ignorance. Their ships are over us, Hlatan. They will not allow you to threaten their people."

"People? They are aliens, Tmoyan, not people. Their lives don't count."

"You're a fool, Hlatan."

"I follow my orders, pilot, and you would be wise to do the same." Hlatan turned away angrily, then back to face Tmoyan again. "You invite me to mutiny! I would have you shot if I did not believe you were sincere in your opposition. I know you've been to the council, as has Nadon and Dsanik. I know this. But you have failed to convince them, and now I have my orders. We will carry them out."

As David watched, the conversation turned, and Tmoyan again walked to his aircraft. Hlatan gathered some of his soldiers around himself, and they began to move uphill.

"Failed again," Ethan said, looking over David's shoulder.

David's NetLink buzzed with a call from *Endeavour*. "Well, that didn't work," Carol said.

David shook his head. "No. I'll talk to Nat about it, but I think we should try this again when they start this way."

There was a pause before she responded. "And if they don't stop?"

David thought for a moment. "I'll have to see what Collins wants to do. My instinct is to engage them here."

"OK. We have them on the IR from the Snooper, so I'll prepare another Bludgeon strike above the lake for about the time they would arrive at the downhill bank."

"That's fine. Thanks for the arty support."

"You're welcome." She paused. "We're headed into perigee soon, so we might not be in position when you need the service. Nat will have to call on *Enterprise*."

David looked at his NetLink for the time. "Right. See you on the other side."

"Be safe."

"Yeah, sure. I'll get right on that."

David dropped the link and walked to the edge of the woods where Liwanu was watching for the 262s with Natalie. John followed close behind.

"Nat, I just talked to Carol. I'd like to drop another volley of Bludgeons in front of them as they come forward."

"Where?"

"Just above the lake as they get to our old position."

Liwanu looked over at him. "Kinda close, don't you think?"

"Maybe. What's your thinking?"

"Either in the lake, which would be impressive or just below it. Bludgeons are pretty accurate, but there is some variation in them."

"Hmm. OK." He turned back to Natalie. "Ask Collins for a strike below the lake, just above our old position, as they reach the edge of the woods."

Natalie nodded and again walked away to call *Enterprise*. In a few moments, she was back.

"If they get to the edge of the forest by your old camp, there'll be a Bludgeon attack just below the lake."

"Fine, thanks." He turned again to Liwanu. "When that clears, I want you to start firing over their heads. Make it three volleys, then stop."

Sabrina, who had been standing nearby watching downhill, leaned into the conversation. "They're going to keep coming, sir. I can feel it."

David nodded sadly. "You may be right. They'll have to narrow down their formation to get above the lake, but once they pass that, I think we need to defend ourselves."

"A few rounds, then back to the cut?" Liwanu asked.

"Yes, likely. We'll just have to see how it all evolves."

Chapter 31

New Traenah
Central Council Meeting Room
Spin 9, Subcycle 3, Cycle 2510

Nadon and Dsanik waited impatiently for the council to come to order. They had requested yet another special meeting about the humans on and above their planet.

The First Counselor looked at her with some skepticism. "We have come into session again to hear your arguments, Nadon. I see you have brought a different warrior. Are you expecting somehow a different result?"

"There is new information, First Counselor. Important— "

"No doubt you refer to the additional alien ships that have just arrived?"

"That, yes, and more. Dsanik wishes to address you."

"Continue."

Dsanik stood before the line of sixteen council members. He looked from left to right and back, the faces familiar from news reports but faces he had never thought to see in person. "I am a warrior, Council, and I have served for and against some of you in my long career. But I have never faced anything like I do now. There is enormous, even overwhelming, power above, it is true. But it has not been unleashed. On the contrary, the power of these aliens has been withheld, used only when necessary, in response to our actions at the direction of this council."

The First Counselor moved in his chair uncomfortably. "You presume to blame the council for the appearance of aliens on our planet?"

"I do. I blame your short-sightedness, your retreat to instinct, to ignorance, and your lack of vision in understanding our new place in the universe."

"Clearly, you have been listening to Nadon. She had made many of these same —"

"Nadon is a scientist, not a warrior. I argued with her, supporting your orders, but I now see that this was unwise, even misguided."

The First Counselor stood quickly. "Guard your words, warrior."

Dsanik moved to directly face the council. "What you have ordered us to do has created the opposite of the desired outcome. We struck the humans to drive them out, and in doing so, we kept them here. We struck them again, at your direction, and they were compelled to escape to the surface for safety. I fully believe had we just left them unmolested they would have left on their own."

"Your words are pointed, warrior Dsanik. We are not your subordinates."

"As you say, but now you compound your errors with this folly of a ground assault. I have seen the scouts' reports. The humans are adept, careful, and well-armed. They can call down death from orbit, just as they did to prevent us from attacking them while they evacuated their ship."

The Second Counselor, an experienced politician from North, answered. "If this Council does not proceed with removing this threat from New Traenah, I shall be forced to remove myself from its membership."

Nadon looked at her. "Then go, for we will be better off with less fear mongering and more rational thought."

The First Counselor, once the leader of East, stood. "We must keep our discourse civil, for we ourselves are not the enemy here."

"There is no enemy here, learned Counselor," Nadon snapped, "*except* us."

The First returned to his seat. "What does the master Gkeze say of all this? Surely, he has shared his thoughts with you, his most revered student?"

"And why is he not here to speak his own words?" the Second asked.

Nadon ignored the First's comment, unsure if it conveyed compliment or condescension. "His disability is becoming worse, and it is now quite painful for him to travel." She paced for a moment before the long Council table. "But, yes, I have discussed this at length with him, and he is in agreement. We must allow the humans to depart peacefully and to return for their disabled vessel as well."

She paused.

"Gkeze said something else which I thought was new and, I hope, persuasive. He says we must treat them as we would want them to treat us were the circumstances reversed."

"We have no such duty," the Deputy replied. "Aliens are a threat and must be removed. There is no question of this."

The First Counselor looked up and down the table at his fellow council members. "Yes, we are in agreement on that point, But it may be that the best solution to the current crisis is to permit them to remove themselves."

He stood and turned to the other members. "We will cancel the attack order and request Hlatan return his force to Traedenath. Then, we will see if these despicable humans will vacate our home on their own as they promise. I have my doubts about their sincerity, but we will give them a chance if only to save our own males from harm."

The Second stood, now face-to-face with the First. "This is cowardice — folly — and I refuse to be a part of it."

The First Counselor watched his former associate as she left, then turned back to the table. "Are there any other objections?" No one moved. "Very well, Dsanik, we direct you to order Hlatan to withdraw his force and return to Traedenath."

Dsanik turned to leave. "I hope that I will be in time, Council. The battle may already be engaged." He rushed out and headed for the airfield.

The First Counselor looked back at Nadon. "Nadon, is there a way to contact the humans?"

"There is the alien Trustee, who has been helpful."

"So now we trust in yet another alien species to avoid disaster?"

"Yes."

"Very well. If you can, send word to them that they may leave and may subsequently return for their vessel."

Nadon took her leave of the Council, following Dsanik to the airfield to contact Tmoyan.

New Traenah
Outside the Evacuation Ship
Spin 9, Subcycle 3, Cycle 2510

Staal looked around as his group of sixteen males, drafted suddenly as soldiers, received its instructions. They would move to the far right, past the lower woods and lake, and into the left side of the humans' position in the upper forest. They were mostly too old for soldiering, and none had been required since their arrival from Traenah. But he'd done his mandatory military training years before and still knew how to operate the standard weapon he'd been handed two spins before. He put on his ammo gloves before carefully loading the ammunition cartridges into the weapon.

They moved to the right, moving slowly but deliberately up the paths the scouts had prepared over the last few spins. As they came to the end of the wood, he could see the lake, blue and inviting in the early morning light.

"Keep moving!" came a quiet voice from behind him. Staal gripped his understanding and started climbing the rocks on the right. The boulder field, clearly fallen from the tall walls of this narrow valley, gave them a hidden approach to the upper woods, behind which were the humans. It was another path clearly marked by the scouts.

Staal wanted to look over the edge, to see where they were, exactly, but his leader kept them moving with their heads down. Better, he said, to not be seen and not get your skull suddenly removed.

As David's command team watched the lower forest, they heard the now-familiar sound of Tmoyan's aircraft. He landed just outside the woods and came quickly uphill. He looked at John.

"I failed to convince Snait. He accused me of mutiny. I have come to stand with you."

John translated for the humans.

David looked at the small alien, so apparently sincere in his desire to avoid a conflict. He was, David realized, as committed to avoiding a fight as he was

233

himself. "Will you not be called a traitor, Tmoyan, if you remain with us and fire on your own people?"

"Yes, I may be charged, and if so, I will lose the chance for the female I desire and the kind of life I was hoping for here. A life without needless conflict."

David listened carefully to John's translation. He looked out at the lake, beautiful in its tranquil setting, framed by the enormous evergreens of the forest just downhill. The star was lighting up the forest now, and it reflected a silver highlight he had not noticed before. He looked at it for a long time, a peaceful tableau undeserving of bloodshed.

He spoke without turning from the delicate beauty before him. "John, tell him to go home. Tell him I want him to live that life he aspires to."

"He says he may yet be able to stop Hlatan here."

"Tell him to go home. Hlatan will not be deterred, but brave Tmoyan may someday convince those in power that we mean them no harm."

John translated, then responded. "He does not wish to abandon you here."

"Tell him we will be fine, but please, please get him to leave."

Another long exchange ended as Tmoyan's made a hard fist and released it just before he turned to his aircraft.

John made a fist in response, then turned to David. "He expressed his thanks to you and said that your actions convince him of your character. He is surprised, and impressed, with your honesty and ethical behavior."

David smiled. "Will that pay off someday, oh seer of the future of cultures?"

"I warned you before about insults."

"And?"

"I cannot say for sure, but what you have done is wise. It may pay dividends later on."

"Good. Time for you to go, too, Guardian."

"I don't understand. Hlatan is coming."

"OK, stay if you wish, but I would rather not be responsible for the last of your thirty thousand sunrises."

"I accepted that possibility when I came here. I will stay."

David reassigned three Marines and pointed at John. "When this is all over, I want him still breathing, understood?"

The three nodded and started moving John uphill, away from danger.

"I'm not ready to go!" he exclaimed.

"OK, fine, stay here until they get closer, Then, John, you go where the corporal tells you, and you stay there. Am I making myself clear?"

"Yes, Commander, you're clear."

"Good."

David looked hard at John as if to reinforce his order, then turned away as a smile escaped his face. The old Trustee had guts. One had to give him credit for that.

Far above on *Enterprise*'s Bridge, Fiona stood behind the Surveillance station, as the IR tech began moving the detector off the 262s' ship.

"What are you doing, Bender?" she asked.

"Something is happening on the left, ma'am. I caught some movement just on the edge of the field." As he moved the focus left of the alien ship and slightly uphill, there were small, warm targets moving along the edge of the woods.

Fiona's stomach seized. "Check the right side." In a moment, she turned to the Comm Station. "Get me Powell."

David dropped the NetLink connection and pressed his microphone switch. "Liwanu, they're moving on the extreme right and left. *Enterprise* says about sixteen each side."

"Understood. Lieutenant Herrera, take the left. I'll take the right."

Sabrina moved quickly, grabbing six Marines to follow her to the left edge of the woods, just inside the woods from the field above the lake. They moved silently, and as they came near the rocks that bordered the wood, she motioned them to stop.

They listened for a minute but heard nothing. If the 262s were approaching, they were doing it very well.

The combat link came alive again with Powell's voice. "Sabrina, *Endeavour* says they're maybe twenty meters from where you're standing. They're just above you."

She clicked the silent microphone switch twice, unable to speak with the 262s so close.

Then, a motion in the rocks caught her eye. A flash of brown against the dark grey of the boulders. She pointed where she had seen it, then lifted her 2K7X and fired one round well above where the brown had been. A warning shot, or so she thought.

They were suddenly enveloped in fire as all sixteen 262s fired at once. Their weapons gave just a sharp *crack* when discharged, and Sabrina was snapped aside by the intense burning in her left bicep. As she turned to move her Marines further left, darkness flooded her eyes, and she felt herself falling. She didn't hear herself hit the ground, for by then, she was no longer there.

Herrera's corporal saw her fall dead, along with two others. That left him in charge, and he knew it.

"GET BACK!" he yelled as he returned fire on the 262s. The four of them moved quickly behind trees and up the slope, 262 bullets hitting all around them but missing.

"God DAMN it!" David yelled as he saw the 262s open up on his people. A full squad moved quickly to support the small detachment, firing on the 262s, who were now isolated in their small boulder-strewn position. Their distraction helped the four who had been with Sabrina get away uphill.

David backed up a few meters. "Liwanu," he called over the combat link, "do not let that probe on the right get any further. Fire on them if necessary." He heard two clicks in response as Liwanu started moving his people to the right.

David turned to John. "You should get back where it's safe."

"I'll stay for now."

"You're not good at taking orders, are you?"

"Yes, I've heard that before."

"Fine. You're on your own now. Go up where it's safe or stay here and get killed. It's all up to you. I'm not going to say it again."

David turned without waiting for an answer and moved toward the fighting on his left.

Corporal Gabriel Charles was no fool, no neophyte. He'd been a young private as they descended the corkscrew ramp into the Preeminent leader's lair, and he'd killed his share of Combatants. But he'd never seen anything like the 262s weapons. Three dead, almost instantly. It couldn't possibly be from the slugs themselves, he thought. They had to have been poisoned somehow.

He motioned his three Marines to move further up into the rocks, looking for a position where they could look down on the 262s, now held in place by the other squad. They hesitated, fearful of the instant death around them, but then moved as ordered, carefully scaling one boulder after another, higher, then closer, then higher again, until Charles motioned them to stop.

Through a narrow slit between rocks, Charles could see the 262s, now twenty meters below them. The 262s weren't looking up but at each other and in the direction of the intermittent suppression fire they were taking. They looked afraid to him, but, really, he had no idea what that would look like on a 262. He showed the others the view, then moved to climb on top.

From there, he could see them all. Sixteen, just as Powell had said. His first instinct was to get the other three up there and just clear out the 262s' position with hot lead. But as he watched, there was one individual clearly in charge, pointing and shoving to get things done.

He pulled out one of the three guided smart rounds from his belt and carefully loaded it. As he moved forward, he re-identified his target, designated it for the GS, and fired.

The 262s' chest exploded, his blood spattered all around, on the rocks, on his soldiers. Charles reloaded regular ammo and fired four rounds over their heads.

Staal recoiled from the mass of blood and flesh that had been his leader. In shock, he looked around for a target as four loud explosions assaulted him from above, and hot chips flew into his face from the rocks around him. Looking up, he saw there was just one human with a weapon pointed directly at his face.

Then, in a teoset, he looked again and there were four weapons looking down on him.

Several of his fellow soldiers started to move.

"STOP!" Staal yelled. "They will kill us if we attack them."

"They killed Tsibet. They will kill us, too!"

Staal dropped his weapon and turned to the others. "Then why are we still alive?" He pointed at the humans. "There they are, four of them. They could have killed all of us, but they didn't."

"What would you do? Surrender?"

"You would prefer to die?"

They argued like this for some time, and while they did, the four Marines above watched the eight others work their way behind the 262s, cutting off their escape. Finally, as if teleported there, the Marines dropped into the position from behind.

The 262s looked at each other, then at Staal. "We're alive," he said quietly. "Let's stay that way. Drop your weapons."

The humans herded The People to one side of the gap in the rocks they had hidden in. They then briefly examined the remains of the leader, picking up his communicator. Staal listened carefully to their speech. It sounded strangely high pitched and liquid coming from such large beings. There was discussion among them as firing erupted again in the distance. Staal knew that must mean the other forward probe was being attacked. He tried to stand to look over the edge but was prevented by one of the humans, who firmly grabbed his shoulder and pushed him back down. The human looked him directly in the eye and spoke quietly. Staal was inexplicably reassured by this gesture. He didn't understand why the human had refused him a view of the field, but somehow, he knew it wasn't out of anger or spite.

The radio suddenly came alive. "Tsibet! Tsibet! This is Hlatan. Do you hear me, Tsibet?"

The humans heard it, too, and began talking quickly among themselves. Staal thought for a moment, then touched the human who had pushed him down on the arm. He looked down, spoke a single word, and moved his hands apart. When Staal didn't reply, he repeated the word. Staal stood slowly, pointed at the communicator, then at Tsibet's crushed and scattered remains, then back to the communicator. The human smiled, which shocked Staal to see a familiar expression on an alien face, then picked up the communicator and took Staal's arm.

"Tsibet!" the radio plead. "Tsibet, you are to retire immediately. The attack has been canceled! Tsibet respond!"

"He's trying to tell us something about the radio message and their sergeant, or whatever he was."

Corporal Charles had made his way down the rocks by now, hearing the discussion as he entered the 262s' position.

"Take him back to Powell. The Trustee can translate."

"Yes, corporal."

"Three of you go."

Charles pointed at the 262 making all the gestures, then at the Marines, then up the hill. The 262 made a fist and turned to follow.

Staal walked behind the most enormous human, who seemed to reach up to the very trees around them. The one beside him was more normal, well, more normal for one of The People, but still half a head taller than himself. He glanced at the one behind, wider, with a flat face. None of them seemed to have much fur, but there was a trace of something under their hard headgear. Their hands, when he could catch a glimpse of one, also had some thin fur on them. Strange beings, he thought. So large and different, but he walked with them up the hill, carrying the communicator, silently hoping he would live to see Kirah again someday.

"We took the position, sir," the tall Lance Corporal reported to Commander Powell. "Charles' crew shot the hell out of their sergeant, and they were confused after that. We took them from behind, and they gave up pretty easy."

David nodded. "Good work."

"This one," he said, indicating the 262 he had brought in, "seemed to be the new leader. I saw him myself tell the others to drop their weapons. No mistaking that, sir."

"Hello, may I have your name?" John's unmistakable voice came from just behind David.

Staal looked up in surprise. *"You are the alien I have heard of? The one that came to Traenah?"*

"Yes, I am. May I know your name, brave one?"

"I am Staal, but I am not so brave. I have been taken captive. I will be killed."

John looked at David. "He thinks he is a coward because he's been captured, and he thinks you'll execute him."

"Execute him?" David decided to let that question go for the moment. "What was he trying to tell the Marines?"

"Staal, I am John. There was a message on your radio. You tried to tell the humans about it."

"It was the commander, Hlatan, trying to tell my leader Tsibet to come back because the attack has been canceled. But Tsibet was already dead."

John smiled as he looked at David. "The attack has been called off."

238

"Say what?"

"The commander, Hlatan, was trying to recall this patrol, but the leader was already dead, and the rest you'd captured."

David spoke into his combat link. "They have canceled the assault. Let them retire if they want. Pull back for now." He turned back to John. "Can we talk to Hlatan on this?"

"Yes, I suppose. Staal will know how to use it."

"Good. Have Staal tell Hlatan that we understand that he is standing down. Use language like that, John, nothing like retreat or defeat, understood?"

"Yes. What else?"

"He may send his people forward to recover their casualties. We will be doing the same."

With Staal's help, John was able to relay David's message to Hlatan. Staal also reported that Tsibet had been killed in an engagement with the humans and that he could clear the field of remains if he desired.

"Hlatan expresses his gratitude and will send parties forward immediately. They may ask for direction."

"That's fine. There are only two sites they need to access anyway." David turned from John and looked at Staal for a long moment, then turned to John. "Tell Staal he is no coward. He has acted well, both for himself and his compatriots. He saved their lives, whether he realizes it or not. He has my gratitude."

The alien listened to John's translation but didn't move.

After a moment, David continued: "Tell him he's free to go. The rest of his patrol as well."

John again did the translation, but Staal remained.

David looked at John, who had no response, then back at Staal. "Was there something else?"

Staal listened to his freedom being restored with mixed gratitude. He could go back to Kirah and his warm little house and make cubs if that was what she wanted. He could go back to his job at the airfield. His life could go back to what it once was only a spin ago.

Except for one thing.

"I killed a human."

Chapter 32

GL 252 (c)
In the Redoubt
Thursday, June 20, 2086, 2010 UTC

David listened to John's translation with surprise tinged with grief.

"He is feeling deep guilt, David. The way he says it is not just a statement of fact. He says it as an indictment of himself."

David thought for a moment as he looked at the small alien. Natalie and Melinda, having overheard John's translation, came closer.

David looked at John, dreading the answer to his next question. "Can he describe the human?"

There was a long exchange where the 262 pointed to David, then at Melinda, then Natalie, then back at the tall Lance Corporal that had led him in. David waited patiently, wondering what all these gestures might mean.

"He says the human was tall and shaped different from you. He says it was shaped more like Melinda and Natalie. He struck it in the arm, so he says."

David looked down at the ground and shook his head. "Dammit all. Sabrina."

"No doubt."

David rubbed his eyes, hoping to keep the tears threatening to flow under control. He was again acutely aware that he couldn't remember what time it was or when he last slept. Everything was a mass of grey and it was only getting worse. He looked up and focused on John.

"How can he be sure, John? All of them had to be firing."

There was a short exchange between John and Staal.

"I stood, I saw the human, I aimed, I fired, it fell. There is no other possibility."

David looked for a chair, finally settling on a portable seat near the table Sabrina had been standing by with him and the other officers just a few hours ago. He motioned for Staal to come to him. John knelt next to David.

"She was a female of our species. Does he understand that?"

"Yes, they are also biologically binary, quite similar to humans, actually, in that way. Socially, somewhat less so, but he understands the concept."

"I regret that it was a female, but it was armed and in uniform."

"That is a risk we all take, Staal. You should feel no special guilt about it. In fact, you should not feel any particular guilt at all. Corporal Charles killed your leader, Tsibet. He did not enjoy that act, but he knows it was necessary."

"I have never done such a thing. It is evil, even for an alien."

David looked away, reaching inward for control of his feelings. After a few seconds, he turned back to Staal.

"She was my friend, Staal, someone I have known for a long time, someone I once trusted with my life. I will grieve her in my own way. Perhaps you have a way to grieve a death?"

"Yes."

"Her name was Sabrina. Perhaps it would help you to recall her name from time to time? To honor her memory?"

The sound that came back from the 262 was not quite 'Sabrina,' but it was close enough that David felt that his message had been received. He looked down at the smaller being with some sympathy. He was just a guy who had been thrown into a fight he didn't start. It wasn't his fault.

"Go home, Staal. Go home and live your life."

After John translated, the Marine took Staal by the arm and led him down into to the wide field above the lake. From there, Staal could see small groups of 262s looking for the missing. He walked forward without looking back or to either side, the shadow of his one act of violence following close behind.

David watched Staal walk away until he had to turn back to his own problems. "He'll never be the same."

"No," John responded. "He has seen both sides of war up close, the killing and the dying, and suddenly he understands the ugly truth of both."

"You knew of Staal? You have met him before?"

"I have not. He is a typical male of his kind but perhaps a bit braver than most. I think he will recover if he has an understanding female."

"Understanding females seem to be a universal requirement."

"In many societies, yes, that is true. In others, well…less so."

Liwanu Harry interrupted David's thoughts. "We have the casualties, sir. Eight in all, including the Lieutenant."

David turned to Liwanu, the anger suddenly plain on his face. "Did you get any of those damned rifles?"

"Twenty, sir, at least."

"Good. I want to know what killed them."

"Yes, sir, I am sure FleetIntel will work that out."

David smiled grimly. "Well, Liwanu, I used to work there, and believe me, your confidence far exceeds mine."

"Yes, sir." Liwanu looked at John, then at the maps on the table. "What now, sir?"

"Now *we* go home." He looked up at Natalie. "Nat, call *Enterprise* and get us the hell out of here."

"Sure, David. Right away." Natalie's somber response, a bit out of character for her, only reinforced David's dark pain over his losses. So futile, so unnecessary.

She dropped the connection. "Two hours."

"Fine, thanks."

"David?"

"What?"

Natalie took his arm and moved him away from John. "She was a Marine officer and a good one. She died in the line of duty."

David shook his head. "She had, well, you know…she felt…."

"Yes, I know. But none of that mattered. The choices the 262s made ran her out of options. It's not your fault."

He looked directly at her for a moment. She was such a strong presence wherever she went, thoughtful, but usually distant and careful with her feelings.

He looked away, to the left where Sabrina had been killed. "Thanks, Nat. I know what you say is true, but still, it's hard to take."

She reached up and hugged him gently, her mouth close to his ear. "You are one of the best men I've ever known, David Powell, and I love you enough to tell you the truth. This isn't on you. Believe it."

David nodded, then turned and saw John watching them.

"I think it is time for me to go."

"You're still here?" David asked.

"I am impressed, Commander. Very impressed."

David ignored the compliment, and looked instead toward the 262s in the distance, looking for their lost brethren. "Someday, I hope, Tmoyan and the female he covets, and others like Staal, will be in charge, and things will be different."

"You're hoping for some future contact?"

"They're not that far away from us, John. We should be able to have a good relationship with them. One never knows when we might need to be there for them or they for us."

"That would be a positive situation for both of you."

David paused, trying to find some hope in the dirt and death all around him.

"So, tell me, John the Trustee, will you be around to facilitate that? Can you come tell us when they're ready?"

"I can't say, David the Human Commander, what the future will decide. I will discuss it with my superiors. If we choose to help, we will find a way to let you know."

"A graceful non-answer. Congratulations."

John turned as if to leave, then turned back. "I have enjoyed our conversations. Give Carol my regards, and the children as well."

David paused just a beat before responding: "Sometimes you do scare the hell out of me, John."

"I know, but I mean no harm. Please do express my affection and good wishes."

"As you say."

John smiled. "And tell Jack Ballard he will be seeing me someday, too." He turned and headed through the woods and was quickly out of sight.

David stared at John's retreating back, wondering how he knew what Jack had said years ago.

Well, he thought, *it's like I told Natalie: I don't know how he knows anything, but he seems to know everything.*

Chapter 33

New Traenah
Home of Kirah and Staal
Spin 15, Subcycle 3, Cycle 2510

Kirah was filled with relief when Staal returned alive and unhurt from the battle with the humans. She was also relieved the next spin as she tracked the humans as they left her planet, presumably going back home. They would be back, she was told, at some time in the future to salvage their damaged vessel.

But during this time, Staal said very little other than that he had been picked to scout the humans' location and that they had killed his leader in a skirmish just before the attack was called off. He was sad that Tsibet had been killed, as he was an experienced and capable leader. Still, he considered that loss a normal consequence of their actions that day.

But he was obviously different, quieter than usual and spending his evenings outside, looking at the stars. He would mutter a strange word to himself from time to time, and it would fill him with emotion.

The evening of the third spin after he returned, she went out to sit with him.

"You have been so quiet; I am concerned about you. I would hear what is so troubling to you."

Staal gently waved away her concerns. "I will be fine. I had an experience that will take some time for me to fully understand."

"Can you talk about this *experience*?"

"Not yet. I have not assimilated it yet myself." He turned away from her, and his eyes returned to the stars.

"I see your pain, what looks like grief, and I don't understand. I would help you through this pain, whatever the cause. You have helped me many times."

"You are a kind and patient partner, Kirah. Please allow me a little more time."

"Do you feel guilty that you are here and Tsibet is dead? Is that it?"

"Please, Kirah, just a little more time."

She remained with him for a spedset in silence, then left for bed. She had her regular shift at the Tracker in the morning.

The next spin, Staal went to work for the first time since the battle. He returned much more himself, even making a joke at dinner and laughing at Selol's latest medical school laboratory misadventure.

But after dinner, he was again outside, looking deep into the night. As Kirah came out to join him, he spoke the strange word again.

"What is that?" Kirah asked gently. "You have been saying that word ever since you returned, and it seems to be a source of grief for you."

Staal gripped his agreement but did not look at her. Finally, he broke his fixation on the sky and turned to her.

"It is a name."

She reached over and took his hand. "A name? It is unlike any name I have ever heard."

He paused a moment. "It is a human name."

"A human name?"

"Yes." His eyes went back to the stars.

"Why would a human name with such a strange sound be so powerful to you?"

"Because I killed her."

Kirah squeezed his hand a little tighter. "This is what has been weighing on your thoughts?"

"Yes. We were caught by the humans, and when we rose to fire back, I saw her and shot her. She fell and was still."

"But Staal, they shot at you first, if I understand what you say."

"Yes, that is true."

"Then they must expect that you would defend yourselves, would they not? I am no warrior, but if I were to attack someone, I should expect a response in kind, no?"

"But it was all pointless. Less than a ductset later, Hlatan was calling off the attack. Both Tsibet and the human Suubnah died for nothing."

Kirah was quiet for a while, letting Staal have time to continue.

"I heard Hlatan calling off the attack on the radio. I tried to tell the humans, but they didn't understand at first. They took me to another alien, the same one as came to Traenah, and he told them what I said."

Kirah thought about that, picturing in her mind Staal's struggle to make an alien race understand him.

"But you did make them understand, am I right?"

"Yes."

"And by telling them this and stopping the fighting, I would think you saved many lives."

"Probably so, yes." He paused for a long time. "They took me to the commander of the humans. When I confessed what I had done, he was very sad and told me Suubnah was someone he had known a long time, someone important to him."

"She was his female, perhaps?"

"I think not. He described her like we would a friend, or a close co-worker."

Kirah thought about that for a moment. "It is interesting to me that they have such relationships, so much like our own."

"Yes, they are more similar to us than one would think just looking at them."

"I think, good Staal, that you acted bravely and only as a warrior must. I am happy, and, honored, to be bonded to such a male."

"You have always been too generous to me, Kirah, but in this, you may be right. I have now thought it all over so many times, and I do not see what I could have done differently at any point."

"Then what have you to grieve?"

Staal looked back at the stars for a moment. "The waste, Kirah, the horrible, stupid waste. Tsibet was a good male, a hard worker, and a brave leader. The human commander was clearly sad at Suubnah's loss, I felt deep sympathy for him, and the rest of them, too. He gave me her name and asked that I remember her from time to time. I will do so, regretful of her loss, but you are correct that it was the consequence of actions I had no control over."

"You are no murderer, Staal, and on that, I know well what I speak."

Staal paused a moment, stood without releasing Kirah's hand, and led her back inside their small cottage.

Chapter 34

Endeavour
En Route Earth
Tuesday, June 25, 2086, 1630 UTC

They were five days away from GL 252 on the way back to Earth, and Wren Freya Thomas could hardly believe her good fortune. Here seated before her in *Endeavour*'s in-port office were both Hansen and Powell, the Fleet power couple of the current era.

David smiled as he turned to Carol. "We should tell her about Fiona and —"

"No, we shouldn't."

"But I really like — "

"Shut up."

"OK, if you insist. Still..."

"David!"

"Fine, fine."

"Fiona?" Thomas asked.

"Never mind," Carol responded as she poked Powell gently, cutting off that diversion.

Thomas turned back to David. "Commander Hansen allowed me to read a portion of your report. Tell me about, um, 'Tmoyan'."

"A very brave person, I would say. He participated in the attacks on *Onizuka*, but he held no real animosity for us once he understood we meant him no harm."

"Having second thoughts?"

"He all but said so, yes. I admired his tenacity in trying to prevent the conflict." He paused a moment. "Ever since we got there, to GL 252, I mean, I felt like I was playing a dangerous game of chess with a very smart adversary. Looking back, I think I saw Tmoyan's mind in that contest."

"Admiration for someone who wanted to kill you?"

David nodded. "Yes, a worthy warrior, I would say."

"But what of your FPI people?"

"Yes, regrettable losses there. They were good people."

"You still don't blame Tmoyan or his cohorts?"

"'Cohorts' is a little harsh, Ms. Thomas. They were afraid of us. They had orders. It wasn't personal."

"And your Marines, Lieutenant Herrera, in particular?"

"I knew Sabrina from the Zeta Doradus mission. She was a fine officer with a bright future. I will miss her."

"Is that all?"

"For you, yes, that's all."

"What will happen to *Onizuka*?"

"We'll go back with a salvage mission. She needs new Drive modules to get her back to Earth."

"Any consequences for her captain based on what happened?"

David paused, Carol looking at him but trying to conceal her amusement.

"Oh, there will be an extended and colorful ass-chewing from CINC, I am sure. Other than that, I don't expect anything official."

"Do you think there will be an outreach from the 262s at some point?"

David shrugged. "I don't really know. If Tmoyan and those around him get some influence, then yes, I could see it happening."

"And, what about the Trustee? Do you expect more contact with them?"

He turned to Carol. "You let her see that?"

"Why not?"

"Jesus, Carol, there's never been any mention of them in public. We can't let her talk about that."

Thomas smiled. "I have to talk about that."

"No, you don't!" they responded in unison.

Carol looked at David, then back to Thomas. "Remember when I said there might be things you can't discuss?"

"But this is...breathtaking. A new, ancient race? It's the kind of story that makes..."

"Careers?" Carol asked.

"I have a career, Commander. I meant to say *news*. I don't need this scoop, but it will get out somehow, and if I break it, it will be told properly and with full context." She paused to take a breath. "This is the first actual contact with them, correct?" She looked from one officer to the other, finally settling on David. "From what you say in this report, you've known they are out there, some of what they've done, but this is the first time you've met face to face, right?"

"Yes."

Thomas looked carefully at David. "What's the problem?"

David leaned back, thinking. "Well, first, there is the law of unintended consequences. Who knows what nutty route the revelation will take? I think we need to look hard at that first. They aren't gods but some might think they are. Second, the Trustees clearly avoid publicity. They work best quietly, only appearing when it's necessary."

"You want to respect their wishes?"

"I think we should, yes," David answered. "And we have previously kept what little hints we had of their existence secret. As I said, there is no telling what effect this will have on society."

When Thomas kept writing, Carol gently reached over and pulled the notebook from her hands. Thomas looked up; her pen left hanging in midair.

"We will need to consult with FleetIntel and CINC before you mention the Trustees slash Guardians. Are we clear?"

"Yes, Commander."

"We had an agreement, Ms. Thomas. I will hold you to it."

She nodded reluctantly. "Yes, Commander."

Carol handed the notebook back.

David looked at Carol. "That must have been some agreement."

"Yes," Thomas said, "it was. I've never made such a concession in all my years in journalism. If my old professors knew what I agreed to, they'd tar and feather me for heresy."

"We get to see the final product, too," Carol said with no small pride.

Thomas sighed. "Just one more humiliation for the opportunistic ambulance-chasing reporter, I suppose."

"Wow. You really are something, you know?"

"Yes, but you already knew that, remember?"

"Oh, yeah, right. We're married."

Thomas looked again from one to the other. "Are you two always like this?"

David gave an emphatic "No!" simultaneous with Carol's "Yes!"

Thomas closed her notebook. "I see why people want to know more about you. I do. You are unlike what most people experience in their lives these days and very unlike what I know in mine."

"We love each other," David said, now completely serious. "And we came very close to missing out on it."

"Oh?"

"If Carol had not reached out to me when she did, it might not have ever happened."

Thomas could not hide her surprise. "Not ever?"

Carol leaned forward. "David and I are in different places on this. I think now that it was inevitable that we would come back to each other at some point. The foundation was there, we only needed to choose to build on it. The war just forced the scales from my eyes at a time when I could do something about it."

"I was always waiting for her, watching and hoping that an opportunity would open for something to happen."

Carol took his hand in hers. "I know."

Thomas, not having written a word throughout this intimate exchange, waited for them to finish. "Thank you both, but I would like to come back to some things in a day or two?"

"Sure," Carol responded. As Thomas rose to leave, the ship phone rang, and both officers reflexively reached for it. Carol beat David to it just as he realized this was not his ship but hers.

"Hansen."

Chapter 35

Network Studio
New York, NY
Sunday, August 11, 2086, 2300 UTC (7 PM EDT)

She sat facing the camera, her attractive features set pleasantly, relaxed but not quite smiling. As the studio lights came up, a picture of Carol Hansen faded up behind her, looking directly into the camera with a small smile, arms crossed. *Endeavour*'s commissioning plaque was clearly visible on the bulkhead behind her, proudly announcing itself as *UCDD-44*. There could be little question who it was, but the silver oak leaves on her collar and the name 'HANSEN' embroidered in white over the right pocket of her grey work uniform removed any doubt. 'ISC FLEET' stood out proudly over her left pocket under her command insignia, a star overlaying a globe, wings on either side.

She paused just a moment to let the picture behind her register before she began. "This is Wren Freya Thomas. As you've heard on this network, nearly every day for the last five months, I have been on assignment. I can now tell you that assignment was aboard the ISC Fleet's Unity Class Destroyer *Endeavour*, under Commander Carol Hansen."

She turned to her left as the cameras switched, and the background image moved to a Fleet-provided 'beauty shot' of *Endeavour*.

"I have much to tell you, including the difficult quest to avoid another interstellar war at the star GL 252, but I must start with my strong impression of the bravery, integrity, and intelligence of *Endeavour*'s officers and crew, and most particularly her captain.

"Carol Hansen was just a young ensign, only six months out of the fleet university when the war broke out at Inor. You've all heard the stories about her and the others of *Liberty*: their survival and their work in Inoria until they were rescued. You may have also heard of their aversion to publicity and refusal of interviews, promotional tours, books, and other less savory proposals. I didn't know before this assignment which of those stories were legend, myth, or just plain fabrication. But after spending these months with them, living and working in deep space, I believe every word.

"That young, raw ensign is now a full Commander, with over a hundred lives in her hands. She is forthright, thoughtful, and tough. She was certainly all of those things when ordered to take this correspondent with her on this mission, or, 'cruise' as she would call it. My presence on her ship was not her first preference, nor, perhaps, even her last. In my first meeting with her, she insisted that this story be about *Endeavour* and its crew and not so much about her captain. Carol Hansen, the Ohio farm girl who graduated second in her high school class and then first in her class at Space Fleet University, never wanted to be famous, as she repeatedly told me in unvarnished terms.

"I have interviewed nearly a thousand individuals in my twenty-five years on this network. I can say with absolute confidence that she is one of the few I have met to so completely embody the legend she has become. Wife, mother, warrior. I have come away from this experience with such deep admiration for this woman, and her amazing crew, it is hard to express it in mere words."

She returned to the first camera, Carol's smile right behind her.

"But, I will try..."

Appendix: Traenah Time

It's always kind of interesting (and fun) to see where your decisions about a planet take you. One of the beauties of writing science fiction is the ability to decide where a planet orbits and how fast it rotates. But once you decide, you gotta stick with it, and if there are issues later, well, you have to work that realistically into the context of the story. This, by the by, is why the Forstmann Drive only goes so fast and SLIP comms are so slow.

In Alert Status One, we have two alien planets to work out, with one society using both. That has some interesting consequences.

A year or 'cycle' on Traenah (GL 262 (d)) is 283.6 Terran days. Since Traenah turns a little slower than Earth, it's 261.8 Traenah 'spins'.

The People of Traenah have four digits on their hands and feet, not five like us, so sixteen is a cardinal number in their system, much as ten is to us Earthlings. Their calendar is therefore based on sixteen subcycles of sixteen days each, with a five-day holiday. Every four cycles, that holiday is focused on the comet's 'Peak Night.'

Keeping with this idea of sixteens, each spin is divided into sixteen 'spedset' (97.5 Terran minutes), which are then divided into sixteen 'ductset' (6.1 Terran minutes). The pattern continues through a 'quatset' of 22.9 Terran seconds and, finally, the teoset, which is 1.4 Terran seconds.

Once they got to New Traenah (GL 252 (c)), things naturally had to change. There, a cycle (year) is 474.8 Terran days, and the planet turns in 21.6 Terran hours. So, they now have 527.6 'new spins' each 'new cycle.' That leaves them with 32 subcycles per cycle with 15 days left over. There's no Peak Night to allow for, so my guess is they'd add a holiday between every other subcyc.

At least, that's what I'd do.

I don't think they would change their time system, as many physical and astronomical measures were in the original units. Imagine us abandoning our hours and seconds just because we moved to Mars! We'd have to write all new physics books. It would be easier to just tack on those extra 39-plus minutes somehow and call it good.

So now on New Traenah, instead of each spin being exactly 16 spedset long, it's 13 spedset plus 4 ductset plus 10 quatset with a 13 teoset kicker on the end.

If you stopped reading somewhere in there, I can't say I blame you. I almost stopped writing.

But I like to lay this stuff out for those who are interested in the details.

Afterword

As always, there are a lot of people and places to acknowledge.

Research on asteroid impacts took me all over the web. One of the best is the 'Earth Impacts Effects Program' at impact.ese.ic.ac.uk. There is another good simulator at convertalot.com/asteroid_impact_calculator.html. A detailed video simulation of the Chixulub impact by Gwillerm Kaldisti can be found at 'https://www.youtube.com/watch?v=ya3w1bvaxaQ.' Fascinating stuff.

As usual, most of my character names are either computer generated from templates (which keeps my Perl programming skills somewhat current), or randomly selected from the latest available list of baby names using Excel. For Alert Status One, I did consult fantasynamegenerators.com for some names of specific geographic origin. It's a great tool.

Carol's paraphrased recital of Romans 8:38-39 is from no specific translation.

And yeah, that's my favorite passage, too.

As always, I value the support of family and friends and the direct and sometimes painful input from my alpha and beta readers. And finally, of course, my editor Kimberly Karshner, who ensures all 'i's have dots and we avoid the odd and most embarrassing uncrossed 't.'

There will be another ISC Fleet book, I promise, but I have not committed to a story yet. Maybe a prequel telling Randy Forstmann's Drive origin story will come out (as a novella?) sometime in 2023. Sign up on the website at iscfleet.com, and I'll keep you posted on my progress.

Thanks again for reading *Alert Status One*. Please leave a review wherever you bought it. I appreciate the time you invest in reading, and I hope you've found it entertaining.

Rock Whitehouse
North Ridgeville, Ohio
August 2022

PS: I am slightly amused that the book ends on page 256. I really wish I could claim that I planned that out!

Printed in Great Britain
by Amazon